Messiaen Studies

The French composer Olivier Messiaen is one of the major figures of twentieth-century music. This collection of scholarly essays offers new cultural, historical, biographical and analytical perspectives on Messiaen's musical œuvre from 1941 to 1992. The volume includes: a fascinating snapshot of Messiaen's life in occupied France; a study of the Surrealist poetics of Messiaen's song cycle *Harawi*; a chapter on Messiaen's iconoclastic path to the avant-garde heritage that he bequeathed to his pupils; discussion on Messiaen's place in twentieth-century music; and detailed analysis of specific works, including his opera *Saint François d'Assise*. The chapters provide fresh insights on the origins, style and poetics of Messiaen's music, and therefore provide an inspiration and foundation for future scholarship. Reflecting and expanding upon the broad range of Messiaen's own interdisciplinary interests, the book will be of interest to students and scholars of music, art, literature and theology.

ROBERT SHOLL is Reader in Music at Thames Valley University, and also lectures at King's College London. His research examines the aesthetic and iconographical inspirations behind Messiaen's music, and the ways in which contemporary spiritual music engages with other discourses. Robert is a member of the 'Theology through the Arts' research project at the University of Cambridge and St Andrews, and is a founding co-editor of oliviermessiaen.net. As an organist, he has given recitals at major European venues (including St Paul's Cathedral, La Madeleine and Notre-Dame de Paris), and has performed most of Messiaen's organ music.

Frontispiece: From Messiaen's *Amour oiseaux d'étoile* (*Harawi*)

MESSIAEN STUDIES

EDITED BY

Robert Sholl

CAMBRIDGE
UNIVERSITY PRESS

CAMBRIDGE UNIVERSITY PRESS
Cambridge, New York, Melbourne, Madrid, Cape Town, Singapore, São Paulo

Cambridge University Press
The Edinburgh Building, Cambridge CB2 8RU, UK

Published in the United States of America by Cambridge University Press, New York

www.cambridge.org
Information on this title: www.cambridge.org/9780521839815

First published 2007

Printed in the United Kingdom at the University Press, Cambridge

A catalogue record for this publication is available from the British Library

ISBN 978-0-521-83981-5 hardback

Felix Aprahamian in Memoriam (1914–2005)

Contents

Contributors

AMY BAUER, University of California, Irvine

ROBERT FALLON, Bowling Green State University, Ohio

ALLEN FORTE, Yale University

STEFAN KEYM, Leipzig University

PAUL MCNULTY, Dublin Institute of Technology

ANDREW SHENTON, Boston University

ROBERT SHOLL, Thames Valley University, London

NIGEL SIMEONE, Sheffield University

JEREMY THURLOW, Cambridge University

SANDER VAN MAAS, University of Amsterdam

ARNOLD WHITTALL, King's College, London (Emeritus)

Acknowledgements

The manuscript used on the front cover and in Chapter 2 is used by kind permission of the Messiaen estate. Throughout this volume all musical examples by Olivier Messiaen are reproduced by permission of Editions Alphonse Leduc, Paris/United Music Publishers Ltd, and Editions Durand.

Examples of poetry by Pierre Reverdy are used by permission of Flammarion, Paris. The poetry of Paul Eluard is reprinted by permission of Editions Gallimard, Paris. Roland Penrose's *Seeing is Believing* is reprinted by permission of the Roland Penrose Collection. Maurice Denis's woodcut is reprinted by permission of the Artists Rights Society (ARS), New York/ADAGP, Paris.

1 Messiaen in 1942: a working musician in occupied Paris

Nigel Simeone

Introduction

While 1942 was not a particularly productive year for Messiaen in terms of new compositions or important premieres, it shows him established as a working musician and as a teacher at the Conservatoire (to which he had been appointed in 1941), participating in numerous concerts, and overseeing the first publication of two of his major works: the *Quatuor pour la fin du Temps* and *Les Corps glorieux*. It also provides glimpses of Messiaen working as a composer of incidental music for the theatre (a little-known aspect of his career), of his dealings with the bureaucracy of the occupying powers and of his struggle to find a publisher for the treatise that was to become his *Technique de mon langage musical*. There are three main sections to this study:

- A documentation of Messiaen performances in Paris during his captivity (from July 1940 to April 1941) and an outline of Messiaen's first few months (from May to December 1941) after his return from captivity and his brief spell in Vichy,[1]

- A detailed examination of Messiaen's musical activity in 1942 as a performer, and critical evaluations of his work, publications, commissions, and the campaign to secure publication of his 'Traité'.[2] His public concert-giving activities are documented in the weekly journal *L'Information musicale* published in Paris during the Occupation – a source not only of listings but also of reviews.[3] Additional evidence can be found in Messiaen's diary (see below), in printed programmes, in studies of cultural

---

[1] This intriguing episode is described in detail in Peter Hill and Nigel Simeone, *Messiaen* (New Haven and London: Yale University Press, 2005), pp. 104–11.

[2] 'Traité' was Messiaen's working title for his *Technique de mon langage musical*, and is not to be confused with his later seven-volume *Traité de rythme, de couleur et d'ornithologie*.

[3] The first issue of *L'Information musicale* was published on 22 November 1940, and the last (no. 158) on 19 May 1944. For a detailed study of this periodical, see Myriam Chimènes, '*L'Information musicale*: une "parenthèse" de *La Revue musicale*?', *La Revue des revues*, no. 24 (1997), 91–110.

life in Vichy France and occupied Paris,[4] in general historical works on the period[5] and from personal communications.[6]

- An annotated transcription of significant entries from Messiaen's pocket diary for 1942.[7] This remarkable document (minutely written in pencil) tells us a good deal about preparations for concerts and publications, future plans, meetings with musicians and others, and, occasionally, something of the obstacle course erected by the occupying powers.[8]

1941: Silesia and the return to Vichy France: Pierre Messiaen tells the story of Stalag VIII-A

Wednesday 15 January 1941 was a landmark in Messiaen's career: the first performance of the *Quatuor pour la fin du Temps* in Hut 27B at Stalag VIII-A in Görlitz (Silesia, Poland). The circumstances of this performance have been the cause of much recent scholarly endeavour.[9] Messiaen's capture and his time as a prisoner of war were recalled by his father, Pierre Messiaen, just three years after the events had taken place. Pierre's book *Images* was published in June 1944, while Paris was still occupied, and provides what appears to be the earliest detailed account of his son's captivity.

> In May 1941, Olivier arrived from Silesia where he had been in captivity. We never grew tired of hearing his stories. He had left Verdun after which he had emptied his powder magazines and burned some petrol depots. He left with some others and

---

[4] These include Myriam Chimènes, 'Alfred Cortot et la politique musicale du gouvernement de Vichy', in *La Vie musicale sous Vichy* (Brussels: Editions Complexe, 2001), pp. 35–52; Manuela Schwartz, 'La Politique musicale dans les territoires conquis par l'Allemagne nazie', in Pascal Huynh (ed.), *La Troisième Reich et la musique* (Paris: Musée de la Musique/Fayard, 2004), pp. 131–40; Jean-Pierre Roux (ed.), *La Vie culturelle sous Vichy* (Brussels: Editions Complexe, 1990); and Hervé Le Boterf, *La Vie parisienne sous l'occupation* (Paris: Editions France-Empire, 1997).

[5] In particular, Jean-Paul Cointet, *Paris 40–44* (Paris: Perrin, 2001); Julian Jackson, *France: The Dark Years 1940–1944* (Oxford University Press, 2001); and Ian Ousby, *Occupation: The Ordeal of France 1940–1944* (London: Pimlico, 1999).

[6] Notably a letter from Pierre Boulez and personal recollections of Yvonne Loriod-Messiaen.

[7] Messiaen's pocket diaries from 1939 to his death are in the private archives of Mme Yvonne Loriod-Messiaen.

[8] For further information about Messiaen's activity in the years 1939–45, see Hill and Simeone, *Messiaen*, pp. 91–141. For specific information on the *Quatuor pour la fin du Temps*, see also Rebecca Rischin's *For the End of Time: The Story of the Messiaen Quartet* (Ithaca, NY: Cornell University Press, 2003) and, for *Visions de l'Amen*, Nigel Simeone's 'Messiaen and the Concerts de la Pléiade: "a kind of clandestine resistance against the Occupation"', *Music & Letters*, Vol. 81, no. 4 (November 2000), 551–84.

[9] See 'Er musizierte mit Olivier Messiaen als Kriegsgefangener: der französische Cellist Etienne Pasquier im Gespräch mit Hannelore Lauerwald', *Das Orchester* Vol. 47, no. 1 (January 1999), 21–3; also cited in Rischin, *For the End of Time*, esp. pp. 61–70; and Hill and Simeone, *Messiaen*, pp. 94–103.

headed for Epinal, with two small boxes of manuscripts and music on the back of his bicycle. They were caught by the Germans, who had a special method of surrounding their enemies with motorcycles and moving them along with rhythmical shouts. Then, ten days in a garage at Nancy; overpowering heat and smells, with no water or any latrines; they fed themselves on tinned food. Then ten more days in a camp at Brabois-Villers. They were herded into padlocked cattle wagons from which they could not escape; four days by rail from Nancy to Görlitz, among the urine and excrement, with nothing to drink and nothing to eat. He caught dysentry and stayed for a month in the hospital run by Polish nuns; each room had a portrait of Hitler between the crucifix and a picture of the Holy Virgin.

Silesia is a sinister place; with a long winter – with no respite from the icy cold, no respite from the east wind, but with a grey sky which was illuminated by sublime colours at dawn and at dusk . . . The morning assembly in the courtyard was terrible and on several of these occasions Olivier fainted. There was food to eat, but it was awful: Olivier still loathes barley soup and cod. How did he manage to write his quartet on the Apocalypse [*Quatuor pour la fin du Temps*] there? He met some old fellow-students from the Conservatoire, he volunteered for all the early morning fatigues so that he might be free during the daytime, and the German sergeant in charge of the mail took an interest since he knew that Olivier was an organist and composer. The first performance took place on Christmas night,[10] in front of fellow-prisoners who were astounded by such complex and original music. There were three types of prisoners at the Block House in Görlitz: the Poles who were despised and treated dreadfully, the Flemish Belgians who were given a semblance of consideration, and the Walloon Belgians and the French who were subjected to a mixture of respect and harshness.[11]

Marcel Dupré's role in securing Messiaen's release was a crucial one. He later recalled how he visited Fritz Piersig (at the Propaganda-Staffel in Paris) in early 1941 to plead the case for Messiaen, and was assured that 'in ten days' time, at the latest, he will be in an office'.[12] Dupré's intervention was clearly effective. An emotional letter from Messiaen to Claude Arrieu announcing his newly found freedom allows us to date his return from Silesia (via Nuremberg and Lyon) to Neussargues in the Cantal. He wrote to her on 10 March 1941:

> I am free! with my wife and little Pascal! in Neussargues! (Cantal). Do I need to tell you what joy this gives me? I am gradually getting used to family life again, in fact to life pure and simple . . . I brought back from over there a *Quartet for the End of Time* in eight movements, for violin, clarinet, cello and piano: I am very proud of it as it was written under such difficult circumstances![13]

---

[10] 'Christmas night' seems – fortunately – never to have been taken up by any other later writers despite being another attractive potential myth to add to the much-mythologised story of this premiere.
[11] Pierre Messiaen, *Images* (Paris: Desclée de Brouwer, 1944), pp. 339–40.

[12] Marcel Dupré, 'Souvenirs', unpublished typescript, dated 'Noël 1956', pp. 126–7; English translation in Hill and Simeone, *Messiaen*, p. 110.
[13] The complete text of this letter is published in Nigel Simeone, 'Offrandes oubliées: Messiaen in the 1930s', *Musical Times* (Winter 2000), 33–41.

Messiaen performances in Paris November 1940 to April 1941

While Messiaen was in Görlitz, his music had continued to be performed in Paris. On 8 November 1940, the Orchestre Symphonique Français, conducted by Hubert d'Auriol, performed the fourth movement of *L'Ascension* (*Prière du Christ montant vers son Père*) in a 'Concert spirituel' which also included the *Prières* by André Caplet and the *Cantique du Soleil* by Jacques Chailley, an occasion briefly reviewed by Suzanne Demarquez in *L'Information musicale* (29 November 1940, p. 49). In the issue of 20 December 1940 (p. 137) there is an announcement for another 'Concert spirituel' given by the same orchestra and conductor, which took place on Sunday 22 December 1940, at the Eglise des Dominicains, 222 Faubourg Saint-Honoré. The soloists include the soprano Claire Croiza (replaced before the concert by Ginette Guillamat) and Ginette Martenot (who was Hubert d'Auriol's wife) on the Ondes Martenot. The programme included Messiaen's 'Oraison: Ondes et orchestre'. Presumably this was an arrangement of the 'Oraison' from *Fête des Belles Eaux* for six Ondes Martenot. A review of the concert appeared in the 3 January 1941 issue of *L'Information musicale* (p. 104) in which Jean Douel's only comment of the work was that 'in Messiaen's "Oraison", it is important not to confuse pianissimo and imperceptibility'.

On Tuesday 18 February 1941, at 5pm, André Jolivet gave a talk on 'Berlioz et les quatre Jeune France' at the Théâtre des Mathurins – the second 'Concert-Causerie' in a series which included (among others) Honegger on Franck and Stravinsky (25 March), Auric on Ravel and Satie (27 April) and Sauguet – the organiser of the series – on Rameau and Bizet (6 May). The programme for Jolivet's lecture (with a cover designed by Jean Cocteau) includes details of the music performed, starting with three songs from Berlioz's *Les Nuits d'été*, and ending with three from Messiaen's *Poèmes pour Mi* ('Epouvante', 'Le Collier', 'Prière exaucée') sung by Marcelle Bunlet, with Irène Aïtoff at the piano.[14]

This appears to be the first concert of music explicitly by members of *La Jeune France* to be given during the Occupation, and several more were to follow.[15] But two months earlier, the Association de Musique Contemporaine (AMC) had included Messiaen's music in its concerts. As an organisation the AMC aspired to fill a gap in the city's musical life under the Occupation:

---

[14]The complete programme is printed in Nigel Simeone, 'Group Identities: La Spirale and La Jeune France', *Musical Times* (Autumn 2002), 33.

[15]Simeone, 'Group Identities: La Spirale and La Jeune France'.

This Association, founded during the war, has resumed its activities with an enlarged scope: it appeals to the most eminent and representative composers of the young Parisian school, without any clique-like attitudes. Within its committee as well as its programmes, the AMC has tried to bring together musicians of every school and every tendency, and those who belong to the principal chamber music societies of Paris, whose activities have been interrupted by the war. These include the [Société] Nationale, Triton, the SMI, the SIMC, the concerts of *Revue Musicale*, Jeune France, Sérénade etc.[16]

The AMC's first five concerts of the 1940–41 season included works by Maurice Jaubert, Daniel-Lesur, Jean Rivier, Arthur Honegger, Francis Poulenc (the premiere of the *Sextuor* in its definitive version, on 9 December 1940), Henri Tomasi, Claude Delvincourt, Pierre-Octave Ferroud, Marcel Delannoy, and Messiaen's *Chants de terre et de ciel* performed by Marcelle Bunlet and Simone Tilliard on 23 December 1940.

The committee of the AMC embraced a wide range of stylistic tendencies, and, indeed, political opinions, and despite the focus on chamber music in its programmes, it included conductors (notably Fourestier and Munch) as well as composers. The Honorary President was Florent Schmitt. Robert Bernard (then also editor of *L'Information musicale*) was the Secretary, and the members were Tony Aubin, Georges Auric, Henri Barraud, Louis Beydts, C. (Eugène) Bozza, Pierre Capdevielle, Georges Dandelot, Marcel Delannoy, Claude Delvincourt, Maurice Duruflé, Louis Fourestier, Jean Françaix, Marius-François Gaillard, André Jolivet, Jeanne Leleu, Raymond Loucheur, Jean Marietti, Charles Munch, Francis Poulenc, Jean Rivier, Henri Sauguet and Alexandre Tcherepnine.[17] This list includes two composers (Schmitt and Delannoy) who became members of the 'Groupe Collaboration'and others whose stance was either apolitical or hostile to the occupying powers.[18]

Messiaen re-establishes himself in Paris

Messiaen's first harmony class at the Paris Conservatoire was on 7 May 1941 (an analysis of Debussy's *Prélude à l'après-midi d'un faune*). He quickly

[16] From the manifesto printed as part of the advertisement which appeared in *L'Information musicale* (22 November 1940), 30, and in several subsequent issues. The SMI was the Société Musicale Indépendante, and the SIMC was the Société Internationale de Musique Contemporaine.
[17] Programmes and list of committee members from *L'Information musicale* (22 November 1940), 30.
[18] For details of members of this group, see, for example, the notice in the clandestine resistance journal *Musiciens d'Aujourd'hui*, no. 6 (June 1943), 4: 'Echos ... La presse communique: La section musicale du groupe "Collaboration", sous la présidence de M. Max d'Ollone auquel s'étaient joints MM. Piersig, Sonnen, Florent Schmitt, Francis Casadesus, Gustave Samazeuilh, Marcel Delannoy, Eugène Bigot, a offert au cercle européen, un déjeuner au célèbre compositeur et chef d'orchestre japonais M. Eki-tal-ahn.'

established a rapport with one of the brightest students in his class, and a note in his diary for 9 June mentions an appointment 'chez Mme Sivade, marraine de Loriot pour *Préludes*'. According to Yvonne Loriod, she had been given a copy of the *Préludes* by her teacher Lazare Lévy, and she had quickly learned them all by heart.[19] Loriod was planning to play them in a private recital at Mme Sivade's home (53 rue Blanche) – which was also to include Jolivet's *Mana* and music by Bach – and wanted to work on them with the composer. Within a few months, she was regularly playing selections from the *Préludes* at public concerts in which Messiaen himself was often also appearing.

Marcel Herrand, co-director of the Théâtre des Mathurins, invited Messiaen (presumably as soon as he was back in Paris) to give a concert there, and arrangements were put in hand for an important Parisian premiere in the theatre (36 rue des Mathurins, near the Madeleine). The concert was to take place during the late afternoon, when the building was otherwise unused, before the main evening performance.[20] On Tuesday 24 June, at 5pm, the first Paris performance of the *Quatuor pour la fin du Temps* 'écrit en captivité' according to the flyer, was given by André Vacellier (clarinet), Jean Pasquier (violin), Etienne Pasquier (cello) and Messiaen (piano), along with songs performed by Bunlet and Messiaen, and the *Thème et variations* played by Jean Pasquier and the composer. Messiaen's diary for 1941 gives the complete programme for this concert (which is not given on the flyer or the large poster):[21]

> 4 Mélodies: 'Le Sourire', 'Epouvante', 'Le Collier', 'Résurrection'
> *Thème et Variations*
> *Quatuor pour la fin du Temps*

Messiaen also noted in his diary that Loriod was the page-turner. The reviews included an enthusiastic response by Serge Moreux in *L'Information musicale*, a largely welcoming one by Honegger in *Comoedia*, and a hostile notice by Marcel Delannoy in *Les Nouveaux Temps*.[22]

In the 'Echos' column of *L'Information musicale* for 11 July 1941 (p. 757), an unsigned article declared that: 'Jeune France is not dead. The proof is to be found in the concert on 18 July at 5 pm, at the Hôtel de Sagonne, given by Olivier Messiaen, Daniel Lesur, Yves Baudrier and André Jolivet ... This overdue event is not only a chance to keep up to date with the activities of "The Four" of La Jeune France, who have some huge projects planned for the new season in October. We will also have another chance to hear the *Quatuor*

---

[19] Personal communication.
[20] Rischin, *For the End of Time*, p. 80.
[21] Copies of both are in the present author's collection.

[22] For more on this, see Hill and Simeone, *Messiaen*, pp. 112–13.

pour la fin des[!] *Temps* by their leader, which was unanimously greeted as a French masterpiece after the recent concert devoted to its composer's music at the Théâtre des Mathurins.' The concert was reviewed by José Bruyr in *L'Information musicale* a week later (25 July, p. 804):

This final concert of the season was the last, but not the least . . .

By Messiaen: a piece from his *Quatuor pour la fin des*[!] *Temps* which, moving as it was in its simplicity, did not achieve the same significance as the whole work from which it was detached; then the broad and well-crafted *Variations* for violin and piano.

By Jolivet: two *Complaintes du Soldat* about which I said so many good things at the first performance (and retract none of them – quite the opposite!), then a Suite for String Trio. Even though this was its first performance, the work is not a very recent one. It seems that the style which increasingly deserves to be called 'Jolivian' is grafted here onto a more conventional base. This is most apparent in the two 'Arias', especially the second which is none the less moving for it. By contrast, the 'Fugue en rondeau', despite its doubly classical form, has vigour, life and freedom: a captivating fountain.

By Daniel-Lesur: a simple Pavane and three *Poèmes* set to music with compelling poetry: how much I would like to hear 'Neige' again! Finally, *Le Musicien dans la Cité* to finish with, which is by Yves Baudrier and which nobody could overlook thanks to the talented dedication brought to it by Nadine Desouches, an intelligent and sensitive interpreter for Jeune France. These four have the advantage of performers of the highest order: it is impossible to imagine the *Complaintes* sung by anyone other than Pierre Bernac, nor the pieces for strings played by anyone other than Jean, Pierre, and Etienne, or by Jean and Etienne alone.

The solidarity of *La Jeune France* was again apparent in a letter written by Jolivet to *L'Information musicale* and published in the issue of 24 October 1941 (p. 207). Jolivet was responding to an article by Armand Machabey published on 3 October (pp. 98–9), in which the author lamented the current state of French music, and the apparent lack of any obvious successor to Honegger. Jolivet's riposte is a stirring tribute to his friend Messiaen:

Mes chers amis,

I read in *L'Information musicale* today the article by M. Machabey entitled 'Arthur Honegger et la Musique Française'. Its oversimplicity is curious. I refer particularly to the final paragraph.

1. Honegger has little chance of rallying the majority.

Nor did Lully, Gluck, or César Franck 'rally' anybody. And of these four, it is Honegger who has tried least hard to 'adapt to French taste', and he is much the better for it.

2. 'We find ourselves in front of a kind of void: the style of the last few years has begun to sound jaded, there are no clear tendencies, no boldness, and not even any magnificent failures.'

M. Machabey limits himself to the names of leading figures, and I suggest just one to him: Olivier Messiaen. He should study, even if he is not able to hear performances, the *Poèmes pour Mi* (in the orchestral version), the *Chants de Terre et de Ciel*, *La Nativité du Seigneur*, 'Le Combat de la Vie et de la Mort', and the *Quatuor pour la fin du Temps*.

It is easy to examine them as all these works are published. M. Machabey should be able to notice that the 'style' is not in the least jaded, that the 'tendencies' are clearly affirmed, that 'boldness' is apparent in every bar, and that the 'magnificence' of this music preserves us from a 'long and mediocre monotony'.

I give my permission for these remarks to be published. Through their blunt brevity they should prevent us from forming the false impression that our generation is incapable of inheriting the legacy of Rameau, of Berlioz and of Debussy.

'Combat de la vie et de la mort', in fact 'Combat de la mort et de la vie', is the fourth movement of *Les Corps glorieux*. Messiaen had completed this cycle of 'Sept visions brèves' on 29 August 1939 (a date printed in the first edition), but it was not published until June 1942. The earliest public performance of any part of the work (two movements) did not take place until 28 December 1941, two months after Jolivet's letter was printed.[23] Messiaen had presumably invited Jolivet to hear him play the work at La Trinité, perhaps on the same occasion that he invited his students to hear it (22 July 1941, according to Messiaen's diary).

By December 1941, conditions in Paris had become exceptionally difficult, with the imposition of curfews, and days when the Métro stopped running at 5.30pm. These developments were recorded in Jean Guéhenno's diary for 8 December, and he continued: 'It is 6.30 p.m. and I am watching evening fall. There's not a sound, not a breath. And this is Paris!'[24]

Messiaen in 1942

The miserable start of 1942 was also noted by Guéhenno. On 7 January he remarked on the desecration of the Parisian landscape:

> One by one the statues in Paris are disappearing: the ball in the Place des Ternes, which Fargue amusingly described as resembling an atomiser, Chappe and his telegraph, the two pharmacists in the boulevard Saint-Michel. The other day in the Place du Panthéon, I saw Rousseau being dismantled. Poor 'citoyen', you are going to become the soul of a canon.[25]

January and February 1942 were also exceptionally cold. On 14 February, Guéhenno described the wretched state of the city:

> Nothing can adequately describe the monotony, the resigned stupidity of life in Paris. It is very cold. Everyone huddles up at home without a fire. The only food is from the provisions sent to those who are fortunate enough to have parents living in the country.[26]

---

[23] Messiaen played 'Joie et clarté des corps glorieux' and 'Combat de la mort et de la vie' at the Palais de Chaillot in a recital on 28 December 1941.

[24] Jean Guéhenno, *Journal des années noires* (Paris: Gallimard, Livre de Poche, 1968 edition), p. 255.

[25] Guéhenno, *Journal des années noires* p. 266.

[26] Guéhenno, *Journal des années noires* p. 275.

The bookseller Adrienne Monnier, in her 'Letter to Friends in the free Zone', dated February 1942, wrote:

> Hardest of all to put up with, we are all of the same opinion, is the cold. In the bookshop, where I have had a wood stove installed, it is bearable, but my apartment, like those of most people, is glacial; I can neither read nor write. Every night I light my kitchen stove, and it is while installed next to this dear stove that I am writing to you today.[27]

The harsh weather and chronic lack of heating inevitably had an impact on concerts as well. In November 1943, when he was 18, Pierre Boulez arrived in Paris to study. His memories of the difficult circumstances in which concerts were given are telling, but, despite the extreme cold, audiences continued to come to concerts in large numbers:

> The working conditions were not terribly helpful, because most of the halls were not heated during the winter and musicians played with their overcoats and mittens on to try and brave the cold. The tuning of the wind instruments was less than perfect, as you can imagine. Nevertheless, people came in large numbers to all artistic events, concert halls were always full, and theatres too. It was the only way for people to resist the drab conditions of life.[28]

For Messiaen, the bitterly cold January 1942 included two important performances. The first was a free concert by the Orchestre de la Société des Concerts du Conservatoire, on Sunday 11 January. Charles Munch conducted three works by former prisoners of war: Jean Martinon (*Stalag IX*), Maurice Thiriet (*Oedipe Roi*, with narrations read by Jean Cocteau), and Messiaen's *Les Offrandes oubliées*. The concert ended with a Munch speciality: Roussel's Third Symphony. An unsigned 'note liminaire' in the printed programme for the concert explains its rationale:

> It is no accident that the names of Jean Martinon, Olivier Messiaen and Maurice Thiriet have been brought together on the same programme. They are united by very strong links ... as brothers in arms and fellow-prisoners ... Jean Martinon and Maurice Thiriet met Olivier Messiaen again at Verdun. All three of them had the good fortune to be liberated at about the same time, bringing back from their exile works which were the result of weeks and months of reflection. Two of these works for orchestra (Martinon and Thiriet) are presented for the first time in public at this concert. We should add that Albert Roussel, whose Third Symphony ends the programme, was a friend who gave encouragement and advice to these three young musicians. He would be delighted by this selection, and the presence of his work at this concert becomes doubly significant.

Less than a week later, on 17 January, Messiaen gave a performance of the work which he had written in captivity. The *Quatuor pour la fin du Temps*

[27] Richard McDougall (ed. and trans.), *The Very Rich Hours of Adrienne Monnier* (New York: Charles Scribner's Sons, 1976), p. 404.

[28] Pierre Boulez, letter to the present author, 3 February 2000.

received its second Paris performance in the music room of the magnficent eighteenth-century home of Comte Etienne de Beaumont, at 2 rue Duroc (7th arrondissement) as one of the concerts for the members of his 'Centre d'échanges artistiques et de culture française'. The printed programme (with a pictorial cover by Valentine Hugo) includes a note by Messiaen and a leaflet of Messiaen's commentaries 'read by the composer before each movement'. De Beaumont was clearly taken with Messiaen's music, as in early June 1942 he sent the composer a cheque for 1,000 francs in payment for a commission. Messiaen wrote to thank de Beaumont on 4 June, and noted the details (a maximum of twenty players, to be delivered by January or February) in his diary, but the work was never written.[29] De Beaumont, however, continued to support Messiaen. He wanted to put on the first performance of the *Vingt Regards* (a plan that came to nothing), but it was in his home that the first, private, performance of *Harawi* was given, on 26 July 1946 by Marcelle Bunlet and Messiaen. Again, the audience was provided with a handsome programme for this event – with a front cover of *The Three Graces* by Picasso, and the titles of the songs reproduced in a facsimile of Messiaen's handwriting.

The cold spell continued, but artistic life was thriving in adversity. On 14 February 1942, at the 169th concert of Le Triptyque in the Salle Debussy, Messiaen's *Trois Mélodies* were sung by Lia Dassil, accompanied by Messiaen. On 21 February, at the next concert in the Triptyque series, Yvette Grimaud played two of Messiaen's *Préludes*: 'Plainte calme' and 'Les Sons impalpables du rêve'. The concert of music by La Jeune France at Mme de Drouilly's on 15 March was probably the first time Yvonne Loriod (aged 18) played any of Messiaen's music in public: two of the *Préludes* (nos 5 and 8). Messiaen played his *Thème et variations* with Malvesin at the same concert.

A 'Concert de musique contemporaine' put on by Le Triptyque on 19 March included a group of 'Six mélodies' performed by Marcelle Bunlet and the composer: *Le Sourire, Prière exaucée, Epouvante, Le Collier, Résurrection* and a relatively rare outing for the *Vocalise-Etude*. The next evening, on 20 March, starting 'à 20 heures *très précises*' (according to the programme), Messiaen was at the Salle de l'Ancien Conservatoire to play his *Thème et variations* with the violinist Henri de Malvesin.

A note in the 'Echos' column of *L'Information musicale* on 27 March 1942 (p. 882) reported an event which had taken place two days earlier, also involving Bunlet and Messiaen: 'The Mass for solo voice, organ and drum by André Jolivet was given its first performance at the Chapel of the Franciscan Brothers [rue Marie-Rose, Paris 14e] by Marcelle Bunlet on

---

[29] This letter is in the Pierpont Morgan Library, New York City. An English translation is printed in Hill and Simeone, *Messiaen*, p. 116.

25 March, with Olivier Messiaen at the organ.' Lucie Kayas, in her recent biography of Jolivet, reveals that this was the first performance of the complete work, and was given only after permission had been obtained from Monsignor Chevrot to use a drum in church. This Mass, composed in 1940, had been given a partial performance at the church in Pressignac (Charente) on 14 July 1940.[30] It was published by Heugel in 1958 with the title *Messe dite pour le jour de la paix*. Messiaen's involvement in the 1942 complete premiere was a clear gesture of his esteem for Jolivet, though it is curious that he made no mention of the occasion in his diary.

On 3 May, Messiaen and Loriod were at Virginie Schildge-Bianchini's home for a concert including two *Préludes* (Loriod) and a selection of songs (Messiaen, with Irène Joachim). The 'Echos' column of *L'Information musicale* (17 April 1942, p. 910) announced the next Jeune France concert, put on by the AMC:

> The AMC (Association de Musique Contemporaine) will give its next concert on Friday 8 May, at 6 pm, in the Salle de l'Ecole Normale de Musique. This evening will be devoted to the group Jeune France and will include works by André Jolivet, played by the Trio Pasquier, Pierre Bernac and Irène Aïtoff, Olivier Messiaen played by Yvonne Loriod, Jean Pasquier and the composer, Daniel-Lesur, performed by Bernac, and Yves Baudrier, played by Yvonne Loriod.

The programme included Jolivet's *Suite* for string trio and his *Trois Complaintes du soldat*; Messiaen's *Préludes* (a selection) and *Thème et variations*; Daniel-Lesur's *Trois Poèmes* and *Pavane*, and Baudrier's *Le Musicien dans la cité*. This was a similar programme to that given on 18 July 1941 (see above), and it involved several of the same artists, but with Yvonne Loriod joining the list of Messiaen's interpreters. A review appeared in the 12 June 1942 issue of *L'Information musicale* (p. 974), by Pierre Capdevielle (a composer who was subsequently head of chamber music at French Radio), who shows himself to be a sensitive critic of Messiaen's music, and who is unafraid to end with a barb aimed at Baudrier:

> The last of the few concerts which the AMC has been able to put on this season was devoted to the four musicians who are happy to unite under the proud and romantic title of 'Jeune France'. Inaugurating this interesting evening, the Trio Pasquier – always outstanding – played for us the String Trio by André Jolivet. I like this work, conceived in a spirit of seriousness, in which the writing is driven by a strong and vibrant imagination, not making the slightest concessions and seeming never to forget the ritualistic origins of our art. More Jolivet followed a few moments later. Pierre Bernac, with an artistic distinction which only he can bring, gave the first complete performance of the *Trois Complaintes* which are the finest work of this war by the composer. There are passages here which are eminently sensitive and moving,

[30] Lucie Kayas, *André Jolivet* (Paris: Fayard, 2005), pp. 284–8.

direct, profoundly humane, with no grandiloquence or pomposity, and which, not only through their modal technique but also through the quality of their inspiration, even go back to and rediscover the expressive language of our medieval musicians.

With the composer at the piano, Pierre Pasquier played the *Thème et Variations* for violin and piano by Olivier Messiaen.[31] This work seems like a block of granite, lofty in scale and disdainful in its substance – but this does not prevent a vibrant light from playing over its contours and over the structure of this large quasi-mineral object, which could perhaps best be described as a sort of enormous philosophical stone. A few moments earlier, Mlle Yvonne Loriod played some of Messiaen's *Préludes* with an authority that was not without dryness. Even though these have resonances of Debussy, they are much more than that, and they even have presentiments of the composer who would be able to conceive and write *La Nativité du Seigneur*.

Pierre Bernac sang the delicate and refined *Mélodies* by Daniel Lesur. The *Pavane* by the same composer, extremely well played by Mlle Loriod, showed the same qualities. Then we had *Le Musicien dans la Cité* by M. Yves Baudrier. But there I must stop myself, tempted to say that contrary to the *Trois Mousquetaires* who were really four, with the 'Quatre Jeune France' . . . there are really only three.

On 9 May 1942, the day after this concert, Messiaen gave an interview to Armand Machabey – who seems to have heeded Jolivet's stern advice from the previous year to take notice of Messiaen. Machabey's profile, derived from this, appeared in *L'Information musicale* on 22 May 1942 (p. 945) as the first of the 'Galerie de quelques jeunes musiciens parisiens'.[32] This is prefaced by an editorial which explains the purpose of the articles:

Our colleague M. Armand Machabey is starting a series of brief studies of some young Parisian musicians who have a role of the greatest importance in our artistic life. We have no doubt that the readers of *L'Information musicale* will follow these with interest and enthusiasm, not only because the articles consider the tendencies of our composers, but also because they will be detailed documents, controlled by the composers themselves, relating to their output, to the most important performances of their principal works and giving a view of their projects (works in progress, planned concerts, etc.).

Despite the limited space available, we have tried to present this project in the way which seems most conducive to promoting the work of our contemporaries, to defend and illustrate their labours, and, finally, to shed light on their sources of inspiration.

As far as possible, we will attempt to publish these 'portraits' to fit with current events. So it is that this gallery begins with a study of Olivier Messiaen whose works have just had the most lively success at the AMC, during a concert devoted to the group 'Jeune France'.

---

[31] This is almost certainly a slip, as Pierre Pasquier was the Trio Pasquier's viola player. Jean Pasquier was the violinist and often played the *Thème et variations* with Messiaen.

[32] This series became a regular feature of *L'Information musicale*. The composers featured included Messiaen, Jean Hubeau, Maurice Thiriet, Marcel Delannoy, César Sautereau, Jean Langlais, Georges Dandelot, Yvonne Desportes, André Lavagne, Emile Passani, Eugène Bozza, Pierre Capdevielle, Maurice Duruflé, Jean-Jacques Grunenwald, Henri Dutilleux and Henriette Roget.

The interviews in this series were later reprinted (with revisions) in book form as part of Machabey's *Portraits de trente musiciens français*.[33] The following translation has been made from the original 1942 publication in *L'Information musicale*.

> Olivier Messiaen makes light of every element of music: among his first prizes are those in harmony, composition and, in passing, the organ; at twenty-two he was appointed organist at the Trinité; at thirty-three, professor of harmony at the Conservatoire; at 34 he is the composer of a body of work which, though certainly not prolific, surprises by its austerity, its profound and complex aesthetic, and its features considered so carefully that it cannot help being noticed.
>
> It is difficult to describe Messiaen's art in words, embracing as it does the most extreme doctrines including that of quarter-tones, and which crossed the boundaries of convention long ago.[34] It is built on a transcendental theory of rhythm and tonality: a use of rhythm which divides up durations in a way that is no longer according to the topsy-turvy laws of our music, but according to the most subtle nuances of thoughts, of words and of auditory sensitivity; a use of tonality in which modes have a life of their own, within a fixed framework which leads them to be described as untransposable[35] by Messiaen.
>
> All that could be nothing more than an arbitrary fantasy, or snobbery – but it isn't: it is a coherent system in which the musical atoms, from the syllable to the chord, are closely interwoven. If Messiaen were to write a '*Traité de composition*' we would see in it, I think, an initial cell develop itself through duration and sound, by virtue of an ineluctable internal logic which can be applied right up to the largest of forms.
>
> There is more: this premeditated technique is itself integrated, as in a superior unity, with the profound religious belief which clothes every aspect of Messiaen's activity, his life, his career as a composer and even his musical style, which is nothing less than an act of faith in which he waits humbly for a sign from God that he has reached his goal. Only then does he face the public.
>
> Until now, he had scarcely needed any more applause; since he was 20 years of age, carefully crafted and refined works have been performed in front of audiences of connoisseurs, of artists and of critics who have fallen under the spell of the powerful originality without, perhaps, being able to determine the causes of what they have noticed. It is difficult to detect on one hearing that the *Poèmes pour Mi*, in which the vocal writing is not so much a linear recitative as plainchant, are written without metrical indications and with a profusion of mind-boggling rhythms which outdo Hindu theories; or that the *Quatuor* for violin, clarinet, cello and piano contains virtually no barlines; or that a particular harmony is necessarily linked to a particular rhythm . . . But these are just the technical details and Messiaen asks the listener only to grasp the finished piece.
>
> He is a singular mystic, indistinguishable in a crowd, but whose heart and spirit are fixed intently on an ideal which reaches way beyond the vast majority of people. It is

[33] Armand Machabey, *Portraits de trente musiciens français* (Paris: Richard Massé, 1949). The Messiaen profile appears on pp. 127–30.

[34] Presumably a reference to the *Deux Monodies en quarts de ton* for ondes Martenot, composed in 1938.

[35] In the 1949 reprint, the word 'intransposables' of the 1942 text is changed to the virtually meaningless 'intransportables'.

important to think carefully before judging this man and his music: even without comprehension or sympathy, it demands the most penetrating attention and presents, through its revelatory visions, the development of Messiaen's talent which cannot be concealed. He has certainly not yet given us the best of himself and, if he has formed his aesthetic, defined his point of view, everything leads one to believe that he has not yet completely imbued every reflex, and that we may need to wait a few years before the composer of the *Diptyque* completely liberates and masters his system in a way which we believe will be without parallel.

For a long time he has been distant from the theatre, whose simplistic psychology offends him. He is the author of all the texts he sets to music. Messiaen admits a few literary influences, in particular those of his mother, the poetess Cécile Sauvage, and of Claudel.[36] For the rest, he withdraws into himself, to his home, and towards God, with whom he associates his slightest gesture. It is from this perspective that he must consider whether he wants to strive for the esoteric meaning of his art.

The last paragraph raises some provocative issues. Messiaen's view of theatre was certainly not as negative as Machabey suggests: from childhood his Shakespeare performances right up to his work on the incidental music for *Dieu est innocent* (at exactly the same time as Machabey's article), Messiaen was involved in theatrical activity, and his passion for opera never wavered. More intriguing is Machabey's view of Messiaen as isolated, his withdrawal 'into himself'. This is perhaps the first suggestion of something that was later to become an *idée fixe* in writings by others about Messiaen: his remoteness from the mainstream of Parisian musical activity. Its timing is particularly curious here, given how busy he was as a teacher and concert-giver during 1942.

Messiaen's success at the Association de Musique Contemporaine, in May 1942, was followed the same month by the first publication of the score and parts of the *Quatuor pour la fin du Temps*, in an issue of one hundred copies. The *dépôt légal* copy in the Bibliothèque Nationale de France has a date stamp of 21 May 1942, and in the 29 May issue of *L'Information musicale* a Durand advertisement states that it has just been published at 200 francs net. The advertisement also includes a 'Note de l'auteur' about the Quartet,[37] and a listing of all Messiaen's works published by Durand up to 1942. The publication was reviewed on 10 July 1942 (p. 1028) as part of the regular column in *L'Information musicale* on 'L'édition musicale', signed by 'Gawann'.

In such a few lines, I will not attempt to give you a faithful idea of the *Quatuor pour la fin des*[!] *temps* for violin, clarinet, violoncello and piano inspired by the Apocalypse of Saint John which M. Olivier Messiaen brought back from his captivity and dedicated to his fellow creators. The magnitude of its proportions, the sincerity, the nobility of its vision is enough to attract the interest even of those who might dispute certain aspects

---

[36] Machabey's revised text makes a curious alteration to this passage. In the 1948 publication it reads: 'il aborde aujourd'hui l'opéra-comique, mais n'admet que peu de collaborations littéraires, comme celle de sa mère ou de Claudel'.

[37] A shortened version of the second paragraph of Messiaen's 'Préface' in the score.

of its style, its harmonic language, its philosophical preoccupations. If certain
rhythmic passages appear a little deliberate and are not exempt from monotony, the
mystical sections, such as the fifth and the last, have a quality and individuality of
realisation which are those of an artist endowed with precious gifts. It must be hoped
that he will know how to realise all his promise beyond any preconceived system.
A work such as this *Quatuor* should gain the attention of interested instrumentalists
and of listeners who are seeking the poetic life of a work beyond mere notes.

In Messiaen's concerts during 1942, we also find him performing the music
of his wife, Claire Delbos. On 3 June, for example, he played for the soprano
Renée Dyonis in the second half of a concert at the Salle Chopin billed as 'Le
Sentiment et la Nature dans le Lied'. Messiaen accompanied the *Chanson du
Galérien* and *Berceuse* by Marcel Delannoy, Delbos's *L'Ame en bourgeon* and
Ravel's *Histoires naturelles*.

In mid-June, *Les Corps glorieux* was published in three fascicles by Alphonse
Leduc, and was sent for *dépôt légal* by 19 June, although it was to be another
eighteen months before the work was given its first complete public performance (by Messiaen at the Trinité, on 15 November 1943). Messiaen spent the
summer with Claire and Pascal in Neussargues working on *Technique de mon
langage musical* (published by Leduc in 1944). The autumn season included
the 200th concert of Le Triptyque, at the Salle de l'Ecole Normale on Tuesday
22 December. The distinguished group of musicians assembled for this
occasion included Poulenc, Bernac and Messiaen. *L'Information musicale*
(18 December, p. 146) included a short article about the event:

> Founded in 1934 by Pierre d'Arquennes with the twin goals of serving the cause
> of French music, especially contemporary music, and of giving young performers
> the opportunity to play in public, Le Tryptique has served music well, and has
> established itself among the most important chamber music societies in Paris . . . In
> 1938, the Ministry of Education lent its support, but Le Tryptique does not benefit
> from any official grant, and pursues its generous aims in complete independence . . .
> On the occasion of its 200th concert, Le Tryptique is giving an evening of exceptional
> brilliance. Once again, it will prove its eclecticism through the diversity of the
> musical tendencies represented by the composers on the programme. The Institut is
> represented by Florent Schmitt, the Conservatoire by Claude Delvincourt, women's
> music by Suzanne Demarquez, the Groupe des Six by Honegger, the Ecole d'Arcueil
> by Sauguet, la Jeune France by Messiaen, and the Independents by Robert Bernard.

It was indeed an evening of extraordinary stylistic diversity: André Pascal and
Messiaen playing the *Thème et Variations* between Honegger's *Poèmes de
Claudel* and Sauguet's *Quatre mélodies*, both of which were performed by
Pierre Bernac and Francis Poulenc. The soloist in Bernard's Cello Sonata was
André Navarra, Aline van Barentzen played Delvincourt's *Bocasserie* and the
Quintette Instrumental Pierre Jamet gave the first performance of
Demarquez's *Variations, Interlude et Tarentelle sur un thème populaire
corse*, and ended the concert with Schmitt's *Suite en rocaille*.

The end of the year brought one piece of very good news. Denise Tual offered Messiaen a commission to write a new work – which would become the *Visions de l'Amen* – for the Concerts de la Pléiade. On 26 December, Messiaen wrote to her formally accepting the terms: 'We are entirely in agreement on all the points. I will write for you a work for two pianos; you will put it on at your third concert. I will be paid 10,000 francs for it, and I have already received your cheque for 4,000 francs on account.'[38]

Music for 'un Oedipe': Fabre's *Dieu est innocent*

The only work Messiaen is known to have completed in Paris during 1942 was listed by its composer in the 1944 worklist of *Technique de mon langage musical* as *Musique de scène pour un Oedipe*, for solo Ondes Martenot. The commission had come at the end of the previous year. Messiaen's 1941 diary concludes with a note, 'Revoir Herrand pour musique de scène pour une œuvre d'Euripide ou un mystère moyen-âge aux Mathurins. *Je ferai musique*'. In the end it was to be neither Euripides nor the Middle Ages. There was a considerable vogue for Greek plays at the time, and at least two new French translations of Sophocles's *Oedipe* were published in 1941;[39] André Gide's *Oedipe* (originally staged in 1932) was republished by Gallimard in 1942 in the first collected edition of his plays.[40] Messiaen's music, however, was not for a play called *Oedipe* at all, but for a new one about Oedipus: *Dieu est innocent*, by Lucien Fabre (1889–1952), which opened on 1 July 1942. The cast list of the first edition (published by Editions Nagel in 1945) states that 'La musique de scène était d'Olivier Messiaen.' In his comprehensive survey of theatrical activity in occupied Paris, Hervé le Boterf singles out Fabre's play for particular praise: 'Of all the works conceived in the Hellenic tradition, the most interesting is perhaps *Dieu est innocent*, put on at the Mathurins by Marcel Herrand. Its author, Lucien Fabre, is best known for his novel *Rabevel ou Le Mal des Ardents*, winner of the Prix Goncourt in 1923 . . . In his striking adaptation, he managed in the space of one evening to dramatise a good twenty years in the life of Oedipus.'[41] What of Messiaen's music? The score remains to be rediscovered, but according to

[38] The complete surviving correspondence with Tual about *Visions de l'Amen* was first published in Nigel Simeone, 'Messiaen and the Concerts de la Pléiade'. For a more recent account, see Hill and Simeone, *Messiaen*, pp. 121–9.
[39] The catalogue of the Bibliothèque Nationale de France includes the following editions of Sophocles's play first published in 1941:

Oedipe de Sophocle . . . Traduction nouvelle et littérale en vers eumolpiques, de Gabriel Boissy (Marseille: R. Laffont, 1941); *Oedipe roi, traduit en vers par J.-René Chevaillier* (Paris: Hachette, 1941).
[40] André Gide, *Théâtre* (Paris: Gallimard, 1942).
[41] Le Boterf, *La Vie parisienne sous l'occupation*, p. 133.

Yvonne Loriod-Messiaen its themes were not allowed to go to waste: they were reused a few months later in Messiaen's largest commission to date: *Visions de l'Amen*.[42]

As we have seen, Marcel Herrand and Jean Marchat, the directors of the Théâtre des Mathurins, had already presented a series of 'Concerts-Causeries' in 1940–41, including Jolivet's on *La Jeune France*, and Messiaen's involvement with the Théâtre des Mathurins went back to the June 1941, when it was the venue for the Paris premiere of the *Quatuor pour la fin du Temps*. But with his commission to write music for *Dieu est innocent*, Messiaen found himself working alongside some of the most influential figures in French theatre. The company which had found its home at the Mathurins in 1939 was the Rideau de Paris, run by Herrand and Marchat, both of whom were also distinguished actors on stage and in the cinema. Herrand is perhaps best remembered for his superb performance as the oily villain Lacenaire in Marcel Carné's *Les Enfants du paradis*, and both can be heard on a recording of Stravinsky's *L'Histoire du soldat* made in 1952.[43] Messiaen worked with Lucien Fabre again in late 1944 and early 1945, recording improvised incidental music (on the organ of the Palais de Chaillot) for Fabre's *Tristan et Yseult*, which opened on 22 February 1945 at the Théâtre Edouard VII (with Danielle Darrieux playing the role of Isolde).[44] Just as *Dieu est innocent* had provided thematic material for Messiaen's next large-scale work, so did *Tristan et Yseult*, the programme of which includes a facsimile of the 'Thème d'amour' which was to find a more permanent home a few months later as the great love theme in *Harawi*.[45]

Political orientations

Putting the events of these months into a broader cultural context, it is worth remembering that the Parisian artistic event of 1942 which attracted the greatest attention at the time was an exhibition at the Orangerie in May, described by Julian Jackson as 'one of the high spots of cultural collaboration'.[46] This was a retrospective of work by Arno Breker (who had the

---

[42] Yvonne Loriod-Messiaen, personal communication.
[43] Marchat is the Narrator and Herrand the Devil; the performance is conducted by Fernand Oubradous and it has been reissued on CD by EMI France (585234-2).
[44] Danielle Darrieux (b. 1917) studied the cello at the Paris Conservatoire before starting an acting career at the age of 14. She is probably best known for her later

film roles, including memorable performances in *Les Demoiselles de Rochefort* (1966) and much more recently in Ozon's *8 Femmes* (2001).
[45] A facsimile of Messiaen's manuscript of the *Tristan et Yseult* theme is in Hill and Simeone, *Messiaen*, p. 143, pl. 83.
[46] Jackson, *France: The Dark Years 1940–1944*, p. 311.

misfortune to be Hitler's favourite sculptor), featuring a number of his heroic marble nudes. Those present at the opening included two prominent members of the Vichy régime: Pierre Laval (the Prime Minister) and Abel Bonnard (the Minister of Education). Two notorious Vichy polemicists, Fernand de Brinon and Jacques Benoist-Méchin, were there along with Jean Luchaire (the ultra-collaborationist editor of *Les Nouveaux Temps*), and artists such as André Derain, Dunoyer de Segonzac and Kees van Dongen. Aristide Maillol (the Grand Old Man of French sculpture) came up from the south of France especially for the occasion. He had been Breker's mentor in the 1920s, and was grateful to Breker for his role in saving Maillol's Jewish model Dina Vierny. Others present included Sacha Guitry, Jean Cocteau (whose 'Salut à Breker' was published in *Comoedia*), Serge Lifar and Arletty. Once the exhibition opened to the public, 60,000 French visitors poured through the doors of the Orangerie to see Breker's work, as did almost all of the occupying forces.[47]

Messiaen's own political position during the Occupation was altogether more distanced (and, as far as possible, disinterested) than those who attended the Breker opening at the Orangerie. His friends included *résistants* and others on the Far Left (notably Roger Désomière and Elsa Barraine). By contrast, his principal publisher at the time, René Dommange (Managing Director of Durand), was an active supporter of the Vichy régime.[48] Messiaen sent greetings (via Claire) to Alfred Cortot in a letter sent from Stalag VIII-A in August 1940, but he was most unlikely to have known at the time of Cortot's recent appointment (in June–July 1940) as an advisor on artistic policy to the Vichy régime.[49] Messiaen could hardly avoid asking for Cortot's support for the Conservatoire post while he was in Vichy during March and April 1941, but I have found no later references to Cortot in Messiaen's diaries during the years of the Occupation (let alone later on), even though Cortot was appointed to the Conseil supérieur de l'enseigne-ment du Conservatoire in July 1941.[50] Messiaen mentions in a letter to Claire from Vichy (12 March 1941) that 'there are several vacant places for har-mony teachers', and presumably he realised that these had arisen because the Vichy régime had just dismissed all the Conservatoire's Jewish staff (includ-ing Loriod's teacher Lazare Lévy, who was reinstated in 1944).[51] Messiaen had just returned from nine months as a German prisoner of war. He was unemployed, but had a wife and child to support, so his eagerness to be appointed to the Conservatoire post is entirely understandable. His position

[47] Information from Cointet, *Paris 40–44*, p. 175.

[48] See Hill and Simeone, *Messiaen*, p. 391, n. 22.

[49] See Hill and Simeone, *Messiaen*, p. 96.

[50] See Chimènes, 'Alfred Cortot et la politique musicale du gouvernement de Vichy', p. 36–7.

[51] Hill and Simeone, *Messiaen*, p. 105.

there was officially confirmed on 17 April 1941, two days after Claude Delvincourt had been named as the new Director.[52]

Once he had taken up his new post at the Conservatoire, Messiaen's main day-to-day concerns during the Occupation were the same as those of most other Parisians: earning some sort of a living and getting by despite the privations of food and fuel shortages, trying to advance his career without compromising his integrity as a Frenchman, and avoiding contact with the occupying Germans if possible. However, it was necessary to ask the Germans for permission to put on concerts, and this is why there are references in Messiaen's diary to Fritz Piersig, Head of the Music Section at the Propaganda-Staffel. Another German with whom Messiaen almost certainly came into contact during the Occupation was the passionately Francophile Heinrich Strobel. It is not surprising that Strobel held no official position with the occupying powers: he had been denounced at the *Entartete Musik* exhibition in 1938 as a supporter of 'musical Bolshevism', and his wife was Jewish.[53] But he worked in Paris as music critic of the German-language *Pariser-Zeitung* (1940–44) and, after the war, while Head of Music at Südwestfunk in Baden-Baden, he was to prove a remarkable source of commissions for Messiaen (*Réveil des oiseaux*, *Chronochromie* and *Couleurs de la cité céleste*).

Messiaen's pronouncements on politics were few indeed, but one is striking: an interview he gave for the de Gaulle memorial volume of the journal *L'Herne* in which he explained his admiration for a man he valued above all as a symbol of France itself rather than as a political figure – hardly a surprising view given Messiaen's evident lack of engagement in political affairs. He recalled his time as a prisoner of war in Stalag VIII-A:

> In our despair, a single name rose up, a name to which everyone clung, and it was that of General de Gaulle. He did not yet have the recognition which was to follow, since he was still a clandestine figure if you like. But despite all the precautions taken by the Germans, the prisoners very quickly found out about him, and put their hope in him. This was a flame which glowed in the darkness. I think those who did not follow him later were wrong – precisely because, whatever their opinions, General de Gaulle represented France. He was someone who truly loved France, who personified France, who symbolised France and who was part of French mythology.[54]

---

[52] See Jean Gribenski: 'L'Exclusion des juifs du Conservatoire (1940–1942)', in Chimènes (ed.), *La Vie musicale sous Vichy*, p. 145.
[53] See Schwartz, 'La Politique musicale dans les territoires conquis par l'Allemagne nazie', pp. 137–8, and Willem de Vries: *Sonderstab Musik: Music Confiscations by the Einsatzstab Reichsleiter Rosenberg under the*

Nazi Occupation of Western Europe (Amsterdam University Press, 1996), p. 137.
[54] Olivier Messiaen: 'Des paroles d'esprit: entretien avec Olivier Messiaen', in *Charles de Gaulle* (Paris: L'Herne, 1973), pp. 44–6; English translation in Hill and Simeone, *Messiaen*, p. 140.

Messiaen's 1942 diary: an annotated transcription of significant entries

Messiaen's pocket diary for 1942[55] provides us with a day-to-day portrait of a busy musician at work during one of the most arduous years of the Occupation. As well as his commitments at the Trinité and teaching at the Conservatoire, 1942 was also a busy year in terms of publications: the *Quatuor pour la fin du Temps* and *Les Corps glorieux* were printed, and Messiaen was hard at work on his 'Traité' (*Technique de mon langage musical*). At the very end of the year, Messiaen was commissioned to write *Visions de l'Amen* by Denise Tual – alluded to only indirectly in the diary, but Tual's address is among those written in the back (see Appendix at the end of the chapter).

This document is not a journal – it is a typical small pocket diary of the sort used to record appointments and write personal reminders, with pages for addresses at the end, but Messiaen sometimes outlines plans for works (including a commission from Etienne de Beaumont, which was never written), and he even writes five lines of music on the last page.

The names that appear regularly include members of Messiaen's family: his wife Claire Delbos (with her pet name of 'Mi' or 'Mie'), his son Pascal (whose fifth birthday was on 14 July) and his father Pierre ('Pio'). Messiaen's brother Alain is also mentioned, even though he was languishing in a prisoner of war camp. Among the numerous musicians, Messiaen's young pupil Yvonne Loriod ('Loriot') is mentioned several times, as a page-turner and as a pianist. Messiaen also records having seen quite a lot of André Jolivet during this year – though surprisingly the diary makes no mention of the first complete performance of Jolivet's *Messe pour le jour de la paix* which Messiaen gave with Marcelle Bunlet on 25 March. Since they appeared so regularly together in concerts, it is no surprise to find frequent references to the singer Marcelle Bunlet. Messiaen also worked on several occasions with Irène Joachim – a partnership which may well have led to the singer mentioning Messiaen to her cousin, Denise Tual, who was to commission *Visions de l'Amen* from Messiaen at the end of the year. Details of two semi-private performances of the *Quatuor* which took place in 1942 (in January at Etienne de Beaumont's, and in December at Virginie Schildge-Bianchini's) are given, and there are numerous references to rehearsals with Jean and Etienne Pasquier and the clarinettist André Vacellier, who had become Messiaen's regular team for the work since they gave the Paris premiere with him on 24 June 1941. Messiaen's diary suggests that he attended at least two of the events during the 'Semaine Honegger' (on 1 and 3 July 1942), during Honegger's fiftieth birthday

[55] I owe a great debt of gratitude to Yvonne Loriod-Messiaen for allowing me and Peter Hill to make a transcription of this diary in September 2001.

celebrations. He also visited Honegger on at least one occasion to discuss his 'Traité'. Apart from Loriod, other pupils include Françoise Aubut, Yvette Grimaud and Virginie Schildge-Bianchini, who also ran a musical salon in her home, at which Messiaen performed. Messiaen's duties at the Trinité required him to find deputies whenever he was away. His regular replacement was Line Zilgien, another Marcel Dupré pupil.

There are frequent references to three major Parisian publishing houses, all of whom were involved with Messiaen during the year: Durand for the *Quatuor* and the 'Traité' (which they declined), Leduc for *Les Corps glorieux* and (by the end of the year) the 'Traité', and Lemoine. Messiaen tried to interest Lemoine in the 'Traité' (again without success), but in the end the firm published Claire Delbos's *Paraphrase sur le jugement dernier* (1939) for organ.

Eric Sarnette is a less familiar figure, who nevertheless also figured in Messiaen's diary. Sarnette held several posts, one of which was as 'cultural officer for Paris' according to *L'Information musicale*. Before the war, he had been a significant figure in French film music (and a contributor to 'Cinéma et musique', a special number of *La Revue musicale* published in 1934). In 1942, he was the editor of the journal *Musique et radio* for which Messiaen wrote an article published in November 1942, with the title 'Technique de mon langage musical', perhaps the first use of the phrase which was to provide the title for the 'Traité' about which we read frequently in the 1942 diary.

Messiaen's spellings of names have been silently corrected (he sometimes referred to de Beaumont as 'de Baumont', for example), with the exception of 'Loriot' for Loriod – an endearing slip, since '*Loriot*' is the French word for a Golden Oriole.

Edited transcript of Messiaen's diary

30–31 December 1941

Elysée 49–53 M. Dommange [Durand] tél de 11 h à midi pour Traité.

Au Comité d'Organisation professionelle de la musique – lui demander [two unreadable words] et lui montrer mon travaille. Traité de 280 pages: coût 50.000 fr. graver tout …

Friday 2 January 1942

A 11h voeux de ma classe chez moi. [appointments all day at home incl.:] 6h [Yvette] Grimaud (compos., analyse).

Saturday 3 January

Les Pasquier [presumably a rehearsal of the *Quatuor*].

Sunday 4 January

9h1/2 gr. Messe [at the Trinité].

Monday 5 January

1h1/2 chez Jean Pasquier pour *Quatuor*.

Wednesday 7 January

1h1/2 chez J. Pasquier. Vacellier.

Thursday 8 January

5h1/2 chez Jolivet.

Friday 9 January:

9h répét. *Offrandes*, R. de Madrid.

Saturday 10 January

9h répét. *Offrandes*, R. de Madrid.

Sunday 11 January

9h1/2 répét. Société rue de Conserv.

5h45 Société: *Les Offrandes*.[56]

Monday 12 January

9h1/2 (demander Loriot tourner *Quat.*)

1h1/2 *Quatuor* répétition chez J. Pasquier avec Vacellier.[57]

Saturday 17 January

Chez de Beaumont 3h1/2 répét avec les 4.

5h1/2 mon *Quatuor* chez M. de Beaumont (2 Pasquier, Vacellier et moi,
   Loriot tourner).[58]

Monday 26 January

M. Lemoine prend *Paraphrase* Mie – Il lui envoie lettre et 1.000 fr. en chèque –
   répondre notre acceptation par lettre (Mie et moi) à M. Lemoine.[59]

Monday 2 Februaryt

Passer chez Durand pour Préface … et 2e épreuves musique *Quatuor*.
   J'achète *Rossignol* (chant piano) Stravinsky – commandé.[60]

---

[56] This concert was given by the Société des Concerts du Conservatoire, conducted by Charles Munch, in the Salle du Conservatoire (see above for details).

[57] Here (as elsewhere in the 1942 diary) Yvonne Loriod's name is spelled incorrectly as 'Loriot'.

[58] Comte Etienne de Beaumont (1883–1956) was a wealthy patron of modern art. He was particularly well-known for his support of ballet, organising the Soirées de Paris in May and June 1924. This remarkable season was arranged with the help of Jean Cocteau and Léonide Massine, who choreographed all the new ballets: Milhaud's *Salade*, Satie's *Mercure* and the Offenbach/Rosenthal ballet *Gaîté Parisienne*. De Beaumont encouraged Messiaen for several years after this concert (see above).

[59] The *Paraphrase* for organ by 'Mi' (or 'Mie'), Messiaen's pet name for Claire Delbos, is a work which Messiaen performed several times, and was published by Lemoine in 1949. Messiaen was dealing with her business affairs, and in several entries in the 1942 diary he mentions discussion of her works as well as his own. In all likelihood, he was already concerned about the early manifestations of Claire's mental illness.

[60] Preparations for the first publication of the *Quatuor pour la fin du Temps* were evidently well under way by this stage. Messiaen noted that he collected the second proofs on 2 February, and the first edition was on sale just over three months later: the work was published on 15 May 1942 (as Messiaen noted on 14 May), and the *dépôt légal* copy in the Bibliothèque Nationale de France has a date

Saturday 7 February

Tél Jolivet, Malvesin.

6h Mme Bianchini chez moi.

Sunday 8 February

2h1/2 Concert Loriot.

Les Pio mangent chez nous.[61]

Saturday 14 February

3 mélodies préparer

5h1/2 Triptyque: J'accompagne mes 3 mélodies.[62]

Sunday 15 February

8h dîner chez Pio – reprendre traduct. *Corps glorieux*.[63]

Tuesday 17 February

Reclamer 2e épreuves Leduc [*Les Corps glorieux*].[64]

Wednesday 18 February

A 1h1/2 voir Dupré.

16–18 February

[note at foot:] Vers la mi-février concert chez Mme Bianchini: choix de
    mes mélodies avec Bunlet (30 min.) Bunlet est absente du 20 fév. au
    10 mars, pas libre aussi fin mars. Bunlet chanta Delannoy et moi pour
    500 fr. (son prix est 1000 fr.).

Monday 23 February

Porter Leduc Index et catalogue français – anglais et Information [for *Les
    Corps glorieux*].

Thursday 26 February

Faire catalogue des mes œuvres avec les dates de composition (pour
    Chailley), organiser / envoyer ... copies lettres et article.

Envoyer Sarnette aux Beaux Arts (préfecture Seine) pour détails progr. 15
    [mars] et liste 20 personnes à inviter.[65]

stamp of 21 May. The paper is of unusually
high quality, though it was in notoriously
short supply: Durand's printing ledgers show
that only one hundred copies were printed.
[61] No concert by Loriod is mentioned in
L'Information musicale on this date, but this
may be a reference to one of the private
concerts she gave at the home of her
godmother, Nelly Sivade (at 53 rue Blanche).
[62] The singer was Lia Dassil. Among the other
works on the programme is the *Sonatine IV sur
des modes hindous* by Maurice Emmanuel,
played by Nadine Desouches.
[63] The translations for *Les Corps glorieux* to
which Messiaen is referring here are the 'Index
and catalogue' in French and English
mentioned on 23 February. However, the first
edition (published on 4 June 1942) contains

no prefatory material, no list of registrations
and no English text. A later issue prints a list of
names of organ stops in French and English,
but this was reprinted directly from the
equivalent list in the first edition of *La Nativité
du Seigneur*.
[64] As with Durand and the *Quatuor*,
Messiaen had an efficient publisher in Leduc
for *Les Corps glorieux*. With second proofs
ready by mid-February, things moved swiftly
to enable publication by 4 June (the date of
the *dépôt légal* for all three fascicles of the
work).
[65] Eric Sarnette introduced the works in this
concert, according to Armand Machabey's
review in *L'Information musicale* (27 March
1942), 885. This explains Messiaen's need to
send him information.

Monday 2 March

[note at foot:] Terminer et recopier Traité (avec un titre plus direct . . .
   cela doit être fini pour le 15 mai – à cette époque le porter à Lemoine.

Acheter Quatuors Beethoven.[66]

Saturday 7 March

17h30 Trocadéro Pasdeloup *Roi David*, places retenues.[67]

Sunday 15 March

A 3 h concert J[eune] F[rance] chez Mme de Drouilly.

[below:] au prép. 15 mars:

1) 2 *Préludes* pour Loriot (Nos. 5 & 8).

2) *Th. et var.* pour Malvesin et Messiaen.

Monday 16 March

billets Triptyque, tél. Malvesin pour répéter.

A 5h répétition chez Bunlet pour Triptyque (parle Bianchini).

Thursday 19 March

Mélodies travailler (Collier) à Bunlet 15h1/2.

Triptyque . . . à 20h15 Salle Chopin – j'accompagne mes mélodies à
   Bunlet. Programme Triptyque: Le sourire (1'), Prière exaucée (3'),
   Epouvante (3'), Le collier (3'), Vocalise (4') Résurrection (3') – (par
   Bunlet et l'auteur) total: 20 min.

Monday 23 March

Beethoven 9e [Symphonie].

9h1/2 Conserv. fugue.

1h1/4 je fais la classe d'orgue Dupré.[68]

Wednesday 25 March

Epreuves à midi chez Leduc [*Les Corps glorieux*].

Saturday 28 March

6h chez Durand.

Sunday 29 March

11h1/4 messe . . . Zilgien vient à midi à la Trin[ité].

Monday 30 March

Départ à Lévigny.

---

[66] This is an intriguing entry. Messiaen's choice of a 'more direct title' for his *Traité* was, of course, *Technique de mon langage musical*. The publisher he was hoping to interest at this stage was Lemoine rather than Leduc, who ultimately took it.

[67] Messiaen had great admiration for Honegger, and *Le Roi David* was one of several Honegger works he discussed in his classes. I am grateful to Jacques Tchamkerten for drawing my attention to a photograph of Messiaen's class which shows the score of *Le Roi David* on the piano.

[68] Messiaen deputised for Dupré's Conservatoire class on several occasions; Dupré's other regular deputy in 1942 was Maurice Duruflé (who was formally appointed to a harmony teaching post at the Conservatoire the following year).

[at foot:] Zilgien me remplace à la Trinité du lundi 30 mars au lundi 13 avril exclu.

Sunday 12 April

[note at foot]: Conserv. devoirs vacances: donné aux élèves. basse No. 64 46 C[hant] D[onné] Nos. 70, 71 et 72 de 87 leçons de Dubois – voir aussi No. 64 bis et aux Nos. 70, 71 et 72 bis déchiffrage.[69]

Monday 13 April

Donne devoirs . . . leçon [et] improvisation à l'orgue à Mlle Aubut au Conserv (100 fr. heur)

Organiser progr. 3 mai Bianchini – Bunlet. Remplir formule invit. – fix et date concert – tél Bunlet et Bianchini.

Tuesday 14 April

1h Durand – Leduc.

2h Pascal.

Week of 13–19 April

[above:] Envoyer à Bianchini formule invitation – envoyer à Bunlet liste mélodies choisies pour Bianchini.

[below:] Faire discuter *Ame en bourgeon* au Tryptique par [Irène] Joachim.

Monday 27 April

Tristan 9h1/2 Conserv.

2h . . . chez Durand.

3h Beaux Arts – papier Blumenthal et identité.[70]

[note below:] écrire Dommange pour parution *Quatuor* en mai . . .

Thursday 30 April

9h répét. chez J. Pasquier.

10h1/2 répét. chez Joachim.

[note below:] Répét. chez Joachim: apporter mélodies *Chants de terre* . . . répét. chez J. Pasquier . . . apporter Sonata Bach et 2 ex. du *Th. et var.*

Sunday 3 May

5h concert chez Mme Schildge: *Préludes* Loriot – mélodies Joachim et moi.

Monday 4 May

5h 8 rue de [unreadable] J. Pasquier et Messiaen jouent: Sonate Bach et *Th.et Var.* métro: Alésia.

---

[69] Messiaen's awareness of his own Conservatoire education, and perhaps of his heritage as a teacher there, led him to use a harmony textbook by one of his most traditionalist predecessors: Messiaen set holiday exercises for his pupils from Théodore Dubois's *Traité d'harmonie théorique et pratique* (Paris: Heugel, 1921).

[70] The 'papier Blumenthal' is presumably a reference to the Prix Blumenthal, given by the Fondation Américaine pour l'Art Français, which Messiaen had been awarded in 1941. The prize was a sum of money, given annually to two writers, two artists, one sculptor, one engraver and one musician.

Tuesday 5 May

Composer solfège.[71]

Friday 8 May

6h concert . . . à l'Ecole norm. – 3 *Préludes* (Nos. 5, 3 et 8 par Loriot) *Th. et var.* par J. Pasquier et moi (cachet).

Thursday 14 May

Ascension. 11h1/4 Messe . . .

5h Vêpres . . .

parle d'Alain à Pio.

[at foot of page:] *Quatuor* paru pour 15 Mai.

Saturday 16 May

départ Lévigny.

[at foot:] dossier papiers Zilgien dans tiroir bureau [Zilgien substituted for Messiaen on 17 May].

Monday 18 May

[at foot:] Bunlet guérie peut chanter à partir du 25 mai.[72]

Tuesday 19 May

Retour à Paris – tél Coedès pour dep. casuel . . . payer Zilgien[73]

Wednesday 20 May

Tél. Bunlet et envoyer progr. 15 juin à Dandelot.

[note at foot:] Curriculum à Landormy

Wednesday 27 May

1h1/2 je fais cours Dupré.

Saturday 30 May

1h1/2 je fais cours Dupré.

4h chez Mme Dyonis

6h répét. chez M. de Beaumont.

[note at foot:] Comité groupant Déso, Munch, Honegger, Poulenc, Delv[incourt] et Françaix 1 concert d'orchestre par mois chef d'orchestre: Désormière et Munch – orchestre Sociéte – *œuvres françaises modernes* – je fais partie[?] comité.[74]

Wednesday 3 June

17h30 Salle Chopin Concert Dyonis . . . accompagne Delannoy – Mie – Ravel – tourneur page [word erased]

---

[71] Presumably an exercise for the end-of-year examinations at the Conservatoire.

[72] Messiaen had been performing his songs with Irène Joachim for several weeks during Bunlet's illness. Since Bunlet was one of Messiaen's most devoted advocates, it is likely that he noted her recovery with some relief.

[73] Coedès-Mongin played the choir organ at the Trinité and conducted the choir.

[74] It is not known what Messiaen was rehearsing at de Beaumont's house, but by 4 June the Count had sent Messiaen a cheque for 1,000 francs for a new work (discussed above). The establishment of a committee to promote modern French orchestral music is fascinating, but it appears to have come to nothing.

Monday 8 June

4h 52 av des Ch. Elysées voir Dr. Piertzig.[75]

[note at foot:] Musique de scène Oedipe prête pour 15 juin – 10 minutes musique pour 1 ondes Martenot (on a un instrument et executant) [erased:] écrit [unreadable] pour cachet.

Tuesday 9 June

Oedipe.

Wednesday 10 June

Oedipe.

Thursday 11 June

à 5h chez Bunlet pour répét (donner invit.)

[note at foot]: Passer Soc. Auteurs [i.e. SACEM] acheter bulletin à 6 fr et déclarer *Quatuor* et *Corps glorieux* (prévenez Leduc).

Monday 15 June

8h du soir – concert E[cole] Norm[ale] organisé par Dandelot – au progr. 10 min de mes mélodies – 2e numéro (par Bunlet et moi) sans cachet. Sourire (1929), Epouvante (1936), Collier (1936), Résurrection (1938).

Thursday 18 June

Écrire letter z.[one] libre pour Delv[incourt].

Friday 19 June

Chailley pour z[one] libre.

6h chez Mme Dyonis (répét)

à 9h aux Mathurins – avec ondiste – répét. gen. [*Oedipe*].[76]

3h1/4 répét. avec Martinon chez Schildge.

4h concert chez Mme Schildge 8 mins de mélodies de Mie par Dyonis . . .

de 5h à 10h du soir *Oedipe* [star].

Monday 22 June

Mathurins à 8h . . . du soir

Th. et var. Martinon et Messiaen, 240 bis bvd St Germain.

Tuesday 23 June

Oedipe. 8h aux Mathurins, apporter musique.

Wednesday 24 June

8h du soir *Th. et var.* avec Martinon et Messiaen même endroit.

Thursday 25 June

Soc. Auteurs déclare *Oedipe* et *Corps glorieux.* 5h. écrire Alain.

---

[75] Fritz Piersig was responsible for the administration of music at the Propaganda-Staffel. Messiaen may have been to obtain permission for a proposed concert programme, or to have a list of guests approved.

[76] Messiaen does not identify the ondiste, but the likeliest candidate is Janine de Waleyne whose name appears (followed by 'ondiste') among the addresses in Messiaen's diary.

Monday 29 June

6h. répét avec Bianchini à la Trinité. 8h. Concert Honegger Ecole normale.

Tuesday 30 June

6h1/4 concert Bianchini à la Trinité.

Wednesday 1 July

20h Gaveau – Festival Honegger.[77]

Thursday 2 July

20h *Oedipe* tous les 3 [i.e. Messiaen, Claire and Pascal?]

Friday 3 July

20h Chaillot – Festival Honegger – 3 places pour nous.[78]

Friday 10 July

8h chez Pio.

Monday 13 July

Jouet Pascal.[79]

Tuesday 14 July

Alain (fête). Écrire Société Auteurs (*Corps glorieux*).

Wednesday 15 July

Trinité Mie.

Monday 20 July

Tél. Zilgien pour vacances Trinité. Trinité Mie.

Oedipe, voir papiers Soc. Aut. Dramatiques.

[at foot:] Écrire œuvre pour petit orchestre (20 musiciens maximum) par M. de Beaumont – payé – on la donnerait chez lui en janvier ou février prochain.[80]

Saturday 25 July

Donner tous papiers à Zilgien. Donner clefs et papiers à la sacristie.[81]

---

[77] The AMC concert for Honegger's fiftieth birthday, with Honegger conducting his *Prélude, Arioso et Fughetta sur le nom Bach*, *Pâques à New York* (with Eliette Schenneberg), *Six Poèmes de Jean Cocteau* (with Pierre Bernac) and *Le Dit des jeux du monde*. The programme also included the Second String Quartet (Bouillon Quartet), the *Trois Psaumes* (Schenneberg accompanied by Francis Poulenc) and the first performance of *Cinq Poèmes de Giraudoux* (Bernac and Poulenc).
[78] The programme consisted of *Regain* (the first concert performance of a film score), *Pacific 231*, the Concertino for piano (with André Vaurabourg) and *Le Roi David*, all conducted by the composer.

[79] A reminder to buy a toy for Pascal's fifth birthday, which was the following day.
[80] This project for a work for small orchestra never came to fruition, but Messiaen mentions it more than once in his diary (see week of 5–11 October), and he wrote to de Beaumont accepting the commission in June (see above).
[81] Messiaen spent the summer at the home of his wife's family in Neussargues (Cantal). It was during this holiday that Messiaen later claimed to have written his *Technique de mon langage musical*. It is clear from earlier entries and numerous earlier references to his 'Traité' that the treatise was already in existence before summer 1942; he is likely to have used the time to revise it and put the work into its final form.

Thursday 30 July

Écrire Alain.

[note at foot:] Zilgien fait P[etit] O[rgue] et G[rand] O[rgue] le 15 août. Vacances Trinité de 27 juillet au 4 octobre. Zilgien fait les casuels GO du 27 juillet au 4 octobre – et dimanche GO et PO du 1er août au 30 août exclus – je tendre traitement pendant vacances et reprends mon service le dim. 4 octobre

Tuesday 11 August

Drap – vin – bois – lait – huile. Alain.

20h départ Neussargues.

Week of 24–30 August

[note at foot:] Écrire Delvincourt et Chailley – et M. Herman[?]

Week of 21–27 September

[note at foot:] Copier pour 20 décembre ... *L'Ascension* d'O. Messiaen: 1 pupitre de 1er violin, 2 pupitres de 2e violon, 2 pupitre d'alto, 2 pupitres de vcl, 1 pupitre de CB.[82]

Wednesday 30 September

[asterisk, then note at foot:] En octobre mon *Quatuor* chez Mme Schildge Bianchini – avec mélodies par Bunlet et des *Préludes*? 500 fr à chaque interprète – Loriod tiendrait le piano pour tout.

Sunday 4 October

Je reprends mon service à la Trinité [star].

Week of 5–11 October

[note at foot:] Voir Munch qui accepte de jouer une de mes œuvres Société des Concerts. Trinité: concert orgue: Pierront (*Corps glorieux*), Zilgien (œuvres Mie au complet), Tobon-Mejia (œuvres Mie).

[another note at foot:] Écrire pour M. de Beaumont œuvre pour petit orchestre (20 musiciens maximum) – payé – on la donnerait chez lui février prochain.[83]

Week of 12–18 October

Envoyer à Sarnette pour 1er novembre: pour no. de *Musique et Radio* qui

---

[82] The orchestral material for *L'Ascension* was still only in manuscript, so Messiaen is probably listing additional parts needed for a planned performance of the work on 20 December. For the work's premiere in 1935, he had enlisted the help of his wife Claire and Claude Arrieu to copy the parts for the work. The score was first published by Leduc in June 1948, and a set of printed orchestral parts was prepared at about the same time.

[83] This entry is a characteristic example of Messiaen's networking with potential performers. Nothing immediately came of his meeting with Munch, though the conductor did perform *L'Ascension* on 3 and 4 February 1945. Noëlie Pierront was an organist who performed Messiaen's music regularly (she was also the first person to play any work by Messiaen in Britain). Line Zilgien was Messiaen's assistant at the Trinité, and he greatly admired her playing. I have been unable to identify Tobon-Mejia, though it is possible that he or she was a relative of the Columbian sculptor of the same name who had died in Paris in 1933.

parait 15 nov, article de tête: 35 lignes sur mon langage musical et ma photo.

Finir Traité et le donner à Leduc avec liste de souscripteurs pour son édition.[84]

Week of 19–25 October

[note at foot:] Jouer pièces d'orgue Mie.

[another note:] Organiser avec Sarnette et Bianchini 2 séances: une pour *Traité* et l'autre pour *Quatuor* (Pasquier) et mélodies (Bunlet) – chez Bianchini.

Week of 26 October–1 November

[note at foot:] Acheter *Corps glorieux* chez Leduc[!].

[another note:] Litaize et Langlais doivent donner à Chaillot le concert après Duruflé – leur proposer 1ere audition *Corps glorieux* – et écrire Pierront pour la même œuvre à la Trinité (Challan, Dandelot).

Thursday 29 October

4h à 6h répét. 15 av. du Maine – pour concert Radio Etat.

Sunday 1 November

6h moins le 1/4: Salle Pleyel, Honegger.

Monday 2 November

Préparer Radio.

Tuesday 3 November

4h1/2 à 5h concert par Radio – 15 ave du Maine (1000 fr). Zilgien tire les jeux.[85]

Friday 13 November

3h Jolivet.

Saturday 14 November

Envoyer liste adresses à Sarnette et Bianchini pour *Quatuor*.

Monday 16 November

Téléphoner Durand pour matériel et partition copiée *Hymne* qui part à Lyon. Sont-ils arrivés?[86]

Wednesday 25 November

Salle E. Normale 20h concert Dandelot 15 min des mes mélodies par Joachim et Loriod.

Saturday 28 November

5h1/2 Triptyque.

Messiaen accompanied a selection from the *Poèmes pour Mi*.

---

[84] Two entries related to the publication of *Technique de mon langage musical*, still described here as 'Traité'. The article for Sarnette is discussed above. The note about Leduc is more surprising. Evidently they needed Messiaen to supply a list of subscribers who could be guaranteed to purchase the work before they would consider publishing it.

[85] I have been unable to establish what Messiaen played for this broadcast. The 'Programmes de la Radio' listing in *L'Information musicale* (28 October 1942), 88, does not mention it at all.

[86] The score and the parts never arrived; Messiaen reconstructed the *Hymne* in 1946.

Sunday 29 November

à 5h chez Honegger (Square Vintimille) avec Traité. Faire article pour
Comoedia.

Monday 30 November

2h répét *Quatuor* chez J. Pasquier. Vacellier vient à 2h1/2.

Wednesday 2 December

8h du soir concert de Mme Bianchini – *Quatuor* – les 2 Pasquier, Vacellier
et moi – entendu.

Week of 7–13 December

Tél. Siohan (*Ascension*) – Printemps pour Baillot[?].

[at foot:] Siohan veut toujours *L'Ascension* à Pasdeloup.

Week of 14–20 December

[note at head:] Mlle Loriot pour 20 min. dans mes Préludes au Triptyque
en fin janvier ou février ... 1/2 heure de ma musique au 2e concert
orchestre pour prisonniers – le 28 janv. 18h – salle du Conserv., orch.
Société avec Girard chef.

Tuesday 22 December

Thème et Variations par André Pascal et moi.

Week of 21–27 December

[note at foot:] M. Méhu, 18–20 place de la Madeleine – Société
cinématographique Synops.[87]

Girard a partition orchestre *Ascension*.

Week of 28–31 December

[note at side and foot:] Voir d'abord à la Préfecture de Police, bvd
Chaptal. 1) M. Leclerc 2) Mme Bourreau 3) M. Moutarde[?] qui décide.
4) Monsieur Nostitz, 6 place du Palais Bourbon ou à l'ambassade
d'Allemagne, 78 rue de Lille (tél dans l'annuaire).

Monday 28 December

Départ Lévigny à 7h 30.

[but also:] 2 January 1943: Départ Lévigny.

[note at foot:] Docteur Piertzig, 52 Ch. Elysées, Propaganda allemande, de
la part de M. de Beaumont.

Appendix: addresses listed in Messiaen's 1942 diary

Messiaen's pocket diary for 1942 lists numerous addresses of musical colleagues and friends, including the following:

---

[87] This entry is connected with the
commissioning of *Visions de l'Amen*. Synops
was the film company of Denise and Roland
Tual. Messiaen visited Denise Tual there on
several occasions and he also corresponded
with Méhu.

Mlle Bernadette Alexandre-Georges, 86 rue du Rocher, 8e

Mlle Françoise Aubut, 16 ave Victor Hugo, 16e

Yves Baudrier, 201 ave de la Californie, Nice

M. Béchet, 7 square de la Dordogne, 17e (disques de Alban Berg, Bartók
   [deleted], Strawinsky, Debussy, Ravel)

Marcelle Bunlet, 89 rue Cardinet, 17e

Marcelle Bunlet, 16 ave Félix Faure, 15e [old address, crossed out]

Henri Busser, 5 rue Eugène Delacroix, 16e

[Pierre] Capdevielle, 51 rue St André des Arts, 6e

Jacques Chailley, 17 rue Alphonse de Neuville, 17e

Comoedia, 2 rue de Saint-Simon, 7e

Conservatoire National de Musique, 14 rue de Madrid, 8e

Georges Dandelot, 32 rue Leconte de Lisle, 16e

Jean Douel, 47 rue Decamps, 16e

André Dubois, 55 blvd Beauséjour, 16e

Maison Durand, 4 place de la Madeleine, 8e

Mme Renée Dyonis, 1 rue Récamier, 7e

Restaurant Espérion, rue St Augustin, 2e

Père François Florand, Couvent du Saint Sacrement

Jean Fournet (chef d'orch), 29 rue Taitbout, 9e

Marius-François Gaillard, 37 rue Marbeuf, 8e

Jean Gallon, 28 bis rue Guillaume Tell, 17e

Noël Gallon, 100 rue Jouffroy, 17e

André Girard (chef d'orch), 12 rue Salneuve, 17e

Mlle Yvette Grimaud, 187 rue Ordener, 18e

Arthur Honegger, 71 blvd de Clichy, 9e, examen de concours harm. 1942

Jean Hubeau, 13 ave de St Mandé, 12e

Georges Hugon, 72 ave de Suffren, 15e

Mme Irène Joachim (Mélisande), 14 place [?rue] de Laborde, 9e

André Jolivet, 30 ave Carnot, 17e

Jean Langlais, tél Ségur 72–05

M. Christian Langlois, 88 rue Lecourbe, 15e. Élève de Grunenwald doit
   rentrer dans ma classe.

Editions Lemoine, 17 rue Pigalle, 9e

Daniel Lesur, 19 blvd Longchamp, Marseille

Gaston Litaize, 14 rue Mayet, 6e

Raymond Loucheur, 12 rue des Écoles, 5e

Pierre Maillard-Verger, 139 Fbg St Honoré, 8e

Henri de Malvesin (violon), 32 rue de Lübeck, 16e

Mme Maurice Martenot ou Mlle Madeleine Martenot, 23 blvd
   d'Argenson, Neuilly

Jean Louis Martinet, 15 rue Bernoulli, 8e

Jean Martinon (violon), 189 rue Ordener, 18e

Henri Merckel (violon), 10 bis rue de Garches, Saint-Cloud

Jean Merry, 18 rue Henri Heine, 16e

Alain Messiaen, no. 81.342, Stalag VII B1, Deutschland (Allemagne) [in same diary given as 'Stammlager VII B1']

Pierre Messiaen, 44 quai Henri IV, 4e

Henri Monet, 10 blvd Emile Augier, 16e

Henri Monvoisin (violiniste), 17 rue de Paris, Pomponne

Raymond Niverd, 81 rue Laugier, 17e

Etienne Pasquier, 237 rue du Fbg St Honoré, 8e

Jean Pasquier, 4 square Gabriel Fauré, 17e

Pierre Pasquier, 33 rue de Moscou, 8e

Docteur Pierzig [Piersig], Propagande Allemande, 52 Champs Elysées, tel. Ely. 18–87

Propaganda-Staffel, Passage Elysée La Boëtie, Paris. Kommandant au 4e étage de l'ancienne Banque Américaine, Métro: Marboef [Marbeuf]

Mme Plé-Caussade, 83 ave Mozart, 16e

Eric Sarnette, 54 rue Fondary, 15e

Mme Schildge-Bianchini, 38 avenue du Président Wilson, 16e

Mme Sivade, 53 rue Blanche, 9e, tel. Trinité 63-04 pour Loriod

Alexandre Tcherepnine, 2 rue [de] Furstemberg, 6e

Mme [Denise] Tual: 9 rue de Beaujolais, 1er

Janine [de] Waley[ne] (ondiste), 9 rue des Lions, 4e

Mme Hélène de Wendel, 106 rue de l'Université, 7e

Mlle Line Zilgien, 42 ave de Suffren, 15e

2 Love, Mad Love and the *'point sublime'*: the Surrealist poetics of Messiaen's *Harawi*

Robert Sholl

... c'est dans l'amour humain que réside toute la puissance de régénération du monde'.[1]

Orientation

' "Messiaen is a poor composer, for he wears collars which are far from being fresh [.]" ... For Nadia and those who shared her opinion, there was only one composer: Igor Stravinsky.'[2] This judgement of Nadia Boulanger, recounted by her student Witold Lutoslawski, was doubtless never intended to see the light of day. Boulanger implies that Messiaen's originality was besmirched by the diverse sources of inspiration present in his music (including Stravinsky) and that, rather than being absorbed into his music or even transcended, these diverse presences came to dominate the substance of his music. While Boulanger's somewhat partisan views may be given some credence – especially, for instance in the obvious similarity between the end of Messiaen's *Poèmes pour Mi* (1936–37) and the end of the *Andante amoroso* of Alban Berg's *Lyrische Suite* (1925–26) – more importantly they identify one of the fundamental aesthetic issues raised by his music: how can we understand Messiaen's fusion of religion and modernism? For it is this Surrealist juxtaposition that underlines the originality and eclecticism of Messiaen's music that, in the 1940s, was straining at the leash of its hetero-geneous inheritance and moving towards fresh ornithological pastures. Certainly in his 'Tristan' cycle, which contains *Harawi: chants d'amour et de mort* (1945), a cycle of twelve songs for 'grand dramatic soprano' and piano, the ten-movement orchestral *Turangalîla-Symphonie* (1946–48), and the *Cinq Rechants* (1949) for twelve voices a cappella, the systematic hybridity of the early Stravinsky was subsumed by a more radical

[1] '... in human love resides all the power of worldly regeneration.' André Breton, 'Arcane 17' (1944–47), *Œuvres complètes*, vol. III (Paris: Gallimard, 1999), p. 62. My thanks to Mary Ann Caws, Anna McCready and Jeremy Thurlow, who all made pertinent observations about this study. All translations are my own, unless otherwise indicated.

[2] Undated conversation with Irina Nikolska in her *Conversations with Witold Lutoslawski* (1987–92), trans. Valeri Yerokhin (Stockholm: Melos, 1994), p. 64.

modernism, imprinted with both the scars of personal affliction and the recent events of the Second World War.

It is perhaps unsurprising, then, that Surrealism should have provided a fulcrum for Messiaen's musical thought. In an interview given in 1961, Messiaen explained that his music of the late 1940s was 'plus ou moins surréaliste' and that, in his own *textes explicatifs* that accompany his works, he had endeavoured to pastiche the writings of André Breton (1896–1966), Paul Eluard (1895–1952) and Pierre Reverdy (1889–1960) – poets who, in the 1920s and 1930s, were at the cutting edge of the Parisian artistic demi-monde.[3] By the late 1940s, when Messiaen counted himself a '*grand lecteur*' of these writers, the Surrealist group had effectively splintered, but their intellectual heritage and spirit of revolution were to remain potent.[4]

The aesthetics of Surrealism seemed to provide Messiaen with both a logical consolidation of his thought and the creative impetus to experiment beyond his musical boundaries. In his own description of his song cycle *Harawi*, a Quechua word used in Peruvian folklore that signifies 'an irresistible and profoundly passionate love, which leads towards the death of the two lovers', Messiaen indicates that:[5]

> There is above all in this work a great rhythmic research (added values, non-retrogradable rhythms, rhythmic canons, 'irrational' values and short notes linked to longer ones [*brèves liées à longues*], inexact augmentations, *personnages rythmiques*, etc.); a great quantity of non-classifiable chords and sonorities (notably the chords of inferior contracted resonance); the pursuit of a melodic line that is vocal, simple, singing, with its own melodic cadences; birdsong; counterpoints of water drops; [and] atmospheric vibrations. It is finally, *and this is the only thing of import, a great cry of love* [Messiaen's italics].[6]

Messiaen's emphasis on research intimates the importance of this work in his development as well as its proto-avant-garde status. In an article entitled 'Querelle de la musique et de l'amour' (printed in *Volontés* on

---

[3] *Entretien avec Olivier Messiaen*, recorded sometime during the sessions for the recording of Messiaen's *Turangalîla-Symphonie*, 11–13 October 1961 and included with that recording on Vega 30 BVG 1363. It is interesting that *Harawi* does not contain any preface or accompanying religious or explanatory texts. While Peter Hill and Nigel Simeone suggest that Messiaen may have done this in order to avoid further public controversy (following the performance of his *Trois Petites Liturgies*), Messiaen may also have felt that the prosaic nature of explanation might have undermined the allegorical and poetic nature of the work. Hill and Simeone, *Messiaen* (New Haven and London: Yale University Press, 2005), 156.

[4] Antoine Goléa, *Rencontres avec Olivier Messiaen* (Paris: René Juilliard, 1960), p. 155. Messiaen states that at the time of composing *Harawi* he was a great reader of Reverdy, Eluard and 'a beautiful work of André Breton on Surrealism and painting. It [*Harawi*] is therefore almost entirely Surrealist, with the exception of certain images taken from the mountains of the Dauphiné . . .' It is important to recognise that, after 1930, Surrealism became both a smaller club, from Breton's viewpoint, and a larger artistic movement that was reaching maturity through a diverse range of artists.

[5] Messaien, *Traité de rythme, de couleur, et d'ornithologie* (*TRCO*), Tome III (Paris: Leduc, 1996), p. 279.

[6] Messiaen, *TRCO*, Tome III, p. 282.

16 May 1945), which was written in the wake of a minor scandal surrounding a concert of Stravinsky's neoclassical pieces, Messiaen not only defended some of Stravinsky's neoclassical music, but (to paraphrase Messiaen) attempted to bring down two distant stars (faith and music) and unite these concepts in 'love'.[7] In stating his preference for the advent of 'a composer who is not neoclassical but who is so profoundly and brilliantly revolutionary that his style will one day be called *classical*', Messiaen opines that:

> There is so much that is dry and inhuman in contemporary music! Will our innovator be revolutionary only in his language? It seems almost certain that he will also bring love. And not these blocks of despair, these uninhabited planets, but Love with a capital L, Love in all its forms: of nature, of woman, of Childhood, and above all Divine Love . . . pray with me to the years, the days and the minutes that they may make haste to bring before us that innovator, that liberator who is so patiently awaited: the composer of Love.[8]

With this, Messiaen not only pours the oil of love onto troubled aesthetic waters (still in turmoil since 'Le Cas Messiaen', the scandal that predated, but was revived by the premiere of his *Trois Petites Liturgies de la Présence Divine* on 21 April 1945), but he points to love as the balm that will perfume his own musical innovations. From this perspective, Messiaen's *Harawi*, with its central topos of love, reveals a composer emerging almost unscathed from this winter of discontent, even more certain of his own mission to re-invigorate music with his faith.

As a high watermark of Messiaen's compositional development, the paradox of *Harawi* is perhaps all the more surprising: it is the first major non-religious work in Messiaen's output. Yet it also subsumes features of many of his earlier works: the ecstatic vision of redemption in *Le Banquet céleste* (1928), the twin souls singing beyond mortality in *La Mort du nombre* (1930), the power of human and divine love in *Poèmes pour Mi* (1936–37), the luminous violence and whirling gyrations of *Transports de joie* (*L'Ascension*) (1933–34), *Trois Petites Liturgies de la Présence Divine* (1943–44) and *Regard de l'esprit de joie* (*Vingt regards sur l'enfant-Jésus*) (1944), the veiled erotic hand in the velvet glove of classicism in *La Nativité du Seigneur* (1935) and the search for the transcendent in *Prière du Christ* (*L'Ascension*) and the *Quatuor pour la fin*

---

[7] In the preface to his *Technique de mon langage musical* (*TMLM*), trans. John Satterfield (Paris: Leduc, 2001), p. 7 (originally published in 1944), Messiaen states his desire for a musical language that might 'take down some yet distant stars'. In 'Querelle de la musique et de l'amour' (printed in *Volontés* on 16 May 1945), 1, he writes: 'I have had only two distant stars shining in my darkness: my faith and my music.' This article is translated in Hill and Simeone, *Messiaen*, pp. 153–4.

[8] Hill and Simeone, *Messiaen*, pp. 153–4. In the preface to *TMLM*, Messiaen uses similar language: 'Let us hasten by our prayers the coming of the liberator.'

du Temps (1940–41). All these works find their harvest home in *Harawi*.[9] But if the presence of God is sedimented in Messiaen's musical language (as he demonstrates abundantly in his *Technique de mon langage musical* (*TMLM*)), then the spiritual entropy of the 'revolutionary language' that Messiaen spoke of in 1945, can be understood as an embodiment of, and an allegory of, a burning eternal desire to be with God, predicated in the Christian ideal of predestination.[10]

   Likewise, if the theological narratives of death and resurrection are implicit in the aesthetics of modernity, then Messiaen's Surrealist musical language, which attempts to move beyond the strictures of what Pierre Boulez refers to as 'recognized "markers" within recognized forms', seems to internalise the poetic raison d'être of *Harawi*: the flight of the lovers from the world of *la vie quotidienne* towards their death, as exemplified both in Richard Wagner's *Tristan und Isolde* (1856–9) and Marc Chagall's *Bouquet with Flying Lovers* (1934–47).[11] As in Chagall's *tableau*, Messiaen's cycle places this flight on a metaphysical and eschatological plane while reflecting

[9] Brigitte Massin, *Olivier Messiaen: une poétique du merveilleux* (Aix-en-Provence: Alinéa, 1989), p. 172. In reference to *La Nativité du Seigneur*, Messiaen states that he wanted to show that it was possible to write organ music without referring to the post-Franck idiom. Nevertheless, this organ music is still heavily indebted (aesthetically) to the 'symphonic' thinking of Charles Tournemire (1870–1939).

[10] Messiaen's ideal of predestination is based on his belief that his mother, Cécile Sauvage's (1883–1927), poetry formed and predestined his future as a musician. Messiaen combines this with the New Testament ideal that predestination is God's loving purpose to make people his sons and daughters. Therefore, for Messiaen, it comes to signify the ways in which, through the loving grace of God, we are brought to God by conforming to the imitation of Christ.

[11] Pierre Boulez, 'Sound, Word, Synthesis' (1958), *Orientations*, trans. Martin Cooper (London: Faber and Faber, 1990), p. 178. 'There is a curve in the ear's response to the greater or lesser differentiation of intervals, a curve that may be established in relation to listening-time, duration and pitch are linked – "measurably" – by this phenomenon. In the case of very small intervals time must be considered as stationary, rather as though the ear were listening through a magnifying glass. Apart from this morphology, we must consider the part played by duration in listening. Western music has ingeniously developed recognized "markers" within recognized forms, so that it is possible to speak of an angle of vision, thanks to a more or less conscious and immediate "memorizing" of what has gone before. But with the object of keeping the listener's attention alerted these markers have become increasingly unsymmetrical and indeed increasingly "unremarkable", from which we may conclude that the evolution of form characterised by such points of reference will eventually end in irreversible time, where formal criteria are established by networks of differentiated possibilities. Listening is tending to become increasingly instantaneous, so that points of reference are losing their usefulness. A composition is no longer a consciously directed construction moving from a "beginning" to an "end" and passing from one to another. Frontiers have been deliberately "anaesthetized", listening time is no longer directional but time-bubbles, as it were.' In this passage, Boulez is not only referring to the ability of the ear to follow music through recognised musical signs, but commenting on the changing hierarchy of musical parameters in music, and the way that the ear responds to this phenomenon. Messiaen's *Harawi* therefore absorbs the 'anaesthetisation' of boundaries, while also providing a reconfiguration or resensitisation to musical time.

on physical and worldly transformation that acts, as a 'radical criticism of the past and a definite commitment to change and the values of the future'.[12]

Perhaps, however, unlike many of the grand-narrative later works, *Harawi* does not attempt to embrace or even embody God, but explores the ontological and spiritual status of humanity caught, as George Steiner implies, between Good Friday and Easter.[13] Any such anxiety is exacerbated at moments of crisis, and *Harawi* bears the scars of Messiaen's life like the scratches on photographic negatives that are only fully revealed when developed. *Harawi* can be considered as a cathartic and consolatory work: a refuge from, and an expression of, Messiaen's love for his first wife (the composer and violinist Claire Delbos, who became increasingly mentally unwell), and a sublimation of his burgeoning admiration for Yvonne Loriod, who had premiered the *Vingt Regards sur l'enfant-Jésus* and (with Messiaen) the *Visions de l'Amen*.[14] As an act of artistic honesty, consistent with what Messiaen had described as an emotional and sincere music, *Harawi* can be understood as a testimonial seismograph that registers Messiaen's emotional volatility in its gestural language, a language that resonates with the aesthetics of Surrealism.[15]

Surrealism and love

Born out of the ruins of Dada and on the wings of a spirit of artistic revolution, Surrealism absorbed, amongst other things, Freudian theory and Hegelian dialectics with the intention to 'transform the world, change life, and remake all things in the understanding of the word human'.[16] In his *First Surrealist Manifesto* (1924), André Breton gave the following 'definition':

> SURREALISM, noun. (masc.) Pure psychic automatism by which it is intended to express, either verbally or in writing, the real function of thought; thought dictated in the absence of all control exerted by reason, and outside all aesthetic or moral preoccupations.
>
> ENCYCL. Philos. Surrealism is based on the belief in the superior reality of certain forms of association thus far neglected, in the omnipotence of the dream, and in the disinterested play of thought. It leads to the definitive destruction of all other psychic

[12] Matei Calinescu, *Five Faces of Modernity* (Durham: Duke University Press, 1987), p. 95.
[13] George Steiner, *Real Presences* (University of Chicago Press, 1989), pp. 231–2.
[14] For more on this, see Hill and Simeone, *Messiaen*, pp. 157–9.
[15] In Messiaen's 'Note de l'auteur' to *La Nativité du Seigneur*, he begins with this statement of aesthetic intention: 'Emotion and sincerity, first of all. But transmitted to the listener by sure and clear means.'
[16] Jean-Louis Bédouin, *Vingt Ans de Surréalisme 1939–1959* (Paris: Denoël, 1959), p. 192, quoted in Mary Ann Caws, *Surrealism and the Literary Imagination: A Study of Breton and Bachelard* (The Hague: Mouton, 1966): 'transformer le monde, changer la vie, refaire de toutes pièces l'entendement humain'.

mechanisms and to its substitution for them in the solution of the principal problems of life.[17]

For the Surrealists, only through revealing the hidden life of our unconscious, by the engendering of a heightened or ecstatic sensibility of automatism, can real truth or a higher state of being be revealed. The destruction of the ego was a necessary predicate of transformation, and this is played out in the eventual desubjectification of the lovers in *Harawi*.

The Freudian struggle between Eros (love) and Thanatos (death) resonates in Messiaen's musical language as much as at the deeper unconscious level of the self represented in the androgynous soprano protagonist, who takes the part of both lovers.[18] Indeed, put another way, the process of desubjectification seems intimately bound up with the continual dialectic between the 'revolutionary' aspects and the sedimented secular meanings of his modernist musical language, and his religious aesthetics. For Messiaen, then, *Harawi* becomes something of a '*cas*' in itself, and this leads to the following questions: Can this dialectical process of overcoming itself be overcome, and does this explain the redemptive trajectory of the protagonist and even the nature of the work's lyricism? Does Messiaen's musical language, together with the eschatological telos of the Surrealist erotic gaze (from the first song), create a progessive sense of overcoming or even *éblouissement* (dazzlement) in which the listener is inelectably drawn towards a resensitisation of his own subjectivity in an encounter with God?

If this is so, then *Harawi* represents much more than a post-Freudian Surrealist gloss, for Messiaen's work is not merely about the revelation of subconscious desire; that is less than half the story. Through music, Messiaen attempts to re-orient the Kantian displacement of God by the sublime. If humanity can becomes like a stained-glass window, pierced by the light of God (mediated by colour in his music), this seems to indicate that music, for Messiaen, was perhaps a means by which God is able to draw us into the dynamic of his redemptive and transforming grace.

This call from God to humanity through the truth of art is an allegory of adoptive filiation (the call of God through his son Christ to us), an allegory realised through the agency of love in *Harawi*.[19] Freudian Eros is usurped by

---

[17] André Breton, '*Manifeste du Surréalisme*' (1924), *Œuvres complètes*, vol. I (Paris: Gallimard, 1980), p. 328.

[18] Wallace Fowlie, *Age of Surrealism* (London: Dennis Dobson, 1953), p. 108. For more on Eros and the 'death instinct', see *The Ego and the Id* (1923), especially Part IV, 'The Two Classes of Instincts', in Sigmund Freud, *On Metapsychology: The Theory of Psychoanalysis*, ed. and compiled. Angela Richards, trans. under the direction of James Strachey (London: Penguin, 1991).

[19] In his *Le Christ dans ses mystères* (Les Editions de Maredsous, 1947, first published 1919), trans. Mother M. St Thomas as *Christ in His Mysteries* (London: Sands and Co, 1924), Dom Columba Marmion, one of Messiaen's favourite theologians, writes: 'It is a wonderful thing that God should adopt us as His children; but the means that He has chosen to realise and establish this adoption is more wonderful still.

Christian *agapē* in *Harawi*, as love and desire are made sacramental through the renunciation and sacrifice of the self. The two lovers become one, but the unity can only be fully realised in death (in the seventh song *Adieu*) and the implication of Christian resurrection in the ninth song (*L'Escalier redit, gestes du soleil*). Thus, even as God is explicitly absent from *Harawi*, his redemptive presence is predicated in the telos of the lovers. Love can be understood therefore as the medium of the lover's transformation, and, allegorically, as a force that draws humanity towards the divine, an activity that is, in a secular vein, fundamental to Surrealism.

Indeed, Messiaen's use of Surrealism is not so much a Christian bourgeoisification as much as a continuation (in ways certainly unforeseen by Breton or indeed by other composers such as Francis Poulenc) and even a critique of its ideals.[20] If Messiaen hoped to overcome and transform modernity from within, and thereby reawaken an awareness of the presence of God in humanity, then Surrealism was an ideal heuristic tool. Messiaen attempts to overcome the wiles of modernity (with its ideals of alienation and progress) by creating his own model of aesthetic modernity though a hermeneutic circle of the interrelated dimensions of time, colour, love and birdsong that, like a stained-glass window, enlace, irrigate and glorify the central logos.[21] His gloss of eschatological aesthetics is well partnered by Surrealism's secular transcendentalism. For the Surrealist, the search for the *marvellous* could only approach the noumenal. What Walter Benjamin called a '*profane illumination*' might be achieved poetically by pushing the limits of language to release semantic serendipity and, most importantly, beauty beyond what was seen as the prosaic domain of reality.[22]

In his *Second Surrealist Manifesto* (1930), Breton seeks to illuminate the point at which the dialectics inherent in Surrealism will be overcome: 'For all

And what is this means? It is His own Son, (p. 49). On p. 149, Marmion explains further: 'The grace of divine adoption, which makes us brethren of Jesus and living members of His Mystical Body, gives us the right of appropriating to ourselves His treasures so that they may be accounted as our own by Himself and His Father.'

[20] In *Surrealism and Painting*, Breton states that 'Everything that is doddering, squint-eyed, vile, polluted and grotesque is summed up for me in that one word, God', *Surrealism and Painting*, trans. Simon Watson Taylor (London: Macdonald, 1972), p. 10, n. 10. The version of this book Messiaen would have known was the Brentano edition of 1946. This has much less material in it than the 1965 edition, which contains essays written by Breton on art in the intervening years.

[21] For more on Messiaen's aesthetics of modernity, see Robert Sholl, 'The Shock of the Positive: Olivier Messiaen, St Francis, and Redemption through Modernity', in Jeremy Begbie and Steve Guthrie (eds), *Musical Theology* (Grand Rapids: Eerdmans, 2008 forthcoming).

[22] Walter Benjamin, 'Surrealism: The Last Snapshot of the European Intelligentsia', in Peter Demetz (ed.), Edmund Jephcott (trans.), *Reflections: Essays, Aphorisms, Autobiographical Writings*, (New York: Random House, 1989), 179. In Claude Samuel's *Musique et couleur: nouveaux entretiens avec Olivier Messiaen* (Paris: Pierre Belfond, 1986), trans. E. Thomas Glasow (Portland, Oregon: Amadeus Press, 1994), p. 14, Messiaen states that 'I'm partial to the fantastic side of Surrealism, to the sort of science fiction that goes beyond reality and science itself.'

doors to belief there exists a certain point for the mind [*point d'esprit*] from which life and death, the real and the imaginary, the past and the future, the communicable and the incommunicable, the high and the low cease being perceived as contradictions.'[23] The impassioned rhetoric of this passage exposes the thin membrane between secular emancipation and religious or spiritual transcendence. So, when Messiaen, echoing Breton, makes the following comment, he implies that, for him at least, his music attempts to reach for a point beyond any semblance of conflict between religion and modernism:

> But if you define Surrealism as a mental vantage-point [*point d'esprit*] where visible natural realities and invisible supernatural realities are no longer in opposition to each other and where they cease to be perceived as contradictions, then I am a Surrealist composer. The disciples of André Breton ... wanted passionately to have on earth a state of the beyond. It did not occur to them to have that through faith. In a present eternity, I glimpse infinite life unbounded by Time and Space.[24]

In his novella *Mad Love* (*L'Amour fou*), Breton states: 'I have spoken of a certain sublime point on the mountain. It was never a question of establishing my dwelling on this point.' Breton goes on to explain that, were he to live at this *point sublime*, he would have ceased to be himself, and that, as such, he chose the role of a guide for others to see and 'in the direction of eternal love ... to identify the flesh of the being I love and the snows of the peaks in the rising sun'.[25] For Breton and Messiaen, love as erotic spiritual desire was an essential part of faith, and was not only the catalyst for an eschatological endgame, but also a point of creative and spiritual *éblouissement*.

The move towards synthesis (or redemption in Christian parlance), in *Harawi*, brings seemingly opposed ideas and images into a dialectical confrontation, and is played out on a number of different levels. As such, Messiaen's fusion of Christian and Surrealist notions of art and love, religion and eroticism, mythic and subjective narrative, consonance and dissonance, formal stability and localised instability, developmental and static temporal paradigms, his juxtaposition and reconfiguration of language, the importation of non-European culture, the iconography of birds, irrationality and radicalism and, most importantly, human and divine love are brought into a higher symbiosis, rather than any Hegelian synthesis. Indeed, from the tensions

---

[23] Breton, *Second Manifeste du Surréalisme* (1930), *Œuvres complètes*, vol. I, p. 781. On pp. 781–2, Breton writes that 'le point dont il est question est *a fortiori* celui où la construction et la destruction cessent de pouvoir être brandies l'une contre l'autre'. For more on this, see 'A Certain Point of the Mind', in J. H. Matthews, *The Surrealist Mind* (London and Toronto: Associated University Presses, 1991), pp. 186–206.

[24] Hill and Simeone, *Messiaen*, p. 167. This quotation derives from an article, documenting a conversation with Messiaen, by Ernest de Gengenbach, 'Messiaen ou le surréel en musique', *Revue musicale de France*, 15 April 1946.

[25] Breton, *L'Amour fou* (1936), *Œuvres complètes* vol. II (Paris: Gallimard, 1992), pp. 780 and 783, translated by Mary Ann Caws as *Mad Love* (Lincoln: University of Nebraska Press, 1987), pp. 114 and 116.

between these elements, and their evident biographical resonances, we can understand something of the essential lyrical radiance of *Harawi*.

For a Catholic such as Messiaen, such musical radiance was a reflection of God's presence (within humanity) that erupts effulgently into the world. Through the media of time and colour, music could act as a means of self-revelation whereby the soul is pushed *jusqu'au spasme* to begin a cathartic process of change and transfiguration, an aesthetic trajectory that is essential to Messiaen's music.[26] The reconfiguration of musical and poetic language and the energy released by that reconfiguration is intended not only to bring humanity towards an encounter with God, beyond the immanence of consciousness and language, but, through the presence of Christ, to transform humanity in his image. One can sense something of this quest for a quasi-religious ontology, albeit in a secular vein, in Salvador Dali's definition of ecstasy:

> Ecstasy constitutes the pure state of exacting and hyperaesthetic vital lucidity: blind lucidity of desire. It is *par excellence* the critical mental state that implausible actual thought – hysterical, modern, Surrealist and phenomenal – aspires to render continuous.[27]

One can sense in *Harawi* that the search for God in art has a 'hyperaesthetic vital lucidity' that attempts to render the implausible, the modern, Surrealist and phenomenal continuously through his output. For the Surrealist poet Louis Aragon, such a heightened sensibility had a combative and even transcendent quality: 'the relationship which is produced from the negation of the real by the marvellous is essentially ethical, and the marvellous is always the materialisation of a moral symbol in a violent opposition with the morality of the world in whose centre it appears'.[28] Messiaen's religious mission to render Christ appreciable to humanity and transform the world married a moral dimension (implicit in the sacramental status of love in *Harawi*) with a radical imperative that inspired a violent transfiguration of conventional musical language.[29]

---

[26] Josephin Péladan, *Le Théâtre complet de Wagner: les XI opéras scène par scène avec notes biographiques et critiques* (Paris: Slatkine, 1981), (first published Paris: Chameul, 1895), p. xi. 'But his [Wagner's] mission was another: to present to the occidental soul the mirrors whereby it has the power to be moved, Wagner had to be exclusively an emotional being. Nobody in historical humanity knew how to act more completely than him; he pushed the aesthetic impression to the point of spasm [*jusqu'au spasme*].'

[27] Salvador Dali, in Paul Eluard, in collaboration with André Breton, 'Dictionnaire abrégé du surréalisme' (1938), *Œuvres complètes*, vol. I (Paris: Gallimard, 1968), p. 743. 'EXTASE. – "L'Extase constitue

l'*état pur* d'exigeante et hyperesthétique lucidité vitale, lucidité aveugle du désir. Elle est par excellence l'état mental critique que l'invraisemblable pensée actuelle, hystérique, moderne, surréaliste et phénoménale aspire à rendre *continue*."'

[28] Quoted by Patrick Waldberg in *Le Surréalisme: sources, histoire, affinités, a catalogue published by the Galerie Charpentier*, 1964; stated in Mary Ann Caws, *The Poetry of Dada and Surrealism* (Princeton University Press, 1970), p. 20.

[29] For a recent exposition of the philosophy of love, see Roger Scruton's *Death-Devoted Heart: Sex and the Sacred in Wagner's Tristan and Isolde* (Oxford University Press, 2004), and, in a different vein, Celia Rabinovitch's

By configuring his modernist music as religious, Messiaen attempted to turn the post-Enlightenment substitution of God for the sublime on its head (a fitting metaphor considering the Roland Penrose painting (see Fig. 2.1) that inspired the cycle).[30] To take the profane hyper-romantic modernist aesthetic of Surrealism and reconfigure it towards God in *Harawi* was, therefore, a most important step in Messiaen's religious-modernist project. As Messiaen himself implies, such a somewhat courageous innovation was surely the task of 'a great artisan and a great Christian'.[31]

Surrealism unbound

If the transfiguration of the world was to take place, then action would be imperative. Such an expectation was elaborated by the philosopher Ferdinand Alquié when he stated that:

> What the Surrealist condemns is beauty as a spectacle, beauty separated from action and from life, a beauty to be contemplated, which does not instantly transform the person perceiving it. For all aesthetic perception of the beautiful supposes precisely an attitude of onlooking, of detachment, of withdrawal.[32]

What was needed was a means of galvanising the listener into a participation in the redemptive process, shocking him out of the ordinary.

Beauty for the Surrealist was present in the irrational and violent juxtaposition of objects and ideas, like Lautréamont's juxtaposition of an umbrella and a sewing machine (*Les Chants de Maldoror*, 1868–69), in order to create new references.[33] The Surrealist search for beauty and truth through opposition and juxtaposition of ideas is axiomatic to Pierre Reverdy's proto-Surrealist poetry and aesthetics.[34] In his essay

---

Surrealism and the Sacred: Power, Eros, and the Occult in Modern Art (Boulder, Co: Westview, 2004). Also Jennifer Mundy and Dawn Ades (eds), with Vincent Gille, *Surrealism: Desire Unbound* (Princeton University Press, 2005), Mary Ann Caws' *The Surrealist Look: An Erotics of Encounter* (Boston: MIT Press, 1999), and Mary Ann Caws (ed.), *Surrealism (Themes and Movements)* (London: Phaidon, 2004).

[30] Roland Penrose's *L'Ile Invisible* (1937) was the Surrealist painting that inspired *Harawi*. It was reproduced in the Parisian magazine *Minotaure* as *Seeing is Believing* in issue no. 10 (Winter 1937).

[31] Messiaen, *TMLM*, p. 7. See also the quotation above from Messiaen's article 'Querelle de la musique et de l'amour', p. 1, translated in Hill and Simeone, *Messiaen*,

p. 154. 'pray with me to the years, the days and the minutes that they may make haste to bring before us that innovator, that liberator who is so patiently awaited: the composer of Love.'

[32] Ferdinand Alquié, 'Le Surréalisme et la beauté', *Surrealismo e simbolismo* sous la direction d'Enrico Castelli (Padua: CEDAM, 1965), cited in Caws, *The Poetry of Dada and Surrealism*, p. 7.

[33] Caws, *The Poetry of Dada and Surrealism*, p. 168. Baudelaire's dictum that 'le beau est toujours bizarre' could easily be superscribed on most of Messiaen's scores.

[34] Messiaen may have become interested in Reverdy as a result of hearing about his conversion to Roman Catholicism in 1921 (baptised on 2 May). This led to Reverdy's story 'La Conversion' in *Risques et périls: contes 1915–1928* (Paris: Flammarion, 1972),

'L'Image', Reverdy makes the following connection between inspiration and emotion:[35]

> The Image is a pure creation of spirit. It is not born of a comparison but of the *rapprochement* of two more or less distant realities. The more distant and pertinent the rapport between the two realities, the stronger the image – the more it will have emotive power and poetic reality . . . But it is not the image which is great – it is the emotion provoked by it; the greatness of the image can be judged by this measure . . . it is the surprise and joy of finding oneself before a new thing.[36]

As intimated previously, the lyricism of *Harawi* is premised on the tensions inherent in a constellation of symbiotic concepts. Of primary concern is the conjunction of Surrealism and sedimented Catholicism. Throughout *Harawi*, these entities are brought together though the erotic, mythical, phantasmagorical and eschatological dimensions of love. This love is a sacramental symbol of the unbreakable bond between man and God, an intimation and longing for reconciliation and redemption that is promised through Christ. Through the lovers in *Harawi*, Messiaen gives an exemplar of the reciprocity of God's love, an intimation of what this should and will be, and therefore an allegory of how we are to follow Christ in this life and the hereafter.

God's presence, normally evident in Messiaen's authorial prefaces to his works and the scriptural indices that accompany them, is latent in Messiaen's own poetic language in *L'Escalier redit, gestes du soleil* (song IX of *Harawi*):

---

pp. 65–82. See Andrew Rothwell, *Textual Spaces: The Poetry of Pierre Reverdy* (Amsterdam and Atlanta: Rodopi, 1989), pp. 204–9. Rothwell reads this story as both a satirical attack on Max Jacob's (Reverdy's godfather) religious insincerity and, at the same time as guilt and the desire for repentance, the problems of fame and recognition and Reverdy's personal progression from poetic idealism to religious faith.

[35] Reverdy's early criticism is marked by an idealist emphasis on discipline and artistic control mixed with a taste for asceticism and a self-conscious individuality that may have appealed to the young Messiaen. Although there is some very slight evidence that Messiaen knew Reverdy, the occasional quotations in Messiaen's writings do little justice to the profound effect of Reverdy's aesthetics and poetry on Messiaen's music. In Guy Bernard-Dalapierre's 'Souvenirs sur Olivier Messiaen', *Formes et couleurs*, nos 3–4 (1945) unpaginated (p. 10), he writes: 'How different from the audience who came to my drawing-room to listen intently to the *Visions de l'Amen*, the *Quatuor* or the *Vingt Regards*! That was a rapt, appreciative audience of young people,

squashed between the narrow walls of the old house and overflowing out onto the staircase, an enthusiastic audience including Georges Braque, Pierre Reverdy, Valentine Hugo, André Jolivet . . .' In addition, Messiaen mentions meeting Reverdy on three occasions during the summer of 1944 in his diary. I am grateful to Nigel Simeone for this information.

[36] Pierre Reverdy, 'L'Image', in *Œuvres complètes: Nord Sud, Self Defence et autre écrits sur l'art et la poésie (1917–1926)* (Paris: Flammarion, 1975), pp. 73–5. (This article first appeared in *Nord Sud* no. 13, March 1918). 'L'image est une création pure de l'esprit. Elle ne peut naître d'une comparaison mais du rapprochement de deux réalités plus ou moin éloignées. Plus les rapports de deux réalités rapprochées seront lointain et justes, plus l'image sera forte-plus elle aura de puissance émotive et de réalité poétique . . . C'est qui est grand ce n'est pas l'image – mais l'émotion qu'elle provoque; si cette dernière est grande on estimera l'image à sa mesure . . . Il y a la surprise et la joie de se trouver devant une chose neuve.' This passage is quoted in Breton's *Manifeste du Surréalisme*, Breton, *Œuvres complètes*, vol. I, p. 324.

'Ma petite cendre tu es là, tes tempes vertes, mauves, sur de l'eau. Comme la mort.' The thirst for the presence of the divine is exacerbated by its absence. Messiaen achieves a distantiation from the Tristan myth through the recasting of Tristan and Isolde as the 'young man' and the 'young girl' (Piroutcha). The otherness of their being, a reflection of the Surrealist adoration of the exotic and of pre-Columbian culture, allows an objectification and idealisation of love that is intensely metaphysical, Surrealist, and essential to the drama of Messiaen's narrative of the *au-delà* in the cycle.[37]

Objectification begins in the first song, where the subject is not the lovers but their gaze: 'L'œil immobile sans dénouer ton regard, moi.' In this first song (*La Ville qui dormait, toi*), the physiognomy of G major is readily detectable (not least though the cadences) in Messiaen's chords; the subtle play of triadicism and dissonance articulates a higher, more eclectic notion of non-traditional 'tonality' in which register, spacing and appoggiatura or added-note dissonances come to challenge if not usurp such traditional distinctions as consonance and dissonance, an ideal of colour that can be understood as analogous to the higher spiritual consciousness of the lovers.

The intensity of their gaze is also intimated in the repeated rhythm, only interrupted at 'L'œil immobile', where the limping non-retrogradable quaver–semiquaver–quaver rhythm is symbolically stabilised by a crotchet.[38] For Eluard and Messiaen, eyes are a reciprocal medium between the imagination and reality; they act as mirrors in which the lovers can see each other, providing a communion of cosmic dimensions:

La courbe de tes yeux fait le tour de mon cœur,	The curve of your eyes encircles my heart,
Un rond de danse et de douceur,	A circle of dance and of softness,
Auréole du temps, berceau nocturne et sûr,	Halo of time, cradle, nocturnal and sure,
Et si je ne sais plus ce que j'ai vécu	And if I no longer know what I have lived through
C'est que tes yeux ne m'ont pas toujours vu.	It is because your eyes have not always seen me.
Feuilles de jour et mousse de rosée,	Diurnal leaves and moss dew
Roseaux du vent, sourires parfumés,	Reeds of the wind, perfumed smile,
Ailes couvrant le monde de lumière,	Wings covering the world of light,
Bateaux chargés du ciel et de la mer,	Boats loaded with the sky and the sea,
Chasseurs des bruits et sources des couleurs,	Hunters of sounds and wellsprings of colours,
Parfums éclos d'une couvée d'aurores	Scents hatched from a brood of dawns,
Qui gît toujours sur la paille des astres,	Which lies forever on the straw of stars,

[37] For more on the exotic and pre-Columbian aspects of Surrealism, see Louise Tythacott's *Surrealism and the Exotic* (London: Routledge, 2003). My thanks to Peter Hicks for his assistance with the translation of the poetry by Eluard and Reverdy in this study.

[38] This hypnotic Hindu rhythm – it is a diminution of Çârngadeva's rhythm *Dhenkî* (crotchet–quaver–crotchet) – is given internal life by subtle changes in harmonic narrative, for instance at bar 5 (*le banc*), and cadential punctuation. For more on Hindu rhythms, see *TRCO*, Tome I (Paris: Leduc, 1994), pp. 273–305.

Comme le jour dépend de l'innocence	As the day relies on innocence
Le monde entier dépend de tes yeux purs	So the world relies on your two pure eyes
Et tout mon sang coule dans leurs regards.[39]	And all my blood flows in their looking.

One can only suppose that the images of love, light, sky, sea, stars, colours and birds, in this poem, must have attracted Messiaen to Eluard's lyric poetry, where birds are associated with freedom and light, as in Eluard's *Au cœur de mon amour*:

Un bel oiseau me montre la lumière	A beautiful bird shows me the light
Elle est dans ses yeux, bien en vue.	It is in his eyes, clearly visible.
Il chante sur une boule de gui	It sings on a ball of mistletoe
Au milieu du soleil.[40]	In the middle of the sunshine.

For Messiaen, birds are a symbol of innocence and luminosity, immortality and transcendence that is threatened by modernity. It is, then, a small step to grasp such resonances in Messiaen's use of the bird as a metaphor for the voice of God in nature, a presence that in *Bonjour toi, colombe verte* (II) and *Amour oiseau d'étoile* (X) attempts to transcends both tonality and *la vie moderne*. In song II, birds symbolise a celebration of love and they represent a means of release from such human bonds ('Étoile enchaînée, ombre partagée . . . chant des oiseaux'), while in song X they have become synonymous with this release ('Oiseaux d'étoile . . . chaînes tombantes vers les étoiles, plus court chemin de l'ombre au ciel') and the realisation of eternal and divine love above the world. The delicate violence of their seemingly irrational arabesques in both songs become what the Surrealists would call a *fil conducteur* between the phenomenal and the noumenal worlds. In *Bonjour toi*, for example, Messiaen's increasingly ambitious ornithological tracery resonates against E♭ major arpeggios, subtly suggesting the immanence of traditional tonal hierarchy while, in turn, their flotsam challenges such imaginary constraints.

Such passages do not merely juxtapose ideas, but use organised irrationality as a modus operandi that implies sense, while ultimately challenging and even confounding it. Boulez perhaps unwittingly points to a fundamentally Surrealist disjuncture of Messiaen's music when he states that '*Messiaen's method never manages to fit in with his discourse*, because he does not compose – he juxtaposes – and he constantly relies on an exclusively harmonic style of writing; I would almost call it accompanied melody [my italics].'[41] If Messiaen's technique can be reduced to 'an exclusively harmonic style of writing' and 'accompanied melody', then certainly the absence of

---

[39] Paul Eluard, from *Capitale de la douleur* (1926), *Œuvres complètes*, vol. I, p. 196.

[40] Paul Eluard, 'Au coeur de mon amour', from *Mourir de ne pas mourir* (1924), *Œuvres complètes*, vol. I, p. 137. These poems were dedicated to Breton.

[41] Pierre Boulez, 'Propositions' (1948), *Relevés d'apprenti* (Paris: Editions du Seuil, 1966), translated by Stephen Walsh as 'Proposals' in *Stocktakings from an Apprenticeship* (Oxford: Clarendon Press, 1991), p. 49.

Ex. 2.1: *Répétition Planétaire* b. 5–17

traditional musical teleological structuring may be keenly felt. Yet Boulez's desire to distance himself from his forbears in his own music of this period somewhat overlooks certain aspects of Messiaen's music, not least the inter-actions between the heterophonic layering of systems, and the ways in which developmental procedures, albeit corrupted or at least perhaps (with relevance to Surrealism) instantiating another element of symbiosis with traditional procedures, may contain elements of stability. For example, this passage in *Répétition planétaire* (VI) presents the layering of several contiguous systems (Ex. 2.1).

Messiaen tells us that the right hand is a repeated pattern of 25 semiquavers (the first b/a dyad occurs twice), and that the left hand repeated Cs (strength-ened by the voice) become shorter from 5–1 semiquavers (marked on the

Ex. 2.2: *Répétition Planétaire* (from r.h. b. 5–7)

score). The seismic *broderies* in between these nodal points are what the composer Charles Tournemire might have called *guirlandes alleluiatiques*.[42] While it would be tempting to make a (Messiaen-like) comparison between such 'garlands' and extended melismas in plainchant, perhaps using the notions of arsis and thesis to reveal the shifting sands of contour in this passage, this sort of aesthetic nostalgia glosses over the reality of this passage, which is much more interesting (and complex).

The right-hand set of 25 semiquavers is divided into a sort of inexact mirror, with the repeated dyad in b. 7 used as the central term. Without wishing to use any number-crunching meta-language, these pitches can be arranged (with a certain license) so that the shape of the mirror formation is clear to the naked eye (see Ex. 2.2).

The top staff (reading left to right) of this reduction refers to the pitches of the bracketed section 1 in Ex. 2.1, i.e. b. 5–7. The bottom staff (reading right to left) refers to the pitches of b. 7–8. My bracketing of pitches in Ex. 2.2 reveals a maximum correspondence between the staves, but in Messiaen's music, such correspondences are concealed by the grouping and the order of the pitches. While both staves use all twelve pitches, these factors, together with the repetition of pitches, reveal the corruption of any twelve-tone ancestry.

What happens in the left hand is somewhat more complex to define. The figurations enact a fan-like permutational quasi-development (see Ex. 2.3). While there is some surface evidence of motivic shapes or groups (as indicated by tendentious ascription of *a* and *b* in Ex. 2.1 and 2.3), the spectre of invariance remains only but an attractive illusion, even more so in a consideration of the whole texture, where the left hand operates as a distinctly separate system from the right hand, so that, for instance, any sense of 'cadence' in the right hand at bars 13–14, where the voice and the right-hand pattern almost coincide, is obviated. The whole section (Ex. 2.1) ends when the rhetorical sense of the expansion of the five-note figure in the left hand at b. 7 seems to o'er extend itself and vault towards the irrational. In such heterophonic music, the disintegration of material (and its reintegration into new patterns) is brought into constructive tension with the overarching hand of rational control. The

[42] Messiaen, *TRCO*, Tome III, p. 293. Messiaen calls these 'groupes broderies'.

Ex. 2.3: *Répétition Planétaire*, l. h. figures from b. 7–17

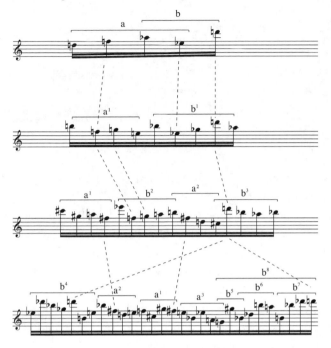

conjunction of systems in b. 5–17 goes further than Reverdy's '*rapproche-ment* of two more or less distant realities': the aural image and the ensuing emotion both promotes Surrealist serendipity and provides an axiom of the lover's eschatological struggle to escape the mortal bonds of modernity.[43]

The quasi-developmental quality of this passage from *Répétition planétaire* is reminiscent of the increasing sophistication and reconfiguration of motives that defines the immanence of Messiaen's birdsong in *Bonjour toi*. Both these examples reveal a dialogue between stability and non-stability, and between sense and irrationality. The extent to which these seemingly opposing concepts can be overcome, then, is premised in the extent to which the improvisational quality of these passages can achieve the proposed image of freedom.

For Messiaen, freedom is given an eschatological meaning in his aesthetics of time. In his musical aesthetics, he adopts the separation of time and eternity (from St Thomas Aquinas). To evoke eternity in his music, Messiaen attempts to confound our human sense of clock-bound time, so, for instance in Ex. 2.1, the conflagration of systems (together with Messiaen's use of pitch and register) combine progressively to give the listener less to hang onto (the 'recognized "markers"' that Boulez speaks of), so that the sense of where the ending might occur is somewhat obfuscated. Yet, even

---

[43] Reverdy, 'L'Image', pp. 73–5.

Ex. 2.4: *Doundou Tchil*, opening

as passages such as this attempt to achieve this they are grounded in their own temporal paradigms; the three birdsong refrains in *Bonjour toi* are 'regulated' by the left-hand E♭ major chords, and the passage in *Répétition planétaire* (Ex. 2.1) by the left-hand Cs. The irony, as always with Messiaen, is that the reality of his music is far more concerned with creating interesting and diverse uses of time than merely the attractive utopian ideal of evoking eternity. The notion, fostered by the composer and other commentators, that his music is static, is a paper tiger speared by the music itself.

The purity of Messiaen's desire to separate time and eternity may be undermined by the musical processes, but what is more interesting is the way Messiaen's music provides a constructive theological engagement with time to present an image of human artifice, struggling with its own limitations, and striving toward the divine, an image that is reconfigured and dramatised in the lover's flight towards death in *Harawi*. There is a sensitivity here and even a reluctance, not always present in Messiaen's music, to attempt to embody the divine in music.

This tension is mirrored in the dialogue in *Harawi* between Messiaen's engagement with more traditional forms of musical discourse, such as verse-refrain and variation form, and the ways in which the content of them attempts to overcome these moulds. Such a tension provides a *locus* for the religious-modernism that Nadia Boulanger seems to have found so distasteful.

The immanent-transcendent dialogue between form and content, and the sense of ordered disorder is exemplified in *Doundou Tchil* (IV), where the left-hand percussive bird *personnage rythmique* forms a self-recontextualising riff (Ex. 2.4). The ever-evolving *correspondences* between the recurring alternation of A/A♭ (in the bass riff of the piano part), their fourth-chord relation with D, G and C♯ (voice), and other notes that destabilise the tendentious quartian hierarchy, engender an ongoing rollercoaster of onomatopoeic dizziness that is exacerbated upon repetition by the addition of a melismatic *merle*. The sense of spontaneity, or as Breton puts it *disponibilité*, entails a dialectic between the conscious and the unconscious, 'reality and dream, presence and absence, identity and distance, intimacy and loneliness, unity and multiplicity, continuity and discontinuity, language and silence, mobility and immobility, clarity and obscurity, and so on', that intimate the essence of Messiaen's style.[44]

Such modernist complexity is suggested by the hybridisation of mode in the first retrograde canon of *Montagnes* (III) of 11, 5 (*dhenkî*), 11, and 7 semiquavers (all prime numbers) (see Ex 2.5).[45] The right-hand from b. 12 uses a tâla of 6 chords in mode 3^1, and the left hand, a tâla of 7 chords in mode 6^4: it is a classic Messiaen passage reminiscent of, but more complex than, that in *Le Verbe* (*La Nativité du Seigneur*) (1935). Like that passage, the chords and modes are not chosen idly. Taken as two sets, the intersection between the modes (five pitches that form a symmetrical mirror around the fulcrum of B: G, A♭, B, D, E♭) are prevalent in the chords Messiaen chooses, and especially in the left hand. The death-mask of tonality is present in this 'centricity' that, together with the superimposition of systems and the diffused and even fractured triadicism that pervades Messiaen's harmony, at best achieves a semblance of stability in its closed circularity. Likewise the canons in *Doundou Tchil* (IV), *Adieu* (VII) and *Dans le noir* (XII) become, in the absence of any controlling tonality, like the disembodied *objets trouvés* of the helmet and spoon that Breton discovers while walking around a flea market with Alberto Giacometti.[46] The serendipity of finding these objects, and their change in 'associative and interpretative qualities' when the spoon is brought back to Breton's house, are, for Breton, allegories of the seren-dipitous encounter of another being, and the love that will change life. As incantations of the Surrealist 'marvellous', these canons take on an auratic quality in the way they distance themselves from the surrounding musical landscape, and the ways in which their 'shuffling' of *personnages rythmiques*

---

[44] Mary Ann Caws, *The Poetry of Dada and Surrealism*, p. 19.

[45] The right-hand canon begins with the second value of the five-semiquaver *dhenkî* (quaver–semiquaver–quaver), while the left hand begins with the third value of *dhenkî*. The canons are always at the distance, therefore, of one semiquaver. What is evident from Ex. 2.5 is that while the left hand is supposedly playing the right-hand durations backwards (i.e. not just the overall number of semiquavers, but the actual durations themselves), the visual effect (in the example) is that the groups are almost superimposed upon one another rather than in canon. Surprisingly, the fact that the final term in the right-hand canon at the end of this section (p. 15, b. 3) is interrupted (Messiaen only uses 6 out of 7 of the semiquavers) can

actually be sensed somewhat in the abrupt return of the opening material from the song.

[46] See section 3 of Breton's *L'Amour fou*, *Œuvres complètes*, vol. II, pp. 697–709. In Mary Ann Caws' translation of *Mad Love*, p. 125, n. 7, she writes: '*L'objet trouvé* is of course the *trouvaille*, the thing found and always turned towards the positive, seeming at once surprising and necessary.' In a letter (lost by Breton), Joë Bosquet identifies the mask as an object used to protect the eyes from death (*éclats d'obus se trouve rattaché à la mort*), while the spoon symbolises sexual desire (*désir amoureux*). These symbols concretise the Freudian principles of Thanatos and Eros. See Breton, *Œuvres complètes*, vol. II, pp. 708–9 and the corresponding note on p. 1696.

Ex. 2.5: *Montagnes* b. 11–21

intimates other possible temporal and ontological dimensions within Messiaen's oneiric vision.[47]

Serendipity is likewise premised in Messiaen's treatment of refrain/couplet and variation form, which become the ordinary vessels that demarcate and innervate Messiaen's transcendent vistas.[48] Indeed the outward conventionality of Messiaen's variation technique in *Répétition planétaire* (*thème de la terre*) – antecedent–consequent phrases, phrase extension and addition of phrases, the close motivic relationship between variations (with the addition of parts, new accompanimental figures, increasing the tactus from quavers and semiquavers to triplet semiquavers (var. 5) to demisemiquavers (var. 6)) – and, in *Katchikatchi les étoiles* (XI), where there is a greater difference between the variations, define the primitive silhouette of the creator's hand. It is not just the (conscious) use of Hindu rhythms (râgavardhana, candrakalâ and lakskmiça) in *Répétition planétaire*, or necessarily the atonality, or the presence of Messiaen's modes that distinguish these variations from their nineteenth-century heritage, but the violent, irrational, and even self-destructive, nature of Messiaen's language, premised in his apocalyptic literary language (*Tourbillon, Etoile rouge, Tourbillon, Planète mange en tournant*), an ideal of 'development' taken further in Boulez's Piano Sonata No. 2 (1946–48).[49]

The variations in *Répétition planétaire* have not only something of the character of automatic writing, but also a markedly regressive infantilism (in the vocal part) that, as in *Doundou Tchil* and the '*Pia*' sections of *Syllabes*, take on the ritual tribal element of play.[50] In one of Messiaen's favourite books of this period, *Surrealism and Painting*, Breton cites Giorgio de Chirico (from 1913) who stated that: 'To be really immortal a work of art must go completely beyond the limits of the human, to where good sense and logic are absent. In this way it will come close to the dream and to the mentality of childhood.'[51] Such a mentality is intimated in the Surrealist

---

[47] In *Montagnes*, the canon provides an antistrophe (to borrow a term Messiaen would use later in connection with *Chronochromie*), a couplet in *Doundou Tchil* (see *TRCO*, Tome III, p. 288), and a contrast from the E♭ major sections in *Adieu* (VII) and *Dans le noir* (XII). The idea of aura derives from Walter Benjamin's essay 'The Work of Art in the Age of Mechanical Reproduction', in Hannah Arendt (ed.), Illuminations (London: Fontana, 1992), pp. 211–44. In Louise Tythacott's *Surrealism and the Exotic* (p. 81), she writes that: 'Objects and places revered by the Surrealists always resonated with auratic qualities. Charged with mysterious power by the ideology of the group, they were ascribed marvellous pedigrees, shrouded in myth, bathed in magic, laden with lingering traces, accumulated latencies.'

[48] 'To win the energies of intoxication for the revolution – this is the project about which Surrealism circles in all its books and enterprises'; Benjamin, *Reflections*, p. 189.

[49] See, for instance, The Book of Revelation 6:12–14 and 8:10–12.

[50] In *TRCO*, Tome III, p. 299, Messiaen states that 'Pia' is a magical syllable used by primitive peoples who would sit around a tree and pass the syllable around the circle very loudly and quickly. While, in Messiaen's piece, the singer sets the tempo for this repetition, the changing chords in the piano signify, for Messiaen, the repetition of the syllable by different voices.

[51] Breton, *Surrealism and Painting*, p. 18 n.

phantasmagoria of *Harawi*, in which gestural affect and colour challenge and attempt to transcend the immanence of form. These paroxysms of onoma-topoeic non-sense are (in the Surrealist sense) intent upon unmasking the irrational drives of the subconscious and, for Messiaen, laying bare the heart of the individual, uncovering and raising up from the abyss the soul which has been covered over by *la vie quotidienne*.[52]

This 'Pia' section, which Messiaen calls 'Syllable Magique' (p. 65), embra-ces a wild effulgence of chords from previous songs, previous works (*Vingt Regards*), along with altered chords of contracted resonance, turning chords and other invented harmonies. Messiaen's chords affect a changing tissue of density, and therefore timbre, which irradiates a lyricism that is in Reverdy's words 'an aspiration towards the unknown, an indispensable explosion of being dilated by emotion towards the exterior'.[53] They are the psychotic and pulmonary murmurs that lead inevitably to arrest.

Vers le point sublime

Like the empty cross, Messiaen's *Harawi* is an exhortation to the Eluardian *dur désir de durer*.[54] It is composed in the liminal space of perpetual leave-taking between presence and absence that is 'ni dynamique, ni statique', but ecstatic.[55] For the Surrealist this state is recognisable as '*dépaysement*: the sense of being out of one's element, of being distorted by the unfamiliarity of a situation experienced for the first time'.[56]

But in Messiaen's cycle, such premonitions of the *merveilleux* take on the cloak of eschatological expectation. The absence of subjectivism becomes the irrigation of the lover's ontological passage in *L'Escalier redit, gestes du soleil* (IX), where the contemplation of physical union is a precursor to a contemplation of the spiritual and divine union in *Amour oiseaux d'étoile* (X). The joy that this inspires is at once Christological and memorialising without any human senti-ment or sense of tragedy. It is present in the memory of her ('ma petite cendre'), and in the litanic metaphors ('du ciel, de l'eau'), that act like elusive footholds for the drowning narrator. The acknowledgement of loss – 'Je suis mort' – is the first dawn of a realisation that leads inexorably to the cathartic – 'Inventons

[52] For more on the concept of the 'Abyss', see Ernest Hello's *Paroles de Dieu: réflexions sur quelques textes sacrés*, texte presenté par François Angélier (Grenoble: Jérôme Millon, 1992, first published 1875), pp. 131–2.
[53] Reverdy, 'L'Image', p. 40: 'Le lyrisme qui va vers l'inconnu, vers la profondeur, participe naturellement du mystère. La part faite au mystère, la conscience qu'on décidé d'en tirer les poètes modernes, caractérisent notre époque.'

[54] Paul Eluard, *Le Dur Désir de durer* (1946), *Œuvres complètes*, vol. II (Paris: Gallimard, 1968), pp. 65–83.
[55] Breton, 'Nadja', in *Œuvres complètes*, vol. I, p. 753.
[56] Jean-Pierre Cauvin, 'Introduction: The Poethics of André Breton', *Poems of André Breton: A Bilingual Anthology* (Austin: University of Texas Press, 1982), p. xvii.

l'amour du monde' – and a lachrymose and therapeutic withdrawal, premised in the motivic repetition and augmentation of values on p. 79 of *Harawi* ('tu es là, toi.'). Memory of mortality is detonated in 'L'Amour, la joie', to depart for a celebration of the hope of resurrection: 'tu es là … Comme la mort. L'œil du ciel.' The eschatological trajectory of *L'Escalier redit* complements Breton's situation of 'love' at the heart of his Surrealist poetics of convulsive beauty:

> This blind aspiration towards the best would suffice to justify love as I think of it, absolute love, as the only principle for physical and moral selection which can guarantee that human witness, human passage shall not have taken place in vain.[57]

If love, for the Surrealist, is the human *point sublime* that life and art aspire to, then the redemptive action of Christ, expressed through a hyper-aesthetic musical language, was for Messiaen the *point sublime* of beauty and truth.

In *Harawi* Messiaen attempts the re-enchantment of the aesthetic with the divine. The female singer becomes both Messiaen's ventriloquist and ventriloquist's dummy(s), almost schizophrenically vacillating between a narrator and his characters to become, in Breton's words, a 'communicating vessel' that metonymically resonates towards the *au-delà*.[58] The narrator (a dramatic soprano) is both present as the idealised woman and absent in the lovers' desubjectified union. Such spiritualisation of women is not only found in Eluard, but also in Breton's *Nadja* (1928), *L'Amour fou* (1936), and in *Arcane 17* (1944–47), where he 'maintains that earthly salvation can come only through the redemptive power of woman'.[59]

In the Surrealist painting that inspired *Harawi*, Roland Penrose's *L'Île invisible* (1937), reproduced in the Parisian magazine *Minotaure* as *Seeing is Believing* in issue 10 (Winter 1937), the women's inverted disembodied head points up through the clouds (Fig. 2.1).[60] Her expression seems to signify a spiritual and visionary domain. Beneath her are outstretched hands, reaching as if to receive the sacrament of forgiveness and redemption. One hand is opaque, as though compromised by the dark satanic mills of modernity pictured in front of them. It is almost as though the hands of the painter

[57] Breton, *L'Amour fou, Œuvres complètes*, vol. II, p. 784, translated by Caws, as *Mad Love*, p. 117.
[58] See Breton's 'Les Vases communicants' (1932), *Œuvres complètes*, vol. II. On p. 164, Breton writes of automatism: 'I hope it will be seen as having tried nothing better than to lay down a *fil conducteur* between the far too distant worlds of waking and sleep, exterior and interior reality, reason and madness, the assurance of knowledge and of love, of love for life and the revolution, and so on'; translated by Mary Ann Caws in *André Breton* (New York: Twayne, 1996), p. 39.
[59] Caws, *The Poetry of Dada and Surrealism*, p. 84.

[60] Messiaen describes, but does not name, this painting in Goléa, *Rencontres avec Olivier Messiaen*, 155–6. In a conversation with the painter's son on 11 June 2003, Anthony Penrose confirmed that Roland Penrose did not have a preference for either title of this painting (currently lost), and that the work dates from 1937. He informed me that it belongs to a period of creative work inspired by Lee Miller, and that it relates closely to an *objet d'art*: *The Dew Machine* (1937). Furthermore, he stated: 'Penrose rarely commented on what his work was about', and he had a 'passion for women and nature'. There is no known extant correspondence between Penrose and Messiaen.

Fig. 2.1: *Seeing is Believing* (L'Ile invisible), Roland Penrose, 1937

are reaching into the painting (from outside), searching or perhaps resisting both the magnetism of the woman and her role in his transformation. As an irrational being (presented upside down), the woman seems to provide a conduit (like birdsong for Messiaen) for man's redemption and a vision of eternity beyond the storm clouds of war and human conflict. She becomes in Reverdy's terms 'The poet [who] is essentially the man who aspires to the real plane, the divine plane, the mysterious and evident creation.'[61]

---

[61] Pierre Reverdy, 'Poésie' (first published in *Le Journal littéraire* on 7 June 1924), in *Œuvres complètes: Nord sud, Self Defence et autre écrits sur l'art et la poesie (1917–1926)*,

Given Messiaen's marital and emotional turmoil, the demands placed on him by his young son, and the professional uncertainty after the end of the war, it is perhaps unsurprising that this painting should have inspired *Harawi*: evidence that, in Reverdy's words, 'Reality does not motivate the work of art. It departs from life to await another reality.'[62]

The eschatological and apocalyptical topos of this painting is specifically located in *Amour oiseaux d'étoile* (X), which looks towards this moment of redemption: 'Chaînes tombantes, vers les étoiles, Plus court chemin de l'ombre au ciel.' Reverdy's *La Jetée* (*Les ardoises du toit*) (1918), quoted by Messiaen in the preface to *TMLM*, seems to prefigure the spiritual dimension of this song with exquisite poignancy:

Les étoiles sont derrière le mur	The stars are behind the wall
Dedans saute un cœur qui voudrait sortir	Inside leaps a heart that wishes to get out
Aime le moment qui passe	Love the moment which passes
A force ta mémoire est lasse	Perforce, your memory wearies
D'écouter des cadavres de bruits	Of hearing the corpses of noises
Dans le silence	In the silence
Rien ne vit	Nothing lives
Au fond de l'eau l'image s'emprisonne	At the bottom of the water the image is imprisoned
Au bord du ciel une cloche qui sonne	On the edge of the sky a bell which tolls
La voile est un morceau du port qui se détache	The sail is a part of a port which can be detached
Tu restes là	You stay there
Tu regardes ce que s'en va	You look upon the thing that departs
Quelqu'un chante et tu ne comprends pas	Someone sings and you don't understand
La voix vient de plus haut	The voice comes from higher up
L'homme vient de plus loin	The man comes from further away
Tu voudrais respirer à peine	You would like barely to breathe
Et l'autre aspirerait le ciel tout d'une haleine[63]	And the other would inhale the sky in one breath

Reverdy's poem expresses the inestimable gulf between life and death, and the sense of spiritual contact and love that bridges this abyss. Messiaen's poem and music register the quiet sense of profound belief that although 'we now see through a glass darkly' with metaphors of hands, birds, stars and

---

p. 206. 'Le poète est essentiellement l'homme qui aspire au domaine réel, le plan divin, la création mystérieuse et évidente.'

[62] 'La Realité ne motive pas l'œuvre d'art. On part de la vie pour attendre une autre réalité.' 'Self Defence', *Critiques-Esthétiques* (1919), in Reverdy, *Œuvres complètes: Nord sud, self Defence et autre écrits sur l'art et la poesie (1917–1926)*, p. 117. This idea of *l'autre* can be seen in the final line of *La Jetée*, the last line of which was used by Messiaen on p. 7 of *TMLM*: 'the liberator. And, beforehand, let us offer him two thoughts. First, that of Reverdy: ' "May he draw in the whole sky in one breath!" ''

[63] This version was published in Pierre Reverdy, *Plupart du temp*, vol. I (Paris: Gallimard, 1945 and 1969), p. 196. Rothwell points out that the revisions Reverdy made in 1945, made as manuscript additions on the first edition copy held at the Fonds Littéraire Jacques Doucet in Paris, reduced the Cubist aspects of these poems by evening out the syntax and regularising the typography (Reverdy's typography was obviously inspired by Mallarmé's *Un Coup de dés*). See Rothwell, *Textual Spaces*, pp. 181–202.

eyes, we may one day 'see face to face'.[64] Messiaen's Surrealist language in *Amour oiseaux d'étoile* charts the interior waters of a soul's longing through a solemn choral-like texture in which his modes and chords of contracted resonance are irradiated by the gentle luminescence of F♯ major.

In *TMLM*, Messiaen posits himself as the man who comes from far off – a man composing in the twentieth century but with a pre-Enlightenment certainty of faith that will, quoting the poem above, 'inhale the sky' and transform the world 'in one breath'.[65] Reverdy's poem implies the necessity of a conduit between the omniscient 'tu' (perhaps the beloved or Christ) 'behind the wall' of mortality and the strife of modernity (*cadavres de bruits*). Music for Messiaen was such a conduit; it attempted to close the gap between seemingly distant images to create a strong emotional or cathartic response in humanity.

Reverdy uses birds as a metaphor for the special qualities that would be required of a man that might lead modernity out of its malaise, qualities that Messiaen believed he possessed:

> There are people in the world who can easily bear the wailing of factory sirens, the blaring of car horns, the stupid barking of dogs, but who are unable to hear birdsong without disquiet.
>
> Birds sing for themselves alone. But it can be that, in order to sing the loudest, certain birds search out the brotherhood of mankind.[66]

Messiaen is surely one of those birds that sing of the fraternisation of humanity. Birds, as the voice of God in nature, are one of the iconic tools he applies to his project of realising the invisible presence of Christ in music. They are a frequent image used in *Les Ardoises du toit* and elsewhere in Reverdy's poetry. In *Réclame*, birds seem to be an image of the possibility of transcendence after the darkness of the crucifixion:

Hangar monté	Barn built
la porte ouverte	The door open
Le ciel	The sky
En haut deux mains se sont offertes	Above, two hands are offered
Les yeux levés	Eyes uplifted
Une voix monte	A voice ascends

---

[64] St Paul's First Letter to the Corinthians 13:12.
[65] Messiaen, *TMLM*, p. 7.
[66] Messiaen evidently knew this quote from Reverdy's works. The section in italic below is used in a small article by Messiaen, 'Derrière ou devant la porte? . . . (Lettre ouverte à M. Eugène Berteaux)', *La Page musicale*, 26 February 1937, p. 1. Pierre Reverdy, *Le Gant de crin* (Paris: Plon, 1927), p. 36: '*Il y a des gens* au monde qui supportent aisément les hurlements des sirènes d'usine, les beuglements des trompes d'autos, les aboiements stupides des chiens, mais *qui ne peuvent entendre sans malaise un chant d'oiseau.*

Les oiseaux chantent pour eux seuls. Mais il arrive que certains oiseaux semblent rechercher, pour chanter le plus fort, le voisinage de l'homme.'

Eluard has also written: 'Il y a un mot qui m'exalte, un mot que je n'ai jamais entendu sans ressentir un grand frisson, un grand espoir, le plus grand, celui de vaincre le puissances de ruine et de mort qui accablent les hommes, ce mot c'est: fraternisation.' 'L'Évidence poétique' (1937), in *Œuvres complètes*, vol. I, p. 520.

Les toits se sont mis à trembler	The roofs begin to shake
Le vent lance des feuilles mortes	The wind tosses some dead leaves
Et les nuages retardés	And the clouds held back
Marchent vers l'autre bout du monde	March towards the other end of the world
Qui se serait mis à siffler	Which would begin to blow
Dans le calme d'un soir d'été	In the calm of a summer evening
Le chant	The song
L'oiseau	The bird
Les étoiles	The stars
Et la lune pour t'écouter[67]	And the moon to listen to you

Through the quasi-sacramental images of an open door, the two hands (as in Penrose's painting), the lifted eyes and the ascending voice, Reverdy's poem speaks of an eschatological desire that cannot reach beyond earthly confines. Only the song of birds and the stars intimate the possibility of eternity. Indeed, lines like 'Ta tête à l'envers sous le ciel', and finally 'Mes mains, ton œil, ton cou, le ciel', in Messiaen's *Amour oiseaux d'étoile* resonate with Reverdy's poetry and Penrose's painting. One only need hear the line 'Tous les oiseaux des étoiles' in *Amour oiseaux d'étoile* (X), engraved on a tablet near the place where Messiaen's ashes were scattered, to realise that Messiaen could have recognised in Reverdy's lines the longing and desire, as in *L'Ascension*, for freedom in the beyond.[68] Considering that this line from *Harawi* was printed in the order of service for Messiaen's funeral, there can be little doubt about Messiaen's interpretation of Penrose. Below Ex. 2.6 Messiaen is quoted:

> After death, during the necessary purification that precedes the definitive vision of God, one cannot remember the joys and pains of this life. One remembers only the good and bad actions. At this moment, I will be upset with all the evil that I have done. But, I will also rejoice in all the good I have been able to do, and this final memory permits me to understand progressively at last the invisible.[69]

Messiaen's hope to join his 'birds of the stars', free at last from the world's torment, is a clear statement of his faith in the hereafter. In the final song (*Dans le noir*) the return to *La Ville qui dormait*, perhaps a vision of the celestial city and the bien-aimée above the ruins of modernity, is marked by the absence of the '*toi*' from the first song. As in *La Mort du nombre*, the lovers are now beyond their mortal coil.

---

[67] Reverdy, *Plupart du temps*, vol. I p. 165. Crucifixion is a recurring image in these poems, especially evident in *Pointe* and in *Au carrefour des routes* from *Etoile peintes* (1921). The line 'Deux bras sont restés etendus' from *Pointe* may have inspired the opening of the text of *Les Offrandes oubliées*: 'Les bras étendus, triste jusqu'à la mort'. See also *Quelque part* from *La Guitare endormie* (1919): 'Les mûrs saignant, au bord du ciel où grimpent les épines. La couronne du monde enserre le front torturé du couchant.'

[68] See also *Départ* from *Les Ardoises du toit*, in Reverdy's *Plupart du temps*, vol. I, p. 179.

[69] Order of service for Messiaen's funeral, 14 May 1992. My thanks to Dennis Hunt for supplying me with a copy of this document.

Ex. 2.6: From *Amour oiseaux d'étoile*

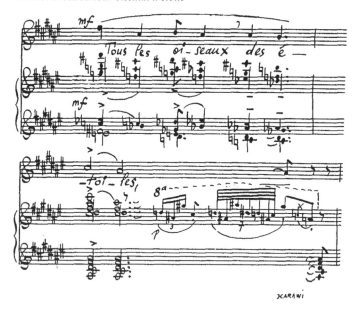

Harawi looks down on the overcoming of the spiritual, emotional and physical struggle inherent in mortality as a necessary rite of passage, a *dépaysement* before the inevitable divine *merveilleux*. Messiaen's 'Tristan trilogy' was therefore a creative necessity, a panacea to the spleen of his dying love and the appeasement of guilt at his burgeoning new paramour.[70] In his novella *Mad Love*, Breton offers this comforting olive branch:

> Is the mirror of a love between two beings likely to be clouded over by the very fact of circumstances totally foreign to love and to be unclouded, suddenly when the circumstances cease? Yes.[71]

More poignantly, Breton himself uses a 'Tristan' allegory in his exegesis of love:

> Death, whence the grandfather clock bedecked with country flowers, as beautiful as my tombstone and stood on its end, will start up again on tiptoe to sing the hours not passing. For a man and a woman, who, at the end of time, must be you and me, will glide along, when it is their turn, without ever looking back, as far as the path leads, in the oblique light, at the edge of life and of the oblivion of life, in the delicate grass running before us to its arborescence. It is composed, this lacy grass, of a thousand invisible, unbreakable links, which happen to chain your nervous system with mine in the deepest night of knowledge. This ship, rigged by hands of children, exhausts the bobbin of fate. It is this grass which will continue after me to line the walls of the humblest room each time two lovers enclose themselves, scorning

[70] Describing the period before her marriage to Messiaen in 1962, Loriod stated: 'So we cried. We cried for 20 years until she died and [we] could marry.' Claire Delbos died in 1959, so the period referred to is 1939–59. 'Her maître's voice', Yvonne Loriod-Messiaen interviewed by Michael White in *Independent on Sunday*, 10 January 1999. [71] Breton, *L'Amour fou, Œuvres complètes*, vol. II, 776, translated by Caws as *Mad Love*, p. 110.

everything that can happen, even the approach of the end of their lives. No rock, no matter how high it reaches, no rock threatening to fall each second, can keep this grass from becoming so dense and around the bed as to hide the rest of the world from two gazes seeking each other and losing each other.[72]

For Breton, as for Messiaen, the grave has no victory, nor is there any sting in death, but only a metaphysical change of appearance. In *Harawi*, the psychological, erotic darkness of night is used as a necessary precursor to the new day: a Christian symbol of redemption where souls will pass beyond human eroticism to divine love. The dreaded flight to reality in Wagner's opera becomes the longed-for new dawn, a symbol of new love and light not only for *les amants*, but for all humanity.

Harawi implies love that is 'a super human joy, overflowing, blind and unlimited', inculcating Breton's ideal that 'Convulsive beauty will be veiled-erotic, fixed-explosive, magic-circumstantial, or it will not be.'[73] This sort of conflict and complementation of images seem to encapsulate perfectly the Eluardian notion of lyricism as a '*développement d'une protestation*', a protestation as much as a panacea, in Messiaen, against a world indifferent to the transfigurative power of love.[74]

Throughout Messiaen's 'Tristan trilogy', and particularly in *Harawi*, Messiaen himself is implicitly autobiographically present, and yet also absent, in the objectification of images. In attempting to take on the Eluardian mantle of the 'poet that inspires rather than who is inspired', he seems to be attempting to galvanise himself out of his own suffering.[75] The listener becomes an eavesdropper on a form of private self-therapy.

In *Harawi*, listening and comprehension enter into the domain of fragmentary apperception that is commensurate with the symbolist notion of synaesthesia, and which attempts to confuse the senses and create a *bouleversement de l'âme*, rather than to overthrow one hierarchy for another.[76] Messiaen's rush of oneiric images is designed to overwhelm cathartically

---

[72] Breton, *L'Amour fou, Œuvres complètes*, vol. II, 749–50, translated by Caws as *Mad Love*, p. 82.

[73] Messiaen, *TRCO*, Tome II (Paris: Leduc, 1995), p. 151. Breton, *L'Amour fou, Œuvres complètes*, vol. II, p. 687, translated by Caws as *Mad Love*, p. 19. The quasi-Stravinskian gyration of *personnages rythmiques*, the superimposition of mode and the *style oiseau*, the use of leitmotifs as objets trouvés, the extreme timbres and fortissimos of the orchestra, fortified by the percussion and the ondes Martenot, all engender an onomatopoeia of spiritual and erotic consummation. The *Turangalîla-Symphonie* represents one of the *points sublimes* of his art that necessitated the search for other avenues of expression such as the *Mode de valeurs et d'intensités* (1949) and the musique concrète piece *Timbres-durées* (1952).

[74] Paul Eluard, 'Notes sur la poésie en collaboration avec André Breton (1936), *Œuvres complètes*, vol. I, p. 477. For more on the idea of love as a protestation against the world, see part II of Breton's 'Les Vases communicants', *Œuvres complètes*, vol. II.

[75] Paul Eluard, 'Ralentir travaux' (1930), *Œuvres complètes*, vol. I, p. 270, and in 'L'Evidence poétique' (1937), p. 515.

[76] Martin Jay, *Downcast Eyes: The Denigration of Vision in Twentieth-Century French Thought* (Berkeley: University of California Press, 1993), p. 178.

the conscious mind and thereby to lead humanity to 'another reality'. This is
the *point sublime* towards which Messiaen was aiming in *Harawi,* the
Turangalîla-Symphonie and the *Cinq Rechants*: a point of departure and a
recognition that love and life were before him – the promise of each coming
hour unravelling 'life's whole secret, perhaps about to be revealed one day,
possibly in another being'.[77]

[77] Breton, *'L'Amour fou', Œuvres complètes,*
vol. II, p. 714, translated by Caws, as *Mad
Love,* p. 42.

3 Messiaen's journey towards asceticism

Paul McNulty

The publication of Messiaen's treatise *Technique de mon langage musical* (*TMLM*) in 1944 marks an important landmark in the composer's position within the history of twentieth-century music. Such an audacious (and perhaps precocious) event illustrated a character brimming with confidence, and it could have been interpreted as a move towards a new 'School' of composition. However, nothing could have been further from Messiaen's mind: his treatise was essentially written for his pupils at the Paris Conservatoire to aid his teaching, and it was dedicated to Guy-Bernard Delapierre, who was a great supporter of Messiaen's endeavours. In focusing entirely on his compositional methodology, or rather the constituent parts that make up his language, and drawing the vast majority of the musical examples from his own works, Messiaen effectively turned his back on the Austro-Germanic canonic tradition as exemplified by Schoenberg and his followers, and, while remaining essentially French in his aesthetics, he expounded compositional traits that would be recognisable instantly as simply 'Messiaen'. That within five years his compositional language could change so drastically with the appearance of the piano study *Mode de valeurs et d'intensités* in 1949 (part of the *Quatre Etudes de rythme*) is therefore perhaps attributable to a series of events, influences and the changing cultural landscape after the war.

The music of Debussy (particularly its rich harmonic language) and Stravinsky (with its rhythmic vitality) represent some of the most powerful influences on Messiaen. From these and other composers Messiaen absorbed what he needed and went on to create something entirely personal and, it could be argued, introspective. The years 1949 to 1951 saw Messiaen move away from the rich, voluptuous sonorities, and the blatant Christian symbolism of his earlier music, to favour a more abstract style, the repercussions of which surprised even Messiaen himself.

The now-legendary story of Antoine Goléa playing Messiaen's recording of *Mode de valeurs* to a young Stockhausen and Karel Goeyvaerts at Darmstadt in 1951 illustrates the ferocious appetite of the next generation of composers for something new. *Mode de valeurs* provided the impetus for the birth of the total serial movement, although, as has been argued by many

63

scholars, the work itself is in no way serial.[1] Boulez, for example, in writing *Structures Ia* for two pianos – a work that is serial in a conventional sense in its deployment of pitch, and also one of the first European attempts at serialising duration, dynamics and articulation – selects the top twelve-tone row (Messiaen uses the term '*Division*') of *Mode de valeurs* as his prime row, not as a direct *hommage à* Messiaen, but to remove 'all responsibility' from the composer (Boulez) in an effort to see how far automaticism could be taken.[2] In *Structures Ia* every detail – from pitch to rhythm, and dynamics to register – is predetermined, so that the act of composition is the unfolding of the processes set in motion; the piece ends when the processes terminate.[3]

The title page of *Mode de valeurs* bears the inscription 'Darmstadt – 1949', a place that was to become a Mecca for the next generation of composers. The founding of the *Internationale Ferienkurse für Neue Musik* in Darmstadt in 1946 by Wolfgang Steinecke was an important occasion that played a part in repairing the damage caused by years of Nazi repression. Initially, this summer festival was dominated by the music of Hindemith and neoclassicism but the arrival of René Leibowitz in 1948 with his 'very controversial' classes heralded the renaissance of serialism, which in turn was one of the major factors that brought about total serialism, and the waning of neoclassicism.[4] Messiaen attended as a guest of the city in 1949 and, despite the inscription referred to above, it has been suggested that he didn't complete *Mode de valeurs* until the following winter.[5] This raises interesting questions about the exact chronology of events surrounding its composition, and the composition of the piano piece *Cantéyodjayâ*.

It is accepted that this work is a precursor to the more elaborate *Mode de valeurs* and for a long time its date of composition was given as Tanglewood, 1948, but it is now accepted that 1949 is a more accurate dating of this work, as this coincides with the dates Messiaen attended the Tanglewood Music Center (then called the Berkshire Music Center), where he taught

[1] See Robert Sherlaw Johnson, *Messiaen* (London: Dent, 1975), pp. 105–7, and Richard Toop, 'Messiaen/Goeyvaerts, Fano/Stockhausen, Boulez', *Perspectives of New Music*, Vol. 13, no. 1 (1971), 141–69.

[2] Pierre Boulez, *Conversations with Célestin Deliège* (London: Eulenburg, 1976), p. 55.

[3] This idea of automaticism is not alien to Messiaen: substantial passages of his works from the 1940s superimpose a series of rhythms on a series of chords in the manner of *color* and *talea*. An excellent example of this occurs in the first movement of the *Quatuor pour la fin du Temps*, the *Liturgie de cristal*,

where the piano has a progression of 29 chords (harmonic pedal) against 17 durations (rhythmic pedal). It would take 493 units (29 times 17, because both are prime numbers) for the cycle to come full circle. An unnoticed missing chord adds further intricacies to this process but this is beyond the scope of the present discussion.

[4] Hans-Heinz Stuckenschmidt, 'Synthesis and New Experiments: Four Contemporary German Composers', trans. Abram Loft, *Musical Quarterly*, Vol. 38, no. 3 (July 1952), 353–68.

[5] Harry Halbreich, *Olivier Messiaen* (Fayard/Fondation: SACEM, 1980), p. 39.

composition alongside Aaron Copland.[6] The Darmstadt summer school took place from 19 June to 10 July, which slightly overlapped with the courses at Tanglewood (4 July to 14 August).[7] It seems reasonable to assume, then, that Messiaen visited Darmstadt full of new ideas and made some preparatory sketches for the *Mode de valeurs*. He may well have then travelled to Tanglewood, where he composed *Cantéyodjayâ*, which in essence belongs to the old Messiaen style but also contains a brief experimental passage (pp. 8–10 *Modéré*) in the form of a scaled-down version of *Mode de valeurs*.

Before highlighting some of the features of *Mode de valeurs*, it is pertinent to examine some of the key events and influences on Messiaen in the 1940s in an attempt to account for this aesthetic shift in his compositional language. Messiaen's appointment as a harmony professor at the Paris Conservatoire in May 1941 can be partly attributed to another teacher's misfortune. Yvonne Loriod recalls that his predecessor André Bloch, a Jew, was due to retire the following September but decided to leave earlier because of the persecution of the Jews.[8] Since Schoenberg and many others had moved to the United States in the 1930s and, since part of the Nazi's cultural policy was to obliterate serialism and reinstate the great German masterworks, it was very difficult for composers to access such works. In addition to the radical policies of the Nazis, there were restrictions on what could be taught at the Paris Conservatoire.

In Messiaen's harmony class there were, among others, Pierre Boulez, Serge Nigg and Yvonne Loriod – later to become Messiaen's second wife – and the desire of these students to learn more about contemporary music must surely have been a huge stimulus to Messiaen. In conversation with Claude Samuel, Messiaen stated that the inquisitive nature of his students compelled him 'to undertake studies I might not have dreamt of, had it not been for them'.[9] Pertinent to Messiaen is the fact that most of the students he taught were composers, and, as such, he felt that all his classes, be they at the Conservatoire, Tanglewood or Darmstadt, were classes in composition.[10] However, just as he was establishing himself as a teacher of some of the brightest students in Paris, France was liberated and a series of events

[6] André Boucourechliev, 'Messiaen', in Stanley Sadie (ed.), *The New Grove Dictionary of Music and Musicians*, vol. XII (1980), 207. See Peter Hill and Nigel Simeone, *Messiaen* (New Haven and London: Yale University Press, 2005), pp. 179–80, who suggest that, given how much was happening in Messiaen's life (including his wife's illness, which can partly account for his focusing on works for solo instrument after the exhausting size of the *Turangalîla-Symphonie*), it is understandable that Messiaen got some dates confused.

[7] Thanks to Bridget Carr, the archivist at Tanglewood, for this information.

[8] Jean Boivin, *La Classe de Messiaen* (Paris: Christian Bourgois, 1995), p. 31.

[9] Claude Samuel, *Olivier Messiaen: Music and Color: Conversations with Claude Samuel*, trans. E. Thomas Glasow (Portland, OR: Amadeus Press, 1994), p. 176.

[10] Antoine Goléa, *Rencontres avec Olivier Messiaen* (Paris Genève: Slatkine, 1984), p. 241.

precipitated a dramatic cultural and aesthetic shift, which would have colossal implications for the evolution of music and Messiaen's position therein.

The emergence of René Leibowitz (1913–72) would cast a shadow over Messiaen's recent good fortune. Claims that Leibowitz studied directly with Schoenberg and Webern have never been confirmed, but what should be undisputed is that he was the champion of the twelve-tone movement in Europe, particularly after the untimely death of Webern.[11] Leibowitz took centre stage when France was liberated in 1944 by conducting a performance of Schoenberg's Op. 26 Wind Quintet. On hearing this piece, Boulez was prompted to seek instruction in twelve-tone technique from Leibowitz.[12] Maurice La Roux, another student who also changed allegiance from Messiaen to Leibowitz, recalled that instruction in serial technique was absent from Messiaen's classes, although Messiaen was better at some aspects of Schoenberg than at anything by Webern.[13]

We can get some sense of Messiaen's knowledge of serialism from his brief thoughts on the subject in Tome III of the *Traité de rythme, de couleur, et d'ornithologie*. He refers to Leibowitz's terminology for codifying the four possible arrangements, of a tone row, taking as his starting point the series used in Schoenberg's *Variations for Orchestra* Op. 31.[14] Messiaen goes on to give examples of how twelve-tone rows can be deployed, and all but two of the chosen musical excerpts (one each by Schoenberg and Berg) are by Webern, perhaps showing Messiaen's predilection for the latter. In conversation with Claude Samuel many years later, Messaien stated that: 'Webern was the "true" serial composer; Schoenberg and Berg were the precursors, and Boulez the realizer and the "surpasser".'[15]

It is interesting that Messiaen chose something from Schoenberg's output that he could criticise. In discussing the opening chords of the Op. 33a Piano Piece, he says: 'Unfortunately, this passage offers too many classified

[11] Reinhard Kapp, 'Shades of the Double's Original: René Leibowitz's dispute with Boulez', *Tempo*, Vol. 165 (1988), 4.
[12] Joan Peyser, *Boulez: Composer, Conductor, Enigma* (London: Cassell & Company Ltd, 1976), pp. 32–3.
[13] Boivin, *La Classe de Messiaen*, p. 37. It is questionable how much music by Webern was available in the 1940s, let alone whether Messiaen attempted to discuss it in any of his classes; La Roux's inclusion of Webern could be clouded by the passage of time.
[14] Leibowitz's 'originale' is renamed 'Le movement droit' by Messiaen; his inversion classification, 'renversement', is renamed 'Le movement contraire'; his retrograde

classification, 'récurrence', is renamed 'Le movement rétrograde'; and his retrograde of the inversion classification, 'récurrence du renversement', is renamed 'La rétrogradation du contraire'. See Messiaen, *TRCO*, Tome VII (Paris: Leduc, 2002), p. 45.
[15] Samuel, *Olivier Messiaen: Music and Color*, p. 192. It is worth noting that some aspects of Messiaen's approach in *Mode de valeurs* (particularly the fixed timbre of pitches) bear an astonishing resemblance to the second movement of Webern's *Variations* Op. 27 for piano. Whether Messiaen knew this work is uncertain, although he tells Samuel (p. 112) that he first encountered Webern's music after the Second World War.

sonorities: the second chord is the second inversion of a diminished fifth and diminished seventh. ...'[16] This is a surprisingly weak criticism on Messiaen's part, since it is inevitable that a multitude of recognisable chords can be found in a serial piece if one seeks them out. In addition, Messiaen's classification of such chords is somewhat ironic, since such chords have resonances that translate to colour for him. This seems to contradict one of Messiaen's fundamental criticisms of serial language: 'it is black! I see it without coloration. Always black, grey, black, grey.'[17] Finally, in response to the serialists' apparent concentration on pitch, as early as 1942 Messiaen proposed the idea of an ordered series applied to the other parameters of sound, namely duration, dynamics, articulation and timbre, ideas that would eventually manifest themselves in his *Mode de valeurs* and be taken up by younger composers.[18]

While the experiment with serialism became a phase in Messiaen's compositional output, it could be argued that, in terms of the future direction of music, Leibowitz somehow backed the wrong horse with respect to serialism. Boulez has made it clear that Leibowitz's teaching did not suit him because he took a rigidly academic approach and seemed to offer no thoughts on how serial music could continue to evolve: 'he was serviceable at the beginning, but I began to resent him when I saw how narrow and stupid he was.'[19] The fundamental difference between Leibowitz and Boulez was that the former was inspired by Schoenberg and the latter by Webern.

Leibowitz never assumed a high-profile teaching position in Paris, but in many ways this was to his advantage because, if he had been at the Conservatoire, he would have been unable to teach serial technique. His sole aim was to resurrect the music of Schoenberg, Berg and Webern. In many ways he succeeded: in 1947 he organised a festival entitled 'Hommage à Schoenberg' in which the music of these composers was brought before the Parisian public. Interestingly, Messiaen was in the audience for the performance (conducted by Leibowitz) of Webern's Symphony Op. 21 at this festival.[20]

Leibowitz went on to write several books on serial music and, to further his belief that serialism should assume its rightful position as the world's new

---

[16] Messiaen, *TRCO*, Tome VII, p. 50. His criticism of Schoenberg in the *Traité* is far from exhaustive or empirical, and once again shows that many critiques were written to suit a particular agenda by choosing material which would corroborate a point while conveniently ignoring anything that might contradict it.
[17] Samuel, *Olivier Messiaen: Music and Color*, p. 241.

[18] Messiaen, *TRCO*, Tome VII, p. 44. A footnote in the text indicates that this section was first drafted in the early 1950s.
[19] Peyser, *Boulez*, pp. 39, 44 and 76.
[20] Boivin, *Messiaen*, p. 62. Incidentally, Webern's *Symphony* Op. 21 was the first work that Leibowitz had brought to the attention of his new 'followers' in 1944.

and most sophisticated musical language, he published an article about one of his pupils, the Italian André Casanova, whom he claimed arrived at a form of serialism despite Leibowitz's deliberate avoidance of discussing this during their meetings.[21] In this article, and his book on Schoenberg, Leibowitz asserts that serialism was the logical outcome of Romanticism. In other words, he believed that serialism inherently formed part of the canon of music because, as he states, '... continuity – not a violent break – is the *principle* [sic] element in the transition from one musical system to another'.[22] What this fails to take account of, particularly in the context of the twentieth century, is that a multitude of factors impinge upon the development of musical language. In pursuing this concept of a singular historical lineage, Leibowitz implies that music that does not conform to this is not historically legitimate.

This belief in the historical imperative of serialism and the 'natural' evolution of music is further projected in Leibowitz's highly charged critique of Messiaen's *Technique de mon langage musical* – 'Olivier Messiaen or Empirical Hedonism in Contemporary Music' – which appeared in the journal *L'Arche* in 1945 just one year after the publication of Messiaen's treatise. Leibowitz states that: 'Above all, to compose music means to participate in an authentic and necessary way for this evolution, without which one perhaps manages to satisfy certain personal needs, but nothing more.'[23] His pejorative use of the word 'hedonism' in the title of the article provides the crux of his central criticism of Messiaen (and others) as illustrated in the above quotation: namely, that the pursuit of a musical language or style outside of the natural evolution of music results in music whose only function is to satisfy the composer himself. The idea that the composer is the only one to gain some level of satisfaction from the music is surely a gross generalisation and simplification of what are complex aesthetic and emotional considerations. Leibowitz also hints that there is an element of selfishness on the part of such composers, and in this respect he stretches the semantics of 'hedonism'. It would also seem that hedonism (where 'pleasure

[21] See René Leibowitz, 'A New French Composer', *Music Survey New Series 1949–1952*, Vol. 2, no. 3 (1950), 148–54.
[22] René Leibowitz, *Schoenberg and his School*, trans. Dika Newlin (New York: Philosophical Library, 1947/1949), p. 22 (italics in original quotation). Leibowitz was not alone in this belief. Adorno also strongly believed in the historical necessity of serialism and regarded Stravinsky's attempts at 'Restoration' as, in part, a product of mass culture. This was all part of an intellectual and aesthetic culture in all the arts whose basic tenet was that,

according to Dahlhaus, for a composer's (artist's) work not to be considered 'superfluous', he had to 'entrust himself to the course of history'. See Carl Dahlhaus, *Schoenberg and the New Music*, trans. Derrick Puffett and Alfred Clayton (Cambridge University Press, 1987), p. 64.
[23] René Leibowitz, 'Olivier Messiaen ou l'hédonisme empirique dans la musique contemporaine', *L'Arche*, Vol. 9 (1945), 132 (all translations from this article are my own). This further contributes to the notion of the 'superfluous' work mentioned earlier.

is the chief good or the proper end of action', as defined by the *OED*) in music that is part of the so-called 'canon' is perfectly acceptable to Leibowitz.

The article begins positively by acknowledging that Messiaen is a much-performed composer in Paris, and one who is not part of the 'degrading musical atmosphere there'.[24] This is presumably a reference to neoclassicism, a movement that both men despised.[25] Whilst initially complimenting Messiaen on striving for a personal language, which is a little contradictory considering that the whole article lambasts such an approach, Leibowitz quickly interjects a word of warning by describing the desire of composers to arrive at all costs at a personal language as one of the great scourges of the time. He argues that the great masters accepted a *universal language* and, despite this, originality never failed them.[26] Leibowitz commends the composers of the tonal period who, despite working within a language whose characteristics or component parts remained unchanged for a substantial period of time, still managed to compose works of great originality. In other words, originality need not imply a radical departure from the idiomatic language of the time, which for Leibowitz perhaps characterised many aspects of twentieth-century music.

From here on the tone of Leibowitz's article becomes at best critical, and at worst vitriolic. He takes Messiaen to task for discussing the individual parameters of music – such as pitch, or rhythm – separately. Leibowitz believed that the act of composition should encompass all the parameters, including timbre, from the outset and simultaneously rather than working on each parameter separately.[27] In *Schoenberg and his School* Leibowitz censures Stravinsky, albeit in a footnote, pontificating that 'the genuine polyphonic tradition *does not admit the idea of rhythm for its own sake* ... the "purely rhythmic" experiments of certain contemporary composers seems to me not only mistaken, but quite meaningless'.[28]

Whilst he pays tribute to Messiaen's rhythmic innovations, Leibowitz suggests that because Messiaen has only a 'partial understanding' of variation form, the arresting effect of something new is lost.[29] He focuses on several

---

[24] Leibowitz, 'Olivier Messiaen ou l'hédonisme empirique dans la musique contemporaine', 130.

[25] See Samuel, *Olivier Messiaen: Music and Color*, p. 195, 'The Renaissance itself was a recreation and not a useless copy ... The principle is totally reprehensible; I'll even say it's a complete absurdity' (Messiaen's response when asked what he thought of neoclassicism).

[26] Leibowitz, 'Olivier Messiaen ou l'hédonisme empirique dans la musique contemporaine', 132 (my italics).

[27] This raises an interesting paradox: as a composer and teacher immersed in serial technique, Leibowitz conveniently ignores the whole act of precomposition involved in composing a twelve-tone row.

[28] Leibowitz, *Schoenberg and his School*, p. 247 (italics in original quotation).

[29] Leibowitz, 'Olivier Messiaen ou l'hédonisme empirique dans la musique contemporaine', 133.

excerpts from *TMLM*. For example, in *Danse de la fureur, pour les sept trompettes*, from the *Quatuor pour la fin du Temps* (Example 13 in *TMLM*), he notes that, despite a relatively complex rhythmic structure, great portions of the material are literal repeats (a valid observation), which proves, according to Leibowitz, Messiaen's lack of understanding of 'variation' and renders the exercise pointless.[30] In Messiaen's defence there are many excellent examples of his use of *variation* in the broadest sense of the word. A case in point is the middle movement *Combat de la mort et de la vie* of *Les Corps glorieux* (1939) in which a jagged, angular theme centred around two tritones is treated in canon, used as a foundation for a violent toccata, chopped up by 'elimination', and finally becomes the basis for a serene slow movement.

On the Modes of Limited Transpositions Leibowitz denounces Messiaen for claiming a new discovery because Busoni, Capellen and others had worked out similar modes at the turn of the century.[31] Leibowitz is correct, insofar as Mode 1 is the whole-tone scale and Mode 2 the octatonic scale, but there is an element of ingenuity on Messiaen's part, since he creates other modes based on the inherent principle of 'limited transposition'. At the root of these modes is a richly chromatic approach to melody and harmonisation – the subtle nuances of which are determined by the symmetrical divisions of each mode and the various transpositions that arise. In addition, the synaesthetic properties of sound translated as colour for Messiaen cannot be overlooked when considering his modes, and, as will be seen shortly, this fascination with colour constitutes a vital part of *Mode de valeurs*. Leibowitz completely ignores this aspect and asserts that, since the entire chromatic range is now available, it is pointless developing such artificial and empirical systems.[32] To further this argument he quotes a substantial passage from Schoenberg's *Harmonielehre*, in which Schoenberg comments on the futility of creating new scales.

The essence of Schoenberg's argument is that creating new scales does not emancipate the composer from the restrictions of the diatonic system: these new scales will have their own restrictions/limitations, which means that the composer is merely substituting one set of conventions for another.[33]

---

[30] Leibowitz, 'Olivier Messiaen ou l'hédonisme empirique dans la musique contemporaine', 133. Indeed these examples are indicative of a criticism Boulez was to make several years later in 1948 in an article entitled 'Proposals', later reprinted in *Stocktakings from an Apprenticeship*: 'he [Messiaen] does not compose – he juxtaposes'.

[31] Leibowitz, 'Olivier Messiaen ou l'hédonisme empirique dans la musique contemporaine', 137.

[32] Leibowitz, 'Olivier Messiaen ou l'hédonisme empirique dans la musique contemporaine', 137. Leibowitz's criticism of Messiaen becomes vindictive and insulting when he adds a quotation from Shakespeare's *Hamlet*, 'something is rotten in the state of Denmark'.

[33] Arnold Schoenberg, *Theory of Harmony*, trans. Roy Carter (London: Faber and Faber, 1978), p. 395 (originally published as *Harmonielehre* in 1911).

Finally, it is worth noting that, in confining himself to a particular mode, Messiaen is no different to the composer who confines himself to one row, and all the restrictions that that brings: after all, there are over 479 million different ways of arranging twelve notes, as Messiaen continually reminds us.

It is highly unlikely that *Mode de valeurs* is in any way a direct response to Leibowitz's criticisms (I doubt Messiaen would have given Leibowitz the satisfaction), but an analysis of the *étude* reveals the composer developing techniques he had been using throughout the 1940s, while at the same time keeping a surreptitious eye on what was happening around him. One such event that had a direct impact on Messiaen's professional life was the premiere of the *Trois Petites Liturgies de la Présence Divine* in April 1945. This produced typically mixed reviews ranging from those waxing lyrical about the composer, to those taking issue with the mysticism, text and sonorities created.[34] Messiaen himself was delighted with the performance, but in many ways it did not further his case for a composition class at the Conservatoire. Indeed, one of the objections raised when Boulez (and others) approached Delvincourt about the possibility of a composition class was the débâcle in the press over Messiaen's *Trois Petites Liturgies*. Given the artistic and cultural climate of the late 1940s, Leibowitz's criticisms, students deserting him, and difficulties at work and with the Press, it was perhaps not too surprising that Messiaen might have tried something radically new.

One more event may have given him all the encouragement he needed. Before embarking on his summer teaching courses in Tanglewood and Darmstadt, Messiaen became acquainted with the American experimental composer John Cage. Between 1946 and 1948 Cage composed his *Sonatas and Interludes* for prepared piano, and in 1949 this work enabled him to obtain a grant to spend six months in Europe. Messiaen invited Cage to play his *Sonatas and Interludes* at the Salle Gounod of the Conservatoire on 7 June with another (private) performance scheduled for 17 June at Suzanne Tézenas's salon.[35] Although Messiaen was in attendance at this second performance, it was his former pupil, Pierre Boulez, who introduced Cage and his works to those assembled. Having explained the concept of inserting various objects between the strings of the piano – that is, the workings and theory of the prepared piano – Boulez went on to say that 'from this he [Cage] deduced the necessity of modifying duration, amplitude, frequency, and timbre – in other words, the four characteristics of a sound'.[36] Cage had observed that by inserting objects between the strings of the piano the four

[34] See Alain Périer, *Messiaen* (Paris, Editions du Seuil: 1979), pp. 80–1 for details of the reviews.
[35] Jean-Jacques Nattiez (ed.), *The Boulez–Cage Correspondence*, trans. Robert Samuels (Cambridge University Press, 1993), p. 5.
[36] Nattiez, *The Boulez–Cage Correspondence*, p. 30.

characteristics of sound were altered and, crucially, in terms of a prepared piano, the timbre of each note was fixed for the duration of the piece.

Boulez's comment before this performance that Cage was 'giving at the outset an originality to each sound' crucially anticipates Messiaen's compositional approach in his *Mode de valeurs*.[37] For in Messiaen's *Mode de valeurs*, each note has a specific timbre (defined by register, duration, and dynamic and articulation markings) fixed for the entirety of the piece, which requires phenomenal concentration and tone control from the performer.[38] The proximity of Cage's performance to Messiaen's working on *Cantéyodjayâ* and *Mode de valeurs* is too compelling for Cage not to have been a vital influence in the creation of these important pieces. Indeed, the performance of the *Sonatas and Interludes* had a profound effect on Messiaen, a fact that is corroborated by Karel Goeyvaerts, a former student, who would shortly experiment with total serialism. Goeyvaerts recalls that 'the crisp sounds of his [Cage's] gamelan piano and the precise rhythm of the sonatas kept us spellbound. Messiaen claimed that this was his most riveting musical experience since he first discovered Çârngadeva's *deçî-tâlas*.'[39]

In a programme note to a performance of *Timbres-durées* in 1952, Messiaen acknowledges Cage's important position in the move towards working with all the parameters of music: 'I must pay homage to the prophets who paved the way – the way which leads from Varèse to Boulez by way of Webern, Jolivet, John Cage and myself.'[40] In concluding that Cage had some influence on Messiaen, particularly with his prepared piano, it is prudent to note that both composers came from polar opposites in terms of their beliefs and aesthetics. The music that both composers produced in the 1940s does not immediately offer itself up to obvious comparison, but sometimes influences can come from the most obscure places. It is abundantly clear that what Messiaen found fascinating about the *Sonatas and Interludes* was their extraordinary exploration of colour and timbre, and how the pieces reminded him of a gamelan orchestra.

---

[37] Nattiez, *The Boulez–Cage Correspondence*, p. 31.

[38] It is worth listening to Messiaen's recording of the *Quatre Etudes*, made shortly after they were written, where the explicit markings in the score are far from adhered to. The defence usually given is that the piano used did not have a middle pedal, thereby making some of the sustaining virtually impossible.

[39] Karel Goeyvaerts, 'Paris-Darmstadt 1947–1956: excerpt from the autobiographical portrait', *Revue Belge de Musicologie*, Vol. 48 (1994), 40.

[40] Hill and Simeone, *Messiaen*, p. 199. It is also worth noting that in his article 'Forerunners of Modern Music' Cage argued for a music structured around duration/rhythm since the only characteristic sound and silence have in common is duration. This puts Cage clearly at odds with Leibowitz but in the same aesthetic world as Messiaen. Written in 1949, the article was translated into French and published in *Contrepoints* later that year. See John Cage, *Silence* (Hanover, NH: Wesleyan University Press, 1961), pp. 62–6.

In order to understand Messiaen's exploration of colour and timbre, and the apparently dramatic change in Messiaen's compositional style it is useful to summarise the main characteristics of his language as expounded in the *Technique de mon langage musical* – melody, harmony and rhythm. Taking melody and harmony together, Messiaen's writing is based almost exclusively on his Modes of Limited Transposition, and in this respect *Mode de valeurs* marks a radical departure. In the rhythmic domain, Messiaen's main interest was in working with the semiquaver as a unit of duration (frequently adding it to what would otherwise be a metrical bar), and building rhythms based on Çârngadeva's *deçi-tâlas* where the emphasis is again on ametrical, rather than conventional Western, structures. From these Messiaen explored augmentation, diminution and non-retrogradability, and a host of other techniques including the *personnages rythmiques*.[41] In working with units of duration, Messiaen developed the idea of chromatic rhythm, whereby a series of durations based on an increasing or decreasing series of values such as 1 to 12 semiquavers was used in *Mode de valeurs*. This plays an important part in Messiaen's compositions from the 1940s[42] and culminates in a technique Messiaen described as *interversions*, whereby the series of numbers is subjected to permutations.[43]

Chromatic rhythm is the foundation on which *Mode de valeurs* is built, but Messiaen goes a stage further by establishing a one-to-one correspondence between pitch and duration, in a manner that attempts to go beyond the serialists' 'unilateral interest in pitch', of which he spoke in the early 1940s.[44] This is first seen in the *Modéré* section of *Cantéyodjayâ*, where Messiaen employs a mode of twenty-four pitches (three divisions of eight), each of which is fixed in register, duration and dynamic.

In the first division (Ex. 3.1) Messiaen uses the demisemiquaver as the basic rhythmic unit, resulting in durations of one demisemiquaver to one

---

[41] The *personnages rythmiques* technique has its roots in Stravinsky's *Le Sacre du printemps*, where one rhythm augments, another diminishes and the third remains unchanged at each repetition. Messiaen uses the metaphor of three actors interacting with each other. See Samuel, *Olivier Messiaen: Music and Color*, p. 176, and Messiaen's analysis of *Le Sacre du printemps* in *TRCO*, Tome II, pp. 93–147.

[42] See, for example, 'Regard de l'Onction terrible', from the *Vingt Regards sur l'enfant-Jésus*, where Messiaen uses chromatic durations to create an effect of simultaneous acceleration (a sequence of durations starting with a long note and decreasing in value by one semiquaver on each subsequent chord) and deceleration (a sequence starting with a

duration of one semiquaver and subsequently increasing by one semiquaver).

[43] The technique of *interversion* involves the reordering of a series of numbers (frequently twelve in Messiaen's case), which yields a finite number of different arrangements before the original returns (much like the 'Charm of Impossibilities' seen in the Modes of Limited Transpositions). For example, rearranging the series 1 2 3 … 12 (the numbers can represent notes, durations or both) by working from the extremities to the centre gives 1 12 2 11 3 10 4 9 5 8 6 7 (this can be seen in Ex. 3.2). By applying the same formula, the next interversion reads 1 7 12 6 2 8 11 5 3 9 10 4 and so on.

[44] Goléa, *Rencontres avec Olivier Messiaen*, p. 247.

Ex 3.1: *Mode de valeurs et d'intensités* Division I

crotchet; the second and third lines use, respectively, the semiquaver and quaver as their units applied in the same way.[45] Many of the notes have similar dynamic markings, since Messiaen only employs five distinct gradations but, unlike in *Mode de valeurs*, there are no articulation markings.

With *Mode de valeurs* the full realisation of the latent possibilities of this technique can be seen: each of the three divisions now has twelve pitches, cumulatively spanning the entire range of the piano (based once again on demisemiquaver, semiquaver and quaver rhythmic units), and each note has one of seven dynamic markings and one of twelve articulation markings. It is worth stressing that this effectively creates a bank of fixed sounds (strongly reminiscent of Cage's *Sonatas and Interludes*)[46] on which Messiaen can draw. Each pitch, with its unique set of parameters, acts as a colour to be placed on a canvas, and Messiaen, like a painter, can mix these colours in an infinite number of ways to create a kaleidoscopic aural feast in two dimensions (the horizontal and the vertical), through individual lines and the resulting amalgamations. The first of the three divisions that make up *Mode de valeurs* clearly shows these practices at work (see Ex. 3.1).

When it comes to writing the piece, Messiaen adheres to the serial practice of avoiding octaves or unisons, but here comparisons with serialism end, since the divisions are not set up to be transposed or treated by any other serial technique. Not surprisingly, then, there are very few occurrences of a total unfolding of a division,[47] but, despite the fact that there is no apparent compulsion to state each of the divisions in their entirety, Messiaen suggests that the piece begins with an almost exact unfolding of each division.[48] There

[45] There is a minor inconsistency in the first bar at the bottom of page 8 of *Cantéyodjayâ*. The final note that makes up the first division is a C, which should have a duration of one crotchet (eight demisemiquavers), whereas in this bar it lasts for only five demisemiquavers. It is difficult to determine whether this is an error by Messiaen or a conscious departure from the mode of durations.

[46] See, for example, *Sonata V*, where the left hand plays a chromatic ostinato (B C C♯ D E♭ D D♭ C) in quavers throughout. By inserting the *same* implements between the strings (bolts and rubber, with the addition of plastic on D and E♭) Cage creates a distinctly percussive effect/

accompaniment that pervades the entire movement.

[47] See Johnson, *Messiaen*, p. 107 for a full account. Messiaen, too, highlights some of these in his analysis in *TRCO*.

[48] Messiaen, *TRCO*, Tome III, p. 128. According to Messiaen, division 2 unfolds from b. 1–9, but its final note (12) does not make its first appearance until b. 13. There are similar problems with the other divisions and Messiaen gives no insight as to why the third line starts with note 9 of the division. Richard Toop's analysis (see footnote 1) of the opening is much more informative and offers an explanation for the pitch selection and ordering.

is in fact only one occurrence in the whole piece where one of the divisions unfolds in its entirety in the order 1 to 12 (see line 1, b. 103–7), but even here the order of the final two notes is reversed.[49] By almost obstinately avoiding a traditional twelve-tone statement, Messiaen seems to deliberately negate the serial aesthetic and instead creates a three-part contrapuntal/pointillist texture devoid of any apparent sectional structure, which was rare for him.[50]

There are many detailed analyses and interpretations of this work available, including Hill and Simeone, who propose that Messiaen takes two approaches (that of unfolding scales and 'chopped'-up scales) which come together at the end of the piece.[51] Despite the seemingly radical nature of such procedures, I hope to show that some aspects of the work draw heavily on processes developed specifically by Messiaen throughout the 1940s. Of particular significance is the use of interversions, discussed above, which provides a strongly disciplined counterpart to the apparent freedom of much of *Mode de valeurs*.

It is interesting to observe that occurrences of such 'structured' material (interversions) are to be seen at significant points throughout: namely, around appearances of the lowest note of division 3 – C♯. From an aural perspective, each tolling of bottom C♯ of division 3 provides the listener with a strong anchor, given its duration, dynamic marking and resonating attributes, and the fact that it is heard only three times in the piece. Its first appearance occurs after much organised activity. From b. 24 in line 1 (top staff of Ex. 3.2) the first occurrence of a total unfolding of a division can be seen; that is to say, no note is repeated until all twelve have been stated.

Messiaen applies the interversion 1 12 2 11, etc. to achieve this effect. Immediately (one demisemiquaver) after the last note of the interversion is sounded (note 7 of the division), the C♯ of division 3 makes its first appearance. Messiaen highlights this note in *TRCO*, where he comments that it is preceded by the shortest note of that division (E♭). In addition he mentions the pitches of line 2 (b. 20–7) as the line is almost a complete retrograde of division 2 (notes 10 and 8 are omitted [not shown in Ex. 3.2]).[52] It will be noticed that the retrograde reading of a division creates a feeling of acceleration (marked in Ex. 3.2), while a feeling of deceleration

[49] The obvious reason for switching the order of notes 11 (F) and 12 (B) in line 1 is to avoid the F making an octave with note 5 of division 2, which sounds in b. 106. However, there is no reason why Messiaen *had* to have an F sounding in line 2 at this point, and it may be that he deliberately chooses to avoid a full twelve-tone statement but unfortunately he doesn't explain why!

[50] The lowest note of line 3 (C♯) is heard only three times during the course of the piece, which gives the work some semblance of a tripartite structure (see Toop, 'Messiaen/ Goeyvaerts, Fano/Stockhausen, Boulez', 144), and its significance will be assessed shortly.
[51] Hill and Simeone, *Messiaen*, p. 191.
[52] Messiaen, *TRCO*, Tome III, p. 128.

Ex. 3.2: *Mode de valeurs et d'intensités* b. 24–8

occurs in line 3 (notes 3 4 5 1 2 1 12 of division 3).[53] Another very striking feature of b. 24–8 is that the notes in lines 2 and 3 begin *piano* and legato, and as such they help to give the interversion greater prominence. As the end of the interversion approaches, a greater sense of urgency is created in lines 2 and 3 with the use of the shortest (and loudest) notes of the divisions, thereby propelling the music to the climactic C♯.[54]

This analysis of a small section of *Mode de valeurs* reveals Messiaen building on what he had already been exploring in earlier compositions. But paradoxically, despite the presence of interversions, the overall effect and impact created by *Mode de valeurs* is in marked contrast to anything he had written before. It shows Messiaen able to create something totally 'new' without abandoning everything from his past, and, although the Modes of Limited Transposition are absent from the piece, the inherent exploration of colour lives on, albeit in a

---

[53] It is surprising that Messiaen doesn't highlight these features (or even the interversion in line 1) considering that in his analyses of the *Livre d'orgue*, *Chronochromie* and other works which use such techniques he laboriously discusses every single interversion. It is not an unfair criticism to say that his 'analysis' of *Mode de valeurs* is far from insightful.

[54] The two other occurrences of C♯ in line 3 are marked as follows: immediately after the end of its second appearance (b. 78–80), line 1 proceeds with a triple interversion, which can be easily read by following the numbers in bold or italics: **8** *1* **1** *12* **7** *2* **11** *6* **3** *10* **5** *4* *9*. Its final appearance (from b. 112) is very striking, as no other note is played after the C♯ sounds and the piece fades away on this single sonority.

more explosive manner. Finally, the overall sense of emancipation or freedom that this piece engenders is quickly quashed and replaced by rigid organisation in *Ile de feu 2* (1950) and in the *Livre d'orgue* (1951–2).

Messiaen's casual dismissal of *Mode de valeurs* to Claude Samuel as being 'musically next to nothing' should not diminish its seminal position as the most important influence for the next generation of composers and, specifically, the total serialism movement.[55] Some aspects of the piece (in particular, Messiaen's use of chromatic rhythm and the exploration of colour) have their roots in earlier works, but the inescapable sense of asceticism, or purging, somehow clouds any obvious precursor, with the minor exception of *Cantéyodjayâ*.

Messiaen's fortunate position at the Paris Conservatoire and his analysis/composition course at Delapierre's gave him the opportunity to work with students who would in turn cause him to rethink his approach to composition. That Messiaen's experimental style was short-lived reveals that his commitment to his own form of serialism was not whole-hearted, although there are passages in his later works, such as *Chronochromie* and *Saint François d'Assise*, in which such techniques are revisited.[56] Other positive factors that could be said to have played a part in the creation of *Mode de valeurs* include Messiaen's experiences as a visitor to Darmstadt and Tanglewood, the success of the *Turangalîla-Symphonie*, and the encounter with Cage. Such positive events are interspersed with mixed reviews of his music,[57] vehement criticisms by Boulez and Leibowitz, and a general sense of marginalisation by his colleagues at the Conservatoire.[58]

All these factors contributed to the shift in his aesthetics. While Messiaen may be more readily remembered for earlier modal music, his use of birdsong, and his commitment to expounding the doctrines of Roman Catholicism, the 'experimental'[59] works of 1948–52, whether a hiatus in his output or an inevitable part of the composer's evolution, clearly demonstrate that Messiaen felt it necessary to move outside his own 'comfort zone', and to take a closer look at what was happening in the musical world of postwar Europe. These works have endured, and remain an important milestone in Messiaen's output.

---

[55] Samuel, *Olivier Messiaen: Music and Color*, p. 47.

[56] In *Chronochromie* the use of interversions, this time based on thirty-two values, governs the structure of the *Strophes*; in *Saint François d'Assise*, Messiaen makes use of a *Modes de valeurs et d'intensités* in the seventh tableau, *Les Stigmates*, from fig. 3 to 4, and from fig. 6 to 7.

[57] See Nigel Simeone, 'Messiaen and the Concerts de la Pléiade: "A Kind of Clandestine Revenge against the Occupation" ', *Music and Letters*, Vol. 81, no. 4 (2000), 551–84 for a detailed account of concerts in the 1940s; and the earlier reference to Périer, *Messiaen*, in footnote 34.

[58] See Boivin, *La Classe de Messiaen*, pp. 74–5.

[59] This is a term frequently used to describe the works of 1949–51. Bearing in mind recent revelations, the upper date should be extended to 1952, given that the *Livre d'orgue* was not completed until then. See Hill and Simeone, *Messiaen*, p. 201.

4 Forms of love: Messiaen's aesthetics of *éblouissement*

Sander van Maas

Je n'ai pas besoin d'être 'intéressé'. Rien ne m'intéresse. Je demande seulement à aimer et à être aimé.[1]

Introduction

Olivier Messiaen often alludes to the subject of love in his works. Many pieces possess a 'theme of love' or a reference to love as a biblical or theological motif. The years between 1945 and 1948 are of especial importance with regard to this subject. During this period, Messiaen created the 'Tristan trilogy', consisting of the song cycle *Harawi*, the *Turangalîla-Symphonie* and the *Cinq Rechants* for choir a cappella. According to the composer, the central concern of this trilogy is love as 'a reflection – a pale reflection but nevertheless a reflection – of genuine love, divine love'.[2] He associates 'divine love' with mythical couples such as Tristan and Isolde, Pelléas and Mélisande and Merlin and Vivian. The trilogy thematises the physical, passionate and spiritual life of an imaginary loving couple, their journeys and their ultimate love-death.[3]

In a musical sense, the 'love music' can be seen as one of the fixed 'types' of music Messiaen's œuvre has generated. In her comprehensive study of his works, Aloyse Michaely gives a description of a number of general characteristics that the various 'love themes' and 'love movements' share.[4] For instance, Messiaen tends to express the subject mostly in a slow or very slow tempo and,

[1] 'I don't need to be "interested". Nothing "interests" me. I only want to love and to be loved.' Claude Samuel, *Olivier Messiaen, Music and Color: Conversations with Claude Samuel*, trans. E. Thomas Glasow (Portland, OR: Amadeus Press, 1994), pp. 46–7.
[2] Samuel, *Olivier Messiaen: Music and Color* 30–1.
[3] On this period, see, for instance, Audrey Ekdahl Davidson, *Olivier Messiaen and the Tristan Myth* (Westport and London: Praeger, 2001). On the interaction between the various

levels of love, see Paul Griffiths, *Olivier Messiaen and the Music of Time* (London: Faber and Faber, 1985), pp. 124–42 and in particular p. 139, and Antoine Goléa, *Rencontres avec Olivier Messiaen* (Paris Genève: Slatkine, 1984), notably chapter 7.
[4] Aloyse Michaely, *Die Musik Olivier Messiaens: Untersuchungen zum Gesamtschaffen*, Hamburger Beiträge zur Musikwissenschaft, Sonderband (Hamburg: Karl Dieter Wagner, 1988), pp. 497–566, especially p. 566.

in his Modes 2 and 3. These 'colour modes' can be associated with a number of major keys. The most important one Messiaen uses for the love music is F♯ major, which is the key of the luscious sixth movement of *Turangalîla, Jardin du sommeil d'amour.*[5] Michaely also describes how Messiaen tends to use overarching melodic curves, and the way in which he ends phrases with a recurring melodic turn, consisting of a rising minor seventh or octave followed by a falling fourth. A beautiful example can be found in *Regard de l'église d'amour*, the last movement of Messiaen's *Vingt Regards sur l'enfant-Jésus* (1944).[6]

However, the subject of love cannot only be found at the level of themes, symbols, allegories, references or performance indications, but also at a much deeper level in his work.[7] This can best be illustrated with works from a later period in which the physical and subjective explicitness of love songs like the *Cinq Rechants* seems to have disappeared altogether. Already in his Tristan works, Messiaen evoked images of a cosmic, non-human nature, but at that time only as a canvas on which to express the romantic condition. After 1948, it seems as though the human subject leaves this romantic subjectivity behind in his work, and becomes in a sense more decentred, indeed more formal. The keyword to the aesthetic of this period is the notion of *éblouissement*, exemplified, according to Messiaen, in his own music, and thereby setting it apart from any other form of religious music.[8] The notion refers to a blinding of the inner senses (a dazzlement), which, he says, some of his works have been especially designed to produce. To Messiaen's (inner) eyes and ears, *éblouissement* represents the epitome of musico-religious experience.

To talk about love is probably as difficult as to talk about music. And it is even more difficult to talk about love, music and religion at once. Yet this is what Messiaen's work demands. Therefore, the challenge is to understand the logic that binds the three together. In an attempt to take a step in that direction, in the following study a number of complementary theoretical

---

[5] In the composer's mind's eye, this key produced, as he expressed it, 'a sparkling of all possible colours'. Almut Rößler, *Contributions to the Spiritual World of Olivier Messiaen, with Original Texts by the Composer*, trans. Barbara Dagg, Nancy Poland and Timothy Tikker (Duisburg: Gilles und Francke, 1986), p. 118.

[6] To my knowledge, it is unknown whether Messiaen had any symbolism in mind regarding the meaning of this melodic figure.

[7] For this latter, see, for example, Messiaen's *Les Offrandres oubliées* from 1930, part of which is to be played 'avec un grand amour'.

[8] Messiaen implies this when he discusses the phenomena of *son-couleur* and *éblouissement* in *Lecture at Notre-Dame, Conférence de Kyoto* and elsewhere. Although he mentions several musical examples of 'musique colorée' in Claude Samuel's *Music and Color* (Wagner, Chopin, Stravinsky, Debussy), he does not give a single musical example of where *son-couleur* and *éblouissement* meet mystically as they allegedly do in his own works (notably, according to the composer, in *La Transfiguration* and *Saint François d'Assise*). See below for further details.

tools will be employed. Following this introduction, in the second section I will briefly describe the topos of *éblouissement* in the writings of Messiaen, and then, in the third section, I will discuss Messiaen's references to musical examples relevant to the experience of this phenomenon. In my fourth section I turn to the aesthetic ideal of the sublime as a possible tool for the analysis of *éblouissement*. Leaving the sublime behind, in a fifth section I discuss *éblouissement* in terms of the French philosopher Jean-Luc Marion's notion of idolatry. In my sixth section I attempt to develop this new approach by using the notion of *Gestalt* from the theological aesthetics of Hans Urs von Balthasar. And in the final section, I will sketch the logic of love from the perspective of the previously discussed four key elements: *éblouissement*, the sublime, the idol and the iconic *Gestalt*.

The topos of *éblouissement*

Messiaen for the first time addresses the question of the experience of *éblouissement* in his *Couleurs de la cité céleste* (1963). In the preface to this score, he refers to its biblical derivation:

> The sound-colours [*son-couleurs*] ... symbolise the 'Heavenly City' and 'He' who inhabits it. Outside of time, outside of space, in a light without light, in a night without night ... That which the Apocalypse, being even more terrifying in its humility than in its vision of glory, designates only by a dazzlement [*éblouissement*] of colours ...[9]

Messiaen often likens *éblouissement* to the stained-glass windows of medieval churches and chapels. It was during a visit to the Sainte-Chapelle in Paris, when he was around 10 years of age that the dazzling effects of these windows first made a deep impression on him.[10] As he later explained, 'when one sees a stained-glass window, one does not immediately see all the figures. One has a sensation of colour, and one is dazzled [*on est éblouit*]. One has to shut one's eyes.'[11] And describing the experience in even greater detail in his Notre-Dame lecture from 1977:

> What happens in the stained-glass windows of Bourges, in the great windows of Chartres, in the rose-windows of Notre-Dame in Paris and in the marvellous,

[9] See score, 'Première note de l'auteur'. Later references to *éblouissement* include the scores of *Et exspecto resurrectionem mortuorum* and the score of *Méditations sur le Mystère de la Sainte Trinité*. Before he ever used the term, Messiaen described aspects of the experience in the preface to the score of the *Quatuor pour la fin du Temps*.

[10] See Samuel, *Olivier Messiaen: Music and Color*, p. 37; Rößler, *Contributions to the Spiritual World of Olivier Messiaen*, pp. 43–4; Messiaen, *Conférence de Kyoto* (Paris: Leduc, 1988), pp. 5–6; Messiaen, *Lecture at Notre-Dame* (Paris: Leduc, 2001), p. 9.

[11] Olivier Messiaen, in *Olivier Messiaen: The Music of Faith*, documentary film dir. Alan Benson (London Weekend Television, 1986).

incomparable glasswork of the Sainte-Chapelle? First of all there is a crowd of characters, great and small, which tell us of the life of Christ, of the Holy Virgin, of the Prophets, and of the Saints: it is a sort of catechism by image. This catechism is enclosed in circles, medallions, trefoils, it obeys the symbolism of colours, it opposes, it superimposes, it decorates, it instructs, with a thousand intentions and a thousand details. Now, from a distance, without binoculars, without ladders, without any object to come to the aid of our failing eye, we see nothing; nothing but a stained-glass window all blue, all green, all violet. We do not comprehend, we are *dazzled*![12]

Messiaen wanted to translate this extraordinary visual experience into music. For this purpose, he was able to make use of his special synaesthetic sensitivity, which gave him a largely involuntary correspondence between colour and sound. Messiaen claimed to see particular colours in his mind's eye when hearing certain combinations of tones: 'When I hear a score or read it, hearing it in my mind, I visualise corresponding colours which turn, shift, and combine, just as the sounds turn, shift, and combine, simultaneously.'[13] In the course of his career, this correspondence proved to be stable enough to be used as a compositional tool.[14] It allowed him to compose pieces like *Un vitrail et des oiseaux*, in which he portrays stained-glass windows and colourful birds.

However, in a number of cases Messiaen does not only imitate the colours of stained glass, but actually attempts to give himself – and probably also his ideal listener – the actual experience of *éblouissement*. His reasons are not merely musical or pictorial, but rather religious and, in a certain sense, even mystical. Messiaen believed *éblouissement* to be a genuinely mystagogical, transformative and religious experience.[15] He chose to use it as a model for a musico-religious aesthetics, turning music into an instrument of transformation:

> Coloured music does that which the stained-glass windows and rose-windows of the Middle Ages did: they give us dazzlement [*éblouissement*]. Touching at once our

---

[12] Messiaen, *Lecture at Notre-Dame*, p. 13 (translation slightly amended). See also his remarks in Samuel, *Oliver Messiaen: Music and Color*, pp. 63 and 139. Messiaen's account of *éblouissement* is also published on CD; see *Olivier Messiaen: Les couleurs du temps* (INA/Radio France, 2000), CD 2, track 4.

[13] Samuel, *Olivier Messiaen: Music and Color*, p. 37. For a general introduction to and bibliography of the subject and cultural history of synaesthetics, see Nicholas Cook, *Analysing Musical Multimedia* (Oxford: Clarendon Press, 1998), pp. 24–56.

[14] For these correspondences, see notably volume VII of Messiaen's *Traité de rythme, de couleur, et d'ornithologie* (*TRCO*) (Paris: Leduc, 2002).

[15] Messiaen, *Lecture at Notre-Dame*, p. 12: 'The more the sounds strike and knock the inner ear, and the more these multicoloured things move and irritate our inner eye, the more a contact is established, a rapport (as Rainer Maria Rilke said) with another reality: a rapport so powerful that it can transform our most hidden "I", the deepest, the most intimate, and dissolve us in a most high Truth which we could never hope to attain' (translation amended).

noblest senses: hearing and vision, it shakes our sensibilities into motion, pushes us to go beyond concepts, to approach that which is higher than reason and intuition, that is, FAITH.[16]

According to Messiaen, this capitalised faith continues into the new life after resurrection. In this new life, the faithful will have been given new, transfigured bodies, and they will undergo an '*éblouissement perpétuel*' in and through which they will know their Lord Christ. However, Messiaen does only refer to this theological idea in his musical works; he actually crosses a line that almost no one before him had crossed. Messiaen links the supernatural experience of *éblouissement* to his own music in an apparently non-metaphorical way, turning it into an exceptional vehicle for religious experience.[17] In a summary of his tenet in the *Conférence de Notre-Dame*, Messiaen explains why he puts the music of 'sound-colour' and *éblouissement* above any other form of religious music: 'Finally, there is that breakthrough towards the beyond [*la percée vers l'au-delà*], towards the invisible and unspeakable, which may be made by means of sound-colour [*son-couleur*], and is summed up in the sensation of dazzlement [*éblouissement*]'.[18]

This idea gradually turned into a topos in his writings. Dazzlement became a highly significant possibility in its own right, a speculative musico-religious event different from its initial association with stained-glass windows. In the last scene of the opera *Saint-François d'Assise*, for instance, when St Francis is taken up into heaven, Messiaen calls upon the notion of *éblouissement* to describe this act of grace. He makes Francis exclaim, 'Lord, illuminate me with your Presence! Liberate me, intoxicate me, dazzle me [*éblouis-moi*] with your excess of Truth …'.[19] After these words, as the stage directions in the

---

[16] Messiaen, *Lecture at Notre-Dame*, p. 15.

[17] The question whether this should or should not be interpreted as a metaphorical relation is crucial. As I argue below, the theological (and, for that matter, musicological) tendency to restrict the scope of musical experience by relegating it to the realm of metaphor does not do justice to the difference Messiaen rightly makes between 'religious music' and 'sound-colour and dazzlement' (see Messiaen's *Lecture at Notre-Dame*). The instability of the border between the 'literal' dimension of religious truth and the 'metaphorical' dimension of its artistic 'representation' is what should interest us here. It is this very problem which makes music, according to Henry Chadwick's *bon mot*, 'indispensable, but dangerous' (for example, because it upsets the *ordo* of signification, literality and truth), and which reveals the truly Augustinian dimension of Messiaen's work. Relegating

éblouissement to the realm of metaphor effectively destroys the significance of his project, turning it into the production of mere 'images', and evading the profound question of religious mediation, see Sander van Maas, *Faith in Music: On Olivier Messiaen* (New York: Fordham University Press, 2008).

[18] Messiaen, *Lecture at Notre-Dame*, p. 4 (translation amended).

[19] Messiaen, *Conférence de Kyoto*, p. 18. It should be noted that Messiaen does not always use *son-couleur* even when the subject matter calls for it. For instance, in the fifth scene of *Saint François d'Assise*, although Messiaen compares it to Saul's confrontation with Christ on the way to Damascus (Acts 9:3–9), St Francis's mystical breakthrough is not accompanied by the music of *éblouissement*. He does not even use the word; according to Messiaen, Saul is blinded (*aveugle*) by the experience, not dazzled (*ébloui*).

score prescribe, the spot where François had laid is to be flooded by a blinding, white light.[20] *Eblouissement* pervades the drama, the stage setting and the music alike, extending possibly to the audience. Later in 1989, Messiaen suggested to Brigitte Massin that 'The summit of contemplation is an *éblouissement*, therefore an excess of truth', and his music, so he seems to suggest, participates in this veritable excess.[21] But how is the musical elaboration of such a religious and mystical possibility to be understood? How does Messiaen actually compose this music of *éblouissement*? What makes music and religion relate so intimately?

The music of *éblouissement*

Messiaen has provided some answers to these and related questions, which give rise to a number of additional, even more pertinent questions. In November 1985 he visited Japan and gave a lecture in Kyoto. In this lecture, published as the *Conférence de Kyoto*, Messiaen again addressed the issue of *éblouissement*. This time, however, he made a remarkable reference to two specific works that, according to Messiaen, are 'directly related' to the experience.[22] One of these is *La Transfiguration de Notre-Seigneur Jésus-Christ*, from which he quotes five particular passages. The following brief analysis of the first of these will offer some insight into the way Messiaen actually composed his music of *éblouissement*.

Messiaen composed *La Transfiguration* between 1965 and 1969. The work is written for seven instrumental soloists, choir and orchestra. Its form is reminiscent of Bach's passions or the eighteenth-century oratorio, consisting as it does of a number of vocal 'recitatives', 'commentary' movements and two closing chorales. Its fourteen movements are grouped into two '*septénaires*', the second running at twice the length of the first. The text of the work is a patchwork of scriptural and theological fragments, all addressing some aspect of the transfiguration of Christ as related in the Gospel of Matthew. In the 'recitatives' of *La Transfiguration*, Messiaen sets the text of Matthew's account of Jesus's transfiguration on Mount Tabor (Matt. 17:1–13). Each of

---

[20]'Everything disappears, everything darkens. The choir positions itself before the backdrop. A single bright white light illuminates the spot where until moments before St Francis had laid. That light should gradually become more intense until the conclusion of the act. When the light becomes blinding [*aveuglante*] and unbearable, the curtain drops'. *L'Avant-scène opéra*, Hors série no. 4, 'Saint François D'Assise' (Paris: Premières Loges, 1992),

p. 100. The music here features a corresponding 'white' C major triad, played by massive orchestral and vocal forces.
[21]Brigitte Massin, *Olivier Messiaen: Une poétique du merveilleux* (Aix-en-Provence: Alinéa, 1989), p. 191.
[22]Messiaen, *Conférence de Kyoto*, pp. 14–16. The other four passages from *La Transfiguration* he refers to are: Part VII (entirely); Part IX, fig. 50–51; Part XII, fig. 9–10; Part XIV (entirely).

these 'recitatives' (in Latin) recounts a part of the principal verses of
Matthew's account. The verse sung in the third 'recitative' (Part VIII) is
the one recounting how Peter, Jacob and John, standing on top of the
mountain and witnessing Christ's transfiguration, were overshadowed by a
luminous cloud: 'He was still speaking when suddenly a bright cloud covered
them with a shadow, and suddenly from the cloud there came a voice which
said: "This is my Son, the Beloved; he enjoys my favour. Listen to him."'[23]

Messiaen's musical setting of this scene reveals a number of details that are
important for a deeper understanding of the music of *éblouissement*. In the
same way as in the other three recitatives, this third recitative is introduced
by a strongly 'syncopated' percussion section passage featuring the temple
block, leading into an enormous explosion of tam-tams, gongs and a long
trill on the chimes. The instrumentation and above all the unusual rhythmic
engagement between the instruments in this section are reminiscent of
Southeast Asian musical traditions. It is an illustration of Messiaen's great
love of metallophones with long and rich resonances which, according to the
composer, 'add a certain mystery' to the music, and evoke an 'unreal
quality'.[24]

After this introductory gesture, the choir of tenors starts singing the
biblical texts. Its musical setting strongly evokes the Gregorian antiphon,
followed by an equally 'liturgical' piece of recitative *recto tono* (on one note
only). This pseudo-monastic passage is followed by eleven measures of
uneven ascending and descending clusters in the strings, some of which are
played in harmonics (representing, according to Messiaen, the moving
cloud). These alienating elements lead to the passage he quotes in
Conférence de Kyoto as being related to *éblouissement*. This passage starts at
fig. 5 and extends into the tenor recitative: '*Et ecce vox de nube, dicens: Hic est
Filius meus dilectus* [And behold the voice of the cloud, saying: This is my
beloved Son]'. At this point in the score (fig. 6), there is a remarkable
footnote referring to the figurative character of the music.[25] In fact, the
footnote adds technical instructions to the general idea of the piece, which
Messiaen had already described in the short analyses that preface the score.
The relevant analysis reads as follows:

> Rhythmical introduction (varied). Continuation of the evangelical text in the
> recitative. The luminous cloud is represented by groups of glissandi in the strings,
> glissandi of various lengths and tempi. The 'Voice' from the cloud is accompanied by
> the multicoloured, undulating chords, the colours of which move at different speeds.

[23] Translation quoted from *The New Jerusalem
Bible* (London: Darton, Longman & Todd, 1990).
[24] Samuel, *Olivier Messiaen: Music and Color*,
p. 57.

[25] Messiaen, *La Transfiguration de Notre-
Seigneur Jésus-Christ* (Paris: Leduc, 1972), Part
VIII, at fig. 6.

The trills of the triangle and chimes join the harmonics of the strings, emphasising the shivering of the light.[26]

Messiaen wants his music to represent a number of things, beginning with the presence of God. He depicts this in a thoroughly apocalyptic way, with the images of shivering light (cloud and Son) and colour (Father), that can be found in Revelation 4:3, and, secondly, the Voice of God coming from the cloud. According to the footnoted instructions in the score, the choir (*ppp*) should sound as if coming from very high up and far away, and remain so. Thirdly, Messiaen's textures are to represent the triumph and glory of the Trinity and the 'victorious third' which refers to the g–b interval in the double basses and the fifth and sixth cellos, which is audible throughout the passage and becomes ever more prominent from b. 42 onwards following the crescendo in the score.[27]

Before this musical depiction comes to life, Messiaen orders a 'moment of silent expectation': a short pause, which he prepared two measures earlier with a two-beat rest. After that, the music gradually builds up with a foreboding recitative and expectant rests, until at figure 6 a sudden clarity ensues. The instrumentation of this *éblouissement* passage consists of sopranos and tenors, first and second violins, violas, double basses and percussion. The richness of timbre as well as the verticality of structure contrast sharply with the sober, unison singing of the tenors that precedes the sudden change. Messiaen fills the vertical space of his sound painting with materials that belong to the tradition of religious music, such as a drone (the B♮ in the lowest and highest strings, used also as a harmonic), organ-like clusters (reminiscent of the voix céleste's effect of arid transparence and harmonic saturation), the fairy-tale sound of the triangle and the 'mystery' of the chimes. In the high and middle registers the strings produce chromatic chords that can be identified as belonging to Messiaen's paradigmatic turning chords (*accords tournants*).[28] The heterogeneous sound image that results from these trills, clusters, resonances and harmonics is relatively stabilised by the identifiable continuity of the drone, and the 'turning chords' that revolve around themselves and saturate the sound spectrum.

The passage, which is only six measures long, is played in a mesmerisingly slow and perfectly constant beat of 20 M.M., so that its timing and form contrast sharply with its context. The creation of this sort of 'window' is typical of most musical passages that Messiaen mentions as examples of *son-couleurs* and *éblouissement*. A situation is created in which a sudden

[26] Messiaen, score of *La Transfiguration*.
[27] Samuel, *Olivier Messiaen: Music and Color*, p. 149, and *Conférence de Kyoto*, p. 15.
[28] See Messiaen, *TRCO*, Tome VII, 277–80 and 166–72. See also Michaely, *Die Musik Olivier Messiaens*, pp. 115–22, in particular her comprehensive harmonic analysis of Part VIII on p. 121.

change in the musical context occurs, which leads into a completely different (contrasting, opposing) musical situation.[29] Immediately after the 'break-through', the music returns to its previous style, which in general is less complex and more homophonic. It could well be argued that besides any consideration of synaesthetic colour, this very window-form itself produces the effect of 'breakthrough'. In Part VIII of *La Transfiguration* (at the begin-ning of the second *septénaire*), after the sudden introduction of the music of *éblouissement*, the music changes back to soprano-and-tenor recitative, and loses all luminosity, complexity and heterogeneity. And, it should be added, it loses all reference to religious 'breakthrough', too, for Messiaen does not even mention his setting of the remainder of God's own sentence, *'in quo mihi bene complacui: ipsum audite* [he enjoys my favour. Listen to him]'.

What is to be concluded from all this? In the first place, it should be kept in mind that, according to Messiaen, *éblouissement* has little to do with the *representation* of religious ideas by visual or musical means. The music of *éblouissement* certainly possesses many pictorial features, but its most impor-tant religious moment lies in the very *erasure* of these figurative elements (the apparent 'content' of the passage), in a way similar to the erasure of the figures in the stained-glass windows. Secondly, on a musical-technical level, it should be noted that the structure of both this and other musics of *éblouissement* employ a strategy of sudden change, by which the form of the passage comes to resemble a 'window' surrounded by sharply contrasting music. This reinforces the impression that the music of *éblouissement* is in fact not to be found in the actual content of the contrasting section, but rather in the enveloping form. In the third place, from Messiaen's references to it in *Conférence de Notre-Dame*, *éblouissement* seems to depend strongly on notions of grace and even of the miraculous (which strongly depend on *singularity*). Yet the effect of *repeatable*, musical-technical structures, of a rhetorical strategy of sorts, seemingly reduces any *éblouissement* to the trick of a musical illusionist.

Should this, in the final analysis, lead to the conclusion that Messiaen's testimony with regard to *éblouissement* is in fact little more than musical theatricality? Or should his testimony be understood as a contemporary reference to a musico-religious *possibility* that Enlightenment aesthetics and certain theologies taught us to forget? What is there to be said about *éblouissement* as a phenomenological or musico-religious figure outside of the confines of musicological interpretation? And ultimately, how can the

---

[29] See the passages Messiaen quotes from Parts VIII and XII in particular. The passage from Part IX also involves a grand scale change in texture, but here the new texture builds up more gradually. Obviously, the concept of sudden change does not apply to the chorals Messiaen mentions (Parts VII and XIV).

formal emptiness of the music of *éblouissement* be related to the theme of divine love, which after all forms the horizon of Messiaen's work?

The shattering of form

The threefold turn to form in the music of *éblouissement* – found in the erasure of specific content, the sudden textural changes and the emergence of rhetorical structures – seems to lead away from notions of interiority, feeling and content typically associated with love. But there is more to be said about *éblouissement*, as well as about music *qua* religion, and about love. On closer inspection, the 'turn to form' that characterises Messiaen's postwar music is not a turn to form as concrete, unified and meaningful, but a turn to form construed as *fragmentation*. This 'shattering of form' that characterises Messiaen's postwar work is present at both the level of musical form – Messiaen likens his juxtapositions of fragments to, for instance, Stockhausen's experiments with moment form – and at the level of musical aesthetics.[30] This multi-level change from unified to shattered form has already been signalled by writers such as Alain Michel and Wilfrid Mellers. Both authors describe Messiaen's music in terms of the sublime, an aesthetic notion that from the late seventeenth century onwards has fascinated philosophers and artists alike. Michel recounts how the lyrics used by Messiaen for the twelfth part of *La Transfiguration* evoke the idea of the mind's movement from visual light to intelligible light. 'In order to arrive at this transition, [Messiaen] uses a quite recent experience of nature. It had only been a short time ago – say, since about the beginning of the romantic era – that European intellectuals had made the effort to perceive the sublimity of the high mountains.'[31] Writing about the same work, but focusing on the effect the music has on its listeners, Mellers observes that 'purely aural sublimity – as distinct from any presumptive psychological "content" – could hardly be carried beyond this point'.[32]

The aesthetics of Messiaen's music very often seem to invoke the sublime. Not only do Messiaen's titles, mottoes and commentaries refer to classical examples of the sublime, such as starry heavens, the abyss or alpine mountains, but also the very style and design of much of his music inclines to typical gestures towards the sublime, such as the overpowering, the majestic

[30] Samuel, *Olivier Messiaen: Music and Color*, p. 187.
[31] Alain Michel, 'La Transfiguration et la beauté: d'Olivier Messiaen à Urs von Balthasar', in *Bulletin de l'Association Guillaume Budé* (December 1974). Reprinted in *Hommage à Olivier Messiaen* (La recherche artistique, November–December 1978), pp. 86–9, especially p. 87.
[32] Wilfrid Mellers, 'La Transfiguration de Notre-Seigneur Jésus-Christ', in *The Messiaen Companion*, ed. Peter Hill (London: Faber and Faber, 1995), p. 458.

and the unimaginable. Messiaen's music is not only a music of beautiful proportion, elegant design and good taste; it very often seeks to transcend human measure. It aspires towards the divine, or at least to the worldly traces thereof, through an arsenal of grand musical gestures, some of which may be quite violent and even repellent to the ear. This music brings forth *negative* forms of representation: it presents that which cannot be presented in positive form (in an analogy from the domain of language: the name of God) through shattered or shattering forms (faltering speech, ineffable words) or by falling silent altogether. Traditionally, the sublime has been thought of as that which overpowers the human mind and may be thought to testify to (and perhaps, as Messiaen suggests, lead the mind towards) the ineffable domains of divine mystery.

In Kant's *Critique of Judgment* – the *locus classicus* of modern aesthetics – the sublime is analysed in a fashion more appropriate to Enlightenment aesthetics, setting a limit to the domain of sense perception with regard to religion.[33] The sublime is construed as a feeling that indicates that the object of perception is unrepresentable to the subject's imagination. The sublime shatters the mind's power to synthesise the intuitions it receives into a unified representation of the object; in other words, to give it a unified form. According to Kant, the first moment of the sublime is characterised by the experience of displeasure (*Unlust*), which accompanies the overpowering of the imagination. After this initial moment, reason responds to this negative moment by making available to the subject its supernatural destiny which is expressed by reason's three transcendental ideas: God, Infinity and Immortality. In this second moment, the subject elevates itself above its finitude and subordination to the forces of nature, and thus pleasurably (*Lust*) overcomes its initial painful break with the world by realising the superiority of its own destiny (i.e. freedom). The idea or feeling of the sublime has been a major source of inspiration for artists, in particular to the Romantic movement of the nineteenth century.[34]

In his classic book on the relation between religion and art, the phenomenologist theologian Gerardus van der Leeuw describes a variety of ways in which the sublime may be present in music:

> Music attains sublimity by slowness of tempo. But this is not the only means, nor does it offer a guarantee for true sublimity, as many 'religious' composers seem to

[33] Immanuel Kant, *Critique of Judgment* (1790), transl. J. H. Bernard (Amherst: Prometheus, 2000), sections 23–9.
[34] See, in particular, Kiene Brillenburg Wurth, *The Musically Sublime: Infinity, Indeterminacy, Irresolvability* (Rijksuniversiteit Groningen, 2002; published on http://dissertations.ub.rug.nl>

(accessed 16 July 2007)) and Jan Christiaens, *"Kunstreligion" en het Absolute in de muziek: Olivier Messiaen's tijdsmetafysica (1949–1951) en het ontstaan van het serialisme* (Karlheinz Stockhausen, Karel Goeyvaerts)', Katholieke Universiteit Leuven, 2003; unpublished dissertation.

think. To slow tempo belongs majestic reserve, chaste restraint. And even this
remains nothing unless everything points to an emotion which admits no more
violent expression . . . If we ask whence it comes that the massive, the sublime, often
moves us religiously, indeed seems to be an expression of the holy, we find that this
lies in its overpowering character. We cannot escape it; we find ourselves in the
presence of the wholly other.[35]

Drawing on Rudolf Otto's classic *Das Heilige* (*The Idea of the Holy*), van der
Leeuw iterates that if art is to express the Holy by means of the sublime, both
of its constitutive moments, the *fascinans* and the *tremendum*, should be
present. It is not enough for art either to 'enchant, captivate, illuminate,
remove a burden from the heart' or to 'oppress, bring fear, cause horror and
terror'. As he puts it, 'it may be that terror dominates, but fascination must
not be absent. It may also be that we are so enchanted that we revel in bliss;
but if every tremor is lacking, it is a false bliss, even if we may be confronted
with real beauty.'[36] It is not difficult to find examples in Messiaen's music
in which either of these elements dominates – or in which some equilibrium
is maintained.[37]

It seems appropriate to apply the problematic of the sublime to much of
Messiaen's work. Not only does his music often use musical-technical
gestures belonging to the tradition of the musically sublime; his imagination
and aesthetic thought also tend to remain within the domain of this notion.
However, the notion of the sublime cannot account for a number of specific
aspects of *éblouissement* as enumerated by Messiaen. Firstly, Kant seems
almost to understand the sublime as an engagement of the subject with itself,
thereby greatly reducing the role of sense experience. Therefore he cannot
account for that which remains of perception in the experience of
éblouissement: the saturation of colour and sound, despite the erasure of
the figurative. Secondly, the sublime does not fully coincide with the religious aspects of *éblouissement*. Even if Rudolf Otto describes the sublime as a
historical 'schematisation' or distant echo of the original experience of 'the

[35] Gerardus van der Leeuw, *Sacred and Profane
Beauty: The Holy in Art* (New York: Holt,
Rinehart and Winston, 1963), 231. For listeners
to Messiaen's music, this may not sound
unfamiliar. Two short examples could be given,
both from his early organ repertoire. The first is
the extremely slow piece *Le Banquet céleste*,
notated in quaver = 52, with its endless final
chord, especially as played on Messiaen's
recording. The second example is *Apparition de
l'église éternelle*, a piece which is characterised by
the gestures of laborious swelling and expansion
from its first seconds onwards, and which
reaches its tremendous, triumphant climax on a
giant C major triad midway through.

[36] Van der Leeuw, *Sacred and Profane
Beauty*, p. 232. In his account of
éblouissement and 'breakthrough' in *Lecture
at Notre-Dame*, Messiaen not only mentions
the dazzling intensity of this experience,
which corresponds to Kant's idea of the
dynamical sublime, but also the
overwhelming number of 'intentions' and
'details' (*'mille intentions, mille détails'*)
included in the stained-glass windows,
which corresponds to Kant's idea of the
mathematical sublime.

[37] See, among many other possible examples,
the seventh scene of *Saint-François d'Assise*
('Les Stigmates'), notably 'la voix du Christ'.

numinous' or 'the wholly Other', these phenomena cannot be reduced to each other.[38] Messiaen does not talk aesthetics; he talks religion. And despite the fact that the difference between the two is not always clear (not in general, and certainly not in a work as 'postmodern orthodox' as Messiaen's), I will argue that this heterogeneity is necessary and constitutive, and that it points towards the ways in which Messiaen's music of *éblouissement* reconfigures the complex idea of 'sacred music'. So, to begin with, what is the specific theological-aesthetic logic behind the music of *éblouissement*?

Reinterpreting *éblouissement*

Messiaen's account of *éblouissement* implies a basic distinction between ordinary and extraordinary aural experiences. The event of dazzlement and 'breakthrough' does not belong to the ordinary range of musical experiences, but is an exception with a more or less transcendent and, to that extent, normative status. This raises the question as to what happens exactly when this exceptional potential of musical experience becomes reality. How does 'normal' audibility change, and how can the specific listening experience of *éblouissement* be characterised? The philosopher Jean-Luc Marion suggests one answer to this question. Elaborating from a phenomenology of the idol, Marion describes a perceptual logic that to a great extent parallels the phenomena Messiaen refers to. As will become clear, this logic reveals a number of aspects that remain hidden when these phenomena are analysed from the perspective of the sublime.

Traditionally, idolatry refers to the religious error of giving divine worship to anyone or anything other than the true God. It may concern the religious adoration of an image or statue that is thought to embody a divinity, or to possess divine powers. Music and the theatre are also sometimes thought to harbour the idolatrous power of substitution for the true object of worship or of leading the faithful astray. Augustine is famous for his concerns about the theatre and the song of 'beautiful voice', which according to him tend to draw attention to themselves rather than referring, through gesture and words, to the ultimate realm of divine truth.[39] In Marion's phenomenology of the idol, however, idolatry is not located in an object (a statue, song, etc.), but in a certain mode of perception.[40] Anyone or anything can become an

[38] Rudolf Otto, *Das Heilige: Über das Irrationale in der Idee des Göttlichen und sein Verhältnis zum Rationalen* (Munich: Beck, 1997), p. 61.

[39] See, for example, Augustine, *Confessions*, Book X, section 33.
[40] Jean-Luc Marion, *God Without Being: Hors-Texte*, trans. Thomas A. Carlson (Chicago: Chicago University Press, 1991), pp. 9–15.

idol when it falls under the régime of the idolatrous gaze. Marion's analysis focuses on visual phenomena in order to criticise the conceptual idolatry of philosophy. This need not concern us here. For present purposes it will suffice to note that the visual is essential in Messiaen's account of *éblouissement*. To this extent, the logic of the idol may help articulate the structure of dazzlement (a term which Marion uses, too), and inspire further analysis of aural phenomena.

In a phenomenological sense, the idol is characterised by its sheer visibility; in other words, by the very fact that it is visible. It does not hold anything back; it gives itself *as pure visibility*. According to Marion, it is this which dazzles the beholder. The idol appears in the field of normal vision, which is characterised by the fact that I gaze beyond it and see nothing in particular. The gaze 'transpierces' the visual; it sees nothing because it renders indifferent all meaningful differences:

> But here the idol intervenes. What shows up? For the first (and last) time, the gaze no longer rushes through the spectacle stage without stopping, but forms a stage in the spectacle; it is fixed in it and, *far from passing beyond*, remains facing what becomes for it a spectacle to *re-spect* [sic]. The gaze lets itself be filled: instead of outflanking the visible, of not seeing and rendering it invisible, the gaze discovers itself as outflanked, contained, held back by the visible. The visible finally becomes visible to the gaze because, again literally, the visible dazzles the gaze. The idol, the first visible, from the beginning, dazzles a gaze until then insatiable.[41]

The idol is the first truly visible phenomenon, and nothing more than that. It saturates my gaze completely with its splendour, i.e. its sheer excess of visibility. It marks the extreme limit of what my gaze can bear in terms of visibility – and it *dazzles* me.[42] The gaze is fascinated, arrested, and moved to adoration by the intense and exclusive sensibility of the idol.[43] Dazzlement is accompanied by, as Marion puts it, a feeling of 'success, glory, joy'.[44] It is associated with the notion of being dazzled by an 'excess of truth' (Messiaen-Aquinas), like the truth of the One whom no one can see without dying.[45] Or by the truth of Ideas: the Light that makes us see worldly

---

[41] Marion, *God Without Being*, pp. 11–12 (italics added).

[42] As mentioned above, dazzlement differs from mere blinding by the fact that it presupposes clear visibility: *éblouir* is the opposite of *aveugler*. See also Jean-Luc Marion, *Etant donné: essai d'une phénoménologie de la donation*, 2nd edition (Paris: Presses Universitaires de France, 1998), p. 285, where he states that 'When my gaze cannot bear what it sees, it suffers dazzlement [*éblouissement*]. For not being

able to bear it is not simply the same as not to see; one first of all has to perceive, even to see clearly, to know what cannot be born. [*Eblouissement*] is about a sight which our gaze cannot bear.'

[43] Jean-Luc Marion, *De surcroît: Etudes sur les phénomènes saturés* (Paris: Presses Universitaires de France, 2000), p. 73.

[44] Marion, *De surcroît: Etudes sur les phénomènes saturés*, p. 73, and Marion, *Etant donné*, p. 286.

[45] Exodus 33:20.

shadows, but which itself can only be seen by those whose eyes have already been filled with Light (Plato).[46] Messiaen, too, interprets the experience as exclusively joyous, beneficial, and as an ascent towards truth.

Marion, however, emphasises that the saturating event of dazzlement leaves an essential thing behind. The idol obfuscates the fact that phenomena are *given*, through maximising their mere *appearance*. The idol prevents any reference to the deeper dimension of divine givenness by prioritising the gripping and immersive power of the sensible spectacle. As Plato put it in the *Phaedrus*, 'for beauty alone this has been ordained, to be most manifest [*ekphanéstaton*] to sense and most lovely of all'.[47] But, one has to add (as Plato did himself) that perhaps this phenomenon is also the most dangerous. For the rapture of beauty may hide the saturating richness of the things that appear before us: their endless historical resonance, their infinitely rich signifying potential, their irretrievable moment of origin, all of which according to Marion do not result from their self-contained autonomy, but from their saturating givenness (by the Other).

Discussing the organ cycle *Les Corps glorieux*, Paul Griffiths once remarked that much of Messiaen's music needs a (correcting) verbal clue in order to realise its religious intentions:[48] 'Indeed, the objects and musical states that Messiaen offers to our inspection in *Les Corps Glorieux* are so very singular that we may well be disinclined to accept them as invitations to meditate on something else, preferring to make of them the centre of our contemplation.'[49] Griffiths here refers to the classic, Augustinian dilemma of idolatry, which should discourage any credulous interpretation of Messiaen's music, the examples he gives of *éblouissement* and 'break-through' included. The examples from *La Transfiguration* given above show precisely the kind of arrest and adoration typical of the phenomeno-logical idol. The most pertinent among these are perhaps the two chorales, which present the listener with densely chromatic chords that saturate the aural spectrum and often seem to contradict the melodic progress of their

---

[46] The reference to Plato pertains to *Republic* 515c and 517a. It is interesting to note that the Aquinas phrase 'excess of truth' Messiaen often alludes to is actually a mixture of several different *questiones*. The most important of these sources is *Summa Theologiae* I–II, q. 101, 2, ad 2, which deals with the relation between poetical and divine realities. With regard to the splendour of the idol, see also Jean-Luc Marion, *De surcroît: Etudes sur les phénomènes saturés*, p. 73.

[47] Plato's *Phaedrus*, 250d, trans. R. Hackforth, in E. Hamilton and H. Cairns (eds), *Plato: The Collected Dialogues* (Princeton University Press, 1996), p. 497.
[48] Messiaen defined the ultimate intention of his œuvre as 'the illumination of the theological truths of the Catholic faith'; Samuel, *Olivier Messiaen: Music and Color*, p. 20.
[49] Griffiths, *Olivier Messiaen and the Music of Time*, p. 70.

form.[50] The fascinating scintillations of these 'sound-colours' draw the ear into their inner world, presenting a phenomenon that does not retain the particular aural negativity found in tonal chord progressions (due to a stress on the functionality of harmonies rather than their sonorous qualities), but exhausts itself in and through its sheer audibility.[51] A similar effect of arrest is put into play in the other three examples, all of which involve a sudden change from linear musical discourse to simultaneous, resonant complexes that arrest and saturate the ear. As Messiaen describes it with reference to the passage from Part XII, the listener is thrown into an 'abyss of sweetness', being arrested by a quasi-falling motion rather than a self-conscious projection of a pathway along the musical trajectory.[52]

However ravishing and totalising these aural experiences of arrest, excess and adoration may be, Marion warns against their hidden limitations. The idol does not come into being through an act of grace, but, uniquely, is produced by the human gaze.[53] It operates as an invisible mirror, which confronts the gaze with its limitations, and thereby reveals that the divine, insofar as it is perceived, has only been perceived according to the measure and capacity of the *human* gaze. In the final analysis, the idol, which articulates the logic behind the experience of *éblouissement*, is constituted by the subject's gaze, which is fascinated and dazzled by the resplendent reflection *of itself* – without knowing it.[54] According to this interpretation, dazzlement is an expression of the exact opposite of what Messiaen and his sources speak of. It results from human incapacity, and could accordingly be interpreted in terms of lack, sin and suffering. It should be well noted that *éblouir* can also mean 'to deceive' and 'to mistake'. The idol does not accomplish the 'conversion' that would reverse the perspective of the gaze

---

[50] My aural analysis based on the CD recording of *La Transfiguration* by Reinbert de Leeuw and others (Montaigne MO 782040). Technically speaking, chromatic saturation can be found in the harmonic sequence of Part XIV, b. 5. It occurs ever more frequent over the course of the piece. What interests me here, however, is found in the same movement, e.g. in b. 9–10 or b. 60–3. In both these passages, another kind of saturation makes its appearance. The harmonies no longer appear as 'harmonic', but rather display an irreducible *aural excess*. Along the horizontal axis, something similar happens to the choral melody: see, for instance, b. 17–18 or b. 40–2, in which the melodic line is disseminated in its ('interior' or 'exterior' – this border becomes undecidable) spectral field, and becomes literally *ecstatic*. In places like these, Messiaen's 'musical language' is not

destroyed; rather, it is saturated, transfigured, it becomes ecstatic, consumed.

[51] The opening chord of *Adoro te* (the first piece of *Livre du Saint Sacrement* (1984) as recorded by Hans-Ola Ericsson on JADE 74321 30295–2) is another example.

[52] Messiaen, *Conférence de Kyoto*, p. 15.

[53] Marion relates it to a certain tiredness, an exhaustion that is caused by the great effort to perceive the divine. 'The idol offers the gaze its earth – the first earth upon which to rest. In the idol, the gaze is buried.' In other words, the idol reveals a shortcoming in the gaze: it prefers, or is forced, to rest, and resting in the idol, it marks the border between the visual (i.e. the idol) and the opening toward another dimension (i.e. the icon and divine revelation), which, however, remains beyond the gaze's idolatrous reach. See Marion, *God Without Being*, p. 13.

[54] Marion, *God Without Being*, pp. 10–11.

and show the human gaze the gaze of the (divine) Other, which constitutes it. According to Marion, this kind of reversal remains the privilege of *the icon*, a figure to which I turn in the next section.[55]

The phenomenology of the idol suggests that the experience of *éblouissement* may well be of a particular nature, but at the same time remains within the coordinates of the modern subject. This it shares with the Kantian sublime. Both the idol and the sublime imply a certain narcissism (a turn of the subject to itself) as well as a certain idolatry. Yet, by reading the idol from the reverse perspective of 'saturation' – i.e. from the wholly different, non-subjective principle of (divine) givenness – Marion at once shows a possible 'breakthrough' towards the beyond of a merely subjective idolatry or sublimity. As seen earlier, Wilfrid Mellers already used the notion of saturation in his discussion of *La Transfiguration*. Marion offers a complement to his description by demonstrating the limitations of the idol as well as of the vision of iconic 'conversion'. However, what remains to be thought through is this vision as such: how can we understand that, according to Messiaen, the dynamics of *éblouissement* do not dissipate before an idolatrous 'invisible mirror' (Marion), but break through to the other side? In other words, does Messiaen indeed gesture towards a *musical icon* beyond the logic of the idol (and, for that matter, a corresponding *transfiguration of the ear*)? And, if so, how should this musical iconicity be understood? For a possible answer to this question, one must turn to the religious thinker whose work has been a major reference point for both Marion and Messiaen, the Swiss theologian Hans Urs von Balthasar.[56]

The iconicity of aural form

A very thin line connects Messiaen to Hans Urs von Balthasar. The latter's name is mentioned only a few times in the texts written by the composer, but whenever he speaks of Balthasar it is in an extraordinarily laudatory tone.[57]

[55] Iconicity *not* understood here in the usual musicographical sense (referring, among others, to musical depiction) but in Marion's sense of 'transparency' and 'reversal of the listening perspective'. That is to say, from a different angle, an experience of music *not* as constituted by the listening subject (as in the case of the musically sublime or the aural idol), but as already *given* (in a phenomenological sense) in the manner of an icon. The theological notion of the 'musical icon', as implied by Messiaen, can also be found in the music of John Tavener and Arvo Pärt.

[56] On the interrelations between the musical thought of Marion and Balthasar, see Sander van Maas, 'On Preferring Mozart', in *Bijdragen: International Journal in Philosophy and Theology*, no. 65 (2004), 97–110.

[57] Samuel, *Olivier Messiaen: Music and Color*, pp. 17 and 211. Massin, *Olivier Messiaen: une poétique du merveilleux*, pp. 73, 105–6, 151. As far as I know, Messiaen has never directly quoted Balthasar in his writings and interviews.

Although the influence of Messiaen's theological reading on his work remains indirect, he appears to have liked interpretations of *La Transfiguration* based on Balthasar.[58]

In a general sense, Balthasar's theology is of import to an interpretation of the arts because he has put the notion of beauty back on to the theological agenda. As Balthasar attempts to show in the first part of *The Glory of the Lord* (*Herrlichkeit: Eine theologische Aesthetik*), the notion of beauty has gradually been marginalised under the influence of protestant theology (Luther's, and more particularly by Kierkegaard's). To many theologians, he contends, the aesthetic has become synonymous with empty appearances and unethical styles of living. As he claims, in contrast to its perfect embedding in the One, True and Good in ancient and Hellenic theology, Beauty has become isolated.[59] In the first volume of *The Glory of the Lord*, entitled *Seeing the Form*, Balthasar criticises the de-aestheticisation (*Entästhetisierung*) of theology and pleads for a revaluation of Beauty in theological thought. He aims to formulate a 'theological aesthetics' in which Beauty is once again thought of as being transcendental, the equal of the True and the Good.

Balthasar describes his theological aesthetics as an attempt to practise aesthetics in the field of, and using the methods of, theology. It sets itself against aesthetic theologies, in which 'the theological content is betrayed and sold out to the usual conceptions of immanent aesthetics'.[60] The early romantic cult, which became known as *Kunstreligion* (religion of art), can be posited as the supreme opposite to this project, but Balthasar does not explicitly mention it. His prime target seems to have been the philosophical aesthetics that was developed from the religion of art, notably by Schopenhauer and Nietzsche. In order to articulate his theological aesthetics, Balthasar relies most heavily on the notion of form or figure (*Gestalt*). As he contends, 'the words that try to express beauty, first of all revolve around the mystery of the *Gestalt* or the created. *Formosus* stems from *forma*, *speciosus* from *species*. But at the same time the question arises of the "great radiance [*Glanz*] from within", which illuminates the form from within. And then there is the created,

[58] To my knowledge, Balthasar himself did not write on Messiaen. Others, however, have attempted to relate his thought to the composer's œuvre. See Michel, 'La Transfiguration et la beauté', and his *La Parole et la beauté: rhétorique et esthétique dans la tradition occidentale* (Paris: Les belles lettres, 1982), 144–5.

See also Pascal Ide, 'Olivier Messiaen, musicien de la gloire de Dieu', *Communio* Vol. 19, no. 5 (September–October 1994), 97.

[59] Hans Urs von Balthasar, *Herrlichkeit: eine theologische Aesthetik* (Einsiedeln–Trier: Johannes Verlag, 1988), vol. I, p. 47.

[60] Balthasar, *Herrlichkeit*, vol. I, p. 35.

and that which makes it radiant, which turns it into something valuable and loveable.'[61]

These two moments of beauty relate to the subjective moments of the perception of beauty and the being enraptured by it: 'For no-one sees truth without being at once enraptured by it, and no-one [can] be enraptured without having perceived it [*wahr-genommen*, (literally) having received the truth]'.[62] According to Balthasar, this dynamics of perception, understood as 'taking the truth', and the kenotic *rapture* (*ecstasis*) of the faithful spectator, firmly links Beauty with the True and the Good respectively.[63] The acceptance of truth in and through the appearance of the *Gestalt* goes together with an ethical 'giving oneself' (*Hingabe*) to, and in the service of, this truth.[64] Balthasar even understands this experience to be the very core of the Christian faith. 'Being swept along [*Hingerissenwerden*]', as he formulates it, 'is the origin of Christianity'.[65] It is the original response of faith to the figure of Christ (*die Christusgestalt*); that is, to the Son who is the image (*eikon, Gestalt*) of the Father.[66]

Criticising the viewpoint that, to the Christian faith, the hearing of the Word is more important than the seeing of the *Gestalt*, Balthasar argues that perception (*Wahr-nehmung*), as 'an acceptance of a Truth that offers itself', comprises and implies both hearing and believing.[67] This primacy of the visual translates into music as a special interest in musical form. According to Balthasar, music's spiritual powers are to be found in the contours of *melody*. A melody, he argues, is both material and – because it can be transposed – spiritual. It embodies the virtues of the *Gestalt*. Melody represents the creational element, which refers beyond itself to the archetype of all

---

[61] Balthasar, *Herrlichkeit*, vol. I, p. 18. See also p. 111: 'The *Gestalt* is only beautiful because the gratification it gives stems from the profound truth and goodness of reality which shows itself as something endlessly and inexhaustibly valuable and fascinating. The appearance as manifestation of the depth is inextricably both at once: true presence of the depth, of the whole, as well as a real reference beyond itself to this depth.'

[62] Balthasar, *Herrlichkeit*, vol. I, p. 10. Here he further contends that 'this is equally true for the theological relation between faith and mercy, because faith, while surrendering itself, understands the *Gestalt* of revelation, and mercy has already taken the faithful up into the world of God'.

[63] The theological notion of *kenosis* refers to the 'self-emptying' of Christ when he took 'the form of a slave, becoming as human beings are, ... accepting death' (Phil. 2:7–8). In the

present context, it refers to an analogical 'self-emptying' on the part of the listener.

[64] See Mario Saint-Pierre, *Beauté, bonté, vérité chez Hans Urs von Balthasar* (Paris: Les Editions du Cerf, 1998), pp. 259–63.

[65] Balthasar, *Herrlichkeit*, vol. I, p. 30. According to Balthasar (p. 114), this experience should not be understood in a merely psychological way, but as 'the movement of the whole of man's Being ... away from himself or herself, by Christ, [in]to God [*in Gott hinein*]'. Accordingly, *Hingerissenwerden* is understood in terms of *eros* and *agapē*.

[66] Balthasar, *Herrlichkeit*, vol. I, p. 442. See also Col. 1:15.

[67] Balthasar in fact resists a certain interpretation of the Pauline notion of '*fides ex auditu*' (Rom. 10:17) as found in Bernard of Clairvaux. See, for instance, Bernard's *Sermones in Cantica Canticorum*, 28:6.

form: the divine creative principle. More generally, Balthasar adheres to a hylomorphic ('Apollonian') model, setting the *Gestalt* against what he understood to be the pantheistic, Dionysian tendencies in Schopenhauer, Wagner and Nietzsche.[68]

As discussed above, Marion proposes the icon as an alternative to the closure of the idol. This figure depends to a large extent on Balthasar's notion of *Gestalt*. Essential to the logic of *Gestalt*, and also of the icon, is a reversal of perspective, which opens up the standpoint of the 'Other'. *Eblouissement*, despite being the effect of an idolatrous relationship between the spectator-listener and the world, refers to the *beyond (au-delà)* of idolatrous closure – as a kind of 'low-water mark' of the divine. The *Gestalt*, or icon, is a theoretical figure that delineates the opening of the beyond (Messiaen's '*percée vers l'au-delà*'), linking the experience of this event to the 'gift' of saturated (and saturating) Form. In the music of *éblouissement* analysed above (in section 3), form contained a variety of levels: forms of musical-pictorial figurations, form in a musical-technical sense, and the formal aspects of repetition and theatricality. Balthasar suggests that we regard these levels as aspects of a single and unified phenomenon ('Form') which expresses the depth and totality of its own givenness.

What, however, does this significant otherness or 'givenness' of Form consist of? It should be noted that the axiom of Balthasar's theology resides in the aesthetico-theological idea that form – and musical form, too, for that matter – is 'revelation from above'.[69] First and foremost form is 'animated and effective [*lebendige und wirkende*]' form, and this animation articulates the 'depth' of form; that is, its theological dimension.[70] The appeal of the theory of *Gestalt* and icon is the ethical appeal of a *living* instance. In music, Balthasar seems to prefer melody because it evokes the human element, as indeed a vocal melody does most strongly. With respect to this preference for animated form, his theological aesthetics approaches Eduard Hanslick's, whose 'tonally moving forms' are animated by a (metaphysical) *Geist*.[71] Balthasar seems often to lay claim to figures which do not unequivocally belong to the domain of theology, turning them into vehicles which, to a certain extent, facilitate the movement across the fields of faith and the arts.

---

[68] It is remarkable and highly telling that the 'pantheistic' Schopenhauer favoured the same musical phenomenon – melody – to articulate his metaphysics of music. The consequences of this parallel are analysed in depth in my study *Faith in Music: On Olivier Messiaen*.

[69] Hans Urs von Balthasar, *Die Entwicklung der musikalischen Idee: Versuch einer Synthese der Musik/Bekenntnis zu Mozart* (Einsiedeln–Freiburg: Johannes Verlag, 1998), p. 48.

[70] Balthasar, *Herrlichkeit*, vol. I, p. 20.

[71] In the first edition of his *Vom Musikalisch-Schönen* (1854) Hanslick appeals to metaphysics. In the second edition he shied away from such references, replacing them with references to the natural sciences. See Carl Dahlhaus, *Klassische und romantische Musikaesthetik* (Laaber: Laaber Verlag, 1988), pp. 291–2.

Moving similarly into the area in between the sacred and the secular, Marion even more consciously avoids committing himself to a theological-dogmatic framework, without sacrificing metaphysical perspectives, however. In his philosophical analysis, the depth of the icon, which reveals its own givenness through saturation, refers to the constitution of the listener. According to his phenomenology, listening to the music of *éblouissement* from the perspective of saturation would mean an encounter with the very origin of oneself in an aural gift that logically precedes any synthetic act of aural cognition. In other words, listening to this music would first of all mean being struck (*éblouit*) by a givenness that precedes and overflows any subjective synthesis of melodies, harmonies or other aspects of musical structure. It opens up a domain of musical experience that resists the division of music into musical languages and genres, such as the 'secular' and 'sacred'. This is the domain Messiaen refers to when he says, 'I believe there is no truly profane music, nor any truly sacred music, but one reality, seen from different angles'.[72] Strictly speaking, the music of *éblouissement* is a sacred music *beyond sacred music*.

Eblouissement and the logic of love

When he speaks of *éblouissement*, Messiaen does not refer to sacred music as a mere matter of musical themes, stylistic features, symbolism or lyrical content. Neither does he refer to allegories or metaphors.[73] Musical *éblouissement* and 'breakthrough' are not, as Paul Griffiths proposes, reducible to, on the one hand, the specificities of a musical structure and, on the other hand, a set of private beliefs.[74] As the notion of the sublime indicates, much more can be discovered about Messiaen's work (and also about music and musical experience in general) than would result from an analysis in terms of 'what parades in sound and time', excluding 'the intentions that may crowd around it'.[75] Messiaen's music is too rich to be reduced to formal structure, and his ideas are too challenging to be reduced to beliefs. Insofar as

[72] Messiaen, in Goléa, *Rencontres avec Olivier Messiaen*, p. 41.

[73] Even the stained-glass windows should not be understood as a metaphor in this respect. In *Lecture at Notre-Dame*, Messiaen accords his music of *éblouissement*, the windows and all the other references equal status according to the open, juxtapositional logic of a metonym – and necessarily so. Firstly, because his 'music' (i.e. *sound-colour*) evades monomedial distinctions which would allow a transfer of a visual 'metaphor' to the aural domain. And secondly, as I have tried to argue, because it exceeds simple distinctions in terms of 'literal-versus-metaphorical'; the relation between Messiaen's music and its referents (truth, *éblouissement*, etc.) calls for a metonymical, participatory and resonant logic rather than a logic of exclusion.

[74] Griffiths, *Olivier Messiaen and the Music of Time*, p. 51.

[75] Griffiths, *Olivier Messiaen and the Music of Time*, p. 51.

his music is understood as sacred music (a notion he himself did not accept as a pure category), it is sacred music beyond 'sacred music' in the derivative sense of music featuring 'religious' themes, purveying symbols of 'religion', etc. Such determinations remain secondary with regard to the events Messiaen refers to as 'breakthrough' and *éblouissement*, as does the trivialising interpretation of these events as musical allegories. The abandonment of the major–minor system may well represent an image of 'experiences beyond the normal', as they take place *outside* of the musical domain (Griffiths), but it does not account for the way these experiences should be thought *within* it.[76]

Love in Messiaen's work is not primarily a matter of theme, emotion or 'content'; it is also a matter of form. It is the depth of form (on numerous levels) that overwhelms its listener with givenness. As Balthasar writes, the experience of love is *ecstatic*; it is a response to a singular gift. The decisive musical expression of this gift is the 'purely aural sublimity' (Mellers) that shatters the unity of form in the technical sense. A technical analysis of this music from its representation in a score can never account for the liminal character of the music of *éblouissement*, which breaks through the score's suggestion of synthetic coherence in terms of time, space and structure. It should be reiterated that this shattering of form has little or nothing to do with might or power. As Messiaen often reveals, the music of *éblouissement* need not be loud or violent in terms of volume or style. Saturating and dazzling a listener does not require deafening him or her. Nor need the music be fragmentary or pure chaos to produce such an effect. The form of the music is not 'broken' from without, but from within, ever expanding the music's universe. Saturating and enveloping the listener with its ecstatic joy, it calls for his or her affirmation through an aural 'leap of faith', a transfiguration of the ear.

Messiaen's music without a doubt is music in the spirit of the *theologia gloriae*, a fact which is sometimes used as an argument against Messiaen's aesthetics.[77] However, such a criticism presupposes that the pitfalls of musical idolatry can be avoided. It approaches Messiaen's work from within the long tradition of suspicion against the powers of theatricality and rhetoric, which certainly remain characteristics of his work. Here a more profound line of questioning presents itself: can theatricality, idolatry, even blasphemy, be avoided, and should they be avoided? This is not the place to begin this discussion, but it would be wise to put Messiaen's work and thought into a context that is as broad as possible. Neither musicology nor theology have

---

[76] Griffiths, *Olivier Messiaen and the Music of Time*, p. 51.

[77] Rößler, *Contributions to the Spiritual World of Olivier Messiaen*, p. 51.

yet recognised the profoundly interdisciplinary and intermedial character of his work.

Fundamental questions are raised by Messiaen's work, which both traditional disciplines must address: with regard to the status of music as a medium (e.g. for 'sacred subjects'), and with regard to religion as a reality independent of (musical) mediation. As I have tried to outline, the phenomenology of *éblouissement*, through the introduction of new analytical strategies, points into new directions. First, it enables the analysis of how Messiaen's music *sounds* and *acts*. It allows the description of the interaction between sound and listener, particularly as a process in which the listener is actively involved, and to which he or she brings a horizon much wider than it is generally assumed to be. And second, paradoxically, it demonstrates the value of a number of figures originating from theological traditions for the analysis of sacred music as *not* just an artistic medium conveying stable religious meaning, but rather as a critical phenomenon residing *in between* music and religion.

5   Messiaen's mysterious birds

Allen Forte

Introductory comments

Olivier Messiaen, unlike many of his twentieth-century predecessors – with the possible exception of Arnold Schoenberg – was an energetic analyst of the music of other composers. The seven volumes of Messiaen's *Traité de rythme, de couleur, et d'ornithologie* (*TRCO*) comprise a remarkable record of his essays, teaching notes and analytical reflections upon a variety of music, including works by Stravinsky, Debussy, Ravel, Varèse, Jolivet, Boulez, Stockhausen and, of course, by the composer himself.

Even more extraordinary was his involvement with the avian kingdom. For example, the two volumes of Tome V of *TRCO*, a total of 1,310 pages, are devoted to *Chants d'oiseaux d'Europe* and *Chants d'oiseaux extra-Européens* (*European Birdsongs and Birdsongs outside Europe*), an incredible documentation that includes rhythmic, but not pitch-structure analyses of birdsongs 'transcribed' by Messiaen during his travels in Europe (that is, regional France) and abroad (especially in Japan), but also in the southwestern United States.

The pillars of Messiaen's philosophical approach to music were mystical Christianity and nature. In the latter category, birds play the central role; they are God's musicians. His lifelong interest in birdsong, however, has elicited various negative responses. Ornithologists and scientifically inclined music critics heaped scorn upon Messiaen's inclusion of bird-calls in his music, pointing out that they were not accurate representations. But early on, in his *Technique de mon langage musical* (1944), the composer had made clear his position with respect to his birdcall transcriptions:

> Since they [birds] use untempered intervals smaller than the semitone, and as it is ridiculous servilely to copy nature, we are going to give some examples of melodies of the 'bird' genre which will be transcription(s), transformation(s), and interpretation(s) of [their] volleys ...[1]

[1] Olivier Messiaen, *The Technique of My Musical Language* (*TMLM*), trans. John Satterfield (Paris: Leduc, 1956), p. 34.

He then gives six examples (the first from the *Quatuor pour la fin du Temps*), without providing any information about the sources from which the pitches of the often enigmatic birdsongs are derived. This hiatus left subsequent writers on Messiaen's music unsupported with respect to the question of the pitch-structure origin of the songs. Foremost among these was Robert Sherlaw Johnson, whose extensive and valuable writings on birdsong do not address that topic. He writes:

> In *Technique de mon langage musical* Messiaen discusses some aspects of pitch-structure
> in his music . . . None of these [intervals, chords, etc.] is of much use in discussing
> the pitch-structure of birdsong . . .[2]

Later on, Johnson becomes more specific with respect to a widely used modern analytical technique: 'Set theory as a method of analysis is of no use in this context [birdsong pitch-structure] either . . .'[3]

Of course it is true, as Johnson points out, that 'set theory' in its most basic phase ignores register, contour, etc. in order to identify set-class origins. Still, as I hope to demonstrate, that basic phase is essential in order to understand the harmonic sources upon which Messiaen drew in his elaborate and often complex birdsongs, often set in a harmonic context supportive of the song itself. In this study I shall take a fresh analytical look at Messiaen's birdsongs, using 'set theory' as a primary tool. Although birdsong occurs throughout Messiaen's very large and diversified repertoire, I shall concentrate upon those in his monumental piano composition *Catalogue d'oiseaux* (1956–58).

The *Catalogue* consists of thirteen pieces, each devoted to a single bird, but including songs of many others, which Messiaen recorded as present in the environment of the primary bird. The pieces are grouped symmetrically (3 1 2 | 1 | 2 1 3) and contain a remarkable total of seventy-eight different birdsongs.

Since each bird is represented by several songs in each piece, depending upon the time of day Messiaen recorded them and other environmental considerations, I have selected one song of each bird, usually the first, for analytical scrutiny. Before launching into these miniature analytical studies, however, I shall present a theoretical basis derived from Messiaen's own writings, intended to dispel the notion that Messiaen's birdsong somehow lie outside the composer's compositional-technical world.

---

[2] Robert Sherlaw Johnson, 'Birdsong', *The Messiaen Companion*, ed. Peter Hill (London: Faber and Faber, 1995), p. 259.
[3] Johnson, 'Birdsong', *The Messiaen Companion*, p. 260. The complete quotation is: 'Set theory as a method of analysis is of no use in this context either [the pitch-structure of birdsong], as it quickly becomes obvious that it cannot account for the features which give much of Messiaen's birdsong its particular character.'

Source harmonies

The musical-technical basis of Messiaen's creative output developed over the course of the composer's creative life to embrace not only the Modes of Limited Transpositions described by Messiaen in 1944, but also all five categories he describes in Tome VII (2002) of *TRCO*. These are: (1) the chords derived from the Modes of Limited Transpositions (including other configurations); (2) the 'accord à renversements transposés sur la même note de basse' (the chord of inversions transposed upon the same bass note); (3) the 'accords à résonances contractées' (the chords of contracted resonances); (4) the 'accords tournants' (the turning chords); and, the grandest chord of all, (5) the 'accord du total chromatique' (the chord of the total chromatic), no doubt included to complete the magic number 12! For practical purposes, however, I will draw upon only the first 11 source harmonies (in bold) listed on Table 5.1, together with their pitch-class set class names and prime forms in standard numeric notation. The pitch-class set names simplify references to the harmonic sources and are more useful for the present study, especially when subsets of the source harmonies are involved, than Messiaen's colourful but sometimes recondite labels.

Table 5.1 provides an overview and summary of the eleven source harmonies and their representations in the thirteen birdsongs of the *Catalogue d'oiseaux*. Among the Modes of Limited Transpositions, Mode 2 is represented most frequently, with Modes 3 and 4 not far behind. Of the non-modal source harmonies, 7–20 leads, while 7–z12 and 8–4, both theoretical possibilities, are not represented in this work.

Category 1   The Modes of Limited Transpositions
Mode 2: 8–28   0 1 3 4 6 7 9 10 (C C♯ D♯ E F♯ G A A♯) 3 transpositions
Mode 3: 9–12   0 1 2 4 5 6 8 9 10 (C C♯ D E F F♯ G♯ A A♯) 4 transpositions
Mode 4: 8–9   0 1 2 3 6 7 8 9 (C C♯ D D♯ F♯ G G♯ A) 6 transpositions
Mode 5: 6–7   0 1 2 6 7 8 (C C♯ D F♯ G G♯) 6 transpositions
Mode 6: 8–25   0 1 2 4 6 7 8 10 (C C♯ D E F♯ G G♯ A♯) 6 transpositions

Although each mode as a whole may have fewer than the normal 12 transpositions, its subsets are not necessarily limited in that respect. For example, Mode 3 (9–12) is symmetric (4 transpositions), but one of its eight-note subset classes (8–19) has 24 distinct pitch-class transpositions, the normal 12 transpositions and 12 inversions.

Category 2   Chord of transposed inversions on the same bass note
7–20   0 1 2 4 7 8 9 (C C♯ D E G G♯ A)
Category 3   Chords of contracted resonances (2 chords)
7–z12   0 1 2 3 4 7 9 (C C♯ D D♯ E G A) 12 transpositions
7–z36   0 1 2 3 5 6 8 (C C♯ D♯ F F♯ G♯)
Category 4   Turning chords (the descriptor 'turning' remains enigmatic) (3 chords)
8–4   0 1 2 3 4 5 7 8 (C C♯ D D♯ E F G G♯)

Table 5.1: The eleven source harmonies in *Catalogue d'oiseaux*

Category	1	1	1	1	1	2	3	3	4	4	4
Source harmony	Mode 2 (8–28)	Mode 3 (9–12)	Mode 4 (8–9)	Mode 5 (6–7)	Mode 6 (8–25)	7–20	7–z12	7–z36	8–4	8–5	8–14
Catalogue d'oiseaux	No. II	No. III	No. I	No. VII	No. I	No. II	None	No. III	None	No. XI	No. XII
	No. III	No. IV	No. IV			No. VI		No. X		No. XII	
	No. V	No. VII	No. V			No. X					
	No. VII	No. VIII	No. IX								
	No. VIII	No. XII	No. XII								
	No. X	No. XIII									
	No. XII										
	No. XIII										

8–5   0 1 2 3 4 6 7 8 (C C♯ D D♯ E F♯ G G♯)
8–14   0 1 2 4 5 6 7 9 (C C♯ D E F F♯ G A) (contains 7–20, Category 2)
Category 5   Total Chromatic (12–1)

In addition, Messiaen lists the following 'Special Chords':
1. The Chord on the Dominant (7–35). This inversionally symmetric septad, one form of which is our familiar major scale, is not a subset of any of the octads listed in the five major categories above.
2. The Chord of Resonance (8–24) – a subset of Mode 3 (In the Second Viennese School repertoire, this is a major sonority in Berg's *Wozzeck*. Three forms of pc set 8–24 [the chord of resonance] are contained within Mode 3 [pc set 9–12]).
3. The Chord in Fourths (6–7). Messiaen points out that it contains all the notes of Mode 5. More precisely, with respect to pitch-class content, it is identical to Mode 5.

Thus, excluding the 'Special Chords' there are exactly eleven distinct Source Harmonies (those I have listed in Table 5.1). I would now to turn to the properties of these source harmonies.

While the rationale for Category 1 (the Modes of Limited Transpositions) is clear from the name Messiaen has assigned to them, the same cannot be said of the other categories. Category 2, which contains a single set class, 7–20, is of special importance in Messiaen's œuvre, as indicated in the birdsong examples in the second part of this chapter and elsewhere, for example, in the *Quatuor pour la fin du Temps*. It is not represented, except perhaps incidentally, in the atonal repertoire of the Second Viennese School, nor in the serial music of the later twentieth-century modernist composers, and in that respect can be said to be 'uniquely' associated with Messiaen's music.

Although 7–20 is not symmetrical from the pitch standpoint – unlike, for example, the Category 3 septad 7–z12 – its interval content has a special 'balanced' property that Messiaen would have recognised. This is apparent from the interval-content vector of 7–20: [433452], which informs us that interval classes 1 and 4 (minor seconds and major thirds) are present in the same number (4), and that the same equivalence obtains with respect to interval classes 2 and 3 (3), leaving the largest number of interval classes in position 5 of the vector – i. e. perfect fifths/fourths, while the tritone is present twice. The large number of perfect fifths here is particularly interesting, since it is the maximum number possible minus 1. Only 7–35, the venerable diatonic scale, but a maverick septad with respect to Messiaen's usage, has 6 perfect fifths. Thus, 7–20 is a rich and diversified sonority, one that for some reason has been ignored in the Messiaen literature.

Extreme instances of this property of balance is evident in the interval content of the two harmonies in Category 3, the 'chords of contracted resonances'. These harmonies are twins (thus, the 'z' for 'zygotic'), sharing interval vector [444342], which tells us that minor seconds, major seconds, minor thirds and perfect fifths are all present in the same number – 4 of each – while interval class 4 ('major thirds') are short-changed by one, and the number of tritones (2) is the maximum number minus 1 with respect to the total of 35 septad set classes.

Intervallic balance is also a property of two of the Turning Chords in Category 4, namely, 8–4, with vector [655552] and 8–14, with vector [555562]. Remarkably, these two numerical arrays contain the same integers, sharing three of the six interval classes in the same number (major seconds, minor thirds, major thirds), while 8–4 has the same number of minor seconds as 8–14 has perfect fifths (6), and both have the same number of tritones. Octads 8–4 and 8–14 are also uniquely related under the multiplication operation M5. That is, multiplying each integer in the pitch-class representation of 8–4 by 5 (modulo 12) will produce 8–14 (and the reverse). Clearly, this emphasises the importance of interval class 5 (the perfect fifth and its companion the perfect fourth), a status which is amply demonstrated in Messiaen's music. Of the three harmonies in Category 4, however, 8–5 does not offer as neatly balanced an intervallic profile as do the other two 'Turning Chords'. Its interval vector [654553] shows that it shares interval classes 2, 4 and 5 (major seconds, major thirds and perfect fifths) with those of 8–4 and 8–14 in the same number (5). The intervallic equivalency stops there, however, since 8–5 is heavier with respect to tritones (3) and lighter with respect to minor thirds (4). Thus, in terms of intervallic balance and equivalencies, the Category 4 octads – with the exception of 8–4 and 8–14 – do not present an altogether cohesive picture, and in terms of theoretical explanations we must resort to some version of Messiaen's 'charm of impossibilities'.[4]

Many students of Messiaen's music may quite understandably have difficulty determining just which of these source harmonies are operative in a particular passage or work. Here are what I believe to be useful guidelines.

As a working axiom, I take the Modes of Limited Transpositions as primary, as they most certainly were in the development of the composer's harmonic sources. Because of their length, it is not possible to reproduce the placement tables I have devised, which provide precise information regarding the location of a particular pitch-class set extracted from a birdsong in

---

[4]In his *TMLM* (p. 13), Messiaen describes 'The Charm of Impossibilities' as residing 'in certain mathematical impossibilities of the modal and rhythmic domains. Modes which cannot be transposed beyond a certain number of rhythmic transpositions, because one always falls again into the same notes; rhythms which cannot be used in retrograde, because in such a case one finds the same order of values again – these are two striking impossibilities.'

one (or more) of the source harmonies listed above. I will, however, make ample use of them in the analytical part of this chapter.

The issue of source harmony identification can be illustrated by the following survey of tetrachords and their modal membership. Three tetrachords belong to only one mode each: 4–1 (chromatic), 4–10 (octatonic), and 4–23 (diatonic). Fifteen tetrachords belong to two modes each. Five tetrachords belong to three modes each. Six tetrachords belong to all four modes. Of those, four are included in all six non-modal Source Harmonies.

To cope with this diversity, a guideline to select primary source harmony membership is needed: preference is given to the source harmony in which a set occurs as a subset the greatest number of times. For example, 6–z12 is represented four times in Mode 6 (8–25). No other source harmony contains 6–z12 as many times. Here it should be noted that, with increase in set size, the number of choices of source harmonies decreases. Tetrachords, in particular, are very gregarious when it comes to membership in Source Harmonies.

Birdsong in the *Catalogue d'oiseaux*

The final part of this study consists of analytical vignettes of each of the thirteen principal birdsongs from the *Catalogue d'oiseaux*. Essential technical references for this survey are of course the source harmonies presented in the previous section. I begin with an example from *Le Chocard des Alpes* (*The Alpine Chough*).

The first musical appearance of the *Chocard des Alpes* (Ex. 5.1) consists of a two-note call, the descending fifth D–A, repeated three times in the symmetric rhythmic-attack pattern two semiquavers | semiquaver quaver

Ex. 5.1: *Le Chocard des Alpes* 2/3/4.

ⓐ 6–z6: {2,3,4,7,8,9} Mode 4 (8-9) only

ⓑ 5–7: {1,2,6,7,8} Mode 4 (8-9)

ⓒ 5–7: {2,3,7,8,9} Mode 4 (8-9)

ⓓ 6–z12: {1,2,4,6,7,8} Mode 6 (8-25)

Ex. 5.2: *Le Loriot 1/1/2–3*

(a)   5-35: {6,8,10,1,3} 7-20

(b)   5-28: {4,6,10,0,1} Mode 2

(c)   5-16: {4,7,8,10,11} Mode 2

(d)   4-27: {4,6,10,1} Mode 2

(e)   4-27: {3,6,8,0} Mode 2

semiquaver | two semiquavers. The harmonic setting of this simple call, however, creates a more intricate supporting structure, one derived almost entirely from Mode 4 (Octad 8–9) as shown in the legend below Ex. 5.1.

Two features of this setting invite special attention: the emphasis upon open fifths in the vertical arrangements of the notes, reflecting the intervallic fifth of the birdcall motive, and the replication of pitch-class set 5–7, a favourite of the composer, which occurs both as the entire right-hand part (c) and also (transposed) as the entire second chord (b).

Mode 4's predominant presence in this setting is challenged by the Mode 6 (8–25) formation of the entire left-hand part (d), whose intervallic content, like that of the first chord (a), emphasises bare fifths, depicting perhaps the rugged alpine terrain that Messiaen describes in his dramatic notes on the environment of the *Chocard* that precede the music notation of its song in *Catalogue d'oiseaux*.

As is the case with many of the birdsongs in the *Catalogue d'oiseaux*, the song of the *Loriot* (Golden Oriole) in movement II is 'diatonic', in this instance forming a complete pentatonic scale, labelled item (a) on Ex. 5.2. With reference to the eleven source harmonies, pentatonic pc set class 5–35 derives only from either 7–20 or from turning chord 8–14. On Ex. 5.2 I have given preference to the smaller set class, 7–20, which is also more prominently represented in Messiaen's œuvre altogether – notably in the *Quatuor pour la fin du Temps*, where it is the primary component of the famous succession of 29 chords at the opening of the *Liturgie de Cristal* movement.

The setting of this pentatonic birdsong, however, is composed entirely of Mode 2 constituents, labelled (b) through (e) on Ex. 5.2, and involving all

Ex. 5.3: *Le Merle bleu* 4/4/2

    (a)   4-13: {8,9,11,2} Mode 2 (8-28)

    (b)   4-18: {9,10,1,4} Mode 2 (8-28)

    (c)   7-z36: {8,9,10,11,1,2,4} `Chord of contracted resonance'

    (d)   5-9: {8,9,10,0,2} Mode 3 (9-12)

    (e)   5-16: {9,10,0,1,4} Mode 2 (8-28)

three transpositions of that mode, to form a very rich accompaniment for the Loriot's simple call.

Clearly, the voices that accompany the *Loriot's* call move with it in parallel contours, but not parallel motion. In particular, the lowest voice is a jagged contour image of the birdcall, matching the bird's descending perfect fifths with descending minor ninths: a spatial difference of a tritone. The closing two-chord succession, however, consists of two forms of 4–27 ('dominant seventh') chords in precise parallel motion, an ordered transposition up a whole-step (T2), reminiscent of a Debussyan succession.

Rhythmically, measured in demisemiquavers, the first part of the song spans eight, followed by a rest of the same duration; that is, partitioning the durational space as 8 + 8. The two concluding chords, at a slower tempo, partition the durational space (again measured in imaginary demisemiquavers) as 4 + 8, from which we conclude that the *Loriot*, consistent with its simple pentatonic melody, also favours simple durational proportions.

Mode 2 (octatonic 8–28), Mode 3 (9–12) and 7–z36 (the chord of contracted resonance) are the highly contrasting source harmonies upon which the composer draws for the brief song of the *Merle bleu* (*Blue Rock Thrush*) (movement III) in my Ex. 5.3. Here, as in many of the birdsongs in *Catalogue d'oiseaux*, the song, in the uppermost voice, is accompanied by its contour image. Both represent Mode 2, but derive from different transpositions of that mode and belong to different set-classes, as indicated in the legend below Ex. 5.3. At the close of the song, item (d), Mode 2 is strongly represented by the lower three voices, effectively expanding the accompanying voice, item (b), to a five-note collection. Item (c) may be attributed to Mode 3 (9–12) or

Ex. 5.4: *Le Traquet Stapazin* 1/1/3 and 1/2/2

ⓐ	6-z43: {2,3,4,7,8,10} Mode 4 (8-9)	
ⓑ	6-15: {0,1,2,4,5,8} Mode 3 (9-12)	
ⓒ	4-23: {0,2,5,7} Mode 4 (8-9)	
ⓓ	6-z41: {8,10,1,2,3,4} Mode 4 (8-9)	
ⓔ	4-13: {7,10,0,1} Mode 4 (8-9)	
ⓕ	6-18: {7,8,9,0,2,3} Mode 4 (8-9)	

to Mode 6 (8–25). In either case the resulting highly dissonant sonority clearly depicts the environment in which Messiaen discovered the *Merle bleu*, with its cliffs, described by the composer with the words: 'Les falaises sont terribles' ('The cliffs are terrifying').

In all, the long movement devoted to the *Traquet stapazin* (Black-eared wheatear) (IV) in Ex. 5.4 contains sixteen of its songs, all different, four of which involve an exchange between two members of the species. Additionally, the crowded avian environment is enlivened by birds of some thirteen other species.

In marked contrast to the 'diatonic' songs of the *Chocard* and the *Loriot*, the first song of the *Traquet stapazin* (Ex. 5.4) is ruggedly chromatic, presenting the atonal hexachord 6–z43 from source harmony Mode 4 as the song (item [a] on Ex. 5.4). Indeed, Mode 4 (8–9) is the predominant source harmony for this song. Only the voice that accompanies it, item b on Ex. 5.4, derives from another source harmony, namely, Mode 3. This voice follows the pattern of all the accompanimental voices in *Catalogue d'oiseaux*, replicating the general contour of the song, sometimes explicitly. Here, with only two exceptions, the contours are identical. Thus, although the underlying pitch-class sets and the source harmonies of the two configurations contrast significantly, their very similar contours create a strong congruence at the surface level of the music.

Details of the counterpoint between primary and secondary lines (items [a] and [b] on Ex. 5.4) can be read from the legend of pitch-class sets and modal membership below the musical notation. The first notational grouping (c) forms diatonic tetrachord 4–23, while the second (d) is one of

Ex. 5.5: *La Chouette Hulotte* 2/4/3

(a)   4-3: {9,10,0,1} Mode 2 (8-28)

(b)   4-10: {9,11,0,2} Mode 2 (8-28)

(c)   4-2: {11,1,2,3} Mode 3 (9-12)

Messiaen's favoured atonal hexachords, 6–z41 (also, incidentally, one of Stravinsky's, as in his ballet, *Agon*).

What complicates the music in this instance, and in virtually all the other song settings of *Catalogue d'oiseaux* is Messiaen's extraction of materials from more than one transposition of the same mode. Here, for example, four forms (transpositions) of Mode 4 occur. Again here we find contour similarities.

In simple terms of ascending and descending direction, contour reversal occurs in only two of the seven instances, and in one (–7 and +7) the interval-span is identical. Nevertheless, systematic transformation of contour seems not to be characteristic of the songs of the *Traquet Stapazin*!

The first song of the *Chouette Hulotte* (*Tawny Owl*), Ex. 5.5, is constructed from source harmony Mode 2, subsets of which parse almost the entire configuration, consisting of the seven-note chromatic 'cluster' that spans the interval from A to E♭. The left-hand part, item (c) of Ex. 5.5a, taken separately, comprises pitch-class set 4–2, from Mode 3, as does the last chord.

Messiaen describes this birdsong as 'tantôt lugubre et douloureux, ... tantôt vociféré dans l'épouvante comme un cri d'enfant assassiné' ('at times lugubrious and sorrowful, at others as vociferous in its fear as the cry of an assassinated child') – a typically surrealistic depiction that reminds us of the composer's extraordinarily creative eccentricity.

Like those of all the featured birds in the *Catalogue d'oiseaux*, the song of the *Alouette lulu* (*Wood Lark*) varies radically depending upon the time of day, vocal inspiration, and no doubt other factors. The song shown in Ex. 5.6 is a beautiful instance of source harmony 7–20: {9,10,11,1,4,5,6}, encompassing the entire song, with pitch class B doubled, so that the eight-notes are

Ex. 5.6: *L'Alouette Lulu* 6/5/3

ⓐ 7-20: {9,10,11,1,4,5,6}

ⓑ 4-24: {9,11,1,5}

ⓒ 4-16: {4,6,10,11}

reduced to seven pitch classes. Here the right hand, item (b), plays 4–24, while the left, item (c), plays 4–16 to produce a charmingly dissonant harmonic counterpoint. Interestingly, the first vertical chord in each pair belongs to set class 4–16, the same set class as all of the left-hand part, with the two forms related by perfect fifth, yet another instance of the pervasiveness of that interval in Messiaen's music.

In his preface to the birdsong in Ex. 5.7, Messiaen writes: 'The entire piece (La Rousserolle Effarvatte [Reed Warbler]) is a large curve, from midnight until three in the morning, the events from the afternoon until night repeating in inverse order the events from night to morning.' Thus, formally, this song is more 'structured' than the others in *Catalogue d'oiseaux*, following the 'interversion' pattern so remarkably instantiated in Messiaen's serial music.[5]

The very length of the song (some fifty pages in the published score) presents a basic problem for the diligent analyst. However, the opening seven bars will give some idea of the source materials that underlie this song – perhaps the most extraordinary in the entire *Catalogue d'Oiseaux*.

From the standpoint of source harmony, the beginning of the song is unambiguous: it presents all of Mode 5 (6–7), one of only three hexachords that contain three tritones. The *Rousserolle* presents these in succession, 'avec volubilité', as B–F (once), E–B♭ (thrice) and finally E♭–A (twice), in an asymmetric numerical arrangement characteristic of Messiaen's rhythmic aesthetic. Moreover, each tritone has a distinctive rhythmic pattern.

In the last two bars the tritone E♭–A merges with the cadential notes C–F, breaking out of Mode 5 into Mode 2. Such a clear statement of a mode is unusual in *Catalogue d'oiseaux*. Even here, however, it is occluded by the accompanying voice, which, except for the first bar, imitates the contour of the song exactly. In its entirety, the left-hand part derives

[5] See Allen Forte, 'Olivier Messiaen as Serialist', *Music Analysis* Vol. 21, no. 1 (March 2002).

Ex. 5.7: *La Rousserolle Effarvatte* 4/1/1–7

ⓐ 6-7: {3,4,5,9,10,11} (Mode 5)

ⓑ 7-26: {6,8,10,11,0,2,3} (Mode 3)

ⓒ 6-27: {6,9,11,0,2,3} (Mode 2)

from Mode 3 (9–12), comprising 7–26, one of the eight septad-classes in that mode.

Modal changes corresponding to the sections of this long birdsong are consistent throughout. For instance, bars 11–13 (not shown in Ex. 5.7) are based upon Mode 2 (only), while bars 14–17 present all of Mode 6 (8–25). Not only is the *Rousserolle effarvatte* an expert singer, it is also in virtuosic command of Messiaen's system of Modes!

The principal song of this bird, *L'Alouette calandrelle* (*Short-Toed Lark*), is brief, consisting of two contour-similar phrases from Mode 2 that together outline a familiar sonority: a B♭ dominant-seventh type chord. Accompanying this simple song, in the left-hand part, is a 'diatonic' segment from Mode 3. Collectively, grouping them according to their congruent contours, both hands form 6–z19 followed by 6–z23, so that the modal succession (Mode 3 followed by Mode 2) is a reversal of the right-hand/left-hand pattern.

Although short, the song of *La Bouscarle* (*Cetti's Warbler*) in Ex. 5.9 is significantly more complex than that of the *Alouette calandrelle* (Ex. 5.8) with respect to rhythm and contour, especially the large leaps in the right-hand part of the first bar, set off by the closing figure, which oscillates between C♯ and F♯. Here, as elsewhere in the birdsongs of *Catalogue d'oiseaux*, the accompanying parts replicate the song's contours, but not its intervallic

Ex. 5.8: *L'Alouette Calandrelle* 1/1/2

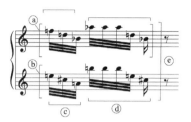

ⓐ   4-27: {2,5,8,10} Mode 2

ⓑ   4-22: {9,11,1,4} Mode 3

ⓒ   6-z19: {9,10,1,2,4,5} Mode 3 (only)

ⓓ   6-z23: {8,10,11,1,2,4} Mode 2 (only)

ⓔ   8-18: {8,9,10,11,1,2,4,5} = c + d

Ex. 5.9: *La Bouscarle* 1/1/1–2

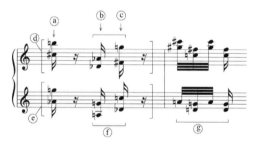

ⓐ   4-z15: {7,8,11,1} Mode 4 (8-9)

ⓑ   4-5: {7,8,9,1} Mode 4 (8-9)

ⓒ   4-9: {6,7,0,1} Mode 4 (8-9)

ⓓ   5-14: {6,7,8,11,1} Mode 4 (8-9)

ⓔ   5-6: {7,8,9,0,1} Mode 4 (8-9)

ⓕ   6-5: {6,7,8,9,0,1} Mode 4 (8-9)

ⓖ   7-7: {6,7,8,9,0,1,2} Mode 4 (8-9)

succession. Despite its surface complexity, both song and harmonic setting are ascribable to a single mode, Mode 4 (8–9), as shown in detail on the legend of Ex. 5.9. In this respect, the closing music of bar 2 (item [g] on the example) is particularly striking, since it presents septad 7–7, an unusual harmony in any event, which belongs only to source harmony Mode 4 and to the turning chord 8–5. For the sake of regularity I have not included 8–5 in the legend of Ex. 5.9.

Ex. 5.10: *Le Merle de roche* 12/3/1–2

(a)   7-20: {0,1,2,4,7,8,9}

(b)   7-20: {11,0,1,4,6,7,8}

(c)   7-20: {7,8,9,11,2,3,4}

(d)   6-z44: {1,2,3,6,7,10} 7-20

(e)   6-z25: {0,1,3,5,6,8} 7-z36

(f)   4-16: {1,3,7,8} 7-20

Although the featured bird in this movement, *Le Merle de roche* (*Rock Thrush*), does not appear until well along in the music, which presents hooting and screeching sounds (*ululements*) of the male and female *Grand Duc* (*Grand Duke*) that set the scene, its first song is long and elaborate. Moreover, in all, there are six *Merle de roche* songs, testifying to its versatility and loquacity.

The chords in Ex. 5.10, the second song of the Merle de roche, derive almost entirely (and again) from source harmony 7–20, including the song, which I have placed last, as item (f) on Ex. 5.10. The exception is the second vertical in the '*ululement*' figure in bar two, item (e), brought about by the parallel 'embellishing' motion in the three upper voices. Especially salient in this harmonic setting are the three successive vertical occurrences of 7–20, in which the first two are related by transposition, while the last, item (c), relates by transposition (ordered) to the first, item (a), and by transposed inversion to the second, item (b).

In the brief answering phrase, the first chord, item (d), also relates to source harmony 7–20, while the second, item (e), represents one of the two 'chords of contracted resonance', 7–z36. Otherwise, the setting derives from the special sonority 7–20, which is so prominent in the birdsongs.

In his preface to the music for *La Buse variable* (*Buzzard*) (see Ex. 5.11), Messiaen describes in some detail its flight and the combat in which it is engaged by other birds in the environment, including six Ravens, in competition for a common prey. The *Buse variable* is not a pretty bird, and Messiaen's music reflects this depiction in the melodic contour of its angular song (tetrachord 4–9), consisting of successive tritones, which I have attributed to turning chords 8–5 and 8–14, an interpretation consistent with the

Ex. 5.11: *La Buse variable* 9/1/1–2

ⓐ   (song) 4-9: {1,2,7,8} 8-5, 8-14

ⓑ   6-z39: {3,5,6,7,8,11} 8-5

ⓒ   8-5: {0,1,2,3,4,6,7,8}

ⓓ   (l.h.) 8-14: {11,0,1,3,5,6,8}

ⓔ   (r.h.) 7-5: {1,2,3,4,6,7,8} 8-5, 8-14

strong representation of those source harmonies in the total context of this setting. Indeed, 8–5 and 8–14 are literally represented in large segments of this setting, as items (c) (8–5) and (d) (8–14).

In the prefeace to the eleventh piece, Messiaen describes *Le Traquet rieur* (*Black Wheatear*), in part, as follows: 'Black, white tail with black designs, the Traquet Rieur is perched on a point of rock at the base of a cliff.' Both the setting and the bird are depicted in its second appearance in the music, with the jagged melodic-rhyhthmic contour of the exceptionally long song, which presents septad 7–6, derived from the turning chords 8–4 and 8–5 only.

The entire setting, however, is more complicated, as indicated by the legend below the music notation of Ex. 5.12. Modes 2, 3 and 4 are the principal source harmonies, with the special septad 7–20 represented on the demisemiquaver and semiquaver figure in the upper stave. Perhaps not surprising, because of its ubiquitous presence in these birdsong settings, this entire figure (item [i]) forms source harmony 7–20. As the *Traquet rieur* ends its song on the high B (a new note in the song), the complete harmony is hexachord 6–2, derived from turning chord 8–5 only.

Messiaen locates the *Courlis cendré* (*Curlew*) (Ex. 5.13) on L'Isle d'Ouessant in le Finistère (a district of northwest Brittany where the composer Charles Tournemire [1870–1939] owned a house and composed many of his works). In a final demonstration of his powers of observation, the composer describes the *Courlis cendré* in his preface as 'a large bird, with striped plumage, speckled with yellow-red, with grey and brown, standing high on its legs, provided with a very long beak, curved in the shape of a sickle or a scimitar.' He continues, describing its song as consisting of 'slow and sorrowful tremolos ascending chromatically, savage trills, and a call in

Ex. 5.12: *Le Traquet rieur* 2/4/1

ⓐ   7-7: {0,1,2,3,6,7,8} 8-5

ⓑ   7-26: {0,2,4,5,6,8,9} Mode 3 (9-12)

ⓒ   4-18: {7,10,1,2} Mode 2 (8-28)

ⓓ   5-29: {8,10,1,3,4} Mode 4 (8-9)

ⓔ   5-z37: {6,9,10,11,2} Mode 3 (9-12)

ⓕ   6-z13: {4,5,7,8,10,11} Mode 2 (8-28)

ⓖ   6-2: {9,11,0,1,2,3} 8-5 (only)

ⓗ   (song) 7-6: {7,8,9,10,11,2,3} 8-5

ⓘ   7-20: {6,7,8,10,1,2,3}

Ex. 5.13: *Le Courlis cendré* 1/1/1

ⓐ   6-14: {3,6,7,8,10,11} Mode 3 (9-12)

ⓑ   6-z23: {10,0,1,3,4,6} Mode 2 (8-28)

ⓒ   5-32: {9,10,1,3,6} Mode 2 (8-28)

ⓓ   5-21: {10,11,2,3,6} Mode 3 (9-12)

a tragic and repeated glissando that expresses all the desolation of the marine landscape.' In the musical example, I have given only the opening music of the *Courlis cendré*, a 'slow and sorrowful tremolo'.

With respect to source harmonies, this music is unambiguous. They are Mode 2 (8–28) and Mode 3 (9–12). These two modes stand in maximum contrast with respect to interval content, Mode 2 emphasising the minor third, while Mode 3 emphasises the major third, a contrast audible at the very surface of the music here. The transpositionally related trichords above the sustained E♭ minor triad are all of the same class: 3–3. Indeed, the significance of the sustained and inexorable E♭ minor triad in the lower register of the instrument is open to speculation in 'extra-musical terms', while the absolutely regular semiquaver motion of the song and its harmonic setting, nine durations in all, requires no explanation, except to remark that its regularity is most unusual among the birdsongs in the *Catalogue d'oiseaux*.

A further regularity – indeed, a symmetry – is evident in the source harmony legend in Ex. 5.13, where the chords oscillate between Mode 3 and Mode 2. Source harmonies then reverse that pattern at the end, oscillating between Mode 2 and Mode 3. This is perhaps the most regular and analytically accessible among the songs of all thirteen birds quoted in the present study.

6 Messiaen's *Catalogue d'oiseaux*: a musical dumbshow?

Jeremy Thurlow

There can be few pieces of music more quixotically determined to depict the scenes and characters of an 'extra-musical' programme – to the bitter end, and to the exclusion of all else – than Messiaen's *Catalogue d'oiseaux* for solo piano (1956–58). In each of the thirteen pieces one principal bird is portrayed amidst its avian companions in its natural habitat. These depictions encompass not only dozens of different birdsongs and calls, each one lovingly delineated and characterised, but many other sounds, sights and sensations, from the croaking of frogs to grand mountain vistas, from the flickering colours of the kingfisher's courtship display to the fearful beating of the composer's heart.[1]

After its heyday in the nineteenth century, the notion of programme music with its accompanying pictorial or narrative gloss gradually became something of an embarrassment amidst increasing insistence on music's absolute status following the First World War, and thus features relatively little in discussion of composers of Messiaen's generation. But the term could be comfortably applied to much of Messiaen's work, with his liking for explanatory prefaces such as the poem at the head of *Les Offrandes oubliées*, which outlines a spiritual and emotional progression corresponding to the mood and feeling of the work's three main sections in much the same way as in a nineteenth-century tone poem like Richard Strauss's *Tod und Verklärung*. And there is a similar programmatic dimension to many movements from the big organ and piano cycles of the 1930s and 1940s. In the *Catalogue*, however, Messiaen develops this programmatic tendency into something much more unusual, where words and sounds are linked in a highly unconventional and rather disconcerting way.

The first unusual aspect of the *Catalogue* pieces, considered as programme music, is the obsessive way in which almost every successive idea in each piece is identified in programmatic terms, amounting to hundreds of annotations throughout the score. Even allowing for the detailed symbolism that had often characterised Messiaen's musical language, it is only in the bird pieces from the

---

[1] See Messiaen's *Catalogue d'oiseaux* VII, p. 3; I, p. 1; IX, p. 5; V, p. 2. Roman numerals denote the different pieces from the *Catalogue d'oiseaux*.

mid-1950s on that he begins this unremitting, step-by-step insistence on determining the pictorial correlation of each individual musical gesture. With the sole exception of the 'colour-chords', which usually appear unlabelled, creating a brief suspension of specific referentiality, the rule which prevails throughout the two and a half hours of the *Catalogue* is that every musical idea represents something particular, and is named: there is no room for music which is at all vague or indeterminate with regard to the programme.

Following on from this, another striking feature of these pieces is the fact that so much of the music consists of short, vivid gestures: individual and distinct, rarely overlapped, simply presented one after the other, often separated by silences, sometimes brief, sometimes long. Short bursts of this kind are a typical feature of much birdsong, of course, and most exceptions to this pattern are found when Messiaen is directing his attention elsewhere: sea, fog, mountains, or the buzzard's mesmerisingly slow, circling flight, for example. Many of these more sustained passages go to the opposite extreme: they present a continuity which is drawn out at some length, and whose length is exaggerated by the deliberate directionlessness of the material, monotonously devoid of phrase shape, cadence or goal (for example, see the opening backdrops of nos I and XI, Ex. 6.5a and Ex. 6.5f). There are a few exceptions, such as in the coda to no. IV, where the sea's theme (borrowed from *Turangalîla*) moves in clearly directed phrases towards the threefold E major resolution provided by the 'mountain-sunset' music, and though the thekla lark and herring gull remain oblivious, their cries are drawn into the overspanning teleology of the progression.[2] But such passages are rare. In general, then, the music comes as a succession of isolated ideas, which rarely lead from one to another. Clearly, music of this kind is much better suited to comprehensive labelling than a more conventional continuity of development would have been.

Take *La Bouscarle* (IX, *Cetti's Warbler*), which begins with a succession of short and striking gestures in different tempos, all separated from each other by silence (Ex. 6.1). Each gesture denotes something specific: brief interventions from the warbler, moorhen and kingfisher; a rising sweep of 'Mode 3' harmony evoking the blue flash of the kingfisher's plumage; some colour chords (unlabelled); then more birdsong.[3] The birds take turns to

---

[2] IV, pp. 24–6. The sea's theme here recalls a flute theme from 'Jardin du sommeil d'amour', the sixth movement of the *Turangalîla-Symphonie*, based on that work's 'flower-theme' (see Robert Sherlaw Johnson, *Messiaen*, London: Dent, 1975, revised edition 1989), pp. 90 and 101–2.

[3] The warbler should more correctly be called Cetti's warbler. Here and later I have abbreviated bird-names of two or more words where the context allows the use of just one without confusion.

   As it happens, one of the gestures in this passage is not individually labelled, but clearly represents another call from the moorhen (b. 15: compare b. 6 in Ex. 6.1 and, later in the piece p. 19, b. 5).

Ex. 6.1: *La Bouscarle* pp. 1–2/3

sing: their songs are not woven together into many-layered tapestries. They are independent of their setting: when we do get a glimpse of the scenery, in the 'watery reflections', it's another image, separate, taking its place in the sequence.

We're used to the idea that Messiaen writes in clear-cut blocks, and rarely develops in the Beethovenian sense. But the tiny fragments which predominate in Ex. 6.1 (and throughout much of the *Catalogue*) are on a totally different scale from the substantial chunks of material which parade by in the *Quatuor pour la fin du Temps* or *Turangalîla*. In the bird pieces the composer's instinct to separate has broken the music right down so that every constituent idea is distinct. Probably the nearest precursor to this, prior to his plunge into wholesale birdsong in *Réveil des oiseaux* (1953), lies in the (distinctly unprogrammatic) neumes of *Neumes rythmiques* (1949), which Griffiths rightly identifies as a crucial step towards the *style oiseau*.[4] But even here the neumes follow one another continuously, without intervening silences, combining to form phrases which grow discursively on each reappearance. If we hear 'blocks' in this piece they are not likely to be individual neumes so much as entire neume-phrases, alternating with the two strongly contrasted refrains. In *Réveil des oiseaux* and *Oiseaux exotiques* (1955–56) short bursts of birdsong become the norm, of course, but even in these works Messiaen regularly combines the different songs in a polyphonic tutti where for a time they are gathered together in a larger communal continuity. The renunciation of such 'choruses' in the *Catalogue* may have been prompted initially by a purely practical concern for the restrictions of the solo piano medium, but it seems almost to have become an aesthetic tenet of the work, and the insistence on separateness is applied not only to the birdsongs but also the landscapes and other images which Messiaen now introduces into his *style oiseau*.[5] Thus in the *Catalogue* the separation of each image becomes a basic premise of the musical style. This has important consequences on its effect as programme music.

In her influential study of narrative in nineteenth-century music, Carolyn Abbate has suggested that even an apparently straightforward piece of story-telling such as Dukas's *L'Apprenti sorcier* only signifies its story intermittently, by means of a succession of distinct motives which 'evoke nodal points in the tale'. The listener instinctively joins these images together into a narrative, just as a reader unthinkingly reconstructs the two-word story told in *Lolita* of how Humbert's mother died: 'picnic, lightning'.[6] Typically in programme music, the motives representing the story's nodal points are woven into a more-or-less-smooth musical continuity of developments and transitions. Like Messiaen's images, these nodal points are often not at all consistent in viewpoint or kind: actions, scenery, objects, emotions, sounds and characters may all play a part. The musical connections between these points cannot function like the narrative ones, but the simple fact of some degree of musical coherence and continuity between the

---

[4] Paul Griffiths, *Olivier Messiaen and the Music of Time* (London: Faber and Faber, 1985), p. 174.
[5] Though there are no choruses in the *Catalogue* and the vast majority of the birds sing on their own, there are a few bird duets. But, like the solos, each duet is self-contained and consistent in texture.
[6] Carolyn Abbate, *Unsung Voices: Opera and Musical Narrative in the Nineteenth Century* (Princeton University Press, 1991), p. 36.

nodal points suggests that one thing leads to another, encourages the kind of narrative joining-up instinctively performed by the listener, and supports the illusion that the music is telling the story.

This floating of programmatic 'nodal points' amid more pictorially indeterminate musical developments may be easier to perceive in an eventful drama like *The Sorceror's Apprentice*, but it is found in mood- or scene-painting programmes too. The process can be seen in a piece like the *Scène aux champs* from Berlioz's *Symphonie fantastique*, whose programme is not dissimilar from those outlined in the prefaces to Messiaen's bird pieces. Berlioz depicts a pastoral scene whose temporal span is measured out by a series of unmistakable sound-pictures: piping shepherds, distant thunder, and the central appearance of the *idée fixe*, that unknowable object of the composer's obsessive fascination. Even the depiction of the composer's own highly emotional response to this image has parallels in the *Catalogue*. But for much of the movement Berlioz's music follows its own course between these nodal points, observing a more generalised 'pastoral' style rather than any more detailed narrative agenda. The way the music evolves seems to bind together the pictures and encourages us to experience the succession of events and moods as a coherent continuity.

As Ex. 6.1 illustrates, Messiaen's approach to his programmes – his way of making music from them – is radically different. The crucial difference lies in the two features observed earlier: the unremitting identification of every image, and the lack of musical continuity between these individual pictures. 'Given any situation in which narrative is expected, the impulse to construct tales from a sequence of single objects is human and irresistible', Abbate writes,[7] and Messiaen seems to recognise this basic impulse, but not respond to it quite as we would expect. In the *Catalogue* he takes every opportunity to make his narrative intentions clear, and quite literally provides 'a sequence of single objects'; but he refuses to write music which parallels and accompanies our urge to join things together. Messiaen's jerky succession of separate flashes creates as many obstacles as footholds for the listener's narrative instinct.

***

In this chapter I want to investigate the relation between the music's rhetorical and topical gestures and its programmatic function, using this as a means to develop a broader interpretation of the work. To help tease out some of the peculiarities and complexities of Messiaen's narrative approach, I intend to weave the discussion around an image of another very unusual kind of narration. Written ten years after the *Catalogue*, Italo Calvino's *The*

---

[7] Abbate, *Unsung Voices*, p. 36. Abbate italicises
the word 'expected'.

Castle of Crossed Destinies serves here as a striking and lucid illustration of narrative operating within particular restrictions which will help to highlight distinctive aspects of Messiaen's programmatic technique in this work.[8] In Calvino's novel the first person narrator, finding refuge at a castle in a forest, discovers that he and everyone else there has mysteriously been struck dumb. They are all desperate to talk and share their experiences. Then someone begins to put tarot cards down on the table, one after another, each card showing an image; in this way, he attempts to communicate his story. Most of the book is devoted to the narrator's accounts of these silent picture-card stories told by the various guests in the castle, none of whom can speak.

The first story told in this way includes the following sequence: a strong man swinging a club; a young man strung up by his foot from a branch; a maiden carrying water. Our narrator interprets the sequence like this: the young man encounters an armed brigand, is robbed and left hanging, then found and rescued by a young woman passing by.[9]

This particular sequence seems to translate into continuous narrative fairly smoothly, but of course there are many difficulties in interpreting a story told in such a way. The main problem is the lack of conjunctions or any kind of syntax, and thus the indeterminacy of the function or role of the next card, and of its relation to the previous ones. Each new picture might represent an action performed by any one of the current characters, or against them; or a new character entering the story; or perhaps not a real event, but a desire, a dream, a threat ... Sometimes the storytellers give a 'spin' to their images with a gesture or facial expression, as when the picture of a king, mournfully set down on the table, is taken to mean that the king has died. And Calvino soon begins to tease us with the narrator's difficulties and doubts in reading his companions' cards, giving alternative hypotheses, hesitating, questioning – 'Was the *Five of Clubs* announcing a path through the forest?' – and sometimes leaving us with unresolved confusion.[10]

The pleasures offered by this writing are diverse and contradictory: the enjoyment offered by the stories themselves is undercut by our delight in the ingenuity of deriving a narrative from a severely restricted set of symbols, our appreciation of the fragility of the communication, the constantly diverging interpretative possibilities, the continual glimpses of the workings and slippages of language.

---

[8] Italo Calvino, *Il castello dei destini incrociati* (Turin: Einaudi, 1973), translated by William Weaver as *The Castle of Crossed Destinies* (London: Secker & Warburg, 1977). Carolyn Abbate mentions the novel as an illustration of narrative process (*Unsung Voices*, p. 36).

[9] Calvino, *The Castle*, pp. 8–9.

[10] Calvino, *The Castle*, pp. 23–4; for instances of confusion, see (*inter alia*) pp. 18–23.

For all the important differences of structure and medium, there are some interesting parallels between the music of Messiaen's *Catalogue* and these picture-stories.[11] Both arise in a situation where narrative intention has been clearly signalled. Both attempt to satisfy the expectation of narrative with a succession of flat images, lacking syntactical connection. Because of this lack, Calvino's pictures are often forced to signify in quite different ways from each other, causing abrupt jumps in the way we interpret them. As we've seen, Messiaen's images similarly lurch between mimesis and metaphor: some give us birds singing, imitating sound with sound; one suggests the visual flash of a bird's plumage in flight, and others emotions such as fear and joy. In itself, this inconsistency of signification is not unusual in programme music, where the interpretative space normally opened up during the music's continuities allows it to be assimilated. But, just as Calvino has devised a situation in which it becomes a problem, acutely noticeable to the reader, Messiaen's musical slideshow similarly draws our attention to the fragile and often rather arbitrary processes by which the narrative is suggested. Both artists enjoy experimenting with the variety of ways that different arrangements and permutations of images can suggest meaning, and, no less, exploring combinations which challenge our narrative-constructing impulse to the limits. (The comparison with the novel also provides an unusual gloss on the performer of these pieces, as the one who recounts his tale of scenery and birds, fear and joy by doling out the musical tarot cards, with an occasional grimace or smile. With his urgent conviction as he presents and characterises each image, and his tension and elation at the (highly uncertain) possibility of communication, Calvino's mute storyteller might make an interesting model for the pianist...)

Though Messiaen has stripped away all connective tissue in the *Catalogue*, he sometimes arranges his musical picture-cards in such a way that elements of a basic interpretative syntax can still be inferred, despite the many stops and starts. We might compare these sequences to the stories that Calvino's narrator finds relatively straightforward to interpret, like the first of the examples given above. A very simple but important syntactical relation that often guides our path through the *Catalogue*'s long catalogue of images is our instinctive tendency, given appropriate hints in the ideas themselves, to make a distinction between a 'background' state and a 'foreground' event such as a call or song. This distinction can be suggested by the musical characterisation, even when the precise pictures invoked would often be unguessable without reading Messiaen's words. Ex. 6.2a represents a specific

[11] In an interview with Almut Rössler, Messiaen has likened his pieces (citing *La Rousserolle effarvatte* as an example) to 'a photograph album from bygone times'. Almut Rössler, *Contributions to the Spiritual World of Olivier Messiaen*, trans. Barbara Dagg and Nancy Poland (Duisberg: Gilles & Francke, 1986), p. 68.

landscape, and Ex. 6.2b an unspecified colour-sensation, but whatever images we may read into them, their softly sustained harmonies unmistakably prepare a background against which the ensuing figures stand out boldly. In this small way, then, the musical syntax supports the verbal narrative by defining the roles of these two images. It is most obvious when the harmonic backdrop is literally sustained behind what follows, as in both these examples. But the different roles can still be felt even when the background harmonies are cut off, with silence intervening before the ensuing figure, as in Ex. 6.2c.[12] Sometimes Messiaen's gaze lingers on the scenery, giving it more weight in the overall sequence, but here he finds a different way to signal its 'background' status, creating a shapelessness and lack of direction which again sets the ensuing action into relief. In this way, even the noisily chaotic mountainscape which opens *Le Chocard des Alpes* (I, *The Alpine Chough*) takes on the status of 'ground', once we get over its fierce initial impact. When it eventually stops, and after the long silence which follows, the decisive appearance of the chough, as 'figure', confirms and completes the hierarchy (Ex. 6.2d).[13]

The relationship between figure and ground is more than just an abstract hierarchical pairing, for it provides a means to influence our impression of the figure itself, and thus engage in the narrative in more subtle ways. For example, colour-chords and other background images typically lend a 'halo' of harmonic illumination to the birdsong they precede. As Messiaen prefers to add fresh layers of harmony rather than merely reinforce what is already there, the relationship is usually complementary to some extent, and often delicately nuanced. The night's dark velvety bass-notes in *L'Alouette Lulu* (VI, *The Woodlark*) set in relief the 'poetic, liquid, unreal' song of the lark high above (Ex. 6.2a). In texture, tessitura and harmony they are completely different (the lark remains atonal over the night's 'B♭ major'),[14] yet the pairing is sympathetic, not at all antagonistic. A wonderfully equivocal example occurs in *Le Loriot* (II, *The Golden Oriole*) just as the sun reaches its apex, arriving on a majestic five-octave chord of E major representing the full glare of midday

---

[12] The other flower/lake refrains in VII provide further examples, such as p. 20 b. 2/3; p. 22 b. 3/4; p. 26 b. 3/4; p. 15 last bar; p. 16 first bar is very similar too. See also p. 9, b. 1–6, where the night's sonorities are cut off before the 'noises in the marsh' (the first of which is surely birdsong!). Here, and throughout this essay, bar numbers are counted from the beginning of the page in question, not from the beginning of the piece.

[13] Further examples can be found in Ex. 6.5b, 6.5c and 6.5g (though the ensuing birdsongs are not shown), and in the opening lake-music of VII.

[14] The left hand's dissonances prevent the right hand's repeated high B♭s from acquiring much sense of tonal definition, I suggest. Later the left hand begins to fix on B♭, but by then the 'night' chords have moved away from their opening 'key' (VI, p. 1–2).

Ex. 6.2a: *L'Alouette lulu* opening

Ex. 6.2b: *Le Loriot* opening

Ex. 6.2c: *La Rousserolle effarvatte* 19/5–20/2

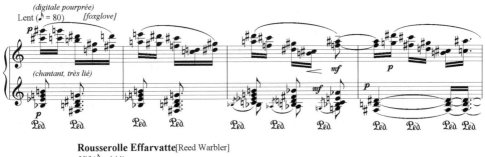

Ex. 6.2d: *Le Chocard des Alpes* opening – 2/3

Ex. 6.2e: *Le Loriot 8/2/3–8/4*

(Ex. 6.2e). At this solemn moment the chiffchaff pipes up, nonchalant and unhurried, the near-bathos of its trivial little figure somehow transforming the grandiosity of its setting into something simpler and more serene.

Sometimes, however, there is opposition between bird and background, if not downright antagonism. This becomes clear straight away in *Le Traquet stapazin* (IV, *The Black-Eared Wheatear*), when the wheatear immediately shatters the peace and harmony of the terrassed vineyards (Ex. 6.3a).[15] The images which follow gently re-establish the peace of the opening, and an important part of this process is the way that their harmonies seem to belong together as if resonating different layers of a rich harmonic field (Ex. 6.3b). Positioned around a core of 'E major' harmonies, this 'field' is a colouristic association of varied sonorities, sometimes shading sharpwards to F# major at the top (in the added resonances of the bunting's song) and sometimes darkening with flat-side fifth-chords in the bass, which encompasses five distinct elements (vineyards, colour-chords, bunting, spectacled warbler, goldfinch). This kind of group is not hierarchical, like the pairing of figure and ground, but associative, and is defined by related attributes of musical characterisation (here, harmony and dynamics).[16]

Nothing bonds a group better than enemies, characterised here by fiercer dynamics and a disrespect for the E-centred harmonic field. While the gull and the raven attempt to sabotage the harmonious little community with

[15] Again, the background/foreground relation of these two opening images is clear, despite the fact that the former is not sustained under the wheatear's song.

[16] The association of 'E major' with harmonies based on whole-tone steps such as F#, D and C in this example also occurs in *Le Loriot* (II), as Griffiths observes (*Olivier Messiaen and the Music of Time*, pp. 184–7). Griffiths' analysis is sensitive and illuminating; one small disagreement I have concerns the 'added resonance' harmonisation of the oriole's song,

which I would characterise, like the bunting's in Ex. 6.3, as elaborating an upper layer centred on 'F# major' over the 'E major' of the left-hand melody. I don't think we can treat the oriole's harmony in successive demisemiquaver slices; with the pedal sustaining, surely the whole group is heard in one.

There are interesting analyses of *Le Traquet stapazin* in Peter Hill (ed.)'s 'Piano Music II', *The Messiaen Companion*, (London: Faber and Faber, 1995), pp. 336–8, and Johnson, *Messiaen*, pp. 139–40. Johnson hears the

Ex. 6.3a: *Le Traquet stapazin* opening – 2/2

wheatear itself as belonging to the group harmony rather than opposing it, and indeed there are good reasons for doing so. Though the wheatear's brief outburst is harsh and disruptive, it can all be accounted for in terms of the lower three staves of Ex. 6.3b: the fifths f–c′/ g–d″ and their descending whole-tone transposition, together with fragmentary remnants of 'E major'. The raven also presents the 'fifths' idea in flattened and distorted form (b. 13). Thus even these birds' antagonism is suggested at least in part by using more remote aspects of the passage's main harmonic field, appropriately characterised, rather than through entirely different harmonic resources.

Ex 6.3b: From *Le Traquet stapazin*

heavy, thuggish squawks, the wheatear himself has nothing to add to his first brief salvo. Indeed, the somewhat aloof 'personality' of our eponymous hero, or anti-hero, leads to a curious but appropriate anomaly of weight and proportion in the piece as a whole, for Messiaen seems to have decided that the best way to portray a taciturn sociopath is to show how rarely he intervenes in the proceedings. The result is that, without contest, the spectacled warbler steals the show, both in terms of the number of his appearances and their sheer charisma, as is already clear in Ex. 6.3. At the end, it is the warbler who bathes in the glow of the sunset, and his song which lingers in the composer's thoughts (as we know from a separate, individually labelled figure – not 'the warbler' but 'a memory of the warbler').

The kind of grouping discussed here concerns the association of elements related by their characterisation (thus contributing to the elaboration of narrative), in contrast to a purely formal grouping based on regular patterns of repetition or alternation regardless of character or style. Groups of the latter kind also occur in the *Catalogue*, and have often been regarded as the primary structural basis of the cycle.[17] Patterns such as couplet-and-refrain are an important and conspicuous basis for much of Messiaen's earlier music, and the prefaces in the *Catalogue* indicate their presence in the organisation of music and programme of at least these two pieces (I and XI). And, indeed, there are plenty of passages where the succession of images clearly invites this kind of understanding.

We can illustrate this by returning to *Le Traquet stapazin*, for the opening passage discussed above is followed by an almost identical succession of images, and then another. If Ex. 6.3a (that is, strophe 1) runs 'vineyards–wheatear–colour–bunting–warbler–gull–raven*–warbler–goldfinch–warbler',

---

[17] The most substantial and thoroughgoing exploration of this aspect of the music is found in Johnson's *Messiaen*, especially the formal diagrams of all thirteen pieces in these terms on pp. 143–58. While these focus on formal arrangements such repetition and alternation, the accompanying 'group structure' charts relate more to the grouping by association of content and character just discussed, as does Johnson's 'concept of mode' (pp. 137–8).

the following sequence (strophe 2) is the same as far as the asterisk, now ending 'colour–goldfinch–gull–warbler', though several birds are given longer this time round (the wheatear remains laconic, of course). Strophe 3 only slightly reshuffles the cards: we hear the same sequence up to the asterisk, now much expanded with gull and raven swapped over, and the ending lengthened to 'colour–goldfinch–warbler–orphean warbler (a new character)–gull–warbler' (see IV, pp. 1–8). Each strophe ends with a long moment of stillness following the warbler's song (and tinted with its still-resonating harmony); these are the longest pauses in the passage (only the wheatear's three-beat silence comes close), and they help to articulate the three strophes of this repetitive, cumulative structure and impose a shape and direction on its thirty-odd constituent images. It is worth noting that the threefold design is nowhere implied in the piece's preface, which simply describes the characters once each, nor could it possibly reflect what Messiaen heard in the field. The formal patterning prolongs the scene and allows further exploration of the different songs, while also helping to quantify and focus our sense of the passing of time.

Typically, Messiaen uses a landscape image to mark repeating structures of this kind, as he does here with the 'vineyards' music. But in *La Buse Variable* (XI, *The Buzzard*) he picks out two mistle-thrush songs from a whole sequence of different birds and soups them up into heroic refrains of resounding grandeur, creating an unmistakable refrain structure in what might otherwise have seemed a relatively arbitrary succession of songs.[18]

Although the formal schemes imposed on these two passages could not in either case be claimed as a direct reflection of narrative events, in helping to define and shape a lengthy string of images they also help to delineate the moment when the narrative moves on. Thus the effect of such formal schemes can be indirectly supportive of the music's narrative dimension. Indeed, passages like these, which recreate Messiaen's earlier large-scale block-forms, get as close as his sound-bite material will allow to the familiar practice whereby programme music prolongs and develops a scene according to formal criteria derived more from musical procedures than from the narrative it is portraying.

So far there has been an apparently smooth consensus between the programme and the music's mosaic design, suggesting perhaps that the abrupt

[18]XI, p. 2 (last system) and p. 7, b. 1. The mistle-thrush's 'ordinary' song is heard on p. 3, b. 3 and b. 6–7 ('la grive draine'), followed by its heroic transformation beginning at b. 11; there are further examples of both versions of the song on pp. 4–6. There is a hint of cyclic repetition in the actual order of birdsongs, but there is no doubt that this would not have been anywhere near so apparent without the refrain's special treatment. It is interesting that in the preface to this piece Messiaen does not attempt to disguise this formal structure in more naturalistic prose, as he does in most of the other prefaces.

disconnectedness of the images is no more than a superficial idiosyncrasy of style. However, up to this point we have only been looking at passages where the choice and order of musical cards helps us to follow their 'story'. In Calvino's novel things are not always so straightforward, not least because his storytellers increasingly find that they have to make their stories from existing 'pre-composed' card-sequences, and I suggest that they are not always so simple in Messiaen's *Catalogue*, either. For each example of helpful, intuitively comprensible 'syntax' discussed above there are also passages where the cards lie more awkwardly, where the images seem to give out ambiguous or even contradictory signals, and like Calvino's narrator we have to wrestle with what is set before us in our attempt to make sense of it.

Problems arise with regard to both the narrative implications and the form. Let's take the formal issue first. Whatever part those strophic and other repetitive formal schemes may have played in the compositional process, the highly inconsistent nature of the unruly mosaics which make up their simple blocks often undermine their supposed identity and suggest conflicting or multiple relations of a much more complex kind.

La Bouscarle, for example, is viewed by Sherlaw Johnson as a strophic form.[19] Certainly the strophic repetitions introduced by the river melody can be heard, but they emerge from and subsequently disintegrate back into a much less predictable sequence. The opening is disorienting in the apparently back-to-front relation of the decisive, fragmentary 'introduction' to the vague shapelessness of the ensuing 'interlude', which sounds more like a belated introduction to what preceded it. In the third 'strophe' the pattern established by its repetition in the second dissolves completely in a string of 'interpolations' old and new.[20] Indeed, despite the clear boundaries between each image, the effect towards the end of the piece is almost a stream-of-consciousness impressionism where strophic and non-strophic ideas intermingle like the watery reflections themselves.[21] In *La Rousserolle effarvatte* (VII, *The Reed Warbler*), recurring refrains do indeed give shape to the middle stretches of this huge piece, as Johnson claims, but the long sequences at beginning and end are arranged around the reed warbler's impressive night-time solos, and Johnson's strophic analysis fails to show how these are very much the equal of the central 'strophes' in weight and importance.[22] In X (*Le Merle de roche*), between the symmetrical scene-setting of beginning

---

[19] Johnson, *Messiaen*, p. 154.

[20] Johnson calls the kingfisher's display (designated by the letters 'pp') a continuation of the strophe, between 'interpolations', but in the context, thanks to its unique character, the kingfisher's display sounds as much like an interpolation as any of the other elements in this passage (*Messiaen*, p. 154).

[21] Peter Hill also hears an impressionistic dissolution of boundaries here: see 'Piano Music II', *The Messiaen Companion*, pp. 340–2.

[22] Furthermore, the first of Johnson's strophes in VII (*Messiaen*, p. 151) has little in common with the others, acting rather as more introductory material which corresponds to

and end, the long pauses do not at all delineate a strophic design, and again
Johnson's supposed strophes seem to account awkwardly for music whose
clearest features are the appearances of the rocky 'interversions' between or
behind the various birds. And in *L'Alouette calandrelle* (VIII, *The Short-Toed
Lark*), despite the repetition of some image-sequences, the effects of contrast
and reprise are felt ambiguously at various different moments in different
ways, thanks to the artful displacement of the opening 'desert-heat' chords
when the opening ideas return, and also to their imaginative transformation
following the duet with the crested lark.[23] It is perhaps in this piece that
Messiaen plays the most interesting games with the disposition of his
picture-cards and the way this changes how they are heard.

As for the programme, the fact of so many separate images and such an ad
hoc, unreliable syntax, together with the structural counterpoint provided by
half-submerged strophic schemes as discussed above, opens up continual
ambiguity and confusion with regard to narrative implications, affecting
even the simplest interpretative decisions. Frequently, Messiaen allows a
bird several different motifs one after another to create a more extended
bout of singing, and because of the *Catalogue's* step-by-step presentation,
some kind of generic characterisation is needed to distinguish whether a
given sequence of ideas represents a monologue or a group conversation. It is
perfectly possible for the music to do this, creating a hierarchy of differences-
within-underlying-similarity (for one bird) against more fundamental differences (for two or more). Sometimes Messiaen does just that, as when, in *Le
Traquet stapazin*, the orphean warbler sings out a whole variety of different
ideas, but his entire song remains distinguishable (by tempo and texture)
from the contrasting styles of the rock bunting and corn bunting before and
after (IV, p. 15–17). But often we find a single bird juxtaposing ideas which
are just as sharply contrasted as those of different birds elsewhere in the piece.
For example, in *Le Merle de roche* (X), the rock thrush, jackdaws and black
redstart each present a highly varied repertoire along with a few obvious
signature songs, and there are often longer silences within their songs than
between them. The red-backed shrike has a bewildering range of gestures,
tempos and dynamics on different appearances (XI, p. 7–11) and the nightingale is often particularly versatile, though in VI this helps to distinguish
him from the very consistent woodlark, the only other bird in this simplest of

parts of the coda, while the 'interlude' just
before the coda surely *should* qualify as a
strophe. Incidentally, in II it seems perverse to
identify the robin as 'refrain' when this role
seems clearly to be taken by the longer
sequences of colour-chords, which also
articulate the garden warblers' strophes in the
following section (see *Messiaen*, p. 144).

[23] When the opening 'desert-heat chords'
return (p. 7, b. 2), this sounds like a turning
point in the piece, although in some senses the
reprise is already under way. A transformed
version of this image is heard on p. 4, last bar.
See also the thoughtful analysis of this piece in
Hill's 'Piano Music II', *Messiaen Companion*,
pp. 329–30.

scenarios.[24] Even the very brief calls in our first example from *La Bouscarle* comprise two different ideas each, contrasting in tempo as well as shape; the moorhen's sudden change of character is particularly disorientating in its suggestion of two quite different birds (see Ex. 6.1 above). The potential confusion of different songs is only really surprising given the context of artificial separation in which they are presented, and as long as important distinctions are maintained – between crow and nightingale, say, or bird and mountain – we may feel is unimportant, or even read it as a small gesture towards realism.

But the bigger and more basic distinctions are no less prone to collapse, as when the rocky 'stegosaurus' music includes a livelier component which is clearly set apart, more like a companion to the black redstart than part of the backdrop (X, p. 5–6); similarly, the 'joy of the blue sea' which sets the scene in XII culminates in a dramatic cry more like a birdsong than a background (XII, b. 3). The issue here is not music's inability to specify certain kinds of particularity without verbal help, which is a trivial feature of all programme music. Rather, it concerns the ambiguities and inconsistencies of these images in terms of the relations and conventions established by their musical context.

Another kind of confusion arises when sharply contrasted images are put one after another as successive representations of roughly the same thing, as seems especially prone to happen with images of water. In *La Bouscarle* we hear a long series of soft atonal chords in irregular rhythms, followed after a lengthy silence by a confident cantabile melody, with clear phrases and cadences, warmly harmonised in Mode 3-inflected A major. Given that they are so different, so completely opposed in style and content, it is disconcerting to find that the first depicts reflections in the water, and the second, only slightly differently, 'the river' itself.[25] Similarly, two adjacent, well-contrasted passages in *Le Courlis cendré* (XIII, *The Curlew*) represent 'the waves of the sea' and 'the water' respectively. And *Le Merle bleu* (III, *The Blue Rock Thrush*) runs to three entirely different textures representing in turn 'the water' (with splashes), 'the blue sea' and 'the waves'.[26] Of course there is an infinite variety of ways to depict the sea, and if these contrasting images were woven into some kind of musical continuity we would probably have no difficulty assimilating them into our own imagined narrative. But when there are no transitions, the sheer contrast will give a strong narrative

[24] Sometimes Messiaen specifies the same bird for two successive ideas, as though aware that their common identity cannot be taken for granted (e.g. VII, p. 37). A narrative situation which his music doesn't so much confuse as ignore is the successive singing of similar songs by two different birds of the same species. Another composer might easily have set these up as call and response from two different singers, but Messiaen's bursts of song follow one another exactly as they would if they were sung by one singer (see IV, p. 13 and XII, pp. 4 and 8).

[25] *La Bouscarle* (IX), p. 2–5 (the watery reflections are shown in Ex. 6.5b).

[26] *Le courlis cendré* (XIII), pp. 13–15; *Le Merle bleu* (III), pp. 5–6.

signal: whatever the first idea represented, the next appears to be announcing itself as decisively different.

We have already observed images of scenery (monstrous rocks, joyful sea) taking on the profile of birdsong. In another subversion of categories a normally passive background image keeps its basic shape, but seems to develop a will of its own, as in VIII, when the background (unlabelled in the score) suddenly becomes much more energetic and aggressive, as if threatening the lark (Ex. 6.4a). Who is this hostile character? Only the fact that the final harmony is sustained under the lark's song indicates that these figures were probably conceived as colour-chords. A spectacled warbler seems similarly threatened in Ex. 6.4b, where the colour-chords keep their usual rhythm, but are quick, astringent, loudly accented, and not sustained under the ensuing song, which has its own colouration. They seem to have taken on an active role, goading the warbler into song.

It's as if Messiaen's tarot pack, like Calvino's, has only a limited number of different suits – musical types such as song textures, harsh calls and noises, rich chordal melodies, chaotic backgrounds, steady two-part meandering, delicate colour-chords, and so on. Within each suit there is a splendid variety of cards, but the overall range of the whole pack is not a continuous spectrum, falling instead into discrete bands. (In this synchronic view of the material, as in its temporal arrangement, there is no continuity, but rather a succession of distinct types.) Sometimes the composer finds himself obliged to use a not-ideally suited card – in Ex. 6.4b, the 'Two of Colours', perhaps – and he presents it with all the rhetoric he can muster to adapt it to the narrative situation, while always being tied to the basic profile of that particular card. One also senses Messiaen refusing to let a limited range of cards compartmentalise his imagination in *Le Merle bleu*. Here he revels in a joyous confusion of related sensations, when certain lively figures (which are unlabelled and may again have been conceived as colour chords) seem to evoke both the preceding images of the precipitous cliffs, and still-to-come evocations of violently crashing waves. The bird itself is also part of the blur, for its undertone of Balinese gongs links smoothly in with these same waves (Ex. 6.4c–e).[27] Ambiguities of function lead to ambiguities of representation in these examples, where one kind of image has to take on several different roles. In all these passages there are serious warps in the pictorial syntax, and if we accept them more easily than, say, the musically opposed depictions of water discussed earlier, it is only because here the ambiguous figures work together (unlike the water images) to create a prevailing mood in each

[27] In the preface we are told that the rock thrush's song 'brings to mind Balinese music', yet in the piece itself Messiaen contrives for the waves to provide the Balinese gong sounds which accompany the song.

Ex. 6.4a: *L'Alouette calandrelle 4/5/3–5/2/2*

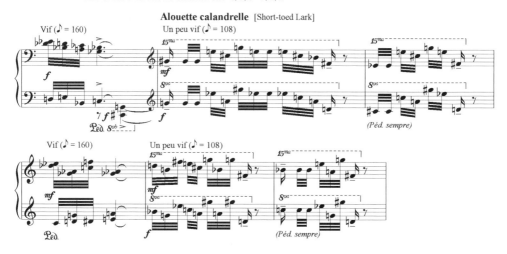

Ex. 6.4b: *Le Traquet rieur 15/3–4*

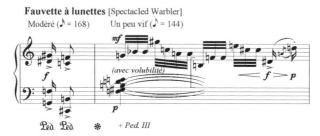

Ex. 6.4c: *Le Merle bleu 4/2–3*

Ex. 6.4d: *Le Merle bleu 6/2–6/3/2*

Ex. 6.4e: *Le Merle bleu* 11/3/2

Ex.(i) 6.4f: *Le Courlis cendré*: (i) 8/1/2 (ii)13/1/1

passage. Similarly, in *Le Courlis cendré* (*The Curlew*) it may seem a nicely impressionist touch that the guillemot's cry is sometimes scarcely distinguishable from the waves (Ex. 6.4f).

Messiaen's persuasive rhetoric, or spin-doctoring, is particularly evident when he comes to deal with the family of images referred to above as 'chaotic backgrounds'.[28] The sophisticated organisation of pitch and especially rhythm underlying passages like the mountain scenes from the first piece serves chiefly to produce a kind of chaos within prescribed limits (Ex. 6.5a). By limiting the rhythmic unpredictability to values based on a perceptible semiquaver pulse, for example, Messiaen allows the passage a kind of rhythmic verve; by allocating just one layer to each hand he provides some sense of contrapuntal

[28] Johnson suggests that this kind of writing is
reserved for scenes which are 'colourless'
(*Messiaen*, p. 135).

dialogue, but still leaves enough space (both in pitch and rhythm) to keep the sounds gaunt and bare; and by fixing the dynamic at an unchanging *forte* he creates from all this an image of implacable, inhuman grandeur. Thus, despite the abstract, non-representational source of the musical techniques, it is relatively easy to make such passages pictorially suggestive. This becomes especially clear if we turn again to *La Bouscarle*'s 'reflections in the river' (Ex. 6.5b). Here in the soft, impressionist haze of water and light we find – surprisingly – more or less the same ingredients as in the jagged cacophony of the mountainscape. The actual notes and rhythms (and their under-lying machinations) are different, but they hardly need to be, for what changes the effect of this passage is terribly simple, if not superficial: the slight adjustment to tessitura, with more middle-range sonorities, the slightly faster tempo and, most importantly, swapping the implacable *forte* for a translucent *pianissimo*.

As this comparison suggests, in passages based on this kind of amorphous twelve-note writing it's the composer's decisions concerning general param-eters which are his chief means of sculpting this somewhat neutral material, not the individual figures, harmonies or rhythms. Such material can be simplified, by reducing the two strands to a single strand of chordal homo-phony, simplified further by replacing the rhythmic invention with equal lengths for every note, and further still by thinning the chords to just two notes. With appropriate choices of dynamic and register, these simplifica-tions can represent (respectively): the chaotic boulders of the Clapier St Christophe – *ff*, repeatedly descending; the gathering darkness and fog – one long *diminuendo* from *fff* to *ppp*, repeatedly descending; and the swirling waters of the sea – alternating *crescendo* and *diminuendo*, rising and expand-ing (see Ex. 6.5c–e). In fact, this final simplification is now close to what I caricatured earlier as 'steady two-part meandering', which usually depicts not swirling waters but the uncanny stillness of circling eagles and buzzards – these are slower, and rise or fall as appropriate (Ex. 6.5f).[29]

Alternatively, such colourless material can be made more complicated by introducing more refined rhythmic distinctions within longer rhythmic cycles, where the underlying demisemiquaver pulse is no longer perceptible. This makes the rhythms seem much more arbitrary than those of Ex. 6.5a, especially when coupled with serialised (and so unpredictable) dynamics, and provides a useful basis for images of fear and mystery, in music of the night (low tessitura here) and the terrifying, grotesque silhouettes of the cirque de Mourèze (Ex. 6.5g–h).

---

[29] See also XI, pp. 16–17, and, for the hovering eagle, I, pp. 2–3 and 7.

Ex. 6.5a: *Le Chocard des Alpes* opening

Ex. 6.5b: *La Bouscarle* 2/3/3–2/4/3

Ex. 6.5c: *Le Chocard des Alpes* 4/4/2–4/5/1

Ex. 6.5d: *Le Courlis cendré* p. 16 b. 1–3

Ex. 6.5e: *Le Courlis cendré* 14/1/1–2

Ex. 6.5f: *La Buse variable* 1/3/3–1/4/1

Ex. 6.5g: *La Chouette hulotte* opening

Ex. 6.5h: *Le Merle de roche* 7/3/3/–7/4/2

In these passages Messiaen took colossal risks. Amidst the *Catalogue*'s cornucopia of vivid and characterful inventions, these images are dangerously low in 'content', and as representations they have the edgy bravado of a confidence trick. (For just this reason, reactions to these passages will be more than usually subjective. Personally, I find the ponderous awkwardness of Ex. 6.5f and 6.5g disappointing, especially by comparison with the lurid and avowedly surreal descriptions of dinosaurs, female corpses, etc., with which they are labelled. The outrageous simplicity of the buzzard's slow circling, on the other hand, has me spellbound.)

Value judgments aside, these passages reveal most clearly the tension between Messiaen's array of musical 'cards' and his narrative agenda. And they occupy a noticeable and significant place in the cycle as a whole, with highly prominent roles in the first and last pieces. *Le Chocard des Alpes* is a curious piece, especially as the opening to a cycle celebrating birdsong, for the three long and noisy mountainscapes massively outweigh the relatively brief outbursts of chough and raven. Perhaps, as in *Le Traquet stapazin*, the proportions are part of the portrait, showing a forceful but tiny bird very much overshadowed by his environment.

The weighting is also odd in the final piece, *Le Courlis cendré*, though in a different way. Like many other commentators, I find the portrayal of the curlew especially haunting. So it is surprising to realise that the curlew himself only appears in the introduction and very briefly in the coda, and is absent from the entire main body of the piece. Instead we have first an exchange of other seabirds calling wildly across the waves, and then at the centre two huge slabs of the amorphous chromaticism discussed above. Most unusually, Messiaen arranges the first of these to lead strongly through into the second in a powerfully directed *crescendo*-cum-*rallentando*, as though arriving at some solemn peroration (Ex. 6.6). It is an intense build-up to a monumental point of arrival, something quite unique in the *Catalogue*. Slowly and grandly the moment passes, the music dies down and the night draws in. The massive boom of the lighthouse introduces a final scene of seabirds before a last call from the curlew and the bleak swish of the surf. It is a desolate scene with which to end. And it is telling that the grand climax reserved for this final piece should be shaped from such amorphous, contentless material, a peroration of empty noise, so different in feeling from the generous, affirmative excess of the big moments in *Vingt Regards* or *Turangalîla*. Even in terms of the programme, there is nothing there: the climax marks merely the first signs of fog and nightfall which will only reach their apex as the music dies to *ppp* some eighty slow chords later.

Is the blankness that rises up so powerfully at the heart of this final movement a reflection, perhaps, of the many empty moments glimpsed throughout the cycle? On this one occasion where the gap between pictures is not merely bridged but completely overwhelmed, is the result, as if in compensation, an eruption of the inarticulacy and emptiness which haunted those earlier silences?

It would be interesting to explore what it means when a writer such as Calvino chooses to write a novel entirely devoted to recounting stories told

Ex. 6.6: *Le Courlis cendré* 15/3/2–16/2/1

by people struck dumb, using pictures alone. Clearly this is well beyond the
scope of this chapter, though the enquiry might begin by considering the
demise of the omniscient narrator, a widespread despair in the idea of language as reliable communication brought into unprecedentedly stark focus in
the wake of the Holocaust, and a fascination with constructivist rigour and
self-imposed constraints which stems in part from Calvino's growing
acquaintance with Oulipo writers in Paris, where he was living at the time.

But we *should* try to address a parallel question. What can it mean that, like
Calvino's novel, Messiaen's *Catalogue* foregoes the discursive and developmental possibilities that would comprise a more 'normal' narrative, and is
reduced to such a bare, flat picture-series, a dumbshow of icons? As I've
argued throughout this chapter, we must surely reject the idea of taking
Messiaen's programmes as if they were being handled conventionally: heard
this way the pieces would surely seem stilted, cranky and even incompetent
by comparison with the superbly maintained illusions of, say, Richard
Strauss, or Messiaen's teacher Dukas. And anyway, even his own earlier
programmatic pieces must have seemed a long way in the past for
Messiaen in the mid-1950s.

Just a few years earlier Messiaen had famously helped to develop some of
the most radical methods of recasting musical language, with pieces like his
influential *Mode de valeurs et d'intensités* (1949) filtering out to the point of
annihilation the impulses of harmonic progression, motivic development,
personal expression and with them what one might call the emotional

narrative drive of Romanticism – in many ways this foreshadowed the ideas (if not the tone) of the Oulipo.[30] But, whereas for Oulipo writers there was always the productive tension of having to 'make sense' grammatically while also obeying the self-imposed rules, for composers it was harder to see what might provide this counter-constraint of grammatical meaningfulness. Messiaen's attitude to his own experiments was ambiguous, and before long he and his former pupils Boulez and Stockhausen were all to step back from absolute pointillism, in which there is no way to set the atomising tendency of the precompositional rules into tension with any kind of discursive continuity. As Paul Griffiths has noted, in their different ways all three composers began to work with 'groups', whose identities were more perceptible. In Messiaen's case, his preferred groups soon became the bursts and flurries of birdsong.[31]

With their vivid and idiosyncratic characterisation, the short and dynamic units of birdsong offered a picturesque distinctness of style and a potential for narrative which may seem a far cry from the utopian abstraction of the *Mode de valeurs*. But they were born out of it, and the questions raised by Messiaen's speculative experiments of 1949–51 continued to haunt the new style. The years of silence which preceded first the *Réveil* and then *Oiseaux Exotiques* give testament to Messiaen's soul-searching at this time, when fears of an aesthetic and technical dead-end must have been greatly compounded by the pain of his wife's long and worsening illness. Even Messiaen's unshakable faith seems to have been under uncharacteristic strain, and it is noticeable that the works following the *Livre d'orgue* show an absence both of the explicit theological content which was so inseparable from his music up to the *Vingt Regards*, and of the human lovers' cosmic certainties in the 'Tristan' trilogy. By contrast, the scenes from the *Catalogue* include only one human, and he is very much an outsider in the world being observed. In its discontinuity the *Catalogue* seems to reflect honestly (if perhaps inadvertently) a reticence, an unwillingness to authorise the reassurance and meaningfulness offered by narrative continuity, falling back into silence rather than providing developments and transitions which would simulate the spinning-out, the *telling*, of the story. Like Calvino's hapless characters, these pieces can't *tell*, they can only *show*.

---

[30] Founded in 1960 by Raymond Queneau and François Le Lionnais, the Oulipo is a literary group devoted to devising constraints and combinatorial procedures as a means of generating literary texts. In 'The Oulipo and combinatorial art', Jacques Roubaud, a member, offers the following definition: 'An Oulipian author is a rat who himself builds the maze from which he sets out to escape' (Roubaud, 'The Oulipo', in *Oulipo Compendium*, ed. Mathews and Brotchie (London: Atlas, 1998), pp. 37–44, 41).

[31] Griffiths, *Olivier Messiaen and the Music of Time*, p. 187.

Because Messiaen's descriptions appear so blunt and absolute, it's easy to assume that the music works in an unambiguous way, almost mechanically. (This is a wider problem with Messiaen's writings about his music, not just with his annotations in the *Catalogue*.) As I have tried to show, the way the *Catalogue* 'narrates' is much more complex, and full of interpretative puzzles. Messiaen treads a fine line here, encouraging the listener to weave together a narrative while also exposing and undermining this instinctive urge. In providing a pattern of suggestive but disconnected ideas, requiring and at the same time drawing attention to the involvement of the listener, he opens up an inviting but also challenging gap between the discursive explanatory tendency of our narrative imagination, and its stimulus – a music of eloquent pictures, struck dumb in its refusal to join them together into a story.

7   The impossible charm of Messiaen's *Chronochromie*

Amy Bauer

Chronochromie occupies a seminal position in Messiaen's œuvre, as both a culmination of the *style oiseau* from 1953 onwards, dominated by transcriptions of birdsong, and as a template for the preoccupation with colour and rhythmic complexity that would mark his later music.[1] At the behest of Heinrich Ströbel, Messiaen wrote *Chronochromie* on commission for the 1960 Donauschingen festival for full orchestra with no keyboards. It premiered to less than universal acclaim, as its riot of twenty-one simultaneous birdsongs in the penultimate movement was apparently more than the audience could bear.[2]

As the composer states in his extensive notes on the work, *Chronochromie* exploits the 'power of impossibility' latent in the colours of the full orchestra; the name stems from the integration of dense seven- and eight-note harmonies with a rhythmic scheme of symmetrical permutations based on thirty-two values in movements 2 and 4 (*Strophes* I and II).[3] These symmetrical permutations, along with the singular harmonies most often called simply 'colour-chords' in the scholarly literature,[4] would appear later in *Sept Haïkaï* (1962), *Couleurs de la cité céleste* (1963) and *Eclairs sur l'au delà . . .* (1988–92). Yet it can be argued that, aside from *Eclairs* and St Francis' 'Sermon to the birds' (Tableau 6 of his opera *Saint-François d'Assise*), *Chronochromie* represents the peak of composed and audible complexity in Messiaen's music, for within it three compositional techniques are juxtaposed in their most arcane forms. *Strophe* I integrates for the first time Messiaen's first fully fledged symmetrical permutation scheme with birdsong from two continents, and three types of 'colour-chord'.

---

[1] The author would like to thank Robert Sholl for his invaluable help in shaping and refining this chapter.

[2] Antoine Goléa, 'Olivier Messiaen, Chronochromie', *Melos*, Vol. 29 (1962), 10; Bernard Gavoty, under the pen name 'Clarendon', wrote 'An excess of brilliance turned everything to grey. So many durations, subtly entwined, ended by obliterating all sense of rhythm'; 'Turangalila d'Olivier

Messiaen', *Le Figaro* (13 October 1961), quoted in Peter Hill and Nigel Simeone, *Messiaen* (New Haven: Yale University Press, 2005), p. 237.

[3] *Traité de rythme, de couleur, et d'ornithologie* (*TRCO*), Tome III (Paris: Leduc, 1996), pp. 7–38. *Chronochromie* is analysed in pp. 79–101 of the same Tome.

[4] See a discussion of this in footnote 13.

In this chapter, I will dissect the harmonic and rhythmic details of *Strophe* I. But I want to address a more universal question: the implacable difficulty of moving beyond simple description to a hermeneutic understanding of Messiaen's music, much less to say anything of its perception and cognition. For, as John Milsom notes, 'Relatively easy as it is to define and describe the technique of Messiaen's "musical language," the extent to which it genuinely operates as a musical "language," expressive both of the concrete and the spiritual, and independent of the verbal exegeses that Messiaen provided, remains a moot point.'[5]

Chronochromie's impenetrability is in a very real sense the sum as well as the measure of the 'power of impossibilities' that Messiaen locates in its rhythmic palindromes and towering chromatic chords.[6] The latter three chord types – the so-called turning chords, chords of transposed inversion over the same bass note, and the chords of contracted resonance (all discussed below) – appear in but nine distinct but unvaried chord voicings. Although these chords are theoretically available at all transpositional levels, Messiaen further limits himself to 65 of the possible 108 forms. The careful presentation and selection of harmonic materials serves as but one example of the theme of limits, or, as Roberto Fabbi calls it, the 'idea of restriction', that informs Messiaen's music at both surface and underlying levels of structure.[7] The composer finds a certain freedom within these restrictive 'impossibilities', be they formal, harmonic or rhythmic:

> It will be noticed that in the 'symmetrical permutations' as in the 'non-retrogradable rhythms,' we find ourselves confronted with an impossibility. A retrograde is impossible, because the rhythm is symmetrical within itself. Further permutations are impossible, because the order in which we read the rhythm – invariably the same one – brings us relentlessly back to the starting-point. These impossibilities endow the rhythm with great power, a kind of explosive force, I would say, a magical strength.[8]

In *Chronochromie*, where nine non-symmetrical sonorities and a thirty-two-member durational series operate in combination, these restrictive impossibilities are neither as limited nor as easily grasped as they were in

[5] John Milsom, Organ Music I', in Peter Hill (ed.), *The Messiaen Companion* (London: Faber and Faber, 1995), p. 62.
[6] Messiaen quoted in Almut Rößler, *Contributions to the Spiritual World of Olivier Messiaen, with Original Texts by the Composer,* trans. Barbara Dagg, Nancy Poland and Timothy Tikker (Duisberg: Gilles and Francke, 1986), p. 41. Messiaen spoke of the 'charm of impossibilities' as early as the *Technique de mon langage musical* (*TMLM*), in reference to the Modes of Limited Transpositions and the non-retrogradable

rhythms; Olivier Messiaen, *TMLM*, vols I and II (Paris: Leduc, 1944), translated by John Satterfield as *The Technique of My Musical Language* (Paris: Leduc, 1956–66), and republished in 2001 in one volume.
[7] See Roberto Fabbi, 'Theological Implications of Restrictions in Messiaen's Compositional Processes', *Messiaen's Language of Mystical Love*, ed. Siglind Bruhn (New York: Garland, 1998), pp. 55–84.
[8] Messiaen quoted in Rößler, *Contributions to the Spiritual World of Olivier Messiaen,* p. 42.

earlier works such as the *Quatre Etudes de rythme* (1949–50; see discussion below). Yet, through an ingenious series of additional limits on his materials, the composer increases the tension between the inherent restrictions of his cyclic materials and their variation.

Analysing *Chronochromie*

The *Strophes* of *Chronochromie* combined for the first time three layers of three different types of non-modal sonorities; each permutation marches asymmetrically beneath percussion accents and French birds (illustrated by winds and keyed percussion) to saturate chromatic, registral and timbral space. The first permutation is given to the first violins, accompanied by three gongs marked *pianissimo* throughout. Tuned bells marked *forte* accompany a second permutation in second violins, while violas and cellos take the third permutation, along with suspended cymbal and tam-tam. The juxtaposition of birdsong adds yet another layer of 'charm' to the whole, a dense combination that would not appear again until the fourth movement of *Eclairs*. That the *Strophes* contain one continuous isorhythm, if permuted and juxtaposed, correlates with their role in Greek lyric poetry: metric movements constructed on the model of Ancient Greek choral song, culminated in a 'polymetric' *Epôde* and were book-ended with a free *Introduction* and *Coda*.

We might question the use of a classical humanist model for such non-teleological, transcendentally expressive music. Is there a musically purposive conflict between those avatars of the 'impossible' – symmetrical rhythms, static harmonies and juxtaposed patterns – and those that represent natural and classical elements? For *Chronochromie* bears more than a passing resemblance to the function as well as the form of Greek choral songs. Early Greek lyric poetry did not distinguish between poetry and song,[9] and featured a great variety of metrical pattern and line length.[10] The most elaborate meters were found in choral songs; these were less intimate than other forms of lyric poetry, and included hymns specifically addressed to the gods, often extolling the virtues of nature.[11] The earliest surviving choral works were by the poet Alcman, who wrote 'I know the tunes of all birds', likely referring to the Greek legend that all music originated in imitation of birdsongs.[12] In *De rerum natura*, Lucretius writes:

[9] David Mulroy, *Early Greek Lyric Poetry* (Ann Arbor: University of Michigan Press, 1999), p. 9.
[10] Mulroy, *Early Greek Lyric Poetry*, p. 10

[11] C. M. Bowra, *Greek Lyric Poetry* (Oxford: Oxford University Press, 2001), p. 6.
[12] Cited in Bowra, *Greek Lyric Poetry*, pp. 29–30.

But by the mouth
To imitate the liquid notes of birds
Was earlier far 'mongst men than power to make,
By measured song, melodious verse and give
Delight to ears. And whistlings of the wind[13]

Chronochromie aligns 'measured song' with the 'liquid notes of birds' until the sixth movement (*Epôde*), when man somewhat artificially surrenders to nature. In *Strophe* I the songs of four different French birds in eight different instruments provide a model for the melodic structure, but also serve to colour and highlight the slower-moving symmetrical permutation scheme. Through a process Messiaen terms 'minting' (*le monnayage*), the faster-moving birdsongs emphasise the demisemiquaver units inside the longer, additive durations in the rhythmic series.[14] Both *Strophes* are based on the same rhythmic cycle, one Messiaen abandons – as did the Greek choral song – after the second Antistrophe. In *Chronochromie*'s culminating *Epôde*, the free rhythm of twenty-one different birdsongs supplants the symmetrical permutations and chord cycles of earlier movements.

The symmetrical permutation series

Messiaen first employed symmetrical permutations of a twelve-note series in *Mode de valeurs et d'intensitiés* (1949), the first of the *Quatre Etudes de rythme*, but they return in a more systematic form in the fourth étude *Ile de feu* II (1950).[15] Messiaen begins with a chromatic scale of durations in which order and duration are equivalent, then re-orders the durations according to a pattern that begins in the middle and works outwards. This pattern is used as an algorithm to generate succeeding permutations (or *interversion*, in his nomenclature) by mapping each new series (renumbered from 1 to 12) according to the permutation. As in the Modes of Limited Transpositions or the non-retrogradable rhythms, Messiaen locates the 'charm of impossibilities' in the inherent limitations his algorithm affords. The cycle in *Ile de feu* II generates only 10 individual duration series (rather than 12) because the values 5 and 10 map on to one another.[16] This technique takes on

[13] Lucretius, *De rerum natura* (*On the Nature of Things*), trans. William Ellery Leonard (E. P. Dutton), 1916, v. 1379–83.

[14] According to Messiaen, the durations of *Strophe* I are 'coloured' in three ways: through timbre, harmonic chord type, and through melodic counterpoint 'qui monnayent plus ou moins chaque durée.' *TRCO*, Tome III, 84–5; cf. *Musique et couleur: nouveaux entretiens* (Paris: Belfond, 1986), Claude Samuel, *Olivier Messiaen: Music and*

Color: Conversations with Claude Samuel, trans. E. Thomas Glasow (Portland, OR: Amadeus Press, 1994), p. 135.

[15] In the last couplet of *Cantéyodjayâ*, Messiaen used a limited serial arrangement; three groups of eight different notes are each assigned a fixed duration, register and intensity, yet employed freely within a three-part texture. See Robert Sherlaw Johnson, *Messiaen* (Berkeley: University of California Press, 1975), pp. 103–4.

[16] Messiaen, *TMLM*, cited in Johnson pp. 108–9.

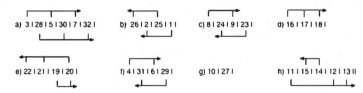

Figure 7.1: The symmetrical permutation series and its partitions

great importance when larger cycles are employed, as explained in exquisite detail at the beginning of Tome III of *TRCO*. Here Messiaen describes how his chosen permutation tames the chromatic cycle that forms the foundation of *Chronochromie*, which otherwise could produce 2.63131×10^{35} permutations. This eight-part formula employs as many transformations as the composer can squeeze out of a thirty-two-note series based on additive durations of a demisemiquaver (Fig. 7.1):[17]

1) the beginning and ends of the series overlap, both right to left (pattern a) and in retrograde (patterns b, c and f);
2) one chromatic segment is retained (pattern d);
3) one chromatic segment is reshuffled internally (patterns e and h); and
4) one large jump (pattern g) from the crotchet tied to a semiquaver that lands on the central node of the formula:
5) the twenty-seventh duration, whose order remains commensurate with its length because it will always map on to itself.

As with the permutation scheme itself, each individual permutation will contain a continuum of variation from the specific to the general. Within the first three permutations, certain durations will be reordered, while others will retain fixed relations of contiguity or order. For instance, the values 19, 20 and 21 will always occupy order numbers 19–21, although each successive permutation of the series will map duration 19, 20 and 21 to a different number of the three-note series. Yet duration 22 will always succeed duration 18, at varying order numbers, while the pairs 14, 13 and 7, 26 will always appear in succession at one duration removed (14–12–13, 14–26–13, etc.). As a recurring feature of the algorithm two numbers in succession will part at the next generation, to be 'reunited' at a different order number in the following series (in permutations 1–3 these pairs are 11, 15 and 31, 6). And finally, at a more general level of 'repetition', values 3 and 6 will always either precede or follow a duration at least nine times or four times its size, respectively

[17] *TRCO*, Tome III, pp. 7–37. The list of 36 permutations is succeeded by 12 superpositions of each of three successive generations in series – permutations 1, 2 and 3; permutations 4, 5 and 6, etc. – with examples of how portions of these appear in *Couleurs de la cité céleste* and the fourth movement of *Éclairs sur l'au-delà . . .*, pp. 39–73.

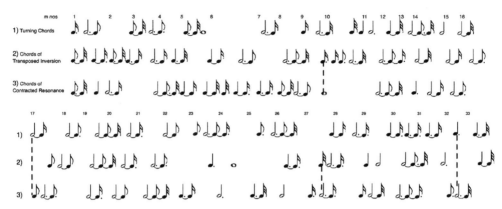

Figure 7.2: Simultaneous attacks between juxtaposed symmetrical permutations, *Strophe* I

(in permutations 1–3 the patterns produced are 13–28, 29–3 and 3–27 and 6–25, 6–25 and 31–6–29).

Messiaen's control of the permutation series assures a mathematical balance between repetition and variation, with a 'quilting point' approximately four-fifths of the way through the cycle, where order and duration merge in a dotted minim tied to a dotted semiquaver.[18] This point of unity among all possible permutations is prepared for by subtle variations on order numbers 19–26, in which the same durations always occupy order numbers 19–21, followed by a five-note segment that continually interlaces durations from opposite ends of the spectrum. Yet the 'charm' of these variations remains largely impossible to hear, and surfaces only briefly at four points within the juxtaposed cycles, during which chords in different layers simultaneously attack (I will return to this point below).

Messiaen has thus chosen his permutational algorithm to achieve a balance between repetition and variety: small and large durations are interwoven throughout each permutation. Each rhythmic cycle has a similar durational arc which peaks approximately two-thirds of the way through with a series of longer durations which in effect 'slow down' the cycle. Yet, when three different permutations are juxtaposed, the combined effect generates a slower-moving rhythm, marked off by those points where two of three cycles attack simultaneously, as shown by dotted lines between layers in Fig. 7.2.

[18]The term 'quilting point' is a translation of Jacques Lacan's concept of *point de caption*, that place in language when the unruly signifier is 'stitched' to the signified to produce meaning, creating a suture in the realm of the symbolic. By using this term to describe Messiaen's permutation series I mean to invoke a double metaphor. As a feature of the series, order and duration are knit together in one central value that serves as a constant through all possible permutations of the duration series. In a larger sense, by assigning a uniform value to the same order number in each permutation, what seems like an arbitrary and contingent pattern proves anything but: the universal recurrence of duration 27 as the twenty-seventh member of the series assigns *meaning* to the permutational algorithm.

Messiaen's chords of many colours

Messiaen scholars have largely ignored the so-called 'colour-chords' that dominate Messiaen's later music in favour of exhaustive description and analysis of his modal harmonies, and those chords that can be easily related to diatonic harmonies.[19] In recent years Vincent Benitez and Cheong Wai-Ling have published studies of these harmonies commensurate with the publication of Tomes III–VII of *TRCO*, clarifying their use and equivalence to earlier harmonies (when that can be determined).[20] No doubt *Chronochromie's* difficulty is enhanced by the fact that its three permutations (permutation 1 in first violin, permutation 2 in second violin, and permutation 3 in viola and cello) are composed of three of these chord types: the turning chord (TC), the chord of transposed inversion on the same bass note (CTI) and the chord of contracted resonance (CCR).[21]

As Wai-Ling notes, the third tome of the *Traité* contains everything we need to construct the latter chord tables of the seventh tome, yet little in the way of explanation regarding their use or derivation.[22] The three TC in the eighth table (Fig. 7.3) are simply presented as A, B and C, eight-note verticalities separated into two tetrachords by pitch content and registration.

[19] The three chord types discussed in this chapter were discussed in Claude Samuel, *Entretiens avec Olivier Messiaen* (Paris: Belfond, 1967), translated by Felix Aprahamian as *Conversation with Olivier Messiaen* (London: Stainer & Bell, 1976), and repeated with more clarity in Claude Samuel, *Olivier Messiaen: Music and Color*. Yet there are few discussions of them in the literature before the publication of the *TRCO*'s first three Tomes in 1994–96. Anthony Pople discusses only modal, 'bimodal' and tonal harmonies in 'Messiaen's Musical Language: An Introduction', in Hill (ed.), *The Messiaen Companion*, pp. 15–50, while Sherlaw Johnson lumps all non-modal chords into the vague category 'colour-chords' (*Messiaen*, pp. 19, 129, 136–7, 168–70, 175). Jonathan Bernard states, 'None of these is ever defined', with regard to turning chords, chords of contracted resonance and chords of inverted transposition, continuing that 'all that is really clear about them is that they are non-modal' ('Colour', in Hill (ed.), *The Messiaen Companion*, pp. 211–12). Most attempts at a broader analysis of Messiaen's harmonic language concern themselves only with the Modes of Limited Transpositions; see especially Christoph Neidhöfer, 'A Theory of Harmony and Voice Leading for the Music of Olivier

Messiaen', *Music Theory Spectrum*, Vol. 27, no. 1 (2002), 1–34.

[20] Vincent P. Benitez, 'Aspects of Harmony in Messiaen's Later Music: An Examination of the Chords of Transposed Inversions on the Same Bass Note', *Journal of Musicological Research*, Vol. 23 (2004), 187–226; Cheong Wai-Ling, 'Rediscovering Messiaen's Invented Chords', *Acta Musicologica* Vol. 75, no. 1 (2003), 85–105, 'Messiaen's Chord Tables: Ordering the Disordered', *Tempo*, Vol. 57, no. 226 (2003), 2–10, and 'Composing with Pre-composed Chords in the Finale of *Et exspecto resurrectionem mortuorum*', *Revue de Musicologie* Vol. 90, no.1 (2004), 115–132; Messiaen, *TRCO*, Tomes I–VII (Paris: Leduc, 1994–2002).

[21] Wai-Ling identifies two forms of the chord of contracted resonance that she dubs the first and second CCR. My use of the term 'CCR' in this chapter is equivalent to Wai-Ling's first CCR. 'Rediscovering Messiaen's Invented Chords', 88ff. She locates TC-like progressions in Messiaen's *TMLM*, using the common perfect fourth in the lowest register as a guide, but does not find the chord described as such prior to the third tome of *TRCO*; 'Messiaen's Chord Tables', 3.

[22] *TRCO*, Tome III, pp. 85–88.

Figure 7.3: Messiaen's eighth table of the turning chords from *TRCO* Tomes III and VII

Figure 7.4: The first sonority in *Strophe* I

These chords in various transpositions generate the first permutation, given to the first violins. The three octachords as presented in *Traité* III share five pitch-classes among them, yet maintenance of a strict vertical spacing between adjacent voices suggests that their connection relies more on pitch and interval-specific connections. Our aural attention is drawn less to the those pitch-classes held in common (1, 3, 4, 5, 8) than to the minor sixth (F4 – D♭5) held invariant between chords A and B, and the augmented octave (E♭4–E5) held invariant between chords B and C.[23] The extreme chromaticism of the TC (set-classes 8–4, 8–5 and 8–14 respectively) is offset by their intervallic arrangement, in which chords A and B share not only the fourth but also a major seventh and compound tritone over the bass.[24] Chords A and C share a fifth over the bass, but the latter has a much more open and expansive sound than the first two chords of the cycle (set 8–14 intersects with the diatonic collection to produce an equal saturation of fourths/fifths). Because of their extreme chromaticism, it is difficult to derive the TC from an extended dominant chord, as Messiaen does with other 'colour chords.' The turning chords occupy the highest register in *Strophe* I; they seem therefore, by virtue of their register, to represent the upper partials of the chords that occupy the lower strata in viola and cello. For instance, Fig. 7.4 is a harmonic reduction of the first sonority in *Strophe* I in which each note of the TC (represented by the cross-hatched grey notehead F♯4 [shared with the CTI] and the white noteheads A4, D5, E5, G♯5, D♭6, E♭6 and G6) can be explained as one of the first seven harmonics of D♭2 or E♭3, or as the first harmonic of A3, D4 and E4 (members of the CCR chord in low strings represented by the seven black noteheads).

[23] Throughout the text I use scientific pitch notation, in which, for example, octave 2 represents the pitches C2 to B2 inclusive.
[24] Throughout this chapter, I use Forte labels for pitch-class sets, as defined in Allen Forte, *The Structure of Atonal Music* (New Haven: Yale University Press, 1973). These are used for comparison only, as Messiaen's chord types are further defined by voicing and registration.

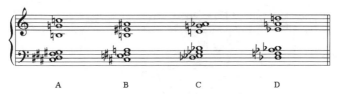

Figure 7.5: The chords of transposed inversion on the same bass note

The four CTI populate the second permutation of *Strophe* I (Fig. 7.5). Unlike their counterparts above and below, all four CTI represent the same set class (7–20). Yet, as their name implies, they appear inverted in the *Traité's* chord tables over a common bass note.

Messiaen describes the genesis of the CTI in detail: the third of a dominant ninth chord built on C♯3 is replaced with its note of resolution a semitone above (F♯3). The ninth is displaced down an octave (D♯3), while two appoggiaturas are placed at a compound tritone and compound major seventh over the root. These resonance elements, as Vincent Benitez describes G4 and C5, are held fast while the chord below is transposed in first, second and fourth inversions (Fig. 7.5: chords B, C and D respectively).[25] The 'virtual' tonic appears as a fourth over the bass in root position, stressing – as in the TC – the foundational interval of a fourth, which characterises both 'root' position, first, and second inversion CTI chords.

The bottom pentachord of the chord pair A and B, and the bottom tetrachord of the chord pair C and D, are related by inversion at T_0I and $T_{11}I$ respectively. As members of set-class 7–20 (characterised by an emphasis on ic5), the four inversions turn the second layer of permutations into a kind of mid-range harmonic ostinato that mediates between the resonant turning chords in octaves 5–7, and the dense chords of contracted resonance in (primarily) octaves 2–4.[26] If we take the content of the 'root' position A chord as representative of the set-class, B appears as chord A transposed at T_{10} or $(A)T_{10}$, C as $(A)T_7$ and D as $(A)T_2$: transpositions of the first chord in the table by intervals with strong functional associations, the major second/minor tenth and perfect fifth. Yet permutation 2 of Fig. 7.7 does not begin with four chords built on the same bass note. Messiaen instead chooses CTI(C) on A3 and follows it with three chords related by T_6, T_4 and T_1.

As with the TC, Messiaen doesn't say much about the chords of contracted resonance. He presents their genesis as a dominant-ninth chord built on E♭, whose third has been replaced with a fourth above the root: A♭ (one assumes, as with the chords of TI, the 'leading-tone' has been replaced with its note of

[25] Benitez, 'Aspects of Harmony in Messiaen's Later Music: An Examination of the Chords of Transposed Inversions on the Same Bass Note', 187–226.

[26] Interval class (ic) 5 represents both the perfect fourth and fifth; set-class 7–20 contains five potential fourths/fifths.

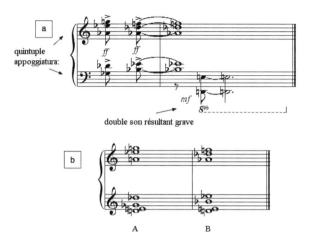

Figure 7.6: The chords of contracted resonance

resolution).[27] This chord is then shown in second inversion, preceded by a quintuple appoggiatura chord that approaches the seventh and ninth (F5 and Db5) from above by whole step, and the remaining tones (Bb, Eb and Ab) from below by major third, whole step and half-step respectively (Gb, Db, A). The goal chord becomes the second chord of contracted resonance, while the appoggiatura notes are 'frozen' as CCR(A). Both chords are then supported by a major ninth from D1–E2, an 'inferior resonance' (*résonance inférieure*) over which the initial chord rings (Fig. 7.6a). The ninth 'contracts' to the fourth octave and is placed under both the appoggiatura chord and the Eb chord in second inversion to produce the first category of chords of contracted resonance (Fig. 7.6b).[28] With only two CCR, this chord type dominates the texture (chord B appears once more than chord A). Both chords share a major seventh and minor ninth over the bass, and, as z-related septachords, CCR(A) and CCR(B) have the same interval vector, <444342>.[29]

All three chord types share several features of utmost importance to Messiaen's later works: they are neither transpositionally nor inversionally symmetrical, and appear only in transposition at specific pitch levels (transpositional levels that occupy a common register). Symmetrical chords, such as those drawn from Messiaen's modes of limited transposition, will duplicate

[27] *TRCO*, Tome III, p. 87.

[28] Wai-Ling clarifies Messiaen's scattered references to this chord, and identifies first and second CCR in *Quatuor* and *Visions*, 'Rediscovering Messiaen's Invented Chords', 87, 89ff. Although Tome III offers a full description of the symmetrical permutations, the complete tables of Messiaen's colour-chords as they appear in *Chronochromie* do not appear

until Tome VII. These tables are referenced in the abstract in Wai-Ling, 'Rediscovering Messiaen's Invented Chords', 103–5.

[29] Z-related chords are two different set-classes of the same cardinality that share the same interval vector (i.e. neither set can generate the other through transposition or inversion, but each contains the same interval classes in equal number).

their pitch content at 1 or more levels of transposition or inversion, but the 'colour chords' offer a maximum of pitch variety: 36 possible TC, 48 possible CTI and 24 possible CCR, with no obvious indication that any particular transposition was favoured over another. At the same time Messiaen exploits chord contrasts by restricting the number of transpositions employed, to feature different chord types over the same bass note (as in the 4 CTI on C♯3 and 2 CCR on D4 in Fig. 7.5 and Fig. 7.6, and the simultaneous use of TC(A) on A4 (white noteheads, Fig. 7.4) and CTI(C) on A3 (cross-hatched grey noteheads, Fig. 7.4). Although each chord has at times appeared as a dominant-type chord in Messiaen's *œuvre*, in *Chronochromie* these chords are divorced from any harmonic function, and form merely an associational network of relations.[30]

Their autonomy is underlined by Messiaen's careful attribution of precise colours for each chord in *TRCO*, Tome III, a quality tied to its intervallic arrangement and, in some cases, its register.[31] Although all six set-classes represented by the chords in *Strophe* I (7–20, 7–z12, 7–z36, 8–4, 8–5 and 8–14) share three pentachords (only one of which is diatonic, 5–29) and thirteen tetrachords, the only inclusion relation among them is 7–20/8–14 (8–4 and 8–5 do not contain any of the septads). The chords CTI(A), CTI(C), CCR(A) and CCR(B) all feature a major second as the lowest interval. Yet all six set-classes feature a relatively even distribution of intervals, which make the aural identification of any distinct chord type particularly difficult (ic5 slightly dominates the interval vectors for 7–z12/7–z36 and 8–14, while ic1 dominates in 8–4 and 8–5).

Messiaen presents the complete transposition tables of all three chord types in Tome VII of *TRCO*, without any apparent link to the pattern of transpositions in *Strophe* I. The transposition of chords within each permutation follows no evident functional or serial scheme. In the same way that the durational permutations include a few segments that retain the order of the original series (Fig. 7.1, segments d, e and h), so there are two spots in which the series of chords follows that of the original chord tables (permutation 2 cycles through all four CTI from table 8 and table 3 at order numbers 10–13 and 19–22 respectively). Fig. 7.7 represents the 'figured bass' of all three permutations: an ordered series of bass notes harmonised by chords drawn from their respective chord tables (Fig. 7.3, 7.5 and 7.6). The combined nineteen-note sonority in Fig. 7.4 is here represented by TC(A) on A4 in permutation 1, CTI(C) on A3 in permutation 2, and CCR(B) on D♭3 in permutation 3.

---

[30] See Benitez, 'Aspects of Harmony in Messiaen's Later Music: An Examination of the Chords of Transposed Inversions on the same Bass Note', 213ff., for illustrations of the CTI in both functional and atonal contexts.

[31] For instance, the three TC have a 'global' effect of 'pale yellow, streaked with white, black and grey, with green spots.' Yet chord A is described as 'pale yellow, mauve, – pinkish copper, pearl grey'. *TRCO*, Tome III, p. 85.

Figure 7.7: The three symmetrical permutations in *Strophe* I represented as an ordered series of bass notes harmonised with chords drawn from the tables in Fig. 7.3, 7.5 and 7.6.

After this simultaneous attack, the rhythmic permutations pull away from one another (the vertical alignment of bass notes indicates chord order *sans duration*); successive notes indicate a transposition of the initial chords, taken directly from the tables in the *Traité*, Tome VII. The dotted lines indicate those four points at which any two of the three permutations attack together.

The three permutations of 32 chords form a resultant series of 96 individual chords distinguished by similar movement from each member to a related chord.[32] Within the registral band occupied by each permutation, bass motions up or down by perfect fifth/fourth (e.g. permutation 1, chords 3–4), or by semitone (e.g. permutation 3, chords 7–8), stand out in this succession. But without a repeated pattern, or a perceptible teleology (beyond completion of the series), the overall scheme is dominated by harmonic stasis and rigidity.

Yet *Strophe* I is the very picture of change: the three permutation cycles meet only at the movement's outset, and the chord types and pitch levels are in constant flux. A range graph of the first 9½ measures of *Strophe* I

---

[32] Parallel motion between two instances of the same chord type occurs five times: twice in permutation 2, between chords 13 and 14 (CTI(B) from G♯3–C♯4) and chords 28 and 29 (CTI(D) from G♭4–B♭4), and thrice in permutation 3, between chords 15 and 16 (CCR(B) from A3–F3), chords 22 and 23 (CCR(B) from C3–F3) and chords 30–31 (CCR(A) from F♯3–E♭3).

(Fig. 7.8) displays permutations 1, 2 and 3 as a sequence of vertical sonorities. The horizontal axis of the graph represents time as an ordered series of attacks, while the vertical axis indicates pitch height in semitones. Varied shades of grey tied to register illustrate the separate yet overlapping range of each permutation (the TC in first violins appear in the three lightest shades of grey, while the CTI in second violins appear in the four medium shades, and the CCR in low strings are marked in dark grey and black). As the graph implies, the homogenous timbre and disjunct spacing of each chord strand blur the identity of simultaneous layers. The confusion between successive and simultaneous shades of grey serves as a visual analogue to Messiaen's emphasis on individual chord 'colour' and resonance at the expense of voice-leading or harmonic connections between chords.

Although 55 different chords appear in *Strophe* I, Messiaen restricts the register and number of transpositional levels allotted to each chord type. Out of 36 possible chords, he uses but 23; TC(A) built on E4 (taken from the first table of the *Traité*) and TC(A) built on C4 and C5 (taken from the fifth) each appear three times, while the following chord types each appear twice – TC(A) from the fourth table, TC(B) from the fifth and tenth tables, and TC(C) from the fifth and ninth tables. Slightly more than half (26) of 48 possible CTI appear, including all the chords in the third and eighth tables, and three chords each from tables 6, 9, 10 and 11. Each of the twelve possible transpositions of set-class 7–20 is represented, but there is a proportional scale that regulates their appearance: four occurrences each of three sets, three occurrences each of three sets, two occurrences each of five sets, and one occurrence of one set.[33] Of 24 possible chords of contracted resonance, 16 different forms appear on only 10 different pitch-classes, but these represent all but two of the chord tables sketched out in Tome VII of the *Traité*.

The harmonic language of *Chronochromie* is steeped in the 'charm of impossibilities': six set-classes, in but nine arrangements, are employed at a limited but evenly graded number of transpositional levels. The chromatic saturation of pitch-space defies us to hear individual chord successions, yet we are conscious of the 'colour of time' as separate strands of percussion highlight each individual chord layer, analogous to the birds in reeds and keyed percussion, whose diminuted songs colour the relentless march of the rhythmic cycle.[34] The shaded registral graph in Fig. 7.8 implies that the

[33] In normal form these would be the collections [1,2,3,6,7,8,10], [3,4,5,8,9,10,0] and [5,6,7,10,11,0,2], four times each; [6,7,8,11,0,1,3], [8,9,10,1,2,3,5] and [9,10,11,2,3,4,6], three times each; [0,1,2,5,6,7,9], [2,3,4,7,8,9,11], [4,5,6,9,10,11,1], [10,11,0,3,4,5,7] and [11,0,1,4,5,6,8], two times each, and [7,8,9,0,1,2,4] once.

[34] Ian Darbyshire suggests that Messiaen chose the term 'colour' in his commentary to suggest the function of the bird songs in obscuring the rhythmic series, as the root of the word 'colour' means 'to hide or cover'; 'Messiaen and the Representation of the Theological Illusion of Time', *Messiaen's Language of Mystical Love*, 33–54; 50, n. 42.

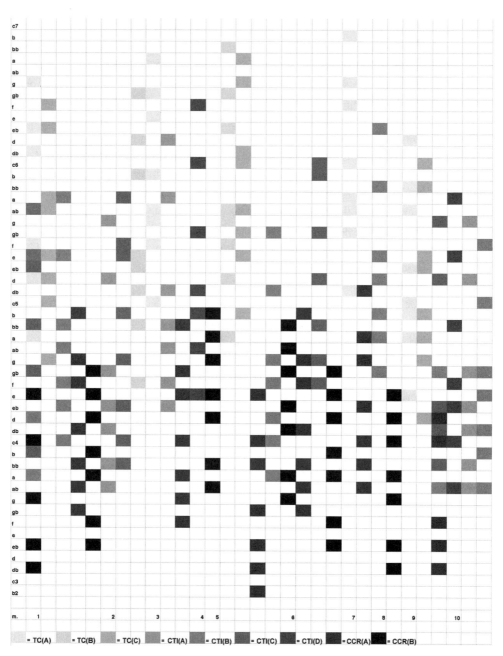

Figure 7.8: Registral graph of the first 9½ measures of the three symmetrical permutations as they appear in *Strophe* I

relative ambitus of each permutation – although it may overlap with its neighbours – is the most audible signifier of each individual cycle; e.g., as only two chord types populate the lowest register, the CCR take on the function of a ground bass, while the mid-range CTI bear the characteristics of a tenor line. The chords of contracted resonance function as a foundation for the shifting chords above, and impart their own subtle harmonic rhythm, as ninety per cent of the time CCR(A) moves to CCR(B) and vice versa. The minting of the permutations through birdcalls, and the perception of a 'passacaglia' bass formed of two chords of contracted resonance, are but shadows of the underlying complexities woven into the harmonic and rhythmic fabric, whose overall substance seems beyond our conscious apprehension. Yet we are also aware, at some unconscious level, that *Chronochromie* offers both freedom and limitation as more than simply a metaphorical representation of the 'charm of impossibilities'.

Understanding *Chronochromie*

Given the evident difficulties composed into *Chronochromie*, we might ask several questions of Messiaen. First and foremost is how we are to understand the 'power' exercised by the mathematical impossibilities inherent in the symmetrical permutations, especially when their overall effect appears to be relatively anodyne. Roberto Fabbi and Jean Marie Wu attempt to deal with the intractable but unavoidable paradoxes inherent in Messiaen's fascination with this power, beginning with the music itself. Why combine symmetrical permutations and schematic chord patterns in such a manner that they are 'probably better understood mentally and felt subliminally than consciously perceived aurally'?[35] Indeed, although (relatively) 'easily seen and understood in the abstract', Messiaen's presentation of both the symmetrical permutations and their accompanying harmonies suggests that their power extends beyond the virtual; that the instantiation in music of non-retrogradable rhythms, modal harmonies and symmetrical permutations have an impact that exceeds their intellectual contemplation as abstract pattern.[36] As Fabbi notes:

> It must be admitted that there is something odd about this 'phenomenon'. Although the expression describing it appears at the beginning of an essay on compositional technique, [the phrase 'charm of impossibilities'] is utterly foreign to specialist jargon, conceptually opaque, paradoxical, and attempts to classify precise technical elements with works of almost poetical resonance. It calls into play types of experience that one normally considers to be of an opposite nature: the sensual and emotional experience of 'charm' and the intellectual, rational experience of 'impossibilities'. It invites us to project technical information onto a wider plane.[37]

[35] Jean Marie Wu, 'Mystical Symbols of Faith: Olivier Messiaen's Charm of Impossibilities', *Messiaen's Language of Mystical Love*, 85–120, 108.

[36] Wu, 'Mystical Symbols of Faith: Olivier Messiaen's Charm of Impossibilities', p. 108.

[37] Fabbi, 'Theological Implications of Restrictions in Messiaen's Compositional Processes', p. 55.

If such restrictions are at the philosophical heart of Messiaen's music, we may indeed project them beyond the parameters of rhythm and harmony, to questions of form and genre. History (in the form of Greek poetics), and nature (in the form of birdsong) place *a priori* limits on the form and melodic scope of *Chronochromie*, as paradigms with strong and timeless associations. And both Greek lyric and the songs of the birds serve as easily available references for the scholar of Messiaen's music. As if to duplicate the transparency and universality of these models, Messiaen lays bare the artifice of his harmonic and rhythmic language in the *Traité*. The third tome records, in paraphrastic detail, every detail of not only *Chronochromie's* composition but also its wider context, as a specific representation of a circumscribed but expressively rich world of possibilities. Over the span of 66 pages (!) we are presented with all 36 possible inversions of Messiaen's original 32-member durational pattern, followed by the juxtaposition of each three successive permutations (*interversions* 1–3, 4–6, etc.).[38] The same tome includes a detailed list of birds and their characteristics as found in each movement, along with, as noted above, a description of each chord type represented in *Strophe* I.

Lest we wonder why harmony receives less attention than rhythm, the final tome of the *Traité* details every possible transposition of each of five categories of colour chords (to produce sixty in total), including the three types that populate *Strophe* I of *Chronochromie*: the chords of transposed inversions, the chords of contracted resonance and the turning chords. Yet Messiaen rarely links the chord to its effect, or compositional purpose.

If we ask why a composer so invested in the mysterious and transcendent would so obsessively document his own work, we are reminded that, as Ian Darbyshire notes, Messiaen writes theological, as opposed to mystical, music.[39] There is a pedagogical insistency to his work, one that seeks to deepen the music's mystery even as he lays bare his materials. Yet how can such utterly personal music, chords that shimmer with a colour only the composer can see, communicate with an audience for whom the 'colour of time' must remain a metaphor, if a very powerful one? Chromæsthesia such as that evinced by Messiaen is not only rare but also utterly unique.[40] The composer answers:

> When I hear music – and it was already like that when I was a child – I see colours. Chords are expressed in terms of colours for me – for example, a yellowish orange with a reddish tinge. I'm convinced that one can convey this to the listening public.[41]

---

[38] *TRCO*, Tome III, pp. 7–38.
[39] Darbyshire, 'Messiaen and the Representation of the Theological Illusion of Time', p. 33.
[40] Discussed in Greta Berman, 'Synesthesia and the Arts', *Leonardo*, Vol. 32, no. 1 (1999), 15–22.
[41] Messiaen quoted in Rößler, *Contributions to the Spiritual World of Olivier Messiaen*, p. 54.

But by comparing his symbolic language to the secret language forged by the early Christians, Messiaen implies that only the initiate can truly grasp his meaning.[42] The composer's own analyses demonstrate this paradox *a fortiori*. Once the symmetrical rhythms and coloured harmonies are described, and their limitations multiplied by the expansion or juxtaposition of materials, one is left to surrender to a rather opaque, all-inclusive notion of spirituality: 'And so, the symmetrical permutations of *Chronochromie* illustrate the mystical experience of eternity that was behind Messiaen's exploration of time.'[43] But how does one begin to grasp the expression of 'everything super-terrestrial, everything that's supernatural'?[44]

The impossible ear

The French empiricist philosopher Gilles Deleuze conceived music as that which materially, in an open system of difference in conjunction with nature, territorialises the world it inhabits. In the form of the ritornello, music is a powerful means of staking out a territory, a region that, as Ronald Bogue defines it, is composed of 'irregular patterns of differential relations that have a certain autonomy in respect to the heterogeneous elements they combine'.[45] Messiaen's concept of music as an expression of the eternal divine may seem a far cry from this definition, yet for Deleuze, Messiaen's music represented the joyful engagement of cosmic forces. Deleuze was concerned with immanence, the empirical real, a philosophical stance that eschews universal essence for analysis of the relations between and among things. An object does not belong to a transcendental category (table, for instance), but has existence in a field or territory; the meaning of a table arises from its interaction with other objects, its social function and the productive relations of which it is a part (e.g. the family sitting down to a meal at home). When one sings a tune, a 'ritornello', one may be marking time while working, or expressing a strong emotion, or

---

[42] 'I've written my theme into the notes, into the music itself, so that future generations will be able to recognise this theme again. I'm like the first Christians who'd invented a secret written language which could be read from top to bottom and the other way around, from right to left and the other way around, from all angles and in every direction, and which always produced a cross-shape with alpha and omega ... they wrote these cryptograms on the walls of the catacombs to make themselves known to each other and, at the same time, to protect themselves from their persecutors.'

Messiaen quoted in Rößler, *Contributions to the Spiritual World of Olivier Messiaen*, pp. 54–5.

[43] Wu, 'Mystical Symbols of Faith: Olivier Messiaen's Charm of Impossibilities', p. 112.

[44] Rößler, *Contributions to the Spiritual World of Olivier Messiaen*, p. 54.

[45] Ronald Bogue, *Deleuze on Music, Painting and the Arts* (London: Routledge, 2003), p. 13; Gilles Deleuze and Félix Guattari, *A Thousand Plateaux: Capitalism and Schizophrenia*, trans. Brian Massumi (University of Minnesota Press, 1987), p. 299.

travelling from one place to another.[46] Music is thus an active agent in defining and establishing territory, an active field of relations that connects history, nation and sound with individuals.

Those three fundamental elements that appear on the surface to co-exist in *Chronochromie* as radical contingencies – birdsong, the symmetrical permutations, and the 'colour-chords' – occupy related roles in Messiaen's music. Deleuze's musical aesthetics likewise revolve around birdsong, rhythm and the role of formal considerations as they relate to temporality. Birdsong establishes continuity among human and non-human species in 'their modes of occupying space and establishing interspecific and conspecific relationships': the way they territorialise their environment and interact with other birds and humans.[47] The autonomous elements that compose a bird's song are a combination of its innate proclivity towards song as shaped by its environment, distinguishing that bird in that place with what can only be called its own 'style'.[48] Likewise the Hindu *deçi-tâlas* favoured by Messiaen in his earlier compositions were once associated with a region, mood and character, but have been 'deterritorialised' within his music.[49]

The territorialisation through song involves a particular relation to time. Time, as divided into *Chronos* and *Aion*, relates sonority, form and rhythm to one another, the first marking off time linearly into units and the second representing a reversible, ametric kind of 'timeless' time. For the Stoics, *Chronos* was a time of bodies, while *Aion* represented the incorporeal. *Chronos* is therefore pulsed time, but, as Deleuze stresses, not periodic time:

> [You] have a pulsed time when you find yourself always before three coordinates. It suffices that there be only one of the three. A pulsed time is always a territorialized time; regular or not, it's the number of the movement of the step that marks a territory: I cover [*parcours*] my territory! I can cover it in a thousand ways, not necessarily in a regular rhythm. Each time that I cover or haunt a territory, each time that I claim a territory as mine, I appropriate a pulsed time, or I beat [pulse] a time.[50]

There are are three general forms of time, of radically different scale. The simplest form of pulsed time is the refrain (*ritournelle*), which occupies a space that is not yet musical: an inchoate musical form with the intent to

---

[46] Deleuze, speaking to Claire Parnet in the documentary by Pierre-André Boutang, *L'Abécédaire de Gilles Deleuze*, 'O comme Opéra', transcribed by Charles Stivale, *Summary of 'Gilles Deleuze's ABC Primer' (L'Abécédaire de Gilles Deleuze, 1988/1995)*, http://www.langlab.wayne.edu/CStivale/D-G/ABC3.html.

[47] Bogue, *Deleuze on Music, Painting and the Arts*, p. 13.

[48] Bogue, *Deleuze on Music, Painting and the Arts*, p. 22; Deleuze and Guattari, *A Thousand Plateaus: Capitalism and Schizophrenia*, p. 319.

[49] Deleuze and Guattari, *A Thousand Plateaux: Capitalism and Schizophrenia*, p. 300.

[50] Gilles Deleuze, 'Vincennes Seminar Session of May 3, 1977: On Music', trans. Timothy S. Murphy, *Discourse: Journal for Theoretical Studies in Media and Culture*, Vol. 20, no. 3 (1998), 208–9.

mark out a musical territory. The second characteristic of pulsed time is 'a time which marks the temporality of a form in development'. There exists a third form, what the Germans call *Bildung*, or what poststructuralists would call 'subject formation'.[51]

On the level of musical structure, the refrain both marks and groups a 'territory', correlating internal impulses with external circumstances, as the autonomous chord structures within *Strophe* I of *Chronochromie* are ordered by the symmetrical permutations, and the permutations in turn are constrained by the seven-part formal design.[52] It is the job of great composers to deterritorialise the refrain in general; that is, to unsettle conventions and invent 'a sort of diagonal between the harmonic vertical and the melodic horizon'.[53] With Messiaen this deterritorialisation of the refrain is even more personal than the calculated juxtaposition of received and natural elements, for it is filtered through his own 'coloured' hearing and his personal experience with birds in the wild. Messiaen deterritorialises the temporal realm by identifying not only a quantitative but also a dynamic and phonetic order of rhythm, as in his analysis of Stravinsky's *Le Sacre du printemps*, and his well-developed notion of *personnages rythmiques*.[54]

A movement of deterritorialisation is at the same time the release (*dégagement*) of a non-pulsed time, in a movement toward becoming something other. Deleuze's prime example of such a 'deterritorialization' was in fact Messiaen's transcriptions of birdsong, through which 'the bird becomes something other than music, at the same time that the music becomes bird'.[55] Messiaen's birds no longer mark a specific territory out there in the world but become 'in sound something other, something absolute, night, death, joy – certainly not a generality or a simplification, but a haececity, *this* death, that night'.[56] The notion of this becoming is neither imitative nor figurative. In much the same way, Messiaen's rhythmic innovations involve a time of heterogeneous durations, no longer pulsed time,

---

[51] Deleuze, 'Vincennes Seminar Session of May 3, 1977: On Music', 209.

[52] Bogue, *Deleuze on Music, Painting and the Arts*, pp. 19–22. I have left out the sticky but perhaps necessary notion of *milieu* as well as the definition of territorialisation as defined by Deleuze and Guattari. They define a *milieu* as 'a coded block of space-time', a code being defined by 'periodic repetition', and describe territorialization in terms of 'rhythm that has become expressive', and 'milieu components that have become qualitative'. Deleuze and Guattari, *A Thousand Plateaux: Capitalism and Schizophrenia*, pp. 313, 315.

[53] Deleuze and Guattari, *A Thousand Plateaux: Capitalism and Schizophrenia*, p. 296.

[54] *TRCO*, Tome II, pp. 97–147. Cf. Gareth Healey, 'Messiaen and the Concept of 'Personnages', *Tempo*, Vol. 58, no. 230 (October 2004), 10–19.

[55] Deleuze, 'Vincennes Seminar Session, May 3, 1977: On Music', 210–11.

[56] Deleuze and Guattari's notion of *haececity* is an attempt to defeat the static and stratifying effect of nouns within language, to remind the reader of the uniqueness of every thing as it is born in the moment. The thing thus disappears, to be replaced by the event, and the thing-as-becoming. Deleuze and Guattari, *A Thousand Plateaux: Capitalism and Schizophrenia*, p. 304.

and no longer dependent on a unifying metrical form.[57] As the composer states:

> The musician possesses a mysterious power: by means of his rhythms, he can chop
> up Time here and there, and can even put it together again in the reverse order, a
> little as though he were going for a walk through different points of time, or as
> though he were amassing the future by turning to the past, in the process of which,
> his memory of the past becomes transformed into a memory of the future.[58]

This non-pulsed time represents the same kind of freedom attained by generalised chromaticism (the free use of all twelve tones) in twentieth-century musical modernism. The notions of sonorous landscape, audible colours and rhythmic characters all represent a process of individuation, part of the floating time that marks becoming: the time of *Aion*, made only of lines, not points.[59]

> [We] might consider the sound–color relation as a simple association, or a
> synaesthesia, but we can consider the durations or rhythms to be colors in
> themselves, specifically sonorous colors which are superimposed on visible colors.[60]

Virtually any bar in *Chronochromie* illustrates this musical becoming that results from the blurring of previously segregated musical parameters. The symmetrical permutation series slows down in b. 22 of *Strophe* I, as the musical texture expands to admit thirteen simultaneous voices in winds and percussion. The permutation series features TC(B) at T5 in first violins, with an attack of duration 20, CTI(D) at T11, in the midst of duration 30, and CCR(A) at T1 near the end of duration 21. A chorus of no fewer than ten birds soar overhead, each with its own unique call, defined by the motivic reiteration of a rhythmic and melodic pattern. Fig. 7.9 illustrates the rhythmic and contrapuntal interaction of seven bird songs with the harmonic/rhythmic 'ground'. The piccolo plays the role of great titmouse, with demi-semiquaver triplet divisions shared by 1st flute, 2nd clarinet and glockenspiel, against the 2nd flute which moves at half speed (in semiquaver triplets). The remaining voices ornament the slow-moving cycle in strings with demisemiquaver and semiquaver overlapping patterns.

At an octave above, the piccolo's (0,1,6) trichord underlines select notes from permutation 1 while emphasising the interval of a minor ninth (the augmented octave A♭6 to A♭7). Each of the black caps in flute has its own unique octatonic collection, and their motives highlight different intervals

---

[57] Gilles Deleuze, 'Conference Presentation on Musical Time, IRCAM, 1978', trans. Timothy S. Murphy; archived at http://www.webdeleuze.com/php/texte.php?cle=113&groupe=Conf%E9rences&langue=2.

[58] Rößler, *Contributions to the Spiritual World of Olivier Messiaen*, p. 41.

[59] Bogue, *Deleuze on Music, Painting and the Arts*, p. 54.

[60] Deleuze, 'Conference Presentation on Musical Time, IRCAM, 1978'.

Figure 7.9: The rhythmic and contrapuntal interaction of seven birdsongs with the harmonic/rhythmic 'ground' in b. 22 of *Strophe* I

while cutting across the harmonic field of all three permutations. The oboe's icterine warbler echoes the piccolo's (0,1,6) at T_0I, and the 1st clarinet's repeating (0,1,3) trichord at $T_{11}I$, which features a minor ninth echo of its higher neighbour. Yet the second marsh warbler in clarinet 2 moves through two and a half octaves and the total chromatic with a scalar passage that shifts from one diatonic pentad to another. The glockenspiel's wren emphasises the same major seventh from C6 to B6 as that of the 1st clarinet, in the context of a (0,1,4) trichord that resonates with permutation 3 in low strings. But the only wind to actually venture into this range is the 2nd clarinet; the remaining voices accent specific pitches within permutations 1 and 2.

Time most obviously 'becomes' colour in the rhythmic 'minting' of sub-divisions smaller than the demisemiquaver, which affect the timbre of under-lying harmonies in much the same way the irrational rhythmic values in Ligeti's canons affect timbre in his works such as *Lontano* (1967).[61] More significant is how the rendezvous and dispersal of avian voices affects our perception of the rigid permutation scheme. As motives converge and diverge, the changing density of rhythmic attack renders time elastic, while each slowly shifting harmony in strings shimmers as various pitches and intervals are doubled in winds and percussion.

Deleuze, as did Messiaen, looked to the late nineteenth century for the liberation of rhythm from the constraints of pulsed time. Wagner's leitmotifs transcended an external character to take on an autonomous life, 'in a floating non-pulsed time in which they themselves became internal characters'.[62] At the end of the nineteenth century music brought to audibility what it had always contained: 'non-sonorous forces like Time, the organization of Time, silent intensities, rhythms of every nature'.[63] Messiaen took the lead in render-ing sonorous those forces that aren't sonorous – which are not even audible – in themselves, making the 'reality of the invisible' palpable to listeners.[64] The aforementioned concept of *personnages* is an example of Messiaen's modernist

---

[61] The first section of *Lontano* begins quietly on a unison A♭ *(pppp)*, a focal point of clarity joined by clarinet and bassoon (b. 1–5), followed by oboe, French horn and trombone (b. 3–8). The minute rhythmic subdivisions of each canonic strand (each line follows a different pattern), and the prescription to *enter with an imperceptible attack* combine to deny any recognisable rhythmic punctuation or periodicity. The ametric entrance of canonic strands in different instrumental bodies causes a pronounced waver in pitch. This effect – when added to the implied vibrato of the expressive marking *(dolcissimo, sempre expressivo)* – causes acoustic beats that add resonance, and shift the overtone structure of the canon. There is no harmonic progression in *Lontano*; rather, triads, octave doublings and stable intervals rise out of the texture and gradually submerge.

[62] Compare Messiaen's observations on the leitmotif: 'There's someone who preceded me

in the search for such possibilities of expression: Richard Wagner with his leitmotif. Later generations have watered down the idea behind the leitmotif by attaching labels to it. This leitmotif's an extraordinary medium of speech and expression, making it possible to depict the past, present and future, all at the same time. This has nothing to do with classical music, or with modern music either, but stands entirely for itself. I owe a great deal to this idea.' Quoted in Rößler, *Contributions to the Spiritual World of Olivier Messiaen*, p. 53.

[63] Deleuze, 'Conference Presentation on Musical Time, IRCAM, 1978'.

[64] 'In my religion, we believe in the reality of the invisible and we believe in the resurrection of the flesh, the resurrection of the dead.' Messiaen speaking in *Olivier Messiaen: A Music of Faith*, London Weekend Television (LWT). First Broadcast on 5 April 1985, transcript – 1986, p. 10.

refashioning of the past. The composer traced *personnages rythmiques* all the way back to Beethoven, who engaged in a 'development by elimination' when he foreshortened the initial cell of the Fifth Symphony.[65] Stravinsky then extended this technique to three simultaneously presented rhythmic figures in which one 'dominates' through expansion, a second 'submits' through contraction, and a third remains immobile throughout, to create a living and breathing musical texture. Having discovered a 'purely rhythmic theme' in Stravinsky, Messiaen himself then extended the concept of *personnages* to melody and harmony in the *Turangalîla-Symphonie*.[66]

Thus a rhythmic technique that was inspired but not fully realised in Beethoven later blossomed in Stravinsky, and was seized on by Messiaen to realise the theatrical potential of rhythm, melody and harmony.[67] By 1960 Messiaen had moved on to a new 'resurrection',[68] reflected by changing his latest work's title from *Postlude* to *Chronochromie*.[69] As Deleuze notes, when the contemporary musician becomes a philosopher, music similarly is no longer a matter not solely for musicians. Neither philosopher nor musician retains interest in simple hierarchy, categorical forms of thought and pure concepts.

> In music, it's no longer a matter of an absolute ear but rather an impossible ear that can alight on someone, arise briefly in someone. In philosophy it's no longer a matter of an absolute thought such as classical philosophy wanted to embody, but rather an impossible thought, that is to say the elaboration of a material that renders thinkable those forces that are not thinkable by themselves.[70]

Messiaen's exploration of the charm of impossibilities in *Chronochromie* renders those abstract charms palpable. Here birds become music, ideas taken on audible form, colours become duration and time becomes colour. If we cannot yet grasp his music as a whole, perhaps it is simply because it is always in the process of becoming, of rendering – through his impossible ear – those forces sonorous, audible, that were not audible in themselves. For the composer, faith in the power of what can't be heard or seen drives that which can, witnessed by the preface to *Un Vitrail et des oiseaux*:

> But the birds are more important than the tempi, and the colours more important than the birds. More important than all the rest is the aspect of the invisible.[71]

---

[65] *TRCO*, Tome II, pp. 401–4.
[66] *TRCO*, Tome II, p. 99.
[67] *TRCO*, Tome II, p. 112.
[68] Messiaen quoted in Antoine Goléa, 'Olivier Messiaen, Chronochromie,' 279.
[69] Hill and Simeone, *Messiaen*, p. 233.
[70] Deleuze, 'Conference Presentation on Musical Time, IRCAM, 1978'.
[71] Preface to *Un Vitrail et des oiseaux* (Paris: Leduc, 1986).

8 Composer as performer, recording as text: notes towards a 'manner of realization' for Messiaen's music

Andrew Shenton

Until the advent of recording technology, the composer's influence as a performer or teacher was continued posthumously only by his or her pupils in an oral (and aural) tradition, and in written sources. By preserving the composer's own performance in an audible form which can be recalled at any time and in any place, we have the equivalent, albeit mediated, of a direct experience with the composer. What we need to decide is how much credence we should give to this information in relation to the score and the other data used to prepare a performance.

This chapter begins by discussing the role of the score and recording in musicological research. It then examines some of the recordings in which Messiaen performs his own music or has had direct or indirect influence on the performance of others, and suggests that these recordings are an invaluable aid to interpretation. Messiaen's own recordings point to a 'manner of realization' for his music, in effect a performance practice (or perhaps better a performance tradition), which will be an axiomatic reference point for future interpretations.[1]

The use of recordings by scholars and performers

The use of recordings in musicological research and as a component of interpretation is receiving increasing attention from scholars and performers. Timothy Day, Curator of Classical Music Recordings at the British Library published an invaluable study in 2000 of the first one hundred years of recorded sound, and musicologists Michael Chanan and Robert Philip have both contributed significant monographs that survey the wide range of recordings available and begin to address their use.[2] José Bowen,

---

[1] The term 'manner of realization' was used by John Milsom in his article 'Organ Music I', in Peter Hill (ed.), *The Messiaen Companion* (London: Faber and Faber, 1995), pp. 51–71, especially p. 60.

[2] Timothy Day, *A Century of Recorded Music: Listening to Musical History* (New Haven: Yale University Press, 2000); Michael Chanan, *Repeated Takes: A Short History of Recording and its Effects on Music* (London

founder of the Centre for the History and Analysis of Recorded Music (CHARM), has worked extensively on performance analysis and has used computers to make comparative investigations of aspects of recordings such as tempo flexibility.[3] This pioneering work has begun to erode our preconceived notions about both performance and interpretation.

To begin to understand the role of Messiaen's recordings in research, it is first necessary to enumerate the ways in which a composer may have a direct or indirect connection with a recording of his or her music. Robert Philip notes that there are seven ways:

1. Recordings performed by the composer
2. Recordings directed/conducted by the composer
3. Recordings made while the composer was present
4. Recordings approved by the composer
5. Recordings made by performers who worked with the composer or who were taught by him or her
6. Recordings made by performers who heard the composer perform or direct
7. Recordings made by musicians of the composer's time and place.[4]

In the case of Olivier Messiaen, six of these categories are relevant – there are no recordings of Messiaen directing/conducting his own music. In the first category, there are a few recordings of Messiaen playing the piano; however, the most significant collection is those in which Messiaen plays the organ. In June and July of 1956 Messiaen recorded all his published organ works (written to that date) on the instrument in La Sainte Trinité, Paris, the church at which he was organist from 1935 until his death in 1992.[5] In June 1972 he recorded the *Méditations sur le mystère de la Sainte Trinité*, also on the organ in La Trinité.[6] This means that, with the exception of the *Verset pour la fête de la dédicace* (1960), the *Livre du Saint Sacrement* (1984) and the three pieces published posthumously (*Offrande au Saint Sacrement*, *Prélude* and *Monodie*), we have recordings of the composer performing his own works on the instrument on which they were conceived.

and New York: Verso, 1995); Robert Philip, *Early Recordings and Musical Style: Changing Tastes in Instrumental Performance 1900–1950* (Cambridge: Cambridge University Press, 1992); Robert Philip, *Performing Music in the Age of Recording* (New Haven: Yale University Press, 2004).

[3] The Centre for the History and Analysis of Recorded Music (CHARM) was initially based at the University of Southampton and then at Georgetown University, and is currently being reconstituted through an AHRB Research Grant at Royal Holloway, University of London. See http://134.53.194.127/bowenja2/CHARM.html

[4] Philip, *Performing Music*, p. 141.

[5] *Messiaen: par lui-même*. Original recording re-released by EMI Classics (Angel Records) CDZD 7–067400–2, 1992.

[6] Messiaen's recording was digitally remastered in 1993 and released by Erato (Radio France). Erato 4509–92007–2.

What can the recording tell us?

With some important exceptions, composers during the first eighty or so years of the availability of recording technology were not quick to realise its potential – often the composer as performer in a recording was only used as a promotional vehicle. In England both Elgar and Britten embraced this technology with success, however, as Philip Stuart notes, it was 'only Stravinsky, starting with acoustic 78s in 1923 and finishing with stereo LPs in 1967, [who] recorded his early works three times, thereby providing a comprehensive picture of how his attitude to the performance of his music evolved ... By the time he retired from performance he had set down his realizations of most of his compositional output.'[7] Stravinsky is quite clear about the value of his own recordings. Writing about his contract with the Columbia Gramophone Company, he notes:

> This work greatly interested me, for here, far better than with piano rolls, I was able to express all my intentions with real exactitude. Consequently these records ... have the importance of documents which can serve as guides to all executants of my music. Unfortunately, very few conductors avail themselves of them ... Doubtless their dignity prevents others from consulting them, especially since if once they knew the record they could not with a clear conscience conduct as they liked.[8]

By asserting his intentions 'with real exactitude', Stravinsky acknowledged that notation, however complex, is imprecise at accurately expressing every nuance intended by the composer, while a recording is, in many respects, capable of documenting more. He also recognised that a recording imposes certain restrictions on future performers, who consequently have some responsibility to the composer's intentions as documented in that recording, but he strongly advocated the use of the recording as an additional and more detailed form of notation. In his autobiography, he wrote:

> Is it not amazing that, in our times, when a sure means which is accessible to all, has been found of learning exactly how the author demands his work to be executed, there should still be those who will not take any notice of such means, but persist in inserting concoctions of their own vintage?[9]

A problem arises if a composer has recorded a piece more than once unless he or she advocates the supremacy of one version, although Stravinsky considers that for his own work 'even the poorest are valid readings to guide other performers, and the best ... are very good indeed.'[10] What he

[7] Philip Stuart (compiler), *Igor Stravinsky – The Composer in the Recording Studio: A Comprehensive Discography* (Discographies, Number 45, Michael Gray, Series Advisor) (New York: Greenwood Press, 1991), p. 1.
[8] Igor Stravinsky, *An Autobiography* (New York: Norton, 1962), p. 150.
[9] Stravinsky, *An Autobiography*, p. 150.
[10] Igor Stravinsky and Robert Craft, 'Contemporary Music and Recording', *Dialogues and a Diary* (New York: Doubleday, 1963), p. 33.

is suggesting, perhaps, is that his recordings set parameters, or a spectrum of authenticity, which performers should be aware of as they determine their own interpretation of a work.

So how should we regard Messiaen's organ recordings? Unlike Stravinsky, Messiaen did not state that he was recording his music for posterity with the intention that they should be studied by others in association with the score. Neither did Messiaen ever claim that he was the best interpreter of his own works. It is far more likely that the original objective of these recordings was to present the pieces to a wider audience (they are in most cases the first recordings of each piece), with the additional cachet that Messiaen was himself the performer.

The *Méditations sur le mystère de la Sainte Trinité* (hereafter referred to as *Méditations*) provide us with a useful case study for exploring the feasibility of using the composer's own recording as part of the 'text' of a piece.[11] Before we consider exactly how the recording might be regarded as part of the text, let us examine how Messiaen's recorded performance of the *Méditations* is changed by the recording process.

The mediated recording

The process which allows us to replay Messiaen's 1972 performance of his *Méditations* today has gone through three main stages of mediation:

MESSIAEN'S PERFORMANCE

1. Analogue recording using 1972 equipment

↓

released by EMI on vinyl, 1973

↓

2. Digitally remastered by EMI

↓

released by EMI on compact disc, 1993

↓

3. Playback (with digital equipment)

↓

LISTENER

The quality of sound reproduction depends on the type of equipment used at each stage of the process, and is subject to a degree of human interference that may have a marked effect on the final product. In addition, organs are notoriously difficult to record because the physical placement of the instruments is often inconvenient for recording: the disposition of the pipes may

---

[11] The *Méditations* are published by Alphonse Leduc (Paris: Leduc, 1973).

be over a wide area, and the building in which the instrument is housed may have acoustic problems (particularly with reverberation and decay time). Placement of microphones, equalisation of sound and remixing all change the recorded sound to suit the taste of the performer, producer and sound engineer, and if a piece is remastered to improve the sound quality and to move it to a new medium (for example, the digital remastering of the original recording of the *Méditations*), the performer may not be involved in this process at all.

Putting aside the technical aspects and assuming that Messiaen was satisfied that the sound recorded in 1972 was an accurate representation of what he wanted for the *Méditations*, there are still two views regarding the degree to which the technology mediates the aural experience of a recorded performance. The philosopher and critic Theodor W. Adorno eloquently expressed them both. In 1927 he wrote:

> The work and its interpretation are accommodated but not disturbed or merged into each other: in its relative dimensions the work is retained and the obedient machine – which in no way dictates any formal principles of its own – follows the interpreter in patient imitation of every nuance.[12]

Here Adorno suggests that technology is storing data which later replicates exactly the original performance. In 1934, however, referring to the phonograph record as 'nothing more than [an] acoustic photograph', he describes the recording as designating a:

> two-dimensional model of a reality that can be multiplied without limit, displaced both spatially and temporally, and traded on the open market. This, at the price of sacrificing its third dimension: its height and its abyss.[13]

In this case, Adorno suggests that technology robs a performance of one of its most important dimensions. He describes this as its 'height and ... abyss', but in addition to commenting on the comparatively poor quality of recordings in the 1930s he is probably also referring to the concept of 'Aura' described by Walter Benjamin in his acclaimed essay 'The Work of Art in the Age of Mechanical Reproduction', which refers to the authentic breath of the work in its own original cultural context.[14] Adorno may also be referring to that intangible rapport between performer and audience which is lost or dissipated in the recording process. He regards the recording as an 'acoustic photograph' because it is infinitely reproducible, and suggests that this

[12]Theodor W. Adorno, 'Nadelkurven' (1927, revised 1965), translated by Thomas Y. Levin as 'The Curves of the Needle', *October*, Vol. 55 (Winter 1990), 50. Reprinted in Richard Leppert (compiler), *Essays on Music: Theodor W. Adorno* (University of California Press: Berkeley, 2002), pp. 271–6, especially p. 272.
[13]Theodor W. Adorno, 'Die Form der Schallplatte' (1934), translated by Thomas Y. Levin as 'The Form of the Phonograph Record', *October*, Vol. 55 (Winter 1990), 57. Reprinted in *Essays on Music: Theodor W. Adorno*, pp. 277–82, especially p. 278.
[14]Walter Benjamin, *Illuminations*, ed. Hannah Arendt, trans. Harry Zohn (New York: Harcourt, Brace and World, 1968).

reproduction undermines the authenticity of the original. This is in a sense the dialectic of every performance: it both erodes the original aura and adds another gilded layer of history to the work.

The lack of direct connection with the audience from a recording can be weighed against the opportunity for something much closer to technical and musical perfection than a live performance, due to the advantages of editing and retakes. This in turn has produced a number of different attitudes of composers and performers to recording technologies which are exemplified in the approaches of the following artists: 1. Glenn Gould, who renounced live performance in favour of the recording studio; 2. Leonard Bernstein, who toward the end of his career had decided the best way to retain music's spontaneity was to record live performances and to compile a recording from multiple takes of a piece; and 3. Benjamin Britten, who, despite a long recording career, consistently advocated the supremacy of live performance. Again it is Stravinsky, writing about what is most important about a recorded performance to a composer, who provides some interesting insight. He suggests that the most important feature of a recording is:

> The spirit of course, the same as in any performance . . . Next to the spirit come the two chief questions of the flesh: tempo and balance. I am annoyed by the violin solo in my *Agon* recording . . . but imbalances of this sort were common in early stereo recordings, and whereas a monaural was a closet, an early stereo was three closets. We also heard things we didn't always want to. Now we have learned to let backgrounds be backgrounds . . . I am even more irritated by an impossible tempo. If the speeds of everything in the world and ourselves have changed, our tempo feelings cannot remain unaffected. The metronome marks one wrote forty years ago were contemporary forty years ago. Time is not alone in affecting tempo – circumstances do too. I would be surprised if any of my own recordings follow the metronome markings.[15]

His remarks on tempo are relevant to this study since Messiaen's printed and recorded tempi are a contentious issue.

The recording as text

So what exactly is the CD recording produced by EMI? In order to answer this we need to examine some of the philosophical and aesthetic issues which are affected by recording technology. In his summary of writings on the ontological status of music, musicologist Peter Kivy suggests that the following four views broadly represent the field:[16]

[15] Stravinsky and Craft, *Dialogues and a Diary*, p. 34.
[16] Peter Kivy, 'Aesthetics', in Don Randel (ed.) *The New Harvard Dictionary of Music*
(Cambridge: Harvard University Press, 1986), p. 16. Kivy has written extensively on philosophical aspects of music. For further reading on issues raised in this essay, see *The*

1. The metaphysical view, expressed for example by philosopher and historian Robin G. Collingwood, that music exists as an object only in the imagination.
2. The physical view that music is, by virtue of sound vibrations, a physical 'object'.
3. The logical view, expressed at its most concise by philosopher Nelson Goodman that '"A score defines a work", and the work is the class of all "compliants" with it.'
4. The neo-Platonic metaphysical view, as expressed for example by philosopher and theologian Nicholas Wolterstorff, that music is a 'nonphysical, Platonic object or "kind", of which its performances are the individual instances.'[17]

The first two of these views are both logical and acceptable. Recordings provide a kind of mediation between the two, and it is because of this that Adorno is concerned about the ways in which the metaphysical dimensions of the work can be consumed, and perhaps also the ways in which mechanical reproduction leads to less practical imagination and effort on behalf of performers and listeners in the process of apprehension of 'truth'.

Moving to Kivy's third and fourth ideas, if we accept Goodman's view that the score defines the work, we are confronted again with the notion that the score is not adequate for fully expressing the composers' intentions. Wolterstorff's concept of 'kind' allows us a certain freedom in actually defining what a piece is; however if we believe that Messiaen, like Stravinsky, had truly represented himself in the recording, then all the 'compliants' of Goodman's score and all the individual instances of Wolterstorff's 'kind' are more limited by the recording in their degree of variation than those permitted by the score alone.

The question of the ontological status of a piece of music can broadly be divided into two further questions: firstly, what exactly constitutes the 'text' of a work of art; and secondly, what constitutes a realisation of the text? Is Mozart's piano concerto in C minor K. 491 the autograph manuscript; the editions by Bärenreiter, Offenbach, or Breitkopf & Härtel; the performances by Levin, Bilson or Tan; all of these; or none of these?

Fine Art of Repetition: Essays in the Philosophy of Music (Cambridge University Press, 1993), *Authenticities: Philosophical Reflections on Musical Performance* (Ithaca, New York: Cornell University Press, 1998) and his *Introduction to a Philosophy of Music* (Oxford University Press, 2002).

[17] There is another view that is relevant to Messiaen's music, which we may call the 'ontological/theological state', in which music that comes to represent the deepest status of personhood may be considered, in itself, divine. However, this aspect is peripheral to the discussion at hand.

Philosopher Susanne Langer believes that a piece of music is incomplete until it is performed. She suggests that a piece of music is a 'physically non-sensuous structure', which:

> has a permanent existence and identity of its own; it is what can be 'repeated' in many appearances, which are its 'performances,' and in a sense it is all the composer can really call *his* piece. For, although he may carry it to absolute completion by performing it himself, and make a permanent gramophone record of his performance so this also may be repeated, the composition nevertheless exists, as something that could be committed to writing or to memory and that might be performed by another person.[18]

Langer takes a similar view to both Goodman and Wolterstorff in her opinion of the way a piece can be 'repeated' or 'performed', but she also argues that it has an identity of its own and is autonomous after it has been created. It is significant that she remarks that a composer may carry it to 'absolute completion' by performing it himself and not 'absolute perfection', acknowledging the possibility of the piece being 'perfected' in an interpretation by another. José Bowen puts it this way: 'each performance is a unique moment during which the individual struggles to convey both a unique message and a specific musical work.'[19]

The philosopher Roman Ingarden asserts that a performance (which is an event), a score (which is an object) and a musical work, are not identical entities.[20] What, then, are the differences between the score and the recording of Messiaen's *Méditations*? One way to answer this is to ask the question: If we did not have the printed score of a piece of music, could we reconstruct one from the recording? The answer for the *Méditations* is 'Yes' – at least in part. However, the reconstructed score would differ from the autograph in certain respects. In the case of the *Méditations* it is likely that the pitches, registration and rhythms could be transcribed in a way that gives a good approximation of the recording; yet, there are certain other pieces of information notated in the score (especially the new 'communicable language' and other written comments) that could not be reproduced because they are not aurally apparent.[21] Since Messiaen's music contains additional semiotic

---

[18] Susanne K. Langer, *Feeling and Form* (New York: Routledge, 1953), p. 120.

[19] José Bowen, 'The History of Remembered Innovation: Tradition and Its Role in the Relationship between Musical Works and Their Performances', *The Journal of Musicology*, Vol. 11, no. (Spring 1993), 158.

[20] Roman Ingarden, *The Work of Music and the Problem of Its Identity*, ed. Jean G. Harrell, trans. Adam Czerniawski (Berkeley: University of California Press: 1986), pp. 9–23, 34–40.

[21] In the eighth *Méditation*, for example, there are parenthetical texts inserted above the staff from St Paul's Letter to the Romans, the Gospel according to St Matthew, and Psalm 54. For more information on the 'langage communicable', a technique devised by Messiaen to transliterate texts by Aquinas into music, see Andrew Shenton, 'Speaking with the Tongues of Men and Angels: Messiaen's "Langage Communicable" ', in Siglind Bruhn (ed.), *Olivier Messiaen: The Language of Mystical Love* (New York: Garland, 1998), pp. 225–45.

elements, their absence in a reconstruction from the recording would rob the piece of key parts, so in this case we must acknowledge that the score and recording are complementary.

There is the view that a recording is not a document available for multiple playbacks, but that Adorno's 'acoustic photograph' should only be listened to once, thereby replicating the experience of a live performance. While there is a logical validity to this argument, it does not serve the scholar or performer, who may derive benefit from repeated hearings. This in turn leads to a further question: is a recording a document of a performance or of a composition? From the musicological point of view, when the composer is the performer it serves as both, and this means that it can be studied as both.

Messiaen and Mozart

If we compare the information we have about the existing primary sources or 'text' of Mozart's piano concerto K. 491 with that for Messiaen's *Méditations*, we see that the main difference between Messiaen and Mozart is that we have more information about Messiaen's music and his intentions.

For both composers we have:

1. The autograph and at least one published score (in Mozart's case, in several editions)
2. Certain theoretical texts and other secondary source material that provides insight into issues of performance practice and interpretation

For Messiaen we have the following additional material:

1. The composer's elaborate written notes appended to the musical score
2. The composer's programme notes about the work and each movement in detail
3. The composer's recorded performance on the organ on which the pieces were conceived (the *Méditations* were developed from a series of improvisations)
4. The composer's imprimatur on the performance of other people (for example, the recordings of the organ works by Almut Rössler)

A good scholarly study of K. 491 would take into account relevant aspects of chronology and biography, and make stylistic comparisons with other concerti by Mozart and his contemporaries; however, even with regards to this type of secondary information we have more on Messiaen thanks to his chronological proximity, and to the greater availability and greater effectiveness of chronicling techniques. This includes specific additional information given by the composer about his musical language, aesthetic and philosophy, along with many instances of specific performance indications. Is this restricting or liberating? For musicologists and performers the situation is the same: the more information we have been supplied with by the composer, the less room there is for either interpretation or speculation unless one chooses to disregard the composer's directions and rely on 'intuition' (itself a difficult and complex notion).

The situation with Messiaen's music is complicated by the fact that much of it is conceived with specific extra-musical (largely religious) connotations. It is possible to take a piece such the *Méditations* as absolute music, though it is not common practice. The performing tradition is to print Messiaen's own notes in the programme to explain the music. If we are prepared to perpetuate Messiaen's programme notes along with his music, should we not, by extension, therefore always take into account what else he says, especially in a form as explicit as a recording?

Comparison of the *Méditations* score and recording

José Bowen believes that, when faced with the problem of synthesising a performing edition from different sources, musicologists have adopted the two schools of recension from classical philology: 'The first school of thought suggests we can do no better than one version (thus we try to determine which version is the most reliable and that is that).'[22] Since we have established that the recording is more accurate at 'notating' nuance and timbre but that the score is also necessary, this approach is not feasible. Bowen describes the second school of thought as suggesting that we can 'create a composite text which resembles none of our samples, but the elements which they share, in an attempt to recover a parent-original'. This is exactly what we need to do with a recording of the composer performing his own works. To create a composite text of Messiaen's *Méditations*, we need to study both the score and recording and make an empirical comparison of the following four basic features of the music: registration, pitch, tempo and rhythm. By selecting the features of each that best represents our perception of the composer's intentions, we can produce a score that can then be subject to the normal considerations of performance such as the instrument and venue, and then to the issues of interpretation that are dealt with further below.

Registration

The choice of the instrument used by Messiaen for his recordings is interesting.[23] It is possible that he chose to record in La Trinité for the sake of

---

[22] Bowen, 'The History of Remembered Innovation: Tradition and Its Role in the Relationship between Musical Works and Their Performances', 144.

[23] It is also interesting to note that Messiaen gave the premiere of the *Méditations* himself,

not in La Trinité but in the National Shrine of the Immaculate Conception in Washington, DC, where he spent three days prior to the premiere choosing the registrations for the piece.

Ex. 8.1: *Méditation VII*, p. 61, b. 7–8

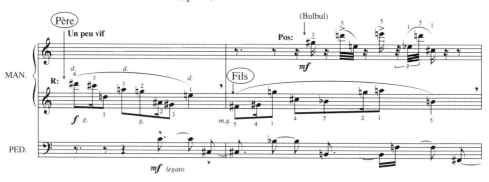

convenience (since he was the incumbent at that church) but, as John Milsom notes, at the time of the 1956 recordings the Cavaillé-Coll organ in La Trinité was in a bad state of repair.[24] By 1972 the instrument in La Trinité had been renovated and expanded, so Messiaen was able to effect more clearly the detailed registration indications in the score that are for that particular organ.[25] Because Messiaen was so specific about his choice of stops it behoves performers to match as closely as possible his intentions for pitch and timbre. Given that there are historical, national and local differences in the sound of organs, Messiaen's recordings give an indication of a French style of organ building which is integral to the sound of his music. Careful study of the recording will help with questions of balance and prominence of parts, particularly in a case such as this passage (Ex. 8.1) from the seventh *Méditation*, where each of the three lines has a different registration, and Messiaen's recording does not make the dynamic distinctions notated in the score (even taking into account the vagaries of recording technique in the 1970s).

In Messiaen's recording there is little difference between the *pp* and *p* markings (in the previous section), and the *f* and *mf* in b. 7 and 8. Given that there is a marked contrast in timbre between the three parts in this example, the dynamic differences may not seem so important. However, since most performers will be making compromise choices depending on the instrument available, having some idea of the relative dynamics of Messiaen's instrument might inform the choice of stops.

[24] John Milsom, 'Messiaen's Organ Music', *Gramophone* (December 1992), 31.

[25] The registrations for the *Méditations* are significantly more detailed than any of the other organ works. Messiaen includes an additional six pages in the score which detail the settings he used for the general pistons, the layout of the console and general remarks on the technical aspects of the instrument and on the timbre of some stops for the Sainte Trinité organ. This degree of specificity reinforces the notion that there is a precise sound world Messiaen wants performers to emulate. The organ has since been modified further. For a history of the organ in La Sainte Trinité, see http://www.uquebec.ca/~uss1010/orgues/france/strinitep.html

Pitch

This study has uncovered some variations in pitch between the score and recording, however, a thorough comparative study needs to be undertaken in conjunction with a study of the autograph manuscript.[26] There is a possibility that these 'wrong' notes represent changes that Messiaen made to the music at the time of the recording, reverting to his role as an improviser (which is how the *Méditations* were conceived). It is more likely, however, that they are accidental. In general, Messiaen's manuscript hand is neat and readable, and, since he was meticulous in proofreading his own printed scores, it is reasonable to assume that he was trying to represent the printed score accurately in his recorded performance.

Ex. 8.2: *Méditation VI*, opening

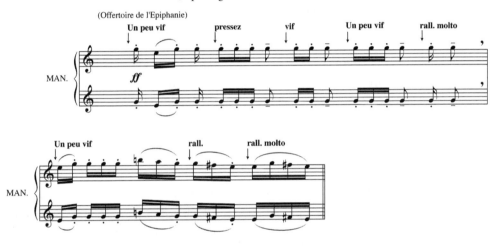

Tempo

With regard to tempi, the first problem is that Messiaen has only given his tempo indications in words (*modéré, un peu vif*, etc.). Absence of metronome markings permits considerable latitude in the interpretation of these tempi, and in the relationship between one tempo and another within the same movement and between movements.

In some places in the *Méditations* the notation of tempo changes is carefully marked, to the extent that small arrows are used to indicate the exact point at which the new indication is to be observed. In the opening of the sixth *Méditation*, for example, there are eight tempo indications over a passage containing thirty-two notes spread over two bars (Ex. 8.2).

---

[26]There are, for example, 'clipped' notes in the section of *Méditation V* that begins on p. 42/2/ 2 of the score.

Here Messiaen seems to be trying to capture the nuance of a sung perform-ance of the plainsong offertory for Epiphany. In Messiaen's recording, the metronome value for the first tempo designation, '*un peu vif*', is around quaver = 64, and all the composer's intentions for the phrase are specific and clear. If an interpreter had not heard the recording, and was to choose a tempo slightly faster or slower than Messiaen's recording, it would not make a significant difference to the relative fluctuations in tempo during these bars. Problems arise where there is a rapid number of tempo changes and where there is less specific designation of the starting point of the different speeds. At the beginning of the eighth *Méditation* for example, six tempo changes are marked in the score within the first twenty-one bars:

un peu vif	(5 bars)
très modéré	(3 bars)
bien modéré	(3 bars)
lent	(3 bars)
modéré	(2 bars)
bien modéré	(5 bars)

The first problem is sorting out a hierarchy for the written tempo desig-nations. Starting with the slowest, the generally accepted order is:

lent
très modéré
modéré
bien modéré
un peu vif

The second problem is deciding to which note value the tempo indication applies, and the third problem is assigning a metronome marking to each tempo indication. These are puzzles about which the recording should be able to provide the answers. Unfortunately, Messiaen's recording only com-plicates the issue further. If we calculate Messiaen's metronome speeds from the recording, using the quaver pulse as a measure for comparison, we get Table 8.1.

Table 8.1: Tempo indications in *Méditation* VIII

un peu vif	quaver = 68
très modéré	quaver = 70
bien modéré	quaver = 84
lent	quaver = 42
modéré	quaver = 25
bien modéré	quaver = 102

Calculating these tempi is difficult because Messiaen does not keep a steady pulse. More problematic is the fact that Messiaen's hierarchy of tempi is different from the accepted order. Based on the information in Table 8.1, Messiaen's hierarchy is:

> *modéré*
> *lent*
> *un peu vif*
> *très modéré*
> *bien modéré 1*
> *bien modéré 2*

It is also remarkable how many of the tempi in Table 8.1 are factors of one another (*lent* is half the speed of *bien modéré*, for example). This means that in Messiaen's recording, during the course of these twenty-one bars there is great similarity in the underlying pulse rather than the diversity one would expect by looking at the score. From an interpretational point of view, without a marked contrast in tempo these small fragments lose all character and comprehensibility. Messiaen's notation therefore seems to be at odds with his intention.

Unfortunately it seems that, even when we have Messiaen's written metronome markings, we cannot take them as wholly accurate. In conversation with pianist Peter Hill, Yvonne Loriod (Messiaen's widow and a distinguished interpreter of his piano music) remarked, 'Messiaen always marked the tempos in his scores only after the work had been performed.'[27] She continued by noting that the tempo in *Regard du Père*, the first movement of the *Vingt Regards*, is possibly marked too slow, and she suggests that in general pianists are technically more proficient now than when the *Vingt Regards* were written. She also observes that tempo is also 'partly a personal matter'. In the same conversation, she announced her wish to make new editions of certain pieces by Messiaen, 'in order to incorporate the tempos Messiaen wanted'.

Discussing the issue of tempo variance in performance Bowen argues that 'the question of how much the tempo must be altered before the musical work is damaged, is cultural and aesthetic, and not theoretical or phenomenological; the answer depends on the composer, the piece and the audience, all of which are linked by cultural traditions', and he concludes: 'it is ultimately audiences who determine whether a performance at a new tempo is still a performance of the work.'[28]

It could be, of course, that we should not be so pedantic about Messiaen's recorded tempi. Surely what Messiaen really wants is for the performer to create his or her own *melos* and engagement with the piece. In this sense,

[27] Interview with Yvonne Loriod on 9 January 1993, published in Hill (ed.), *The Messiaen Companion*, p. 288.

[28] José Bowen, 'Tempo, Duration, and Flexibility: Techniques in the Analysis of Performance', *Journal of Musicological Research*, Vol. 16 (1996), 128.

Messiaen's recording is but one solution. Now the discussion plays into a broader context of the distinction between performer as *executor* and performer as *interpreter*. This dichotomy is eloquently discussed in Robert Fink's article on the forging of a modernist performing style.[29] Contrasting nineteenth-century 'vitalist' performances with modern 'geometric' performances, Fink notes that 'geometric performing practice brings with it a self-consciously objective stylistic ideology based on metronomic, unyielding tempos and a horror of excessive rubato.'[30] He continues by using Stravinsky's distinction between the idea of interpretation, which 'implies the limitations imposed upon the performer or those which the performer imposes upon himself in his proper function, which is to transmit music to the listener', and the idea of execution, which 'implies the strict putting into effect of an explicit will that contains nothing beyond what it specifically commands.'[31] The crux of the matter for Stravinsky is that 'every interpreter is also of necessity an executor. The reverse is not true.'[32] Fink elaborates, noting that:

> the ideal modernist performer [i.e. one who performs strictly notated 'modern' music] is an executor who voluntarily submerges his or her personality and adds nothing to the composer's intentions. The executor ignores spurious emotional or 'spiritual' promptings, keeps the scenic or programmatic element firmly in its place, and remains aloof from all hermeneutics, preferring to base performance decisions on purely musical, purely material considerations.[33]

This was not the case for a Romantic interpreter, for whom personal expression was the key, transmitting, as Fink says, 'not the notes but what was between and behind them: the sense of a living, feeling consciousness at work.'[34] For any performer of Messiaen's music the decision is whether to be an executor or an interpreter, or to find some acceptable middle ground. Messiaen's music is laden with 'spiritual promptings' and cries out for hermeneutic analysis from the performer, so one cannot merely be an executor. However, since his instructions are explicit and musical instructions are reinforced by verbal instructions, one cannot be just an interpreter. His recordings help a performer balance the two approaches.

---

[29] Robert Fink, ' "Rigoroso (eighth-note = 126)": The Rite of Spring and the Forging of a Modernist Performing Style', *The Journal of the American Musicological Society*, Vol. 52, no. 2 (1999), 299–362. Fink bases much of his discussion of 'vitalist' versus 'geometric' performance on Richard Taruskin's article 'The Pastness of the Present and the Presence of the Past', in Nicholas Kenyon (ed.), *Authenticity and Early*

Music (Oxford University Press, 1988), pp. 137–207.
[30] Fink, "Rigoroso", 308.
[31] Igor Stravinsky, *Poetics of Music in the Form of Six Lessons* (Cambridge, MA: Harvard University Press 1970), p. 163.
[32] Stravinsky, *Poetics of Music in the Form of Six Lessons*, p. 163.
[33] Fink, '"Rigoroso"', 308.
[34] Fink, '"Rigoroso"', 309.

Rhythm

Turning back to our comparative analysis of Messiaen's recording and the score of his *Méditations*, the issue of rhythmic deviations in Messiaen's performance reveal a similar dilemma to the problems of tempi. The rhythm *miçra varna* (No. 26b of the 120 *deçi-tâlas* according to Çârngadeva) is used twice (identically) in the eighth *Méditation* (p. 70, b. 17–21 and p. 72, b. 1–5) (see Ex. 8.3).

Ex. 8.3: *Méditation VIII*, p. 70, b. 17–21, the rhythm *miçra varna*[35]

Messiaen uses articulation marks for each chord, and marks the five-bar phrase *bien modéré*. One would expect that using this distinctive rhythm would imply the need for strict accuracy in execution. As there are no further tempo indications, one would also expect that the rhythm would be free from distortion and played at a consistent speed throughout. In his recorded performances, however, Messiaen is lax about the dotted semiquavers, and he inserts a huge rallentando during the last two bars.[36] This therefore seems to make a mockery of his own notation of such a precise rhythm. Messiaen is consistent in the way he plays it each time, but it is another clear example of the dilemma between notation and intention, which would not have been apparent without the recording.

In discussing the problems with Messiaen's performance of the *Méditations*, writer Paul Griffiths comments that: 'There are similar problems in his recordings of the earlier organ works, but they seem particularly crucial in the case of the *Méditations*, since the recording was made within a year of the first performance [which Messiaen gave himself], and should therefore, so one might suppose, capture the music in a state close to that it had achieved when it was notated.'[37] His point is valid. Perhaps

[35] In this example, Messiaen repeats the rhythm twice. The rhythm is then presented in retrograde in the fourth bar (while augmenting the first two values of the retrograde version). The final bar effectively does the same thing, except that the dotted-crotchet value of the fourth bar now comprises a crotchet and quaver, and the final two values of the retrograde are augmented from two semiquavers to a crotchet rest. Changes in organ registration (not marked)

further complicate the effect of Messiaen's rhythm in the final two bars of this example.
[36] Paradoxically Loriod also claimed that Messiaen 'detested' rubato because he believed that it 'kills' rhythm. See Rebecca Rischin, *For the End of Time: The Story of the Messiaen Quartet* (Ithaca, NY: Cornell University Press, 2003), p. 124.
[37] Paul Griffiths, *Olivier Messiaen and the Music of Time* (London: Faber and Faber, 1985), p. 221.

we should be able to take the recording as an accurate representation of the composer's intentions at the time of the recording. Unfortunately, as Griffiths also notes, we have only one recording of Messiaen playing the music of another composer (Debussy), so, with this one exception, we are unable to compare his performance of his own work against that of others in order to determine the extent to which his technique is responsible for the discrepancies between score and recording.[38]

The question of interpretation and realisation

The ultimate question regarding the use of the recording as an adjunct to the score is: does the recording give any authoritative interpretation of the piece? John Milsom devotes a short section of his essay in *The Messiaen Companion* to a discussion of the musicological use of Messiaen's 1956 recording of a movement from *Les Corps glorieux*.[39] He asks a number of interesting questions about Messiaen's recording, including how the poor state of the instrument may have adversely affected the recording. He also asks: 'what status does Messiaen's 1956 recording have in defining the identity of *Les eaux de la grâce*?' Milsom dispenses with complex arguments and moves straight to the logical conclusion of any such debate. His answer is simply that 'fact gives way to opinion'.[40] Ultimately he concludes that, like Bowen, it is the opinion of the listener that is the final arbiter of the definition of any piece and its performance. It is clear that the more we know of Messiaen's wishes, the more our expectation of a performance is shaped by these views. Our level of satisfaction with a given performance depends on how these expectations are realised.

Milsom goes on to discuss recordings by Messiaen's students, and suggest that 'they do not replicate Messiaen's own solutions, but they do broadly adhere to what we might call his *manner of realization*'.[41] Milsom defines the phrase 'manner of realization' by noting that, in addition to markings in the score, 'Messiaen seems to have taken a certain style of performance practice and range of sonorities for granted, and when asked for advice by other organists would guide them towards those solutions.' This 'manner of realization' is a key concept for lovers of Messiaen's music.

It is apparent that, with *all* the available source material for one of Messiaen's pieces – including the score, the composer's programme notes and comments,

---

[38] Messiaen plays the piano in a recording of Debussy's *Cinq Poèmes de Charles Baudelaire*, on the same disc as a live recording of his own song cycle *Harawi* with soprano Marcelle Bunlet, recorded 13 September 1954. INA, Mémoire Vive, IMV04–4.

[39] Milsom, 'Organ Music I', p. 58.

[40] Milsom, 'Organ Music I', p. 60.

[41] Milsom, 'Organ Music I', p. 60 (my italics).

the composer's own recordings and those of his pupils – there is the basis for a school of playing. Performers now have some responsibility to negotiate all this extra material to arrive at a satisfactory performance. Robert Philip, in answer to the question as to what authority we should now base our performing styles and habits, notes that 'the menu of possibilities, from current period and conventional practice, from new and old scholarship, and from a hundred years of recordings, is vast', and he concludes that 'we can pick what we like, as long as we make it sound neat and tidy and sell it in an attractive package'.[42] This is perhaps slightly cynical – there are sensible and musical ways to approach the myriad possibilities of re-creating a work that will contribute something fresh to our knowledge of it.

Let us briefly turn to another example from Messiaen's œuvre. As of the spring of 2006 there are more than thirty available recordings of his *Quatuor pour la fin du Temps*, including a 1957 recording with Messiaen himself at the piano, and 1990 recording which features Yvonne Loriod in the same role. The 1957 recording of the *Quatuor*, in which Messiaen is joined by André Vacellier (clarinet) and Etienne and Jean Pasquier (cello and violin respectively) was the first recording. Etienne Pasquier regarded this recording as definitive, saying: 'those who want to play the piece; they can listen to this recording for the tempi, the dynamics, those kinds of things. Because Messiaen himself was at the piano, and he was very demanding. And we did exactly what he requested. It's authentic.'[43] Yvonne Loriod makes a similar claim for the 1990 recording for which she was the pianist, and recalls that Messiaen 'always took notes on his writing pad and would have us restart when something wasn't good.' She recalled:

> in general I remember that he gave bowing advice in the '*Louange*' movements, so that the tempi would be slow enough . . . He would demand that everything be in the exact tempo that he wanted. And sometimes, we would record several versions so that afterward he could choose the best sonority and the best dynamics . . . I think that this was a really good recording because, as Messiaen was present, the tempos and dynamics are exactly the ones he wanted.[44]

These accounts provide us with yet another important source of information for a manner of realisation, both in the comments of the performers and in the recordings themselves.

A successful use of all this material is found the recording of the *Quatuor* by Jonathan Cohler, clarinet; Ilya Kaler, violin; Andrew Mark, cello; and Janice Weber, piano.[45] In the sleeve notes to the CD, Jonathan Cohler writes that their decision to record the piece was taken after he had surveyed the

[42] Philip, *Performing Music*, p. 250.
[43] Quoted in Rischin, *For the End of Time: The Story of the Messiaen Quartet*, p. 93.
[44] Rischin, *For the End of Time: The Story of the Messiaen Quartet*, p. 124.
[45] Ongaku Records Inc., 2004, 024–119.

existing recordings and discovered that 'none of them, including Messiaen's own, had realized some of the most critical aspects of the piece.'[46] Cohler took all the available information from the composer, included comparative analysis of several recordings, and with the other players in his group made key performance decisions about aspects of the music such as the selection of tempi and the use of vibrato. As a clarinettist, Cohler was particularly interested in the third movement, *Abîme des oiseaux*, which is for clarinet solo. Cohler's comparative analysis of the timings of several recordings noted 'huge variability' in the duration of this particular movement. He wrote:

> On Messiaen's recording, it runs just 5 minutes and 10 seconds. When played exactly as written, the calculated time is 7 minutes and 18 seconds. Most recordings of this movement fall in the seven to eight minute range. On this Ongaku recording [Cohler's version], however, I took into account Messiaen's admonition to Akoka [the clarinettist at the premiere] to hold the E whole notes 'until you can't blow anymore' instead of simply playing the whole notes at eighth-note = 44.

Cohler's performance of the movement lasts an astonishing 9 minutes and 29 seconds – almost twice the length of the composer's own version. It illustrates an important point about the use of recordings and supplemental material in making performance decisions: defining a manner of realisation that is stylistically appropriate still leaves considerable scope for individual expression while maintaining fidelity to the integrity of the composer. One cannot ignore Messiaen's own performance of the *Quatuor* or the ones at which he was present and about which he commented, however, for sheer enjoyment, many may prefer the Ongaku recording.

Conclusion

In *Music and Discourse* Jean-Jacques Nattiez writes: 'the musical work is not merely what we used to call the "text"; it is not merely a whole composed of "structures" . . . Rather, the work is also constituted by the procedures that have engendered it (acts of composition), and the procedures to which it gives rise: acts of interpretation and perception.'[47] The composer as performer and the recording as text will become increasingly integral to acts of interpretation and perception.

Summarising his computer-assisted analysis of tempo, duration and flexibility in the work of several conductors, Bowen noticed that 'even the most

---

[46] Ongaku recording sleeve notes, 5.
[47] Jean-Jacques Nattiez, *Music and Discourse: Towards a Semiology of Music*, trans. Carolyn

Abbate (Princeton University Press, 1990), p. ix.

"improvisatory" conductors seem to retain a single conception and execution of the piece despite the effects of age, geography and personnel', and he concludes that 'it should be possible to discover the characteristics of a conductor's style which are independent of any single work'. This is what will happen with Messiaen and successive composers who find new ways to notate their intentions for performers.

Clearly, there is still much to be done to define a manner of realisation for Messiaen's music. Bowen suggests that 'future performance studies should look on the one hand at period, geographical, institutional, generic, instrumental and individual artistic styles, and on the other, at specific traditions in the performance histories of individual musical works.'[48] The performance history for Messiaen will be based to a large extent on the recordings with which he was directly or indirectly involved. Doubtless the degree to which these recordings dominate interpretations will change, and the next few years may see a strong reaction against Messiaen's manner of realisation as performers seek to make his music personally and culturally relevant. Even now, though, when used intelligently, the recording is an essential element of an holistic approach to interpretation that can be used to enhance our comprehension of the piece to the advantage of the composer.

[48] Bowen, 'Tempo, Duration, and Flexibility: Techniques in the Analysis of Performance', 149.

9 'The art of the most intensive contrast': Olivier Messiaen's mosaic form up to its apotheosis in *Saint François d'Assise*

Stefan Keym

'In music, form is not very important, neither tonality nor serialism . . . The essential is what you have to express.'[1]

'Indeed, I think that I have not done much research on questions of form. Perhaps my best works are those that have no form, in a strict sense.'[2]

Introduction

These statements, taken from two interviews in the 1980s, clearly express Olivier Messiaen's ambivalence to matters of musical form, at least in its traditional sense. An examination of his theoretical writings seems to confirm this impression. In chapter 12 of *Technique de mon langage musical* (*TMLM*), Messiaen dwells on certain technical procedures of conventional forms, such as the episode and the stretto of the fugue or the development of sonata form, but he shows no interest in their formal functions.[3] In his exhaustive *Traité de rythme, de couleur, et d'ornithologie* (*TRCO*), there is no chapter dedicated to formal problems at all. Early commentaries on Messiaen's works created a consensus that form was the least original aspect of his musical language. Some writers such as André Hodeir blamed him for 'formal failure' and 'total inability' in the formal field,[4] and even Messiaen's former pupil Harry Halbreich found an 'absence of global perspective of musical form, in favour of a local perspective'.[5]

---

[1] Olivier Messiaen, in Edith Walter, 'Entretien-dossier Olivier Messiaen', *Harmonie – Panorama Musique*, no. 36 (November 1983), 18 ('En musique, la forme est peu importante, que ce soit la tonalité ou le sérialisme . . . L'essentiel est ce que l'on a à exprimer.').

[2] Patrick Szersnovicz, 'Olivier Messiaen: la liturgie de l'arc-en-ciel', *Le Monde de la musique/Télérama*, no. 102 (July/August 1987), 30 ('Je pense qu'effectivement je n'ai pas fait tellement de recherches sur les questions de forme. Mes meilleures œuvres sont peut-être celles où il n'y a pas de forme, au sens strict.').

[3] Olivier Messiaen, *Technique de mon langage musical* trans. John Satterfield (*TMLM*) (Paris: Leduc, 1956), p. 40.

[4] André Hodeir, *La Musique depuis Debussy* (Paris: Presses Universitaires de France, 1961), p. 97. Hodeir also wrote a rather conventional 'Formenlehre': *Les Formes de la musique* (Paris: Presses Universitaires de France, 1951).

[5] Harry Halbreich, *Olivier Messiaen* (Paris: Fayard/SACEM) 1980, p. 189 ('absence de perspective globale de la forme musicale, au profit d'une perspective locale').

Yet, as this study will reveal, despite and even because of Messiaen's reticence about conventional concepts of musical form, he developed a new, highly original form perfectly suited to express the religious message of his music. By the juxtaposition and frequent recurrence of many short contrasting modules, he created a formal structure resembling a mosaic. This 'mosaic form' is to be found especially in Messiaen's later works and reaches its apotheosis in his opera *Saint François d'Assise*. However, its structure is already announced in his earlier works and remains rooted in a specifically French tradition of refrain forms.

Before discussing the evoluton of Messiaen's formal thinking, it is worth considering why Messiaen thought that his music had 'no form, in a strict sense'.[6] What Messiaen seems to be indicating is that his music avoided a certain formal concept that ruled European music for a long time, one that still seems to dominate the formal perception of many writers on music. This is the concept of 'organically evolving form' which, based mainly on thematic and tonal development, creates the illusion that the composition is not an artefact, but a living organism.[7] This concept was developed and theoretically described in the time of Viennese Classicism and preserved during the era of Classic-Romantic music, especially in Austro-German countries. In the twentieth century, it was maintained by the members of the Second Viennese School and used by many subsequent composers.

From the beginning of his career, Messiaen kept a considerable distance from the tradition of Austro-German music, especially from composers such as Bach, Beethoven, Brahms and Schoenberg, whose music was (and is still) regarded as axiomatic exemplars of 'thematic work', 'developing variation' and 'musical logic'. In the pantheon of Messiaen's favourite composers, there are only two Germans: Mozart and Wagner. Yet, it was certainly not their treatment of form that attracted Messiaen, but some of their harmonic, timbral and rhythmic techniques, and the use of symbolic motives. Indeed, the 'art of the finest, most gradual transition' ('*Kunst des feinsten, allmählichsten Überganges*') that Wagner counted amongst his highest achievements is just the opposite of Messiaen's formal devices.[8] In Messiaen's music, transitions are quite rare, especially in his later works, where he juxtaposes sections contrasting on almost every parametric level. The change from one section to the next usually occurs suddenly without any preparation.

---

[6] Patrick Szersnovicz, 'Olivier Messiaen: la liturgie de l'arc-en-ciel', 30.

[7] See Lothar Schmidt, *Organische Form in der Musik: Stationen eines Begriffs 1795–1850* (Kassel: Bärenreiter, 1990), and Lotte Thaler, *Organische Form in der Musiktheorie des 19. und beginnenden 20. Jahrhunderts* (München/Salzburg: Katzbichler, 1984).

[8] Wagner used this expression in a letter to Mathilde Wesendonck from 29 October 1859, cited in Carl Dahlhaus, *Wagners 'Kunst des Überganges'*, in: *Vom Musikdrama zur Literaturoper*, 2nd edition (München/Mainz: dtv/Schott, 1989), pp. 150–61.

Messiaen's additive and discontinuous formal treatment was recognised early and often criticised: 'he does not compose, he juxtaposes', Pierre Boulez wrote in 1948.[9] The concept of 'composition' underlying this statement is clearly indebted to the German tradition of organic form (transmitted to Boulez via Schoenberg and Leibowitz). The same can be said of a statement by Karlheinz Stockhausen, who in 1982 compared Messiaen's forms with the structure of a tapeworm that can be cut into several pieces without damaging the whole.[10] Stockhausen claimed that this supposedly 'inferior' formal concept was rooted in a specifically French tradition. In fact, there is a certain veracity in Stockhausen's somewhat pejorative description. The concept of additive, cumulative form with two or more contrasting and recurring elements, as used by Messiaen in his early compositions, is clearly related to refrain and rondo forms.[11] These forms were used in many countries, but there seemed to be a special penchant for them in France from the music of Couperin and Rameau to Debussy and Satie.[12] However, these forms constitute a tradition that already existed in medieval liturgy as well as in Baroque dance and concerto movements, and survived into the nineteenth century (and its large 'developing forms' of sonata and symphony) in the guise of rondos and character pieces.

The adaptation of refrain and rondo forms by a young French composer mainly devoted to organ and piano pieces is certainly not surprising, nor very original. However, Messiaen soon began to develop and refine the concept of additive refrain form. He composed pieces with two or three recurring elements of equal importance, and in so doing rejected the hierarchy that exists in traditional refrain forms between the refrain and episodes. Messiaen also reflected on this theoretically in *TMLM*. In chapter 12, he described the seventh movement of his *Quatuor pour la fin du Temps* (1940–41) as: 'variations of the first theme, separated by developments of the second'.[13] In this movement, entitled *Fouillis d'arcs-en-ciel, pour l'Ange qui annonce la fin du Temps*, two contrasting themes alternate three times to convey the following pattern: a–b–a–b–a–b–a. At first, there is no common point and no bridge between the two themes. By their third occurrence, however, each of them is transformed by absorbing some features of the other. While this structure could still be attributed to a traditional formal scheme (the double variation used, for example, in Haydn's late *Andante varié* in F minor for

[9] Pierre Boulez, 'Propositions', in *Relevés d'apprenti* (Paris: Editions du Seuil, 1966), p. 68 ('il ne compose pas, il juxtapose'). This article was first published in *Polyphonie*, no. 2 (1948), 65–72.

[10] Karlheinz Stockhausen, *Texte zur Musik*, vol. VI (Köln: DuMont, 1989), p. 406.

[11] See Messiaen's *Préludes* no. 3 (*Le Nombre léger*) and no. 4 (*Instants Défunts*).

[12] See Couperin's and Rameau's *Pièces de clavecin* (which contain many *rondeaux*); Satie's *Trois Gnossiennes, Le Fils des etoiles, Prélude no. 3* and *Sonneries de la Rose + Croix*; Debussy's *La Soirée dans Grenade, Reflets dans l'eau* and *Hommage à Rameau*.

[13] Messiaen, *TMLM*, pp. 41–2.

piano), another piece analysed in *TMLM* shows a more complex structure. *Dieu parmi nous*, the last piece of Messiaen's organ cycle *La Nativité du Seigneur* (1935), is described by him as the 'development of three themes, preparing a final issue of the first'. The three themes of this piece are much shorter, and their several recurrences form a more irregular pattern. With each recurrence, the themes are more developed and thus get longer. The last part of the piece, a brilliant toccata on the first theme, fills as many pages in the score as the others altogether. These two examples of refrain form analysed by Messiaen in his *TMLM* show two things:

- The additive formal concept of free recurrence and variation of contrasting elements allows for significantly different realisations.
- Despite the non-linear and rather static character of this form that results from its discontinuous, repetitive structure, Messiaen tends to create a sort of intensification in the second half of the pieces.

In the 1930s and 1940s, Messiaen preferred to compose cycles of many contrasting pieces of moderate duration (ranging from about four to ten minutes). Most of these pieces consist of about six to twelve sections that can be attributed to between two and five different section types or themes. In the 1950s and 1960s, however, Messiaen composed some larger single-movement works consisting of much shorter sections.[14] The section types of these works can no more be called 'themes', because their main characteristics (which enable the listener to identify a section type and to distinguish it from both its predecessor and following section) often do not rely on the melodic structure, but on other parameters such as texture, timbre and tempo. In this text, the section types of Messiaen's works since 1950 will be called 'modules'. Through the frequent recurrence and variation of the modules, Messiaen creates different patterns that are combined to form a sophisticated and flexible musical mosaic. It is certainly not by chance that most of these works draw on 'natural' material of birdsong imitations: *Réveil des oiseaux*, the *Catalogue d'oiseaux* (especially *La Rousserolle effarvatte*), *Oiseaux exotiques* and *La Fauvette des jardins*. While three of these compositions depict the daily course in a specific landscape, *Oiseaux exotiques* (1955–56) has a clearer, more architectural structure. This piece consists of thirteen sections that can be attributed to seven different modules (section types) and form the pattern a–b; c–d–c–d; e–f–e–g–f; b–a.[15] The mosaic is built around two

[14] This new type of form is already anticipated in the piano piece *Cantéyodjayâ* (1948). By using the titles '1er refrain', '2e refrain' and '3e refrain' in the score (pp. 10–26), Messiaen himself reflects the transformation of simple refrain form into a complex mosaic form with several recurring elements of equal importance.

[15] The form of Messiaen's *Oiseaux exotiques* is as follows: a (p. 1–3) – b (4–5); c (6–8) – d (8–9) – c (9–12) – d (13); e (14–15) – f (16–57) – e (58–61) – g (62–65) – f (66–83); b (84) – a (85–86).

highly contrasting module groups (c–d–c–d and e–f–e–g–f), the second of which is much longer and more complicated than the first. These two module groups are preceded and followed by a very striking and thus easily recognisable pair of modules (a–b; b–a) that provides the piece with a symmetrical frame.

Mosaic form in *Couleurs de la cité céleste*

The most refined mosaic form of Messiaen's instrumental music is to be found in *Couleurs de la cité céleste*, written for an ensemble of wind instruments, percussion and piano (1963; see Table 9.1). Though not much longer than *Oiseaux exotiques*, *Couleurs* contains no fewer than forty-six sections; some of them are so heterogeneous that they could still be further divided (for example, modules a, f, i). The whole mosaic is clearly structured into seven 'module groups', as has been already shown by Robert Sherlaw Johnson.[16] While Johnson calls the groups 'sections', I prefer to reserve this term for the little basic units of Messiaen's mosaics. I use the term 'group' for the patterns built by the grouping of different modules (section types), thus stressing the additive and repetitive structure of the patterns. In *Couleurs de la cité céleste*, there are three main module groups (groups II, IV, V), which display different strophic patterns; these three groups are framed by an introduction (I) and a coda (VI). Between the first and the second main groups, there is an intermezzo (III) consisting of three striking new modules that recur at the end of the work (VII).[17]

   The seven module groups show many significant interrelationships and differences. The first two main groups stand in stark opposition to each other, whereas the third group and coda combine elements from both of them. The most important module is a plainchant melody, the 'Alleluia du 8e dimanche après Pentecôte'. It occurs in four groups (I, II, V, VI) and thus functions as a sort of 'refrain' for the whole work. After its exposition in I, the plainchant melody is juxtaposed three times with highly contrasting material (birdsong, colour-chords) in II. In V, the melody recurs in its original shape and is simultaneously combined with other contrasting material (Indian rhythms from IV, a new plainchant melody, colour-chords from II), which provides an effect of recapitulation, but also of intensification. This effect finds its peak in group VI, where the 'Alleluia' is superimposed above Indian rhythms from IV and new birdsong. This coda group also recapitulates

[16] Robert Sherlaw Johnson, *Messiaen*, 2nd edition (London: Dent and Sons, 1989), p. 180.
[17] Johnson calls this intermezzo 'refrain'. This is misleading since the intermezzo occurs only twice in the whole piece. The term 'refrain' should be reserved for the 'Alleluia du 8e dimanche après Pentecôte'.

Table 9.1: *Couleurs de la cité céleste*: mosaic form (46 sections)

page	1	2	2–4	5	6–7	7	8	8–9	9–10	11	12	12–13	13–14	15	16	16
module	a	b	a	c	d	e	c′	e	d	c′	e	c′	d	e	c′	e
type	bs	bs	bs	pc	bs	cc	pc	cc	bs	pc	cc	pc	bs	cc	pc	cc
strophe	–	–	–	–	strophe 1				strophe 2				strophe 3			
group	I: introduction				II: first main group											

17–18	19	20–21	21–25	25	26	26–31	32–37	38	38–39	39–40	40	41–48
f	g	h	l	j	k	l	i	j	k	m	k	l
ss	bs	pc	bs	ss	pc	rp	bs	ss	pc	bs	pc	rp
–	–	–	strophe 1				strophe 2					
III: intermezzo			IV: second main group									

48–49	49	50–51	52	52–54	54	55–58	58–59	59–60
c	c′+l	c′+n	c′+l	c′+n	c′+l	c′+e	c′+l	c
pc	pc+rp	pc	pc+rp	pc	pc+rp	pc+cc	pc+rp	pc
V: third main group (various superimpositions)								

61	62–65	66	66	67–69	69–71	72	72–73
b	c′+l+o	p	j	d	f	g	h
bs	pc+rp+bs	bs	ss	bs	ss	bs	pc
VI: coda (recapitulation; culmination point)					VII: recapitulation of the intermezzo		

Modules (16)
a: three different birdsongs presented successively (Tui, Benteveo and Mohoua)
b: Troglodyte barré (birdsong; piano solo cadenza)
c: Alleluia du 8ᵉ dimanche après Pentecôte (brass)
c′: the same, played by three 'xylos' (xylophone, xylorimba, marimba)
d: Oiseau-cloche (several timbres)
e: colour-chords
f: l'étoile qui a la clef de l'abîme (several striking sound gestures)
g: Stournelle (birdsong; piano solo cadenza)
h: Alleluia du Saint-Sacrement (brass choral)
i: eight different birdsongs presented successively (e.g. Araponga, Saltator cendré, Benteveo)
j: l'abîme (resonance effects)
k: Alleluia du 4ᵉ dimanche après Pâques (*Klangfarbenmelodie* of clarinets, horns, bells)
l: superimposition of different rhythmic patterns (Indian and Greek rhythms, permutations)
m: unlabeled section in birdsong style
n: Alleluia de la Dédicace (brass)
o: six birdsongs presented simultaneously (e.g. Troglodyte à long bec, Râle takahé, Saltator cendré)
p: Moqueur de Venezuela (birdsong; piano solo cadenza)

Module material types (5)
bs: birdsong (8 modules: a, b, d, g, i, m, o, p)
cc: colour-chords (1 module: e)
pc: plainchant (4 modules: c, h, k, n)
rp: rhythmic patterns (1 module: l)
ss: sound symbols (2 modules: f, j)

---

birdsongs from I and II and the sound-symbol of 'the abyss' (*l'abîme*) from IV. Further interrelationships between the groups can be discovered by reducing the modules to five types of material:

1) Plainchant is present in all seven groups.
2) Birdsong is omitted only in V.

3) Colour-chords are used in II and V, thus building an arch.

4) Sound-symbols of the abyss occur in III, IV, VI and VII.

5) Indian and Greek rhythms are introduced rather late (in IV), but then continue through V up to the peak of superimposition in VI.

The mosaic form of the whole composition shows a very carefully balanced kaleidoscopic structure that can be seen as a further differentiation and refinement of the simpler additive refrain forms of Messiaen's earlier works. This structure is not easy to follow for the listener. While the break between two juxtaposed modules is normally clear, the aural recognition of the highly sectionalised and repetitive groups demands several hearings as well as a good memory.

What is the sense of this new and rather sophisticated formal concept? As we may conclude from Messiaen's statements cited at the beginning of this study, the composer certainly did not invent his 'mosaic form' for its own sake.[18] On the contrary, he developed it in order to express an extra-musical, religious message. *Couleurs de la cité céleste* depicts the magnificent colours of the walls of the 'Holy City' as described by St John in Chapter 21 of the Apocalypse. According to Messiaen, these colours are symbolised musically not only by harmonic means (colour-chords) but also in the form of the composition:

> The form of this work depends entirely on colours. Melodic and rhythmic themes, complexes of sounds and timbres evolve like colours. In their permanently renewed variations, there can be found (by analogy): hot and cold colours, complementary colours influencing their neighbours, colours brightened to white or darkened by black.[19]

This means that every module of the work is to be seen as a characteristic musical colour and that these colours are juxtaposed and superimposed in order to create maximal contrast. This concept of form, based on intensive contrasts, was obviously inspired by two of Messiaen's favourite models from the plastic arts: the stained-glass windows of medieval cathedrals, and the modern paintings of Robert Delaunay.[20]

It is important to stress that, in Messiaen's music, colour contrasts between modules (and chords) not only suggest a figurative function (such

---

[18] The parallel between Messiaen's music and the structure of a mosaic has been already stressed by Johnson, *Messiaen*, p. 167, and Halbreich, *Olivier Messiaen*, p. 419.

[19] Olivier Messiaen, *Couleurs de la cité céleste*, orchestral score (Paris: Leduc 1967), *Première Note de l'auteur* ('La forme de cette œuvre dépend entièrement des couleurs. Les thèmes mélodiques ou rythmiques, les complexes de sons et de timbres, évoluent à la façon des couleurs. Dans leurs variations perpétuellement renouvelées, on peut trouver [par analogie] des couleurs chaudes et froides, des couleurs complémentaires influençant leurs voisines, des couleurs dégradées vers le blanc, rabattues par le noir.').

[20] See Messiaen's *Couleurs de la cité céleste*, and his *Conférence de Notre-Dame* (Paris: Leduc 1978), pp. 7 and 12.

as the depiction of the 'Holy City') but also produce a strong sensuous impact on the listener: an *'extase colorée'* and a sort of sonic 'dazzlement' (*éblouissement*)[21] that, according to Messiaen, offers him the possibility to feel a presentiment of the Beyond.[22] This impact is not restricted to the sphere of colour, but also affects another very important dimension of Messiaen's music: the perception of time. Messiaen often announced his will to suspend the listener's sense of time. However, in explaining the musical methods used to achieve this aim, he typically referred to microstructural techniques (such as ametrical additive rhythms or modal harmony).

The preface to *Couleurs de la cité céleste* ends with one of Messiaen's rare statements on the temporal aspect of his mosaic form: 'the work does not end – having never really begun: it turns on itself, interlacing its temporal blocks, like the rose window of a cathedral with its flamboyant and invisible colours … '. This means that the mosaic form – because of its open, discontinuous, non-linear, repetitive (and thus unforeseeable) structure – provides a feeling of timelessness. The temporal aspect of this form was accurately described by the young Karlheinz Stockhausen in his article *Momentform*:

> In recent years, musical forms have been composed which are remote from the scheme of goal-directed dramatic forms … These forms are immediately intensive and remain present at an equal level; … they are in a state of always having already commenced and could go on as they are eternally; … in these forms, an instant does not need to be just a particle of linear time, of measured duration. This concentration on the present moment – on every moment – can make a vertical cut, as it were, across horizontal time perception, extending out to a timelessness I call eternity.[23]

This musical 'moment form' that attempts to put the listener in a state of an 'eternal present' presupposes some aspects of information theory. Messiaen and Stockhausen were both convinced that the perception of

---

[21] Messiaen, *Couleurs de la cité céleste, Premiere Note de l'auteur* ('l'œuvre ne termine pas – n'ayant jamais commencé vraiment: elle tourne sur elle-même, entrelaçant ses blocs temporels, comme une rosace de cathédrale aux couleurs flamboyantes et invisibles …').
[22] See Messiaen's *Conférence de Notre-Dame*, pp. 12–15, and Sander van Maas's study (Chapter 4) in this volume.
[23] Karlheinz Stockhausen, *Momentform* (1960), in *Texte zur Musik*, vol. I (Cologne: DuMont, 1963), pp. 198–9 ('Es sind in den letzten Jahren musikalische Formen komponiert worden, die von dem Schema der dramatischen finalen Form weit entfernt sind; … die vielmehr sofort intensiv sind und – ständig gleich gegenwärtig … die immer schon angefangen haben und unbegrenzt so weiter gehn könnten; … Formen, in denen ein Augenblick nicht Stückchen einer Zeitlinie, ein Moment nicht Partikel einer abgemessenen Dauer sein muß, sondern in denen die Konzentration auf das Jetzt – auf jedes Jetzt – gleichsam vertikale Schnitte macht, die eine horizontale Zeitvorstellung quer durchdringen bis in die Zeitlosigkeit, die ich Ewigkeit nenne.'). For the concept of 'moment form' and 'moment time', see also Jonathan D. Kramer, *The Time of Music* (New York/London: Schirmer/Macmillan, 1988), pp. 201–20.

musical time depends on its informational density.[24] According to Barbara Barry, in classical music there is usually a balance between new and recurring elements, and thus a continuous middle level of information. On the contrary, Messiaen (like other modern composers) preferred extremes.[25] In his musical mosaics, the listener is first confronted with a large quantity of new information (three or more contrasting modules exposed quickly one after the other). Later on, these modules often recur and the level of new information decreases significantly. Paradoxically, both extremes tend to confuse the (traditional) sense of time and of form; they hinder the listener's ability to get a clear idea of the order in which events are happening. This effect (which could seem to be a defect in the perspective of classical linear formal concepts such as the sonata allegro) is intended by Messiaen to communicate his idea of a state of timelessness that he believed all Christians shall reach in the Beyond. Moment form and mosaic form, timelessness and 'extase colorée' are two sides of the same coin in Messiaen's religious art. They are the basic principles of his music, especially from the 1950s onwards.[26]

Mosaic form in *La Transfiguration de Notre-Seigneur Jésus-Christ*

In the orchestral works following *Couleurs*, the highly sectionalised single-movement form used in that work did not develop further. In *Et exspecto resurrectionem mortuorum* and *Des canyons aux étoiles*, the composer returned to the more conventional concept of a cycle of pieces of moderate duration and simpler module patterns. However, he transferred his mosaic form into the reign of vocal music, thus enriching this form with a new type of 'colour': the sound of the human voice. In his huge oratorio *La Transfiguration de Notre-Seigneur Jésus-Christ* (1965–69), Messiaen used vocal sections clearly modelled after aspects of ancient liturgical chant, such as a cappella recitation and choral unison singing (often with unison instrumental accompaniment). These vocal sections call to mind that the tradition of refrain forms originally stems from vocal liturgical music, and this also underlines the suitability of Messiaen's mosaic form to the expression of religious messages.[27]

---

[24] See Olivier Messiaen, *Traité de rythme, de couleur, et d'ornithologie (TRCO)*, Tome I (Paris: Leduc, 1994), p. 10, and Karlheinz Stockhausen, 'Struktur und Erlebniszeit' (1955), in *Texte zur Musik*, vol. I, pp. 86–98.

[25] Barbara R. Barry, *Musical Time. The Sense of Order* (Stuyvesant, NY: Pendragon Press, 1990), pp. 167–232.

[26] See Stefan Keym, *Farbe und Zeit: Untersuchungen zur musiktheatralen Struktur und Semantik von Olivier Messiaens Saint François d'Assise* (Hildesheim: Georg Olms, 2002).

[27] In fact, Messiaen showed some interest in the refrain forms of plainchant already in *TMLM*, pp. 44–6.

Table 9.2: *Configuratum corpori claritatis suae* (*La Transfiguration*): mosaic form
(25 sections)

page	35–36	37	38	38	38	38	39	40–41	42–43	44	45	45	46	46	46–47	48–49
module	a	b	c	d	e	f	g	h	a	b	c	d	e	f	g	h
type	inst.		vocal		instrumental			vocal	inst.		vocal		instrumental			vocal
group	first strophe (8 modules)								second strophe							

50	51–53	54	55	56	57	58–59	59	60–62
a	i	a	i	a	i	e	d	a
inst.	voc.	inst.	voc.	inst.	voc.	inst.	voc.	inst.
alternation form (core of the message)						recapitulation/coda		

Modules (9)
a: Grand Indicateur (birdsong; wind instruments)
b: Bulbul (birdsong; woodwinds, horns, strings)
c: sopranos and tenors, unison singing (with chordal woodwind accompaniment)
d: tenors, psalmodic recitative (based on one orchestral chord)
e: Grive grise (birdsong; piano solo cadenza)
f: high register unison melody (strings)
g: *fortissimo* unison and chords (winds)
h: unison choir (with unison woodwind accompaniment)
i: choral (unison and chords; chordal tutti accompaniment)

Text sources (2)
'Salvatorem exspectamus Dominum nostrum Jesum Christum, qui reformabit corpus humilitatis nostrae
configuratum corpori claritatis suae' (Phil. 3:20–21)
'Candor est lucis aeternae, speculum sine macula, et imago bonitatis illius. Alleluia' (Wisd. 7:26)

Text distribution
'Salvatorem exspectamus'. (c1+d1)
'Candor est lucis aeternae, speculum sine macula. Alleluia.' (h1)
'Dominum nostrum Jesum Christum, qui reformabit corpus humilitatis nostrae' (c2+d2)
'Et imago bonitatis illius. Alleluia.' (h2)
'Qui reformabit corpus humilitatis nostrae, configuratum corpori' (i1)
claritatis' (i2)
'claritatis suae' (i3)
'Exspectamus …' (d3)

La Transfiguration includes seven 'meditation' movements with refined
mosaic forms (II, III, V, IX, X, XII and XIII). Movement II, for example,
includes twenty-six sections that can be attributed to nine different modules
(four vocal and five purely instrumental modules; see Table 9.2). The mosaic
consists of four module groups. The first group is a strophe comprising no less
than eight very short modules (a–h) exposed immediately one after the other.
This is a striking example of the 'informational overload' that occurs at the
beginning of Messiaen's mosaic forms.[28] Two orchestral imitations of birdsongs (a, b) are followed by two short vocal sections with chordal accompaniment (c, d) and three instrumental sections with contrasting timbres (e, f, g);
the strophe ends with a longer vocal phrase accompanied by unison woodwinds (h). The whole strophe then recurs in the same order (with a new text),
with some modules varied and extended. The Latin text is also structured as a

---

[28] Barry, *Musical Time*, p. 262.

mosaic of juxtaposed and intermingling elements; it is based on two biblical citations, the first of which is recited in modules c and d, and the second in h.

In the third group, an already well-known module (a) alternates three times with a new one (i – a solemn choral which finally introduces the key word of the whole text: '*claritas*'). Sections i2 and i3 are not repetitions or variants of the melody of i1, but its continuation. This shows that, in Messiaen's mosaic form, the attribution of several sections to the same module does not so much depend on similarity of melody as on aspects of texture, timbre and tempo. The revalorisation of these parameters (that are strongly linked with Messiaen's concepts of 'colour' and 'time'), at the expense of melodic-thematic features, is one of the main differences between Messiaen's mosaic form and the above-mentioned German music tradition, which focused primarily on melodic *Gestalten*, and their more or less 'organic' development, in preference to instrumental colour. Movement II of *La Transfiguration* finishes with a recapitulation of three modules from the first strophe (e, d, a), which serve as a sort of conclusion, and they provide the movement with a symmetrical frame.

The mosaic form as used in *La Transfiguration* differs considerably from the structure of Messiaen's earlier vocal compositions. Of course, these earlier works also have additive refrain forms, but there is much more stylistic and temporal continuity between the different elements. For example, the first part of the third *Petite Liturgie de la Présence Divine* (*Psalmodie de l'Ubiquité par amour*) (1943–44) is built on three elements (repeated two times) that share the same tempo and the same vivid, enthusiastic character. Their three strophic occurrences are followed by a development section in a similar tempo, which leads steadily, by means of tonal modulation and a permanent increase of dynamics and textural density, to an impressive denouement. In the mosaic forms of *La Transfiguration*, on the contrary, there is no common element to connect different modules. They are set against each other like parts of a stained-glass window or a static solemn liturgy, both of which express divine eternity and grandeur. The musical mosaic is dominated by the orchestra: the vocal modules stand as islands within the much more varied and colourful instrumental sections. They are comparable to figures within a church window structured mostly by abstract colour forms, or to the text in a richly ornamented medieval bible.

Mosaic form in *Saint François d'Assise*

The concept of mosaic form with alternating vocal and instrumental modules reaches its apotheosis in Messiaen's only opera, *Saint François d'Assise* (1975–83). Each of its eight tableaux is a huge musical mosaic ranging from seventeen to forty-four minutes and comprising a very large number of sections (usually more than a hundred!). It is the only instance in Messiaen's œuvre where his originally instrumental, abstract and non-linear mosaic form is combined with dramatic action (that retraces the spiritual progress of a saint). This interference of musical mosaic form and narrative dramaturgy is one of the most fascinating aspects of Messiaen's opera. The action affects not only the grouping of the modules, but also the use of each module. Many modules are not limited to one tableau, but recur in several scenes like Wagnerian leitmotifs. Some modules are related to persons, others to ideas, and others to the natural environment (birdsong). The big repertory of modules can be classified into the following groups:

1) vocal modules:
   a) solo recitatives (mostly a cappella; this is the 'normal' way of singing in this opera)
   b) solo melodies with unison instrumental accompaniment
   c) solo melodies with chordal instrumental accompaniment
   d) choral singing (different types from unison up to clusters, but no conventional polyphony)
2) instrumental modules (most of these modules are called 'themes' by Messiaen in the prefaces to the eight tableaux of the orchestral score):
   a) melody-inspired modules (e.g. the *thème de Saint François*, the *thème de la joie* and the *thème du lépreux*)
   b) two-note motives (e.g. the *thème de la décision*, the first *thème de Frère Elie* and sigh motives in tableaux I and III)
   c) sound-inspired modules (several chord themes, but also polyrhythmic superimpositions of different sound layers)
3) instrumental birdsong imitations:
   a) short calls (e.g. Chouette hulotte (Tawny Owl), Fukuro, Notou)
   b) repetitive strophes (especially the New Caledonian Gerygone, a musical attribute of the Angel)
   c) complicated long songs (e.g. Alouette des champs (Skylark), Fauvette à tête noire (Blackcap))
   d) birdsong tutti

As in Messiaen's instrumental compositions, the modules are combined into groups displaying characteristic patterns.[29] The simplest group type is the alternation of two contrasting elements. In *Saint François d'Assise*, this type is

[29] A detailed analysis of the module groups in *Saint François d'Assise* can be found in Keym, *Farbe und Zeit*, pp. 207–31 and 280–309. The mosaic form of this opera is also evoked by Camille C. Hill, 'The Synthesis of Messiaen's Musical Language in His Opera *Saint François d'Assise*', Dissertation, University of Kentucky (Lexington), 1996, but she refers to all module groups as 'verse-response forms' (pp. 245–6), and does not develop any further classification of them.

mostly used for long monologues. Vocal melodies with (usually chordal) accompaniment alternate with a purely orchestral module (often birdsong).

A typical example is Francis's sermon to the birds (VI, 214–253)[30] in which the protagonist's singing alternates twelve times with motives of his favourite bird, the '*Fauvette à tête noire*' (imitated by a homorhythmic texture of eighteen woodwinds). Francis's singing incorporates five different elements, which recur irregularly. In the birdsong sections, there is almost no thematic repetition at all. The whole group has a very static character, and its order is difficult to grasp. On the other hand, this musical form is perfectly suited to the situation. The text of the sermon has no discursive, linear structure; it is a simple enumeration of praise (like many other texts by Messiaen).[31] The function of the music here is simply to create a pastoral and contemplative atmosphere by the aid of sonic symbols of the two protagonists: Francis and the birds.[32]

Other situations require more refined module patterns. In the narrative monologue of Brother Bernard (IV, 149–167), the climax (a short conversation between Jesus and Bernard) is musically underlined by a change of accompaniment from unison to chords and a decrease in tempo (IV, 159/166). The formal frame of alternation between vocal sections and birdsong (such as that of the Philémon, a New Caledonian bird) is preserved, but the different modules have a similar pulse so that this group resembles a traditional opera aria with ritornello structure.

In Francis's second prayer (V, 31–49), his increasing religious ecstasy is expressed through an irregular alternation of his vocal sections with three of his orchestral signature motives (*thème de la décision, thème de la joie, thème de l'appel*). There is more continuity, but no linear direction in this module group.

Francis's monologue before his death (VIII, 113–137) consists of two similar strophes, each of which has a clear linear structure that leads to a final culmination point symbolising the desired passage of the Saint to the Beyond. However, the intensive emotions of this scene are channelled by the stylised mosaic structure: Francis's singing alternates with a superimposition of the instrumental *thème des cloches*, and non-verbal choir clusters. These two elements represent the outer and the inner sphere of the dying protagonist (ringing church bells and voices from the Beyond) and thus they are

---

[30] Roman numerals refer to each tableau, Arabic numerals to the pages in the orchestral score: Olivier Messiaen, *Saint François d'Assise (Scènes franciscaines)*, 8 vols, (Paris: Leduc, 1988–92).

[31] See, for example, the text of the last of Messiaen's *Trois Petites Liturgies*, or the enumeration of religious works of art in his *Conférence de Notre-Dame*, pp. 5–6, or the enumeration of different conceptions of time in *TRCO*, Tome I, pp. 8 and 18–20.

[32] A similar group is that of the monologue of the Angel (V, 88–113), which alternates seven times with the birdsong of the Gerygone.

meant to be understood as simultaneous with Francis's words. However, Messiaen prefers to present these different aspects of the same moment successively in the guise of a repetitive alternation form in order to maintain the quasi-liturgical, solemn character of the work.

Another type of module grouping is that of a strophe which consists of more than three modules repeated several times in a regular way. The most prominent example is the morning liturgy of the Franciscans (II, 9–35). As in a medieval responsorial chant, solo singing (Francis's *Cantique des créatures*, accompanied by orchestral chords) alternates three times with choral sections (a male a cappella choir reciting another poem of St Francis in an austere psalmodic style on one single note). These two contrasting vocal modules are framed by three instrumental elements: the *thème de Saint François* played in unison by the strings, a birdsong (the Merle noir [Blackbird] played by the woodwinds), and a mysterious unison bass motive played by the Ondes Martenot. This static and solemn group reminds us once more of ancient liturgical refrain forms.

However, the use of this group type is not limited to scenes representing a liturgy. It can also be found in the second dialogue between Francis and the leper (III, 106–119: five modules recurring three times), in Francis's farewell monologue (VIII, 9–42), and in the first group of the opera (I, 1–49). This big group contains 77 sections, is built on 11 different modules and lasts about ten minutes (see Table 9.3).

The core of its structure consists of an alternation between two vocal modules: Brother Leo's arioso song about the fear of death alternates three times with Francis's contemplation of 'perfect joy', presented mostly as unaccompanied recitative (except for the final key idea *la joie parfaîte*, which is underlined by colourful chords). The group is enriched by four instrumental modules: the *thème de Saint François*, a sigh motive and two different imitations of the same birdsong (Alouette des champs (Skylark): three 'xylos' versus eighteen woodwinds). This material is presented two times in the same stylised manner (2 × 17 sections). In the third strophe, however, the quasi-liturgical procedure is interrupted by an emotional outburst by Francis, who passionately seeks for the right path to perfect joy (I, 31–35): 'O Cross! O Impossible thing! But were I to lean on you, sacred tree, what strength would you give me . . .' This break is underlined musically by the exposition of new material (a dissonant 'anticipation' of the *thème de la joie*) and by the development of the *thème de Saint François*. After Francis's outburst, the third strophe continues, but is enriched by several interventions of the *thème de la joie* and by the further development of Francis's theme, both strongly increasing the intensity of contrast and expression. This is a striking example of the interaction between discontinuous, quasi-liturgical form and linear dramatic movement in the musical mosaic of the work.

Table 9.3: *Saint François d'Assise*, tableau I, first module group: mosaic form (I, 1–49; 77 sections)

First and second double strophe (2 × 8 modules and 17 sections)

page	1–2	3–5	6	7	7	8	8	8	9	10	10	10	10	10	10	11	11
	12–13	14–17	18	18	19	20	20–21	21	22–23	23	24	24	24	24	24–25	25	25
module	a	b	c	d	e	d	e	f	c	d	g	d	g	d	g	d	h
type	inst.	vocal	inst.	voc.	inst.	voc.	inst.	voc.	inst.	voc.	inst.	voc.	inst.	voc.	inst.	vocal	
from	prelude	Leo	inter-mezzo	Francis / alternation group					Leo	inter-mezzo	Francis / alternation group						refrain

Brother Leo's third strophe (2 modules; 2 sections)

26–28	29–30
a	b
inst.	vocal
prelude	Leo

Francis's emotional outburst (7 modules; 15 sections)

31	31	31	32	32	32	33	33	34	34	34	35	35	35	35
d	i	g^v	e	j	k	e	d	j	k	j	g^d	e	d	f
vocal	inst.	vocal	inst.		vocal	inst.	vocal	inst.	vocal	instrumental		vocal		
'O Croix'		'O chose impossible!'		'Mais si je m' appuie sur toi'		'puissance'		'arbre sacré'					'Frère Léon?'	Leo: 'Mon Père?'

Francis's third strophe (7 modules; 26 sections)

36–39	39	40	40	40	41	41	41	42	42	42–43	43	43	43	43	44	45–46	46	46	47
c	g^d	e	j	d	g^d	d	g^d	e	j	d	j	d	j	d	g/g^d	k	j	d	g^d
instrumental				voc.	inst.	voc.	instrumental			voc.	inst.	voc.	inst.	voc.	inst.	vocal	inst.	voc.	inst.
intermezzo				alternation group						alternation group									

Francis's third strophe (continuation)

47	47	47	47	48	48–49
j	d	j	d	j	h
inst.	voc.	inst.	voc.	inst.	vocal
alternation group					refrain

Modules (11)
a: Alouette des champs (three 'xylos': xylophone, xylorimba, marimba)
b: Brother Leo's song about the fear of death (with chordal string accompaniment)
c: Alouette des champs (eighteen woodwinds; other material as in a)
d: Francis's contemplation of 'perfect joy' (unaccompanied recitative)
e: instrumental sigh motive (three ondes Martenot, strings)
f: Brother Leo's recitative (unaccompanied)
g: *thème de Saint François* (original texture: unison strings)
g^v: vocal version of the *thème de Saint François* (with chordal accompaniment)
g^d: development of the *thème de Saint François* (with chordal accompaniment)
h: Francis's arioso refrain '*la joie parfaîte*' (with chordal accompaniment: three ondes Martenot, strings)
i: tritonus motif (could be attributed both to Brother Leo's song and to Francis's theme; trumpet and strings)
j: *thème de la joie*, anticipation (brass)
k: Francis's vocal lines with unison accompaniment (low woodwinds, etc.)

The third type of module grouping consists of large groups with the irregular repetition of some modules. This type is mostly used for the representation of monologues and dialogues expressing a sharp conflict. A significant example is Francis's first prayer (II, 51–83), in which he overcomes himself to beg God to meet and love a leper. This module group is divided into three different sub-groups: a regular group containing a formal address to God (II, 51–56) is followed by a very heterogeneous and descriptive group (II, 57–71), which depicts a long enumeration of beautiful and ugly creatures and leads to the terrifying idea of the leper, expressed by a shrill twelve-tone-cluster. In the third sub-group (II, 71–83), modules of both preceding groups combine with new elements in order to express the climax of tension and its sudden release at the end of Francis's prayer. The whole monologue is one of the most dramatic and linear groups of the work.

The first dialogue between Francis and the Leper (III, 8–89) shows as much dramatic tension, but a less obvious linear development. The text, which consists of six statements by each person, corresponds to the musical mosaic which is structured as twelve attributable or character-specific sub-groups of modules.[33] Both persons mostly sing unaccompanied recitatives; only very important or emotional words and phrases are 'coloured' by the orchestra. On the other hand, the statements of both figures are often interrupted by short instrumental modules. Messiaen uses mosaic form to express significant features and changes within the dialogue. The leper, who is much more emotional and upset than Francis, has a bigger repertory of modules (18:15). Also, his module groups are longer, especially in the middle of the dialogue when he attacks Francis with fierce reproaches.

At the beginning, the two men seem to be enclosed in two completely different, incompatible spheres; their module groups have no common element. A change in their relationship begins after Francis has called the leper to penance. Here, Messiaen introduces new material (III, 59–61: nonverbal cluster-glissandi of the choir) and recapitulates some modules from the orchestral introduction of tableau III. These elements cannot be clearly attributed to either of the two persons. According to Messiaen's preface in the score, the cluster-glissandi express fear. But is it the leper's fear of penance or Francis's fear of leprosy, or both? From this moment, the two men are related by a similar feeling. This relationship is further expressed by

---

[33] Division of the dialogue (28 modules/119 sections altogether): III, 8–24 (= Leper's sub-group I; 5 modules/17 sections); III, 25–29 (= Francis's sub-group I; 5 modules/7 sections); III, 30–33 (Leper II; 3/7); III, 34–38 (Francis II; 5/11); III, 38–47 (Leper III; 6/20); III, 48–50 (Francis III; 4/5); III, 50–57 (Leper IV; 7/8); III, 57–58 (Francis IV; 3/5); III, 59–61 (this module cannot be clearly attributed to one of the two protagonists); III, 62–67 (Leper V; 6/14); III, 68–71 (Francis V; 2/4); III, 71–83 (Leper VI; 4/15); III, 84–89 (Francis VI; 5/5). See the table in Keym, *Farbe und Zeit*, pp. 504–7.

the birdcall of the Fukuro which occurs in module groups of both men (III, 71–73/77). Sequences and crescendos within this module prepare the powerful rising movement accompanying Francis's solemn and hopeful prophecy of resurrection which concludes this dialogue and provokes the intervention of the Angel. The whole dialogue is one more striking example of the interaction between quasi-liturgical alternation and dramatic development.

While this large module group is dominated by the text, the first dialogue between Francis and Brother Masseo (VI, 35–125) is divided into four sub-groups, each of which is characterised by a different birdsong. An exceptional case is that of the second part of the 'choir monologue' expressing the voice of Christ (VII, 71–113). This group comprises ten different modules that are presented one after the other without any recurrence in order to express the overwhelming, unexplainable power of the revelation of the Absolute.

Each of the eight tableaux of *Saint François d'Assise* consists of several module groups. Their number varies from four groups (tableau II: orchestral introduction – responsorial morning liturgy – Sanctus choir – Francis's first prayer) up to nine groups (tableau VI). Sometimes, the 'grouping of groups' creates patterns similar to the internal structure of the groups. For example, in tableau VI the instrumental intermezzi, built on birdsong, alternate irreg-ularly with dialogues between Brother Masseo and St Francis, and ecstatic monologues of the latter; these alternations result in the pattern a–b–c–b–a–c–a–b–a. In tableau IV, the strophic recapitulation of some module groups is rooted in the dramatic action: as in a liturgy, the Angel asks the same question to Brother Eli and to Brother Bernard. The ceremonial appearance and disappearance of the Angel is also accompanied by the same modules.

These examples demonstrate how Messiaen adapted his instrumental mosaic form to his opera, and how he further developed and refined it in *Saint François d'Assise* in order to represent the dramatic action. By doing this, he created a completely new musical form of opera perfectly suited to express the religious message of the work. In fact, the mosaic form in *Saint François d'Assise* fulfils a double function. On the one hand, it allows the music to follow closely the narrative action; on the other hand, it provides the work with a purely musical, abstract architecture dominated by sharp contrasts that produce a strong sensuous impact on the listener. This double strategy corresponds to Messiaen's description of stained-glass church win-dows which tell a story and at the same time dazzle the observer by their abstract play of colours and light.[34] Through the aid of mosaic form, Messiaen also finds a convincing and highly original solution to the problem

---

[34] See Messiaen, *Conférence de Notre-Dame*, pp. 12–15.

of how to express religious topics on the opera stage in an adequate, dignified way that keeps enough distance from the conventions of secular opera. In fact, the music of Messiaen's opera often expresses a high degree of human emotion, but only within the tight limits of single modules.[35] By the constant breaks between the modules and by their non-linear juxtaposition and repetition, Messiaen isolates these emotional moments and puts them in a stylised, severe structure reminiscent of the frozen architecture of stained-glass windows and the solemn, repetitive course of liturgy.

Viewed from a purely formal perspective, the mosaic form in *Saint François d'Assise* occupies a middle position between the traditional (Baroque and Classical) opera consisting of separate numbers, and the Wagnerian through-composed music drama.[36] The modules in *Saint François d'Assise* are as autonomous as the numbers in conventional opera. However, they are so short and open-structured that they can easily be grouped into a through-composed (though discontinuous) mosaic. In writing his only opera, Messiaen's main aim was certainly not the reform of operatic structure, but the expression of his Christian faith through the representation of the spiritual quest of a saint. However, in pursuing this theological-dramatic goal with the help of techniques developed previously in his purely instrumental works, he succeeded in creating one of the most original formal concepts in twentieth-century opera.

---

[35] There are some exceptions to this rule in the third and seventh tableaux that show a more linear musical structure (and dramaturgy) than the other scenes.
[36] Both of these form types were used in several twentieth-century religious operas. The Baroque 'number structure' was revived by Arthur Honegger in *Le Roi David* (1921). The form of through-composed music drama was chosen by Arnold Schoenberg in *Moses und Aron* (1930–32).

10 Two paths to paradise: reform in Messiaen's *Saint François d'Assise*

Robert Fallon

At the premiere of *Saint François d'Assise* (1975–83), Messiaen instructed his Parisian audience on the concept behind his new opera: 'Tout au long de la pièce, on doit voir les progrès de la grâce dans l'âme de Saint François' ('Throughout the work, one should see the progress of grace in Saint Francis's soul').[1] He elaborated the idea to Claude Samuel: 'At the beginning, he's Francis. Then, little by little, he becomes Saint Francis, and even super-Saint Francis. The series of eight scenes explains it.'[2] A glance at the libretto reveals, however, that Messiaen's narrative bears little resemblance to the unfolding of scenes in the opera. Despite impressing his intention on the audience, the progress is clear only in the first act: Francis defines perfect joy, then prays for it, and then partially finds it by overcoming his revulsion from the Leper. But in the long second act, Francis makes no progress along the path to perfect joy. So what purpose does the second act serve? Furthermore, how did Messiaen expect the histrionic art of opera to portray the most private movements of an invisible interiority?

To begin, the idea that the eight scenes show a soul's progress requires refinement. I suggest instead that the opera unfolds two principles of a theology of preparing for the Final Judgment. The first principle prescribes the road to perfect joy. As shown in Table 10.1, the opera opens with Francis's definition of perfect joy as the denial of the self and the acceptance of suffering, a definition based on Jesus's dictum in Matthew 16:24 (echoed in Luke and John): 'If any want to become my followers, let them deny themselves and take up their cross and follow me.' Francis fulfils the first requirement, the denial of the self, when he overcomes his fear and embraces the Leper, and he fulfils the second requirement, taking up the cross, when he accepts the suffering of the stigmata in scene 7. By dying in scene 8, he attains the perfect joy of union with God.

---

[1] Olivier Messiaen, untitled note in the programme book to his *Saint François d'Assise* (Paris: Théâtre National de l'Opéra de Paris, 1983), p. 15.

[2] Claude Samuel, *Olivier Messiaen: Music and Color: Conversations with*

Claude Samuel (Portland, OR: Amadeus Press, 1994), p. 214. For the original French interviews, see Samuel, *Permanences d'Olivier Messiaen* (Arles: Actes Sud, 1999).

Table 10.1: Scenes 1, 3, 7 and 8 present the theology of perfect joy, and scenes 2, 4, 5 and 6 present the theme of beauty

Theme	*Scene*							
	1	2	3	4	5	6	7	8
	The Cross	Lauds	The Kissing of the Leper	The Journeying Angel	The Angel-Musician	The Sermon to the Birds	The Stigmata	Death and the New Life
Perfect Joy	Perfect joy is overcoming self and suffering		Francis overcomes self by kissing Leper				Francis suffers stigmata	Perfect joy in death by union with God
Music leads to God		Chanting		Knocking	Viol	Birdsong		

Asserting that music leads to God, the second principle is summarised by a line found in scenes 5 and 8: 'Dieu nous éblouit par excès de Verité. La musique nous porte à Dieu par défaut de Vérité' ('God dazzles us by excess of Truth. Music leads us to God by lack of Truth'). This second path to paradise is introduced in the second scene and developed in the second act. It progresses from the chanting of scene 2 to the knocking at the door of scene 4 and the angelic music of scene 5, and culminates with the *concerts d'oiseaux* in scene 6. Francis reiterates the two themes in two valedictory statements before he dies. First he teaches that self-denial brings perfect joy: 'Blessed are those whom the first death will find submitting to Divine Will: the second death will do him no harm.' Next, he acknowledges that music carried him to God: 'Music and poetry have led me to Thee: by image, by symbol, and by lack of Truth.'

The slippage between Messiaen's opera and his description of it suggests that his work's symbolism is richer than even he allows. *Saint François* is not a biography but an operatic theology. The opera unfolds its two ways to save a soul not by its action, but by its contemplation, and not by a disengaged transcendence, but by its incorporation of history in its form and content to increase the significance and relevance of salvation.

Reflecting the pattern of Church reform in twentieth-century France, *Saint François* seeks to reinvigorate lost faith by reconstructing lost origins. This was also the project of a group of theologians in the middle decades of the twentieth century. Two of Messiaen's favourite theologians, Romano Guardini and Hans Urs von Balthasar, were important practitioners of this movement that they termed *ressourcement*. Through pervasive quotation from the Bible, and avoidance of the most stageworthy moments of Francis's life, *Saint François* evokes the origins of Christian drama and updates them for the contemporary opera house. Its similarities to the Orpheus myth recall the story that launched opera, but alter it to convey a Christian message. Emphasising joy and beauty basic to Franciscan faith, its theology relates these issues to twentieth-century problems and filters them through the ideas of twentieth-century writers. Like the theologians preferred by Messiaen, the opera aims to reform the world by addressing an urgent issue among postwar French Catholics – the absence of God in people's lives.

Musical prophecy

Messiaen's opera, which interprets the past within a Christian teleology that ends with the apocalypse and Final Judgment, shares Guardini's view that 'history's sense lies in the fulfillment of salvation'.[3] Such eschatological

[3] Romano Guardini, *The Lord*, trans. Elinor Castendyk Briefs (Washington, DC: Regnary Publishing, 1982), p. 603.

thinking was facilitated by the Cold War's threat of global incineration. In 1983, the year *Saint François* premiered, when Ronald Reagan unveiled his 'Star Wars' plan and terrorism and occupation convulsed the Middle East, Messiaen observed that 'Everybody's scared nowadays, scared of atomic war and the destruction of the earth.'[4] The opera's point of departure is this fear of death, whether from existentialist angst, nuclear Armaggedon, or the apocalypse. Messiaen personified fear in the character of Brother Leo, whose refrain 'J'ai peur' rings throughout the opera. The opening pages of Hans Urs von Balthasar's book *Der Christ und die Angst* (1952, translated into French as *Le Chrétien et l'angoisse* in 1954) acknowledges that the fear of death is at the root of 'the cosmic anxiety of the modern, secular era.'[5] His answer to fear is, of course, faith. 'Human fear', he says, 'has been completely and definitively conquered by the Cross.'[6] Francis, too, offers the Cross to Brother Leo in order to liberate him from fear.[7]

Messiaen's concern for death and the end of the world makes his voice prophetic. Yves Congar, a prominent *ressourcement* theologian, described prophets as 'the first among reformers' and named Francis among them.[8] Before even settling on Saint Francis for a subject, Messiaen seems to have considered reform a worthy subject: 'I chose to consecrate my opera to a prophet,'[9] he told Rolf Liebermann, director of the Paris Opéra. Messiaen's own prophetic doomsaying is exposed in this preface he wrote in 1970:

> The most famous of the 'signs' preceding the upheavals of the agony of the world: the return of the Jews to Israel – this sign is accomplished. [And] the Holy Virgin herself

---

[4] Almut Rößler, *Contributions to the Spiritual World of Olivier Messiaen with Original Texts by the Composer*, trans. Barbara Dagg, Nancy Poland and Timothy Tikker (Duisburg: Gilles and Francke Verlag, 1986), p. 124.

[5] Hans Urs von Balthasar, *The Christian and Anxiety*, trans. Dennis D. Martin and Michael J. Miller (San Francisco: Ignatius Press, 2000), pp. 31 and 39–44.

[6] Balthasar, *The Christian and Anxiety*, pp. 31 and 81.

[7] Balthasar, *The Christian and Anxiety*, p. 42. Balthasar also quotes a passage on death from the end of Ecclesiastes that Messiaen paraphrased in his opera. Brigitte Massin is incorrect in claiming that the words 'J'ai peur, j'ai peur sur la route' are cited from Ecclesiastes; see her *Olivier Messiaen: une poétique du merveilleux* (Aix-en-Provence: Alinea, 1989), p. 195. Although the words 'J'ai peur' are Messiaen's, they may have been suggested by the Jerusalem Bible's note 'b' of Ecclesiastes 11: 'For Quheleth, old age is not happiness but fear of death,' which appears three verses after the

source of the line 'quand s'agrandissent et s'obscurcissent les fenêtres' (Eccles. 12:6).

[8] Yves Congar, *Vraie et fausse réforme dans l'Eglise* (Paris: Les Editions du Cerf, 1950), p. 201: 'Les prophètes sont-ils comme les premiers parmi les réformateurs.' Congar counts Francis among reformers in his *Vraie et fausse réforme*, pp. 59–59, 252, 556, and his *Les Voies du Dieu vivant: théologie et vie spirituelle* (Paris: Cerf: 1962), p. 255. He counts Francis among the prophets in *Vraie et fausse réforme*, p. 222. Unless otherwise noted, all translations are my own.

[9] See Stefan Keym, *Farbe und Zeit: Untersuchungen zur musiktheatralen Struktur und Semantik von Olivier Messiaens* Saint François d'Assise (Hildesheim: Georg Olms, 2002), p. 38, n. 17: "J'ai choisi de consacrer mon opéra à un prophète." Cf. Thomas Daniel Schlee and Dietrich Kämper, eds., *Olivier Messiaen: La Cité céleste–das himmlische Jerusalem: über Leben und Werk des französischen Komponisten* (Cologne: Wienand Verlag, 1998), p. 205.

showed herself time and again . . . There was Pont-Main, Beauring, Banneux, and very close to us: Barabandal (where she spoke of the end of Time), San Damiano . . . Of course, no one is absolutely obliged to believe these things . . . But the whole Bible is there, entirely inspired by the Holy Spirit, wholly an article of faith. And everywhere . . . everywhere it is the same cry of alarm, reclaiming the conversion of everyone before the terrible convulsions that will precede the Resurrection of the flesh and the Final Judgment . . . The end of Time, the end of Space, the entrance into Eternity: all this is coming to us in great strides – and beforehand, the procession of terrors: the antichrist, the cataclysms, the deceptive triumph of the Beast of the Apocalypse.

It is prudent to prepare yourself . . .[10]

The fervour and conviction of this quotation compel critics to consider how Messiaen manifested his faith in his music of the 1970s and, specifically, how *Saint François d'Assise* prepares for the end of time.

Messiaen's apocalyptic 'prepare yourself' begins *La Prophétie musicale dans l'histoire de l'humanité* (*Musical Prophecy in the History of Humanity*), by his student Albert Roustit, who mixes numerological interpretations of music theory and the music of the spheres with figural interpretations of world history. 'The order of the harmonics of resonance', he wrote, 'precisely determines historical epochs.'[11] Roustit argues that, like biblical prophecy, music history foretells world events. For example, he determines that the golden section between Luther's era and the year 2000 falls at the time of Beethoven and Berlioz, when a period of decadence began that he says will culminate in the apocalypse. The progress of music history, he claims, is directed toward exhausting the twelve tones of the octave and depleting everything known as dissonance. When this occurs, as the book says it did in the 1950s, then the return of Christ is imminent. Roustit chooses the year 2000 for the date of the Resurrection and the end of the world.

In 1971, the year after his warning to 'prepare yourself', Messiaen wrote the preface to another book, Jules Chaix-Ruy's *Du féerique aux céleste* (*From*

---

[10] Olivier Messiaen, preface to Albert Roustit, *La Prophétie musicale dans l'histoire de l'humanité* (Roanne: Editions Horvath, 1970), pp. 10–11: 'Le plus célèbre des "signes" précédant les bouleversements de l'agonie du monde: le retour des Juifs en Israël – ce signe est accompli. La Sainte Vierge elle-même s'est montrée à maintes reprises . . . Il y a eu Pont-Main, Beauraing, Banneux, et tout près de nous: Barabandal (où elle a parlé de la fin du Temps), San Damiano . . . Bien sûr, personne n'est absolument obligé de croire à ces choses . . . Mais toute la Bible est là, tout entière inspirée de l'Ésprit-Saint, tout entière article de foi. Et partout, des Prophètes de l'Ancien Testament à l'Apocalypse, en passant par Saint Paul et les paroles même de notre Seigneur Jésus-Christ dans les Evangiles, partout c'est le même cri d'alarme, réclamant la conversion de tous avant les terribles convulsions qui précéderont la Résurrection de la chair et le Jugement Final. Ce qui pouvait paraître relativement loin aux Prophètes d'Israël et à Saint Paul lui-même, tout nous en annonce la proximité. La fin du Temps, la fin de l'Espace, l'entrée dans l'Eternité: tout cela vient vers nous, à grands pas – et avant, le cortège des terreurs: l'antichrist, les cataclysmes, le triomphe mensonger de la Bête de l'Apocalypse.

Il est prudent de se préparer . . .'

[11] Roustit, *La Prophétie musicale*, p. 235: 'L'ordre des harmoniques de la résonance détermine avec exactitude les époques historiques.'

the Fairytale to the Celestial).[12] Chaix-Ruy cites many themes and references that appear in later works by Messiaen: the fairy-tales of Madame d'Aulnoy, the 'diaphanous bubble' of Hieronymus Bosch's *Garden of Earthly Delights*, and the medieval mysticism of Jan van Ruysbroeck's *Brilliant Stone*. He even discusses Francis of Assisi, Maurice Denis's woodcuts for the *Fioretti*, and indeed Messiaen himself.

The following year, 1972, Messiaen imported his fascination for Chaix-Ruy's *Du féerique aux céleste* into his own work, *Des canyons aux étoiles . . . (From the Canyons to the Stars. . .)*, the last work he composed before *Saint François d'Assise*. He was smitten with Chaix-Ruy's title because he adored the fantastical elements of fairy-tales. By changing Chaix-Ruy's titular 'aux céleste' to 'aux étoiles', he evoked Henri Duparc's tone poem of that name. Each of these titles derives from the Latin adage 'Per aspera ad astra' ('Through suffering to the stars').[13] Like *Saint François d'Assise*, *Des canyons* focuses on Christian themes such as suffering, fear, grace, resurrection and the healing power of the beauty of creation (see Table 10.2). Most strikingly, both works are about uniting earth with heaven, whether by transforming the canyons of despair into the stars of paradise or by sanctifying a man into a saint. Both scores employ instruments meant to evoke the wind (the aleophone) and the earth (the geophone); both are in the form of a triptych; both use natural harmonics in the strings to represent the music of the spheres; both end with a joyful peeling of bells, and both refer to the stars as resurrected souls based on a paraphrase of 1 Cor. 15:35–41: 'For one star differs from another star in glory. So also is the resurrection of the dead.' In both works, Messiaen admonishes his listeners to prepare themselves in order to shine brightly and find joy in the hereafter.

Ressourcement and contemplation

While the fatalism of Roustit and the Franciscan wonder of Chaix-Ruy contribute to the opera's immediate intellectual context, the theological project of *ressourcement* colours the opera's intellectual background. By the 1920s, generations of anticlerical sentiment had left French society ignorant of the Roman Catholic faith and disenfranchised from a Church hierarchy dismissed as aloof and authoritarian.[14] To combat these attitudes and reform

[12] Jules Chaix-Ruy, *Du féerique au céleste* (Grenoble: Roissard, 1971).
[13] The notion that salvation is achieved through suffering is symbolised in the 'u'-shaped contour of Saint Francis's Theme.
[14] In their discussion of the book *France, pays de mission?* (1943), which asserted that France required evangelisation, Jean-Marie Domenach and Robert de Montvalon cite the demographics that led Catholic intellectuals to regard the French laity as ignorant of their faith: 'Although nearly 85 per cent of Frenchmen were baptised, two-thirds of them quickly abandoned religious practice

Table 10.2: Themes common to *Des canyons aux étoiles . . .* and *Saint François d'Assise*

Theological subject	Des canyons aux étoiles . . .	Saint François d'Assise
Nature		
Creation	Utah parks, birds, stars	Canticle of Brother Sun, birds, stars
Stars	*Des canyons aux étoiles . . .* (title); 'What is written in the stars . . .' (III)	'He is departed . . . like . . . a golden butterfly that flies from the Cross to go beyond the stars . . .' (scene 8)
Birdsong	Omao, Leiothrix, Elepaio, Shama (XI): compared by Messiaen to Sermon to the birds in his opera	Sermon to the birds (scene 6)
Unity of heaven and earth	*Des canyons aux étoiles . . .* (title unites earth and heaven)	'The birds await the day when earth and heaven unite' (scene 6); progress of grace (human to saintly)
Life on earth		
Fear/Awe	'Cedar Breaks and the Gift of Awe' (V)	'I'm afraid' (scenes 1, 2, 4, 5)
Suffering	'O earth cover not thou my blood and let my cry have no place!' (VI)	'That I may feel in my body the pain that you endured at the hour of your cruel Passion' (scene 7)
Sin	'Man deformed by himself' (IX)	'Thy heart accuses thee . . .' (scene 4)
Grace	'When we enter the state of grace, we receive from the Holy Spirit a new name, which shall be eternal'. (X)	Progress of grace in path leading to perfect joy
Death and afterlife		
Death	Death is implied in the journey from canyons to resurrection (VIII) to stars	References to death in scenes 1, 4, 5, 7, 8
Predestination	'What is written in the stars . . .' (III); Woodthrush symbolises our predestination in heaven' (X)	'What do you think about predestination?' (scene 4)
Resurrection	'The Resurrected and the Song of the Star Aldebaran' (VIII)	References to resurrection in scenes 3, 5, 6, 8
Glory	'For one star differs from another star in glory. So also is the resurrection of the dead.' (VIII)	'For one star differs from another star in glory. So also is the resurrection of the dead.' (scene 8)

the Church, theologians, clergy and laity targeted the unreligious urban poor and the rural faithful for evangelisation in the 1930s and 1940s. Catholic Action – an umbrella term for lay organisations that receive Church

and lived as pagans . . . At Montreuil in 1939, only about two thousand people out of a population of seventy thousand went to Mass on Sunday.' See Jean-Marie Domenach and Robert de Montvalon, *The Catholic Avant-Garde: French Catholicism Since World War II* (New York: Holt, Rinehart and Winston, 1967), pp. 51–2.

sponsorship – organisations like the Jocistes and clerical involvement in the worker – priest experiments, which planted priests among the laity in their workplaces, energised the Church to a degree unprecedented in modern French history. According to Jean-Marie Domenach, editor of *Esprit*, the Occupation intensified the desire for reform:

> Men naturally turned back to essentials, to find reasons for living and dying . . . In the ordeal, there began a re-examination of every aspect of Catholicism, to rediscover the foundation of the Church.[15]

Messiaen echoes this movement in his opera through his method of returning to the roots of Catholic tradition.

Pursuing their agenda of *ressourcement*, a loose confederation of mainly French theologians historicised the New Testament, the Church Fathers, Thomas Aquinas and other medieval standard-bearers of the Christian spirit (including Francis of Assisi) in order to ensure current reforms were consistent with the defining origins of Christianity. Besides Guardini and Balthasar, other key figures included Yves Congar, Henri de Lubac, Marie-Dominique Chenu and Jean Daniélou; collectively they formed the *nouvelle théologie*. Today they are credited with enabling and shaping the reforms of Vatican II. Congar attributed the origin of the term '*ressourcement*' to these words of Charles Péguy:

> A [true] revolution is a call from a less perfect tradition to a more perfect tradition, a call from a shallower tradition to a deeper tradition, a backing up of tradition, an overtaking of depth, an investigation into deeper sources; in the literal sense of the word, a 're-source'.[16]

Arguing that '*ressourcement* is a completely different thing than a return to the past, than a "repristination",'[17] Congar said that it reinterrogates the texts of early Christianity and, as Thomas Aquinas had done with Aristotle, synthesises them into contemporary society – a society that in 1950 was desperate for authenticity.[18]

Francis of Assisi was enlisted by the reform movement's social activists, who saw his most important legacy to the modern world in his compassion and good works, rather than his devotion and obedience. They admired Francis for renouncing his bourgeois life, aiding the sick and the poor and 'rebuilding the fallen church'. As early as 1956, Joseph Lortz, a contributor to the series *Présence de Saint François*, which Messiaen used to write his

---

[15] Domenach and de Montvalon, *The Catholic Avant-Garde*, p. 6–7.
[16] Congar attributed the coinage to Péguy in his *Vraie et fausse réforme*, p. 602, as quoted in Marcellino D'Ambrosio, '*Ressourcement* theology, *aggiornamento*, and the

hermeneutics of tradition', *Communio* Vol. 18 (Winter 1991), 537.
[17] Congar, *Vraie et fausse réforme*, p. 337: '[*ressourcement*] est tout autre chose qu'un retour au passé, qu'une "repristination".'
[18] Congar, *Vraie et fausse réforme*, pp. 51–3.

libretto, asserted that 'Francis is the most authentic image that one can find of Catholic Action.'[19]

Just three years before Messiaen set to work on *Saint François d'Assise*, the perception of Francis as a man of social reform was popularly portrayed in Franco Zeffirelli's film *Brother Sun, Sister Moon* (1972). Ending after Pope Innocent III approves Francis's Order of the Friars Minor, the film depicts only the beginning of the saint's life in order to draw a parallel between the early Franciscans and the contemporary counterculture, thus contrasting the poor spiritual life of the materially wealthy with the rich spiritual life of the outcast poor. Messiaen's opera, on the other hand, presents the latter part of Francis's life, highlights his contemplative nature and avoids social commentary.

Not surprisingly, the *ressourcement* theologians, too, enlisted Francis of Assisi in their efforts to reform the church. But like Messiaen, they focused on Francis's legacy of prayer and contemplation, not his actions. In his *Vraie et fausse réforme dans l'Eglise*, Congar argued that Francis was a model reformer:

> A good 'ressourcée' theology and especially a good ecclesiology are one of the most efficacious guarantees of a faithful reform ... The reforms that are successful in the Church are those that are made according to the concrete needs of souls, in a pastoral perspective, by the route of holiness.
>
> The standard of such reforms is found in the action of a Saint Bernard as well as a Saint Francis of Assisi.[20]

Though he promoted social action, Congar saw in Francis a man whose prayerfulness was a prerequisite for social ministry:

> When a man truly realises this pure vertical [personal] relationship to God that we come to encounter in Francis of Assisi, he changes or creates something in the order of horizontal [social] relationships.[21]

Guardini, too, was unequivocal about the primacy of contemplation over action. Referring to the need for individual development to precede social development, he believed that the crisis of modernism partly resulted from the inverted priority that contemporary Catholics gave to social and

[19] Joseph Lortz, *François l'incomparable*, translated from the German by Jacqueline Gréal (Paris: Editions Franciscaines, 1956), p. 82: 'François est l'image la plus authentique que l'on puisse trouver de l'Action Catholique.'

[20] Congar, *Vraie et fausse réforme*, p. 252: 'Une bonne théologie "ressourcée" et surtout une bonne ecclésiologie sont une des garanties le plus efficaces d'un réformisme fidèle ... Les réformes qui ont réussi dans l'Eglise sont celles qui se sont faites en fonction des besoins concrets des âmes, dans une perspective pastorale, par la voie de la sainteté.

Le type de telles réformes se trouverait dans l'action d'un saint Bernard ou encore d'un saint François d'Assise.'

[21] Congar, *Les Voies du Dieu*, p. 255: 'Dès qu'un homme réalise de façon authentique cette pure relation verticale à Dieu que nous venons de rencontrer chez François d'Assise, il change ou crée quelque chose dans l'ordre des relations horizontales.'

political activism over contemplation. His ideal, instead, was the life of prayer:

> The absolute priority that was assigned to the contemplative life over the active . . . stands out as the fundamental attitude of the Middle Ages, which took the Hereafter as the constant and exclusive goal of all earthly striving.[22]

Guardini's most widely read book, *Der Herr* (*The Lord*, translated into French in 1945), probably guided the theology of Messiaen's opera as it had *Des canyons aux étoiles* . . .[23] He writes that only Francis approaches Jesus in holiness,[24] and that, while it is impossible to write a biography of Jesus, it is possible to write a biography of Francis.[25] Similarly, Messiaen wrote: 'I had always thought that the Passion of the Christ could not be staged, but Saint Francis could at least approach it.'[26] Emphasising Jesus' spirituality over his ministry, Guardini writes that Jesus' intention in treating the sick was to lead people to God, not to relieve their pain:

> He is no social reformer fighting for a more just distribution of material wealth. The social reformer aims at lessening suffering; if possible at removing it . . . For Jesus the problem is quite a different one. He sees the mystery of suffering much more profoundly – deep at the root-tip of human existence, and inseparable from sin and estrangement from God. He knows it to be the door in the soul that leads to God . . . This is obviously what is meant by his words about taking up the cross and following him (Matt. 16:24).[27]

Guardini's focus on the spiritual significance of suffering resonates throughout Messiaen's opera. Not only does the libretto use the same quotation from Matthew, but Francis also echoes Guardini's view of suffering when he tells the Leper in scene 3 that 'Les infirmités du corps nous sont données pour le salut de notre âme. Comment comprendre la croix, si on n'en a porté un petit morceau?' (Bodily infirmities are given us for the salvation of the soul. How should one understand the cross if one hasn't carried a small piece of it?).

Although Messiaen claimed that he was never involved in any religious group, telling Brigitte Massin: 'I have never even simply flirted with any group small or large – whether Thomist or not – of religious thought',[28] his

---

[22] Guardini, *The Church and the Catholic; and The Spirit of the Liturgy* (New York: Sheed & Ward, 1935), pp. 200–1.

[23] Messiaen inscribed the eighth movement of *Des canyons* with a quotation from Guardini's *The Lord*.

[24] Guardini even authored a testimonial on Francis; see his 'St. Francis and Self-Achievement' (1927) in *The Focus of Freedom*, trans. Gregory Roettgar (1966), originally published as *Der heilige Franziskus* in 1951. See also Guardini, *The Lord*, pp. xv–xvi.

[25] Guardini, *The Lord*, p. xvi.

[26] Massin, *Olivier Messiaen: une poétique du merveilleux*, p. 189: 'J'ai toujours pensé qu'on ne pouvait pas mettre en scène la Passion du Christ, mais saint François pouvait au moins s'en rapprocher.'

[27] Guardini, *The Lord*, p. 58. For a similar viewpoint, see Balthasar, *The Christian and Anxiety*, 39.

[28] Massin, *Olivier Messiaen: une poétique du merveilleux*, p. 179: 'Je n'ai même jamais simplement flirté avec aucun groupe ou groupuscule, thomiste ou non, de réflexion religieuse.'

sympathies appear to have favoured the *ressourcement* theologians' preference for contemplation over social engagement. The opera's deliberate, undramatic pace reprises the contemplative mood of his oratorio *La Transfiguration de Notre-Seigneur Jésus-Christ* (1965–69). Christopher Dingle has argued convincingly that *La Transfiguration*'s Latin texts, chant imitations and interpolations from Thomas Aquinas indicate that Messiaen wished to preserve threatened elements of the Tridentine (pre-Vatican II) liturgy.[29] As *La Transfiguration* responds conservatively to the Council's liturgical reforms, *Saint François d'Assise* responds conservatively to its social teachings. Messiaen's esteem for contemplation helps to explain the opera's lack of drama and avoidance of the issue of Francis's love for Lady Poverty. For example, in 1972 a Dutch theologian charged Messiaen with failing to engage with the suffering and social crises in the contemporary world. Messiaen responded by defending the need for faith, saying: 'We must direct our gaze towards the life hereafter and try to forget about this life.'[30] This detached attitude resurfaces in Francis's instruction to Brother Masseo in scene 6 not to worry about material needs because God will provide for his needs as He provides food for the birds.[31] Furthermore, Messiaen portrays Francis at prayer in scenes 2, 3, 5, 7 and 8 and has him perform only one miracle among hundreds enumerated in his early hagiography.[32]

When Messiaen wrote his libretto in 1975, the agenda of the *nouvelle théologie* remained topical. Its greatest influence on Vatican II (1962–65) is probably the document *Pastoral Constitution on the Church in the Modern World (Gaudium et Spes)*, which sought to bridge the division between social action and contemplation: 'Let there be no false opposition between professional and social activities on the one part, and religious life on the other.'[33] But in the years following Vatican II, the divisions in the Church deepened. The Marxist Dominican Jean Cardonnel started "l'affaire Cardonnel" in 1968 after delivering a sermon entitled 'Evangelism and Revolution'. Travel writer John Ardagh reported that a Dominican had lamented the rift between

---

[29] Christopher Dingle, ' "La statue reste sur son piédestal": Messiaen's *La Transfiguration* and Vatican II', *Tempo* 212 (April 2000), 8–11.

[30] Rößler, *Contributions to the Spiritual World of Olivier Messiaen*, p. 53.

[31] Messiaen, *Saint François d'Assise*, scene 6: 'N'oublie pas, petit brebis: le bel exemple que nous donnent ces oiseaux: ils n'ont rien, et Dieu les nourrit. Remettons-nous toujours du soin de notre vie à la Divine Providence: cherchons le Royaume, le Royaume et sa justice, et le reste nous sera donné par surcroît.'

[32] A further source for Messiaen's appreciation of contemplation may be Thomas Merton's *The New Man*, translated into French in 1969 as *Le Nouvel Homme* (see Samuel, *Olivier Messiaen: Music and Color*, p. 169). Merton's book argues that rebirth through contemplation is necessary in order to find one's true self and discusses suffering, decision, and the mystic John of Ruysbroeck (1293–1381), all elements important to Messiaen's works of the 1970s.

[33] Catholic Church, *Pastoral Constitution on the Church in the Modern World (Gaudium et Spes)* (Boston: St Paul Books & Media, 1965), paragraph 43, 43.

militant Marxist lay catholics and the Church hierarchy in France: 'Some of the faithful complain . . . that we priests don't talk about God any more, we talk about the housing crisis.'[34] Among conservatives, Gabriel-Marie Garrone and the Abbé de Nantes publicly criticised Vatican II in the early 1970s. But perhaps the most outspoken French detractor was Archbishop Lefebvre, who resigned in 1968 when he was instructed to celebrate the Mass in the vernacular and who controversially ordained priests in 1975 according to antiquated rites. Pope Paul VI called Lefebvre the greatest cross of his pontificate.[35] Adding to the unrest, the divisive encyclical *Humanae Vitae* (1968) engendered an *à la carte* approach to Catholicism by forbidding the use of contraception.[36] An article published in 1971 in *Esprit* attributed the turmoil to the Church's philosophy of reform:

> The current crisis is not a crisis of faith, but of a metaphysics behind which the Church thought it could entrench itself in order to face modern culture – metaphysics linked, moreover, to social systems that the Church agreed to regard as sacred.[37]

Such a rebuke of the *nouvelle théologie* demonstrates its continued role in Church politics into the 1970s.

Ressourcement theology's search for the authentic Christian spirit influenced the sources that Messiaen adopted in his libretto. Père Louis Antoine's *Lire François d'Assise: essai sur sa spiritualité d'après ses écrits* (1967) provided a motherload of references that enrich the opera, including discussions of perfect joy, a leper, fear and awe, the alpha and omega, freedom from worry, Thomas Aquinas, and art as a path to God.[38] Père Antoine worked to uncover the original Franciscanism 'by going back to [Franciscan] sources purely and simply':[39]

> Thus our thought process joins naturally into the immense movement that carries the entire Church to return to the living sources of the Gospels and the Bible in order to bring the face of God and Christ in its truth back up to date – the famous *aggiornamento*.[40]

[34] John Ardagh, *The New French Revolution* (New York and Evanston: Harper & Row, 1969), p. 386.

[35] *New Catholic Encyclopedia*, 2nd edition (Detroit: Thomson Gale, 2003), s.v., 'Paul VI, Pope', p. 32.

[36] Sandy Tippett-Spirtou, *French Catholicism: Church, State and Society in a Changing Era* (New York: St Martin's Press, 2000), p. 74.

[37] Jacques-J. Natanson, 'Langage, existence, communauté', in *Esprit* (November 1971): 'La crise actuelle n'est pas une crise de la foi, mais celle d'une métaphysique derrière laquelle l'Église a cru pouvoir se retrancher pour affronter la culture moderne – métaphysique liée d'ailleurs à des systèmes sociaux que l'Église avait accepté de sacraliser.'

[38] Père Louis Antoine, *Lire François d'Assise: essai sur sa spiritualité d'après ses écrits* (Paris: Editions Franciscains, 1967).

[39] Antoine, *Lire François d'Assise*, pp. 5–6: 'en remontant à ses sources purement et simplement'.

[40] *Aggiornamento*, meaning 'updating', was the theme of Vatican II. Antoine, *Lire François d'Assise*, p. 6: 'Ainsi notre démarche s'inscrit naturellement dans l'immense mouvement qui porte l'Église tout entière à revenir aux sources vives de l'Évangile et de la Bible afin de remettre à jour – le fameux "aggiornamento".'

A 'return to Saint Francis is needed', he said, and even claimed that Popes
Pius XII and John XXIII had encouraged it.[41] Messiaen's libretto quotes from
the same scholarly translation of the *Fioretti* by Alexandre Masseron that
Père Antoine had used.[42] It also quotes from the Jerusalem Bible, another
product of the spirit of *ressourcement*. The *Ecole biblique* in Jerusalem
translated this French Bible from the original languages after the encyclical
Divino Afflante Spiritu (1943) promoted historical-critical methods in biblical studies. Messiaen's detailed stage directions, set designs, costumes and
imitations of birdsong and church bells he heard in Assisi further attest to his
desire for authenticity.[43]

Generic fundamentalism

Lacking lovers, murders or subplots to provide intrigue, and with only hints
of villains and comics to offer entertainment, the genre of *Saint François* has
been a matter of debate since the work's premiere. Admitting it is not a
'veritable opéra' ('genuine opera'), Messiaen once insisted it is a 'spectacle
musical'.[44] Others have suggested it lies between an opera and an oratorio.[45]
I find that the opera retrieves medieval drama as the source of modern
theatre and invokes the Orpheus myth as opera's first muse. Messiaen's
turn toward medieval drama was anticipated in musical settings of mysteries
and miracles by Jules Massenet, Claude Debussy, Igor Stravinsky and others
(Table 10.3).[46] Neither tragedy nor celebration, the miracles and mysteries
are a sort of Christian realism, or, as Erich Auerbach put it, a mixture
of '*sublimitas* and *humilitas*'.[47] *Saint François* offers an *aggiornamento* of
the medieval miracle play, a genre that depicted a saint's life. Messiaen's

---

[41] Antoine, *Lire François d'Assise*, p. 7: 'Ce
retour à saint François s'impose.' Antoine
may be thinking here of Pope John Paul
XXIII's letter *Cum natalicia* (4 April 1959),
addressed to the Friars Minor, printed in
P. Stéphane-J. Piat, *Saint François d'Assise:
A la découverte du Christ pauvre et crucifié*
(Paris: Editions Franciscaines, 1968), p. 368.
[42] Antoine refers to Masseron in *Lire François
d'Assise*, p. 8, n. 6.
[43] For more on Messiaen's visits to Assisi, see
Keym, *Farbe und Zeit*, pp. 41–3.
[44] Samuel, *Permanences d'Olivier Messiaen*,
p. 34.
[45] See, for example, Robert Sherlaw Johnson,
Messiaen, new edition (Berkeley and Los
Angeles: University of California Press, 1989),
p. 186.

[46] For a list of some 130 French works on
religious subjects for the musical stage, see
Keym, *Farbe und Zeit*, Appendix 4:
'Französische Musiktheaterwerke mit
religiösem Sujet im 19. und 20. Jahrhundert',
pp. 523–5. Paul Hindemith's ballet on Saint
Francis, *Noblissima Visione* (1938), may also
have been a point of reference for Messiaen.
There is no standard of nomenclature for the
genres of medieval drama. I call those dramas
that derive from the Bible *mysteries* and those
that refer to saints' lives *miracles*.
[47] Erich Auerbach, *Mimesis: The
Representation of Reality in Western Literature*,
trans. Willard Trask (Garden City, NY:
Doubleday, 1957), pp. 132, 141. For further
discussion of the opera's genre, see Keym,
Farbe und Zeit, pp. 1–6.

Table 10.3: Prominent dramatic settings of mysteries and miracle plays, 1875–1968

Composer	Title	Date
Jules Massenet	Eve	1875
	Grisélidis	1901
	Le Jongleur de Notre-Dame	1902
Georges Hüe	Le Miracle	1910
Claude Debussy	L'Enfant prodigue	1884
	Le Martyr de Saint Sébastien	1911
Ildebrando Pizzetti	Sacra rapprezentazione	1917
	d'Abram e d'Isaac	
Henry Février	La Damnation de Blanchefleur	1920
Vincent d'Indy	La Légende de Saint Christophe	1920
Arthur Honegger	L'Imperatrice aux rochers: un miracle	1925
	de Notre Dame	
Frank Martin	6 Dialogue aus Jedermann	1944
Joseph-Guy Ropartz	Le Miracle de Saint Nicholas	1958
Benjamin Britten	St Nicholas	1948
	Noye's Fludde	1958
Igor Stravinsky	The Flood	1962
	Abraham and Isaac	1964
Niccolò Castiglioni	Three Miracle Plays	1968

familiarity with medieval drama may have begun with his father's 1948 introduction to and translation of Ernest Rhys's *Everyman and Other Interludes, Including Eight Miracle Plays* (1926).[48] But Edmund de Coussemaker's famous text-and-music edition of mystery plays provides an account of medieval drama that uncannily describes Messiaen's opera:

> Note well that one finds that neither passions, intrigues, nor scenic movements play the principal role in secular drama. What dominates is calm, simplicity of speech, high and noble thought, purity of morals. Music, destined to translate similar sentiments and to add stronger feeling to them, should necessarily have the same character. Also, it need not seek a rhythmic or measured line appropriate to accompany secular passions, but a simple melody, built according to the rules of

[48] Pierre Messiaen, *Théâtre anglais: moyen age et XVIe siècle* (Bruges: Desclée de Brouwer, 1948), pp. 11–66. Messiaen had also taught Adam de la Halle's *Le Jeu de Robin et Marion* to his Conservatoire class in 1947. See Jean Boivin, *La Classe de Messiaen* (Paris: Christian Bourgois, 1995), p. 435.

the modes of plainchant, submitted in all cases to certain laws of rhythm and accentuation that have nothing in common with the precise division of time.[49]

Messiaen acknowledged the opera's debt to medieval drama when he told Almut Rößler that the scenery was designed to evoke 'the medieval system' of representing earth, heaven and hell at the same time, 'just as in the mystery plays of the Middle Ages'.[50]

The opera's allusions to medieval drama focus on heaven and hell. Angels in medieval drama often play the role of consoler, as when one tells Mary 'Ne timeas' ('Do not be afraid') in the *Annuntiatio*, or when another comforts Rachel upon her *planctus* in the *Ordo Rachelis*. Messiaen's angel, too, offers consolation. Francis interprets the mysterious voice for the Leper, saying: 'C'est peut-être un Ange envoyé du ciel pour te reconforter' ('Perhaps it's an Angel sent from heaven to comfort you'). By contrast, Messiaen located the Leper's scene in a metaphorical hell.[51] In his tirade in scene 3, the Leper recovers the practice in medieval drama of representing not only the lamenting soul but also the Harrowing of Hell, the Easter week play that depicts Jesus entering purgatory after his death. Miracle plays often include choirs of angels, conclude with a Te Deum, and quote freely from the scriptures. *Saint François*, also, includes a large chorus of heavenly voices, concludes with a choral praise to God, and quotes liberally from biblical and other sources in what Messiaen called a 'mosaic'.[52] Finally, in the related genre of the mystery play, one common subject was the *Peregrinus*, or the encounter of the Apostle Luke and Cleophas with the resurrected but unrecognised Christ on the road to Emmaus. In a chapter entitled 'Mystère et miracles', Chaix-Ruy describes Christ in this scene as a traveller, who walks 'si léger qu'il ne semble pas toucher la terre' ('so lightly that he appears not to touch the ground'). This was undoubtedly Messiaen's source for his stage direction for the Angel:

[49] E[dmund] de Coussemaker, *Drames liturgiques du moyen âge* (Paris: Librairie Archéologique de Victor Didron, 1861), pp. xii–xiii: 'Remarquons bien qu'on n'y rencontre ni les passions, ni les intrigues, ni les mouvements scéniques qui jouent le principal rôle dans le drame profane. Ce qui y domine, c'est le calme, la simplicité des récits, l'élévation et la noblesse des pensées, la pureté des principes moraux. La musique, destinée à traduire de semblables sentiments et à y ajouter une expression plus puissante, devait nécessairement avoir le même caractère. Aussi n'y faut-il pas chercher une mélodie rhythmée et mesurée, si propre à seconder les passions profanes; mais une mélodie plane, établie d'après les régles de la tonalité du plain-chant, soumise toutefois à de certaines lois de rhythme et

d'accentuation, qui n'ont rien de commun avec la division exacte des temps.'
[50] Rößler, *Contributions to the Spiritual World of Olivier Messiaen*, p. 126.
[51] Messiaen calls the Leper 'méchant' (wicked) (Samuel, *Permanences d'Olivier Messiaen*, p. 377) and situates him in hell (Rößler, *Contributions to the Spiritual World of Olivier Messiaen*, p. 126).
[52] Messiaen calls his libretto a 'mosaic' of texts in Massin, *Olivier Messiaen: une poétique du merveilleux*, 71. Numerous sources for Messiaen's libretto are provided in Camille Crunelle Hill, 'The Synthesis of Messiaen's Musical Language', Ph.D. dissertation, University of Kentucky, 1996), pp. 90–121, and in Keym, *Farbe und Zeit*, Appendix 3, Table 2: 'Zitate und sonstige intertextuelle Bezüge im Gegangstext', pp. 487–91.

'Il évolue sur le chemin en ayant l'air de danser sans toucher terre' ('He walks on the path appearing to dance without touching the ground').[53]

Messiaen's version of the Sermon to the Birds draws its own generic background from the medieval bestiary. As there had been musical settings of miracle plays earlier in the century, so were there prior settings of Apollinaire's *Le Bestiare au cortège d'Orphée* by Francis Poulenc and Louis Durey. Widely used as natural history texts in the Middle Ages, bestiaries have been regarded as the forerunners of modern zoological texts. Their lists of observations of the natural world provided coded lessons in morality. Messiaen's Sermon to the Birds may even attribute the roots of ornithology to Hugh de Fouilloy's all-bird bestiary, sometimes called the *Aviarium* (ca. 1152), which was written explicitly for moral instruction of monastic novitiates.[54] When Leo asks Francis, 'And that one who makes a mistake? He descends the scale before climbing it!', Francis answers, 'That's our brother Scaleclimber. We, too, after the resurrection, we will climb the steps of heaven, appearing to descend them.'[55] Later, Francis again moralises in the medieval homiletic tradition of the *exempla*: 'Do not forget, little lamb, the good example that these birds give us: they have nothing, and God feeds them. Let us always put the cares of our life in Divine Providence: let us seek the Reign, the Reign and its justice, and the rest will be extra.'[56]

Messiaen's return to fundamentals in *Saint François d'Assise* also draws inspiration from the prototypical operatic myth of Orpheus, particularly from Gluck's *Orfeo ed Euridice*, which had played a key role in Messiaen's musical education, since its F major aria in Act 1 was the first music he ever heard in his head by reading (not playing) the score.[57] Orpheus has been the quintessential classical hero for Christian opera because his descent into the Underworld has long been interpreted as analogous to Christ's harrowing

---

[53] Chaix-Ruy, *Du féerique au céleste*, p. 203.

[54] See *The Medieval Book of Birds: Hugh de Fouilloy's Aviarium*, edition, translation and commentary by Willene B. Clark (Binghamton, NY: Medieval & Renaissance Text & Studies, 1992). Clark cites a passage from chapter 44 in order to note that the book was written for monastic instruction: 'Observe how the life of religious can be taught through the nature of birds' (p. 205).

[55] The bird Messiaen refers to in this scene has never been properly translated in the musicological literature. It is the Fan-tailed Cuckoo (*Cacomantis flabelliformis pyrrophanus*), in French called the 'Coucou à éventail' or the 'Monteur de gamme'. English has no equivalent for the latter name, which Messiaen used and which I render as 'Scaleclimber'.

[56] *Exempla* were anecdotes in medieval sermons that illustrated moral points. Francis is responding to a question from Brother Leo as follows: 'Et celui-là qui se trompe? Il descende la gamme avant de la monter!' *Francis*: 'C'est notre frère Gammier. Nous aussi, après la résurrection, nous monterons les échelles du ciel, en ayant l'air de les descendre.' *Francis*: 'N'oublie pas, petit brebis: le bel exemple que nous donnent ces oiseaux: ils n'ont rien, et Dieu les nourrit. Remettons-nous toujours du soin de notre vie à la Divine Providence: cherchons le Royaume, le Royaume et sa justice, et le reste nous sera donné par surcroît.'

[57] This anecdote is recounted in Samuel, *Olivier Messiaen: Music and Color*, p. 110.

of hell.[58] No doubt, Orpheus also appealed to Messiaen because of his power to communicate with animals, as Francis did.[59] In both *Saint François d'Assise* and the Orpheus myth, music bridges the divide between life and death. For Gluck, music is the key to Elysium in the Underworld; for Messiaen, music leads to heaven, in the world above. The operas also share the phenomenon of dying twice that made the myth congruent with Christian theology. Eurydice dies first from a snakebite and again upon Orpheus's backward glance. Orpheus dies when he crosses the River Styx and again when he is torn apart by the maenads. Similarly, the Leper dies once to his spiritual disease and again in body. Francis, too, dies first in himself, giving his life to Christ, and dies a second time in scene 8. Like Francis, Orpheus must conquer fear, overcome desire, and endure suffering in order to enter the next world. But, instead of a barrier like Calzabigi's River Styx, Messiaen offers a road, the path to perfect joy. Whether river or road, the border in both operas is lined with cypress trees to symbolise death. Once in Elysium, Orpheus hears bird-songs in Gluck's 'Che puro ciel' of Act II, an association of birds with paradise very much like the juxtaposition of the Angel's music with the Sermon to the Birds in *Saint François*. Finally, at the end of Gluck's opera, Love (Amor) sings 'Compensa mille pene un mio contento!' ('An instant of bliss may compensate for an age of pain!'). Messiaen corrects this moral when the Chorus, representing Christ in scene 7, sings: 'Est-il de pénible qu'on ne doive supporter pour la vie éternelle?' ('Is there any pain which one would not bear for Life Eternal?'). Messiaen's reform opera clearly paraphrased Gluck's reform opera.[60]

Perfect joy

In addition to returning to generic origins, *Saint François* also resurrected messages of joy and beauty as answers to the angst of *après-guerre* modernity in France. When Brother Leo announces his fear of death[61] – the death when

---

[58] See, for example, John Block Friedman, 'Orpheus-Christus in the Art of Late Antiquity', in *Orpheus in the Middle Ages* (Cambridge, MA: Harvard University Press, 1970), pp. 38–85.

[59] Similarly, one of Messiaen's favourite poets, Rainer Maria Rilke, had compared St Francis to Orpheus, the subject of his famous *Sonnets to Orpheus*, in his poem *The Book of Poverty and Death*.

[60] For more on Gluck and operatic reform, see Daniel Heartz, 'Gluck and the Operatic Reform', chapter 3 in *Haydn, Mozart and the Viennese School, 1740–1780* (New York: W. W. Norton & Company, 1995), pp. 143–235 and 188–210. Gluck's famous preface to *Alceste* is anthologised in Oliver Strunk (comp. and ed.), *Source Readings in Music History: From Classical Antiquity through the Romantic Era* (New York: W. W. Norton & Company), pp. 673–75, and in Piero Weiss and Richard Taruskin, *Music in the Western World: A History in Documents* (New York: Schirmer Books, 1984), pp. 301–2.

[61] Messiaen's mother's papers relate that, as an eight-year-old speaking about suns, planets, ants and skeletons, he had confessed: 'I like everything that creates fear'. See Cécile Sauvage, *Œuvre complètes* (Paris: Editions de la Table Ronde, 2002), p. 244. His mother further describes an incident when Messiaen's younger brother, Alain, cried one morning: 'J'ai peur, j'ai

Ex. 10.1a: The symmetrical leitmotif of Francis

Ex. 10.1b: The wandering leitmotif of Brother Leo

J'ai   peur,   j'ai   peur,   j'ai   peur   sur   la   rou - - - - te.

a poinsettia loses its colour or when a Tiara flower loses its scent – Francis instructs him on perfect joy, as if to say he ought to prepare himself for death and divine judgment.[62]

The relationship between joy and fear, between Francis and Brother Leo, is captured in their respective leitmotifs (Ex. 10.1a and 10.1b). Both themes begin similarly, with a repeated descent from C♯ to G. In Saint Francis's Theme, the leitmotif continues further downward before vaulting up at the end to achieve equilibrium. By contrast, the Theme of Brother Leo loses its way, always changing direction and leading nowhere. Francis's equilibrium is symbolised by the theme's symmetrical arrangement of pitches centring around F♯, a note with a fourfold meaning. F♯ is the key Messiaen frequently used to symbolise God's love, as in the 'Theme of God' from the *Vingt Regards*. In Catholic thought, God's love is most intensely manifest in Jesus, the Son of God. The French word for son, *fils*, is nearly homophonous with the German word for F♯, *Fis*. In addition, 'F' is the letter that corresponds to Francis's own name and 'sharp' in German is *Kreuz*, or cross. What pitch could better represent the centre of Francis's life? But only one passing F♯ appears in the harmony of Brother Leo's theme, which is never transposed or developed. Messiaen's musical symbols tell us that Brother Leo is perpetually lost and without a centre; he will not become a saint.

The musical and theological bond between joy and fear is strengthened by Messiaen's having composed scene 1 immediately after scene 8, because the first scene defines perfect joy and the last scene achieves it.[63] In addition, Brother Leo's confession of 'J'ai peur' alliterates with Francis's penance to

rêvé de chiens' ('I'm afraid. I dreamed about dogs'). Could Messiaen have been thinking of his brother Alain when he assigned the words 'J'ai peur' ('I'm afraid') to Brother Leo?
[62] Messiaen probably first encountered the Tiara flower in Tahiti while en route to New Caledonia to transcribe bird songs for the opera. In Tahiti, the Tiara (*Gardenia tahitensis*) is customarily worn as an

ornament. Used in this anachronistic and unrealistic way, the Tiara flower anticipates Saint Francis's reference in scene 6 to birds from New Caledonia. Like Gauguin, Messiaen uses the South Pacific as an earthly metaphor for paradise.
[63] Messiaen describes the sequence in which he wrote the scenes in Samuel, *Olivier Messiaen: Music and Color*, p. 216.

pursue 'la Joie Parfaite'. In order to highlight the dramatic ambiguity in the struggle between joy and fear at Francis's death in scene 8, Messiaen begins the scene with only the first two notes of Francis's leitmotif in the iambic rhythm of Brother Leo's leitmotif. At the hour of his death, it seems that Francis could be afraid, but when his entire theme finally sounds it is clear that he remains centred in his faith.

Christian theology of joy derives from the Bible, especially the Psalms, Isaiah, the Nativity scenes and the Gospel of John. In a letter from 1932, Messiaen identified his favourite passage in the Bible as John, chapters 14 to 17, when Jesus preaches at the Last Supper 'so that my joy may be in you, and that your joy may be complete' (15:11).[64] Complete joy in Christian theology can be found only in union with God. Joy is therefore a destination almost synonymous with heaven; on earth, joy can be known only imperfectly. It is reserved for the Blessed, the dead saints whose spiritual journey has ended in union with God. In the words of Patrice de la Tour du Pin, one of Messiaen's favourite authors, joy involves a quest, a progress of a soul, a life of a saint.[65]

Both St Francis of Assisi and St Thomas Aquinas took up the biblical theme of complete joy, but called it *perfect joy*. Franciscans have always distinguished themselves through their commitment to living joyfully. Francis was known to admonish a fellow friar who was prone to sulking and his most famous words, after the Canticle to Brother Sun, are in his definition of perfect joy. The opera emphasises joy throughout. Scene 1 defines perfect joy. In scene 5, Francis says: 'All these glories of which the Apostle speaks ravish me. But still more the joy of the blessed, and the infinite happiness of meditation.' Later in the scene, the Angel plays her violin 'with great joy' so that Francis may 'know the joy of the blessed by gentleness of color and melody.' Finally, the opera concludes with the words: 'He [God] resurrects Power, Glory, and Joy!!!'

Messiaen had studied not only the major sources for the life of St Francis, but also the works of Thomas Aquinas, inscribing passages into many of his compositions, setting portions of the *Summa Theologica* in his oratorio *La Transfiguration* and paraphrasing him in interviews. In its passion for truth, *Saint François d'Assise* is one of his most Thomistic compositions. Like Francis, Thomas was careful to distinguish *perfect* from *imperfect* joy. 'The perfection of joy', he writes in the *Summa Theologica*, 'is peace in two respects. First, as regards freedom from outward disturbance; for it is impossible to rejoice perfectly in the beloved good, if one is disturbed in the enjoyment thereof ... Secondly, as regards the calm of the restless desire: for

---

[64] Nigel Simeone, 'Offrandes oubliées: Messiaen in the 1930s', *Musical Times* Vol. 141, no. 1873 (Winter 2000), 34.

[65] Patrice de la Tour du Pin wrote a book of poetry entitled *La Quête de joie* (Paris: Gallimard, 1967).

he does not perfectly rejoice, who is not satisfied with the object of his joy.'[66] Both Francis and Thomas imprinted Messiaen with a sense that perfect joy is found only in Christ.

Transcendent beauty

The second theological principle of the opera – that the beauty of music leads to God – is most clearly presented by the Angel's music in scene 5, played so that Francis may 'know the joy of the blessed by gentleness of color and melody', and by Francis's assertion in scene 6 that 'everything beautiful should lead to freedom, the freedom of glory.' Messiaen was sympathetic to Francis's belief that the beauty of the stars, mountains, and oceans shows the glory of God. 'In this sense,' he said, 'I'm very Franciscan.'[67]

To express the idea that music – or more generally beauty – leads to God, parts of scenes 2, 4, 5 and 6 present music diegetically.[68] The friars' chanting in scene 2 communes with the voices of heaven sung by the Chorus, those 'formes noir indistinctes' ('indistinct black shapes') who are placed 'à droite et à gauche de la scène' ('to the right and left of the stage'). The Angel's terrifying knock in scene 4, which Messiaen called 'l'entrée irrésistible de la grâce' ('the irresistible entry of grace'), precipitates a second encounter between the earthly friars and the heavenly Angel, while the Angel's serene viol solo of scene 5 answers Francis's prayer for a foretaste of heaven. Messiaen said that a woodcut by Maurice Denis had inspired this melody, whose piety and ethereal simplicity suits the picture he had owned as a child (see Fig. 10.1).[69] Finally, the bird choruses of scene 6, which Francis

---

[66] Thomas Aquinas, *Summa theologica* (New York: Benziger Bros, 1947–48), part I, 2nd part, Q. 70, art. 3, 'On how the fruits of the Holy Spirit are related to the virtues'. Cf. Thomas on joy in the *Summa theologica*, part I, 2nd part, Q. 26, art. 2.

[67] Samuel, *Olivier Messiaen: Music and Color*, p. 211.

[68] The term 'diegetic' was popularised in film theory. Referring to whatever occurs within the frame of a narrative, diegetic music is perceived as music not only to an opera's audience, but also to its characters. For example, Walther von Stolzing's 'Morgenlich leuchtend in rosigem Schein' and Cherubino's 'Non sò più cosa son, cosa faccio' and 'Voi che sapete che cosa è amor' exemplify diegetic music because they are songs heard by other characters as music rather than dialogue. Diegetic music has also been called

'phenomenal' music in Carolyn Abbate, *Unsung Voices: Opera and Musical Narrative in the Nineteenth Century* (Princeton University Press, 1991), p. 5, and 'representational' music in reference to drama and the liturgy in Susan Rankin, 'Liturgical Drama', in *The New Oxford History of Music*, vol. II, *The Early Middle Ages to 1300*, ed. Richard Crocker and David Hiley (New York: Oxford University Press, 1990), pp. 316–20.

[69] Messiaen confesses his inspiration from Denis in Samuel, *Olivier Messiaen: Music and Color*, pp. 230–1 (*Permanences d' Olivier Messiaen*, p. 385): 'Quand j'étais jeune, je possédais une très belle édition des *Fioretti*, dont le texte avait été traduit en vieux français pour évoquer l'ombrien parlé par les franciscains à l'époque de François. Or, cet ouvrage était orné de gravures sur bois de Maurice Denis, dont l'une représentait un

Fig. 10.1: The woodcut by Maurice Denis that inspired Messiaen in scene 5, from *Les Petites Fleurs de Saint François d'Assise*, trans. André Pératé (Paris: Librairie de l'art catholique, 1926), p. 255. © 2004 Artists Rights Society (ARS), New York / ADAGP, Paris.

compares to the speech of angels, turn his thoughts to the idea (derived from Matt. 6:26) that, though the birds possess nothing, they remain in God's care. In each scene, the characters personally experience music that transforms them. In scenes 2 and 4, the friars encounter immortality across the threshold of music, while in scenes 5 and 6 Francis enters into rapture through music. The physical presence of this diegetic music leads the characters who hear it toward a greater knowledge of God.[70]

The music in these four scenes becomes increasingly complex, beginning with the monotone chant, continuing with the monochordal rhythm of the knock, then the monody of the Angel's slow viol, and culminating with

ange jouant de la viole devant saint François en totale extase. Cette image, qui m'avait beaucoup frappé, m'est revenue lorsque j'ai décidé de composer mon opéra. C'est pour cela que je me suis aussitôt rendu à Florence afin de rechercher le costume de l'Ange dans les tableaux de Fra Angelico.' Fig. 10.1 appears in St Francis of Assisi, *Les Petites Fleurs de Saint François d'Assise*, trans. André Pératé, illus. Maurice Denis (Paris: Librairie de l'Art Catholique, 1926), p. 255.

[70] The rhythm of the knocking recurs at the imprinting of the stigmata in scene 7, but it sounds only once instead of twice, is not heard by Francis or anyone else, and is not the subject of dialogue, as it was in scene 4. Similarly, the so-called songs of Brother Leo ('J'ai peur') and Francis (the Canticle of Brother Sun) are never apparently heard as song by any character. The music in these passages is therefore not diegetic.

Ex. 10.2a: Focus on pitch in the chanting at rehearsal number 16 in scene 2 (reduction)

Ex. 10.2b: Focus on rhythm in the Angel's knock at the door in scene 4 (reduction)

Ex. 10.2c: Focus on melody in the Angel's viol at rehearsal number 86 in scene 5 (reduction)

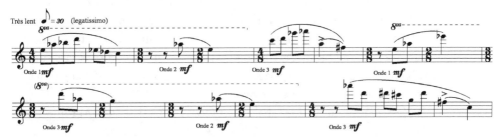

Ex. 10.2d: The *Alouette des champs* begins the *Grand Concert d'oiseaux* in scene 6 (reduction)

the Concerts of Birds, the greatest music in Messiaen's cosmology (Ex. 10.2a–2d).[71] These scenes represent the elements of music: pitch (chant) and rhythm (knock) together create melody (viol); melody with

[71] The rhythm in Ex. 10.2b is played by the full orchestra, though not every instrumental family plays every measure and the accents on notes vary among the families. The reduction of parts does not show that the bass clarinet sometimes plays a descending figure comprised of chord-tones; this figure, however, is barely audible on recordings. For the sake of clarity, the reduction has replaced Messiaen's C♭ with a B♮. The melody in

itself is polyphony (birdsong). In Messiaen's view, birdsong recovers the source of music itself:

> The noises of rain, falling stones, branches being broken . . . there were all sorts of noises, and birds imitated them, and it was through imitating these noises that the birds became musicians, but they were singing a long time before us.[72]

While the chanting, knocking and viol playing are set apart from the surrounding music, the birdsong of scene 6 is disturbingly different. If it is heard as music, then the birdsong throughout the opera could be diegetic music, too. Like the Chorus, which is often present but invisible, the birdsong gives the impression that a narrative voice, the music of the invisible, has been present and communicating all along.

The four scenes about beauty (scenes 2, 4, 5 and 6) develop not only musically, but also theologically. There is progressively less of a human presence in the music. Even in scene 2, which alone offers music produced by people, half of the chanting is from the celestial Chorus, not the friars. Both the knock at the door and the viol solo are the work of the Angel, and the birdsong issues from creatures who, like the Angel, are feathered and non-human. The lack of human agency contrasts with the role of human will in the path to perfect joy. Joy is the reward granted to those who deny their will in favour of God's and who suffer as Jesus suffered. The two paths to paradise, joy and beauty, are therefore paved in different directions: human will prepares the ascent to perfect joy, but only God and God-in-creation can bestow beauty on the world below.

Messiaen found the idea that beauty leads to God in Père Antoine's *Lire François d'Assise*, which discusses the Franciscan view that the beauty of nature reflects the beauty of God.[73] He also discovered the motto for his opera in the book's quotation from Thomas Aquinas: 'Poetic realities cannot be grasped by reason because of their lack of truth; divine realities, because of their excess of truth.'[74] In the *Summa Theologica*, the quotation seeks to justify the decorative trappings of Jewish worship. Substituting music for the ceremonial decoration, Messiaen strongly paraphrased this quotation in

---

Ex. 10.2c is given a faint harmonic context by a held pianissimo C major chord played by the violins, violas and cellos.

[72] Olivier Messiaen, *Entretien avec Claude Samuel*, October 1988, trans. Stuart Walters, sleeve note to Erato CD 75505. Messiaen elaborated this view in his *Traité de rythme, de couleur, et d'ornithologie*, Tome V, Vol. I (Paris: Alphonse Leduc, 1999), p. 15.

[73] Antoine, *Lire François d'Assise*, p. 73. The role of Père Antoine's book in Messiaen's

paraphrase of Thomas Aquinas is discussed in Camille Crunelle Hill, 'Saint Thomas Aquinas and the Theme of Truth in Messiaen's *Saint François d'Assise*', in Siglind Bruhn (ed.), *Messiaen's Mystical Language of Love* (New York and London: Garland, 1998), pp. 146–8, and in Samuel, *Olivier Messiaen: Music and Color*, p. 211.

[74] Thomas Aquinas, *Summa theologica*, part I, Q. 84, response to section 7.

scene 8 with words he quoted so often that they effectively became his artistic credo: 'Dieu nous éblouit par excès de Vérité. La musique nous porte à Dieu par défaut de Vérité' ('God dazzles us by excess of Truth. Music leads us to God by lack of Truth').

An important source for Père Antoine's chapter on beauty and art was another work from the 1960s, Balthasar's ground-breaking study of theological aesthetics entitled *Herrlichkeit*, which was translated into French in 1965. For Balthasar, beauty belongs to the order of transcendental properties, like truth and goodness. Because traces of transcendental beauty are found in all of creation, the beauty of the finite serves as a window on to the infinite:

> What is the creation, reconciliation, and redemption effected by the triune God
> if not his revelation in and to the world and man? Not a deed that would have its
> doer in the background unknown and untouched, but a genuine self-representation
> on his part, a genuine unfolding of himself in the worldly stuff of nature, man, and
> history.[75]

For Balthasar, God is transcendentally beautiful, but the beauty in a thing can reveal the beauty of its form only if one surrenders to its revelation. He credits the Franciscans for their particular appreciation of beauty as a transcendental property.[76] Similarly, in *Saint François d'Assise*, beauty belongs only to God and cannot be fabricated in human music. But in surrendering to beauty, the music of heaven becomes audible.

Operatic histories

Guided by *ressourcement* theology, *Saint François d'Assise* unfolds its moral messages by renovating genres, myths and ideas associated with early sources. The miracle play becomes opera; Orpheus becomes Christian; joy becomes the solution to contemporary anxiety; beauty becomes cutting-edge theology; birdsong becomes music. Advanced in years and surely feeling that his own end was imminent, Messiaen staged the paths to paradise in order to demonstrate how to survive Judgment Day. His historical imagination interpreted the founding of the state of Israel, the increasing reports

---

[75] Hans Urs von Balthasar, *The Glory of the Lord*, vol. I, *Seeing the Form*, trans. Erasmo Leiva-Merikakis (San Francisco: Ignatius Press, 1984–86), p. 119. Messiaen recognises Balthasar's influence on Antoine and on his own conception of the beauty of all creation in Samuel, *Olivier Messiaen: Music and Color*. That Messiaen read Balthasar's *La Gloire de Dieu* [*The Glory of God*] was corroborated by a parish priest and doctor of philosophy; see P. Pascal Ide, 'Une rencontre décisive', in *Messiaen: Homme de foi* (Paris: Trinité Média Communication, 1986), p. 76.

[76] Balthasar, *La Gloire de Dieu*, Book IV, 'Le Domaine de la Métaphysique' (Paris: Aubier, 1982), pp. 54–5 and 58.

of visitations by the Virgin Mary, and the ensuing millennial year 2000 as signs that the end was nigh.

Because he began his career by opposing neoclassicism and defining the avant-garde, Messiaen's look backward to basic principles at the culmination of his career is an irony of music history. His three late homages to Mozart – *Chant dans le style Mozart* (1986), *Un sourire* (1989) and *Concert à quatre* (1990–91, unfinished) – offer additional retrospective glances. In this context, *Saint François* begins to look like the negative image of Messiaen's favourite opera, *Don Giovanni*.[77] Mozart's opera is dark and Messiaen's is light. The Don's hellbent, hedonistic excess is inverted in Francis's heaven-bound, afflicted humility; the Commendatore's murder is inverted in the Leper's new life; and the Statue's supernatural, grey stone is inverted in the Angel's supernatural, rainbow-coloured immateriality.

Messiaen may also have been conscious of a recent incarnation of the diabolic Don in Stravinsky's *The Rake's Progress*.[78] While Messiaen claims to have traced the progress of Francis's soul to sanctity, Stravinsky's opera portrays the progress of a soul to the purgatory of insanity. Both composers drew heavily from the past, but Stravinsky did not adapt the sources of his neoclassicism to a decidedly 'forward-looking' musical idiom. 'My plan of revival', he wrote in 1964, 'did not include updating or modernizing ... I had no ambitions as a "reformer", at least not in the line of a Gluck, a Wagner or a Berg. Can a composer re-use the past and at the same time move in a forward direction?'[79]

Not only does Stravinsky not define 'forward', but he also avoids the issue. *Saint François*, however, offers a direct response, declaring that a composer *can* reuse the past and also move forward – not in the style of neoclassicism, but with the method of *ressourcement*, which updates older traditions for the sake of present-day reform. In 1956, Joseph Kerman predicted that the future of opera would incorporate history:

> Our age is more likely to develop its concepts of drama by investigating the tradition, musical or non-musical. It is a historically and juridically minded age, both for the creative artist and for the audience, and we may as well make virtue out of necessity.[80]

---

[77] Messiaen regarded *Don Giovanni*, the first opera he encountered, as 'le plus grand chef-d'œuvre du genre' ('the greatest masterpiece of the genre') (Samuel, *Olivier Messiaen: Music and Color*, pp. 207 and 178).

[78] Coincidentally, Stravinsky claimed he was inspired to compose his *Oedipus Rex* after reading Johannes Joergensen's biography of St Francis. The story was christianised by Cocteau, whose libretto was translated into Latin by Jean Daniélou, the future *nouvelle théologien*.

[79] Igor Stravinsky, '*The Rake's Progress*: The Author Asks for a Moratorium on Value Judgments' (1964), sleeve note to *The Rake's Progress*, conducted by Igor Stravinsky (Sony SM2 K 46 299), p. 4.

[80] Joseph Kerman, *Opera as Drama* (New York: Vintage, 1956), p. 269.

Messiaen's opera quite literally makes virtue from tradition and his late, retrospective style may well be his final response to neoclassicism. It is a response to history that interprets figurally, conforming the past to fit the needs of the present for the sake of the foreordained future. But, surprisingly in a work about transcendence, it is also a response to history unfolding around him, a history that was preparing for the end of time by combating fear and faithlessness in its own time.

11 Messiaen and twentieth-century music

Arnold Whittall

A network of contexts

Wide-ranging comparison – with precursors, contemporaries, successors –
is a common procedure for musicologists seeking definitive historical place-
ments for their subject-composers. Jonathan Cross provides a succinct
example where Messiaen is concerned: 'Messiaen was intimately familiar,
as revealed through his teaching, with the work of the leading composers of
the first part of the twentieth century – Bartók, Berg, Schoenberg, Webern –
while the influence of Debussy, and to a lesser extent Ravel, is self-evident.
However, it is Stravinsky who, according, to Boulez, "occupies a leading
place". This is borne out by Messiaen's own writings . . . [a]nd in his music,
too, though such ideas and techniques may in general be identified as
characterising early-modern music, the specific influence of Stravinsky is
irrefutable.'[1] Moreover, just as Messiaen, while taking 'rhythmic and formal,
ritualistic and dramatic' ideas from Stravinsky, was able 'to mould them into
something new and distinct', inventing 'a music of epic proportions and
effect which is undeniably his own',[2] so we can conclude that a number
of younger composers who came under Messiaen's spell in their formative
years – Boulez, Stockhausen, Xenakis and Birtwistle among them – are far
from mere imitators. As Cross writes elsewhere of Messiaen and Birtwistle,
'the general parallels . . . are obvious enough: bold, block structure defined
by repetition; an interest in musical ritual and ceremony; structures where
rhythm is the primary organizing parameter; a sophisticated modality; an
interest in ancient, medieval and non-western forms and practices'.[3]

Another example of such constructive contextualisation within broad cultural trends is provided by David Clarke's proposal of a degree of parallel
development between Tippett's late style and 'roughly contemporaneous
tendencies found in figures as diverse as Boulez, Messiaen, Ligeti, Penderecki
and Maxwell Davies. In the later work of these composers and others we find

---

[1] Jonathan Cross, *The Stravinsky Legacy*
(Cambridge University Press, 1998), p. 46.
[2] Cross, *The Stravinsky Legacy*, p. 55.

[3] Jonathan Cross, *Harrison Birtwistle: Man,
Mind, Music* (London: Faber and Faber, 2000),
p. 57.

evidence of a kind of postmodernization definable not as a rejection of modernism but as a later phase of it: a retraction from some of modernism's previous extremes, amounting to a measured assimilation of previously outlawed codes and channels of meaning from the past.'[4]

Simply because Messiaen, like Tippett, had rather less to do with the tradition-rejecting 'extremes' of modernism than most of the other composers in Clarke's list, it becomes possible to conclude, with Cross, that Messiaen's own achievement can only be adequately evaluated when his music is placed in the perspective of the full range of twentieth-century compositional initiatives. The century, of which Messiaen lived through all but the first eight and the last eight years, has often been characterised as a period of special diversity, or plurality, in keeping with the aesthetic and culture of modernism: and the presence of challenging extremes in compositional style and technique were as clear in the year of Messiaen's birth, when the radically different idioms of Debussy and Schoenberg could be experienced (with Stravinsky waiting in the wings), as they were in the year of his death, when composers as disparate as Elliott Carter and John Adams, Harrison Birtwistle and Arvo Pärt, were prominent. It is perilous in the extreme to generalise too broadly from such century-spanning diversity – at least on the level of style – but in terms of what we might call the aesthetics of structure, the notion of a modernism consistently exploring interactions between traditional and innovatory, stable and unstable, fixed and free, can be deployed as a heuristic critical tool, especially for commentaries which aim to consider, and even to balance, theory with hermeneutics. Such thinking lies in the background of this study – and will even rise to the surface from time to time.[5]

While asserting Messiaen's importance to the world of twentieth-century music has long been uncontroversial, the basics of that importance and the manner of its emergence have yet to be fully explored. My rather arbitrary starting point (in a context where matters of length preclude extended technical comparisons between Messiaen and other composers) aims to establish the central topic of this enquiry: Messiaen's relation to, or distance from, the idea of a 'tradition'. Back in 1946, Edward Lockspeiser was in no doubt that 'Messiaen is the composer in France today who has provoked the most controversy'. But that controversy was not the consequence of a radicalism that suppressed all contacts with the past. 'His style is extremely

---

[4] David Clarke, *The Music and Thought of Michael Tippett: Modern Times and Metaphysics* (Cambridge University Press, 2001), p. 224.

[5] For extensive additional commentary along these lines, see Arnold Whittall, *Exploring Twentieth Century Music: Tradition and Innovation* (Cambridge University Press, 2003).

decorative and improvisatory, but the underlying sentiment would seem to be less an expression of religious mysticism than an echo, heavily disguised, of Massenet and Gounod'.[6]

Lockspeiser's attempt to separate the 'expression of religious mysticism' from echos of Massenet and Gounod seems rather pointless today, but it is worth noting his point that those echoes – however heavily disguised – are of French composers. The irrelevance of other traditions to Messiaen is rather taken for granted, and it was not possible in a brief essay called 'Anglo-French Relations' to raise questions about Messiaen's response to German or Russian music. In a more extended and refined commentary on Messiaen, first published eight years after Lockspeiser's, David Drew pugnaciously declared that 'passing reflections of Franck, . . . Massenet, Debussy, Satie, Ravel and Fauré are only significant in so far as they prove how deep are his roots in tradition'. Yet Drew does not attempt to suggest that Messiaen's music makes more sense when placed within a wider European context. Here is a composer for whom 'the traditional patterns of harmonic tension and relaxation are no longer operative', as the kind of connections with 'Oriental practice' Drew finds in a seminal work like *Le Banquet céleste* confirm.[7] Drew was in no doubt that 'in Messiaen, France once again has a composer whose seriousness of aim and range of musicianship is that of a master, and whose courageous indifference to the scorn of the pompiers is worthy of Berlioz':[8] and the degree of expressionism Drew finds in Messiaen's 'fiercely subjective' emotions, and in the 'essential violence' of harmonies which are denied their 'proper resolution', might have been laying the foundations for seeing other European developments in terms of Messiaen rather than the other way round. If so, such an interpretation found its fulfilment in the early twenty-first century, when Célestin Deliège (echoing Jonathan Harvey's view of Messiaen as a 'protospectralist') could offer a Messiaen-centred view of the years since 1945, contending that his thinking about rhythm and form had had a defining influence on music after 1950 (not only in France), and that his thinking about harmony might prove even more significantly central to the new music of the new age.[9]

---

[6] Edward Lockspeiser, 'Anglo-French Relations', *Penguin Music Magazine* 1, ed. Ralph Hill (1946), 33.

[7] David Drew, 'Modern French Music', in Howard Hartog (ed.), *European Music in the Twentieth Century*, revised edition (Harmondsworth: Penguin, 1961), pp. 300–1.

[8] Drew, 'Modern French Music', p. 305.

[9] Célestin Deliège, *Cinquante Ans de modernité musicale: de Darmstadt à l'IRCAM: contribution historiographique à une musicologie critique* (Sprimont: Mardaga, 2003). For Harvey's comment, see *In Quest of Spirit* (Berkeley and Los Angeles: University of California Press, 1999), p. 42.

Chords under analysis

When Robert Sherlaw Johnson was drafting his book on Messiaen, first published in 1975, the composer's 'latest work' was *La Fauvette des jardins* (1970). Johnson describes the 'unusual' feature of the way in which 'phrases representing the lake at different times of day 'climax on a common chord without any added notes'.[10] Commenting that he had already noted this feature in *La Transfiguration* (1965–69), Johnson wrote that 'common chords do occasionally feature in *Catalogue* [*d'oiseaux*], but never in a stressed context', and 'the transformations which this phrase undergoes during the course of the piece recall the four paintings by Monet of Rouen Cathedral, in which he captures the play of light on the Cathedral at different times of the day' (p. 175).

Wisely, Johnson did not spend much time at the end of his book speculating on what Messiaen might do next, and whether or not the stressing of common chords might regain the prominence it had had in the composer's earlier years. Similarly, in a brief conclusion headed 'Messiaen: A Historical Placing', Johnson did little more than note the composer's situation as 'a successor to Debussy and Stravinsky', confirming that he lay 'outside the symphonic tradition' (p. 182). Well-nigh three decades later, we cannot only invoke the perspective of all Messiaen's compositions after 1970, but also that of the seven-tome *Traité de rythme, de couleur, et d'ornithologie*, in which the chordal construction of the 'lake music' from *La Fauvette des jardins* receives special attention.[11]

Messiaen's discussion of 'Son-couleur' in Tome VII of the *Traité* takes us to the heart of his intensely personal understanding of harmony as focused on the character and quality of individual chords.[12] Anyone approaching this text in terms of Germanic concerns with the larger context and the relation of

[10] Robert Sherlaw Johnson, *Messiaen* (London: Dent, 1975), pp. 174–5. Further references are given in the text. It is worth noting here that what was in many ways the most stimulating discussion of Messiaen in English between David Drew and Robert Sherlaw Johnson is found in Wilfrid Mellers, *Caliban Reborn: Renewal in Twentieth-Century Music* (London: Gollancz, 1968), pp. 98–128. The first edition of Roger Nichols's short study appeared in the same year as Sherlaw Johnson's book.

[11] Now that publication of Messiaen's *Traité* is complete, critical commentaries can be expected to proliferate. At the time of writing the principal attempt to interpret his thinking about chords was to be found in three articles

by Cheong Wai-Ling: 'Messiaen's Triadic Colouration: Modes as Interversion', *Music Analysis*, Vol. 21, no. 1 (March 2002), 53–84; 'Rediscovering Messiaen's Invented Chords', *Acta Musicologica*, Vol. 75, no. 1 (2003), 85–105; and 'Messiaen's Chord Tables: Ordering the Disordered', *Tempo*, Vol. 57, no. 226 (October 2003), 2–10.

[12] This is found on pp. 102–7 of Messiaen's *Traité de rythme, de couleur, et d'ornothologie* (*TRCO*), Tome VII (Paris: Leduc, 2002). The sections on 'Accord à renversements transposés sur la même note de basse' and 'Tableaux des couleurs de l'accord à renversements transposés sur la même note de basse' cover pp. 135–47. Further page references are given in the text.

Ex. 11.1: *La Fauvette des jardins* (from final page)

part to whole is likely to have eyebrows permanently raised. But for that very reason it provides an invaluable perspective from which to consider the technical and aesthetic issues under scrutiny in this chapter.

Near the end of the section concerned with the seven-note 'accord à renversements transposés sur la même note de basse', Messiaen quotes three bars from the final page of *La Fauvette des jardins*, which depict 'the great lake of Laffrey' in moonlight, and he makes the point that the chords in question pervade that piece, 'non seulement dans la grande marche d'harmonie qui représente le lac ... mais aussi dans les traits innombrables de chaque strophe de Fauvette, où ils sont parfois avoués et souvent sous-entendus' (p. 139) (see Ex. 11.1).

Messiaen's example is certainly striking for the purity of its chordal content, with the three bars using all four chords from the t3, t6 and t9 versions of the chord respectively, as shown in the *Traité's* relevant 'Tableau' (pp. 142–7). There, each of the chords given for each transposition level is assigned a specific colour combination – for example, the first chord of the first bar of the example shows 'bandes verticales: vertes, violettes, bleu foncé' (p. 143); the first chord of the second bar, 'jaune, taché de blanc et de vert pâle' (p. 145); and the fourth chord of the third bar, 'récif de corail rouge, entouré de rose, de gris, et de vert pâle' (p. 146).

In *Traité* VII, Messiaen presents a sequence of five chords for each transposition level, the fifth identical to the first, as if to suggest a closed succession which might have something in common with a linearly coherent progression in tonal harmony moving away from, and back to, a focal chord. Earlier (from p. 136), he explains the basic character of the chord in question in terms of alterations to a dominant ninth on C♯. Nevertheless, it seems clear that the significance of such chords is not so much connected to their derivation from diatonic sources as to their independence of such sources. These altered dominant ninths are not explicitly required to resolve, as they would be in tonal contexts; even if, in Schoenbergian terms, they fall into 'the sphere of accidental harmonies' which can 'still be brought into [the tonal system] without losing the control provided by the root progressions',[13] the initial

[13] Arnold Schoenberg, *Theory of Harmony*, trans. Roy E. Carter (London: Faber and Faber 1978), p. 345.

validation they acquire from being thought of as types of 'dominant ninth' – that is, as structures built from a root note of the same type as those in Schumann, Wagner, Bizet and Debussy to which Messiaen refers – those roots no longer need to confirm their original structural function.

So confident was Messiaen in the musical potency of these chords as distinctive and separate structures that he never felt the need to provide a theory of progression to complement his lexicon of chordal types; as he notes in this connection, 'ce n'est pas la musique en mouvement'. Given his implicit acceptance of the principle of emancipated dissonance, we might therefore conclude that what he valued most in this new harmonic world was precisely the freedom it gave him to move between the post-tonal harmonic poles of 'fixed' and 'floating' textures, noting that, for many twentieth-century composers, 'fixity' can imply the kind of relatively stable harmonic centring which does not regress to the focused use of pure triads, or allude in any evident manner to traditional principles of voice-leading or harmonic progression: indeed, for many 'mainstream' twentieth-century composers, to do more than touch in passing on such sonorities or such procedures, outside the expressive sphere of parody, would be to court incongruity and banality.

This is the crux for Messiaen, the point at which the assumptions he makes about the aesthetic purpose and character of his music come into play to balance the way he talks about chords in the *Traité*. The topic of 'Son-couleur' in relation to altered dominant ninths makes it possible for him to take those three bars from the last page of *La Fauvette des jardins* and not only ignore their place within the four-bar phrase indicated by the printed slur, but also ignore the climactic harmonic material of the fourth bar, where 'alteration' takes a very different form, in that a first inversion F major triad is followed by a first inversion F minor triad (separately pedalled) (see Ex. 11.2).

As this shows, the ascending three-bar sequence of colour-chords is balanced by the descending three-bar sequence of major/minor alternations, rooted on F, D and A respectively. And, although no further pure triads are heard in the piece, the harmonic character of the last ten bars indicates a focused non-triadic emphasis on A as a suitably strong cadential gesture to round off a thirty-minute single-movement structure. (A more complete analysis of *La Fauvette* would obviously need to consider the relations between this ending and the explicit use of rooted D and A chords earlier in the work, on p. 49 in particular.)

The major/minor triads in *La Fauvette* may not share in the special aura Messiaen assigns to ninth-derived sound-colour harmony; but that does not make them irrelevant to Messiaen's musical theology. Even if we are not justified in reading a generic allusion into his reference to 'la grand marche

Ex. 11.2: *La Fauvette des jardins* (end)

d'harmonie qui représente le lac', it is hard to repress the generic association between this material, as it recurs and evolves through the piece, and those chorale-like affirmations, often involving emphatic major triad resolutions, which can be found in such scores as *La Transfiguration de Notre-Seigneur Jésus-Christ, Des canyons aux étoiles* … and *Saint François d'Assise*. These moments join hands with the world of earlier works like the *Trois Petites*

Ex. 11.3: *Psalmodie de l'Ubiquité par amour*, 4 bars before fig. 1, movt III of *Trois Petites Liturgies de la Présence Divine*

Liturgies de la Présence Divine, and demonstrate how Messiaen could avert banality – a close run thing at times, it must be said – suggesting through these resolutions to unadulterated fundamentals his own unshakable faith in the transcendent power of divine love and truth.

The emphasis Messiaen gives to 'higher consonance'[14] – various sevenths and ninths, often altered and added to by neighbouring notes or appoggiaturas – might suggest a particularly French version of emancipated dissonance, throwing formal and expressive weight on to the individual sonority and leaving its role within the phrase, as a sequence of linear events, outside the realm of harmonic theory. The clearest sense of chord colouring melody tends to be found in phrases where bass and melody move in exact parallel, and where pure diatonicism leaves the chromatic inner voices in a haze of decorative resonance. In the phrase from *Trois Petites Liturgies* (Ex. 11.3) the sudden break with linear conformity at the final cadence reinforces the sense in which the formal identity and semantic functioning of the phrase still require relatively consonant closure, as the most effective way of conveying a sense of spiritual fulfilment.

When Messiaen returned to such cadencing, in the chorales of *La Transfiguration*, there is a distinct polarity between melody and bass, and a use of voice-leading to approach the cadential consonance by way of appoggiatura-type chords whose chromatic density serves to dramatise the human struggle between darkness and light as the grandeur of God is celebrated (Ex. 11.4).

As already noted in connection with the references in *Traité* VII to *La Fauvette des jardins*, Messiaen's theorising says little about progression, little or nothing about the kind of relations between dissonance and consonance, vertical and horizontal, which these examples illustrate. But the melody/bass

---

[14] I introduced this term, a parallel to the familiar 'higher dissonance', in Arnold Whittall, *The Music of*   *Britten and Tippett* (Cambridge University Press, 1982, revised edition 1992).

Ex. 11.4: *Choral de la Sainte Montagne* b. 1–16, movt VII of *La Transfiguration de Notre-Seigneur Jésus-Christ*

polarity, in contexts where 'accords à renversements transposés sur la même note de basse' move to plain, if inverted triads, acquires a significant degree of ambiguity through the character of the voice-leading. For example, in the 'model' statement of the 'lake music' in *La Fauvette* (p. 4, system 4), the stepwise bass descent from F to E (and on to E♭) helps to support the interpretation of the four F-based higher consonances, not as altered dominant ninths in B♭, but rather as enriched higher dominants of C in third inversion, root G, resolving to C major (then minor) tonics (Ex. 11.5).

This ambivalence of function and character creates the possibility of interpreting the music in terms of a kind of Schoenbergian extended tonality.[15] It might even be seen as fulfilling the prophecy of the important nineteenth-century French theorist François-Joseph Fétis, who, as Bryan Hyer has noted, offered a gloomy prediction of the future course of music: 'he believed that the chromaticism of the *ordre pluritonique* [which, in Mozart and Rossini, "represented the culmination and perfection of *tonalité moderne*"] would dissolve into the ambiguous enharmonicism of an *ordre*

[15] See in particular Arnold Schoenberg, *Structural Functions of Harmony*, revised edition, ed. Leonard Stein (London: Ernest Benn, 1969), pp. 76–113.

Ex. 11.5: *La Fauvette des jardins* p. 4, systems 4–5

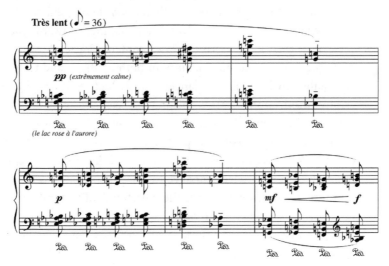

omnitonique, premonitions of which could be detected in music as far back as Mozart. Fétis, however, listened in on "the insatiable desire for modulation" in the omnitonic music of Berlioz and Wagner with revulsion: in their music, the intense appellative energies of pluritonic music neutralize and even negate themselves, weakening the gravitational forces on which *Tonalité moderne* – with its clear references to the tonic – relies. For Fétis, *musique omnitonique* was sensual, decadent, and dangerous. It was music in historical decline.'[16]

Between tonal and atonal

However we categorise their individual elements, Messiaen's characteristic harmonic procedures are technically implicated in the grand twentieth-century strategy of simultaneously echoing and challenging such traditional elements as consonant/dissonant, diatonic/chromatic. As suggested above, Messiaen's procedures could also be aligned with the kind of dramatisation of fixed and free polarities (as an evolution from Schoenbergian, late Romantic distinctions between functional and vagrant harmonies) found widely in music which explores ideas about centredness and 'tonality' in the context of the emancipated dissonance, rather than simply reproducing the kind of traditional techniques that allowed Schenker to distinguish between

[16] Bryan Hyer, 'Tonality', in Thomas Christensen (ed.), *The Cambridge History of* *Western Music Theory* (Cambridge University Press, 2002), p. 748.

music and non-music.[17] Yet Messiaen's methods contrast radically with those of another central twentieth-century figure, Elliott Carter, whose comprehensive system of chord types tends more towards the atonal universe of set theory.[18] As virtually exact contemporaries, Messiaen and Carter prove significantly complementary in both aesthetic and technical respects and, although it would be dangerously reductive to suggest that Carter's creative motivation is entirely abstract, it seems clear that Messiaen's motivation is, in essence, poetic, æsthetic: to do with the expression and celebration of religious faith. In particular, his use of the common chord in chorale-like passages seems to suggest the calm ecstasy of spiritual fulfilment, its visionary effect enhanced rather than impeded by non-diatonic, non-functional contexts. While there is abundant textural and formal contrast in the juxtaposed materials of, for example, *La Fauvette des jardins*, Messiaen never risked the starker tension that would arise between entirely diatonic chorales and modal or atonal textures from which the constraints of traditional voice-leading and harmonic progression had been totally excised. Such extreme oppositions have tended to be used by later twentieth-century composers mainly for purposes of parody – a quality for which Messiaen had no creative need.[19]

Attempting to generalise 'twentieth-century music' in terms of harmonic theory and practice can seem a supremely quixotic enterprise, since post-tonal harmony appears to reject not only codifiable chord construction (in other than abstract, set-theoretic terms) but also voice-leading procedures relatable to the rules of strict counterpoint. Indeed, 'non-functional' remains the term most commonly used for twentieth-century post-tonal harmonic practice. There is nevertheless evidence of considerable classificatory ambition, stemming from Schoenberg's *Harmonielehre* and echoed a little later in the chordal systems devised by Joseph Schillinger and Elliott Carter.[20] The materials set out in Carter's *Harmony Book* might seem to represent everything in that Boulanger-educated composer's life and work which is opposed to Messiaen's, not least because one suspects that Carter would regard Messiaen more in terms of Ivesian naivety and transcendentalist primitivism than of a truly evolved (post-Schoenbergian) modernism.

---

[17] For discussion of 'emancipated dissonance', see Arnold Whittall, 'Tonality and the Emancipated Dissonance: Schoenberg and Stravinsky', in Jonathan Dunsby (ed.), *Models of Musical Analysis: Early Twentieth-Century Music* (Oxford: Blackwell, 1993), pp. 1–19.
[18] *Elliott Carter: Harmony Book*, ed. Nicholas Hopkins and John F. Link (New York: Carl Fischer, 2003). See also Appendix A of David Schiff, *The Music of Elliott Carter*, new

edition (London: Faber and Faber, 1998), pp. 324–7.
[19] Berio's *Rendering* (1988–90), which involves realisations of sketch material by Schubert, is a distinguished example of a relatively recent work which uses quotation without parody.
[20] Schillinger's most influential text is the two-volume *System of Musical Composition*, revised edition (Cambridge, MA: Da Capo Press, 1977).

Nevertheless, and in contrast to the set-theoretic treatises of Allen Forte, David Lewin and others,[21] Carter's *Harmony Book* 'does not present or even imply a compositional system', still less 'claim to set forth a general theory of atonal practice whether for purposes of analysis or composition'.[22] This is in essence because Carter's music treats his chords as 'background' source materials, even if they are also occasionally explicit surface phenomena. Nevertheless, their existence, and their value to Carter himself, underlines the harmonic essence of his mature musical manner, and also indicates why he has attached such importance in his teaching to the exploration of how streams or successions of chords might be satisfactorily composed. Hence the pedagogical – and even, on occasion, the truly compositional – value of 'writing chorales ... with great attention to issues of common tones and voice leading'.[23] Here we have a clear indication of how a post-tonal composer seeks equivalents, or substitutes, for those generally valid 'good continuations' that lie behind the harmonic progressions of tonal composition.

For Carter, and those who share his desire to stand at a clear distance from traditional harmonic thinking, the generic context of 'chorale' is little more than semiotic shorthand for rhythmically regular homophony, and however fervent the tributes to the imperishable greatness of J. S. Bach, neither the religious context nor the textural features of melody/bass polarity found in Bach's chorales will count for much. Messiaen could hardly be more different, and one result of his use of pure triads in chorale-like textures is the orientation of such passages towards the traditional (tonal) chorale. A wealth of ambiguity then arises from the interaction between the characteristics of that genre and Messiaen's personal world of harmony and texture. In the case of the two-bar model of *La Fauvette's* 'lake chorale', perhaps the main ambivalence concerns the sense in which what Sherlaw Johnson terms the 'climax' chord has as its bass a pitch – E – which is passing between F and E♭.[24] If E is indeed the goal of the bass-line succession, then the E♭ (and its superstructure) become transitional rather than cadential, introducing the next stage of the segment. At the same time, however, the temptation to view the first two bars as moving against the background of traditional voice-leading is made problematic by the uncompromising way in which the four F-based chords – despite their reliance on common tones and conjunct motion – resist interpretation in linear terms. Such interpretation might be applied to the outer two-voice melody/bass lines: if the (whole-tone) melody

[21] For comprehensive references, see John Roeder, 'Set', in Stanley Sadie and John Tyrrell (eds), *The New Grove* 2nd edition (London: Macmillan, 2001), vol. XXIII, pp. 164–8.

[22] David Schiff, 'Review of Elliott Carter: Harmony Book', *Tempo*, Vol. 57, no. 224 (April 2003), 54.

[23] Schiff, 'Review of Elliott Carter: Harmony Book', 55.

[24] Johnson, *Messiaen*, p. 176. See again Ex. 11.5.

is parsed as two motions on to C – first by step (E, D, C), then by leap (F♯, upper C, lower C) – the bass reinforces the differences by supporting the melodic steps with repetitions of the F and the melodic leaps with conjunct descent from F to E♮ and then E♭. But the role of the inner parts must be presumed to be colouristic: their function is to contribute to an atmosphere, the textural smoothness appropriate to the spirit of 'extreme calm' which supports Griffiths' perception concerning Messiaen's 'joy that the old chains of cause and effect have been forgotten, and that chords can be moved about in a symmetrical universe that imposes no single flow of time'.[25] Even in the 'lake chorale', however, the use of sequence, and the wider formal context with its contrasts and juxtapositions, brings time back into the picture – and into the experience – so that Messiaen can't quite escape from all contact with his more earthbound modernist contemporaries and their preference for the Schoenbergian 'cry of distress'.[26]

Teaching tradition

Messiaen's lack of interest in matters Schoenbergian and Schenkerian is well documented, and opinions will inevitably vary as to whether his faithfulness to French theoretical conventions (as Alexander Goehr described it, 'harmonic analysis was purely academical, following the French tradition, in which each individual chord is analysed') created limitations which adversely affected his own compositions.[27] What from a Boulezian perspective counts as 'embalmed academic harmony' and 'rhapsodic long-windedness' need not come across that way, and it is worth emphasising the details of his analytical approach in order to clarify certain matters of compositional design.[28] Goehr was deliberately adopting a Germanic perspective when he commented that 'there is little overall interest in the long-term workings of tonality, nor in the relation of individual phenomena to the whole. Each chord is identified according to its constituent tones and then described, as, for example, a dominant seventh (implying but not necessarily receiving a tonal resolution), a modal chord or pair of chords implying a mode, a whole-tone chord, etc. Analysis thus progresses from chord to chord.'[29] Not only did Messiaen recognise 'no idea of musical levels: all was surface' (p. 51), but he was

[25] Paul Griffiths, *Olivier Messiaen and the Music of Time* (London: Faber and Faber, 1985), pp. 16–17.
[26] Willi Reich, *Schoenberg: A Critical Biography*, trans. Leo Black (London: Longman, 1971), p. 56.
[27] Alexander Goehr, *Finding the Key: Selected Writings*, ed. Derrick Puffett (London: Faber and Faber, 1998), p. 48.
[28] Gerald Bennett, 'The Early Works', in William Glock (ed.), *Pierre Boulez. A Symposium* (London: Eulenberg, 1986), pp. 52 and 54.
[29] Goehr, *Finding the Key*, p. 48. Further references appear in the text.

'perfectly satisfied to perceive isolated events, or to imagine and compose them. He did not, like most other composers of our time, feel any desire to construct them into organic wholes' (p. 54). This eccentricity was compounded for Goehr by the fact that Messiaen practised an 'absolute and unbroken continuity ... between tradition and the study of the most advanced concepts and sounds ... In dealing with the most complex new music, he saw no reason to learn new techniques or concepts of analysis, and was quite satisfied to listen and describe what he had heard in the technical language he was accustomed to use' (p. 55). This closeness to a particular type of tradition finds its fulfilment in the *Traité*, and it is tempting to suppose that (like Schoenberg detailing his debts to a list of German masters culminating in Wagner and Brahms) Messiaen saw no need to distance himself from Massenet, Debussy, Dukas, Dupré or Tournemire, because he never felt himself to be slavishly imitating them.

Goehr's sense of Messiaen's rejection of Germanic organicism finds a potent echo in Boulez's celebrated early claim about juxtaposition rather than composition.[30] Much later Boulez repeated the judgement in connection with a perceived link with Varèse: 'like many French people, he does not know how to develop ideas; he just juxtaposes them. And Messiaen is the same, for instance. There is no development in the sense of the Germans, who develop musical ideas: Beethoven, Mahler, and also Wagner, of course'.[31] Even if we dismiss this as too sweeping, and seek (following Cross) to demonstrate that Messiaen's mosaic structuring, following Stravinskian models, does not exclude all variational and transformational procedures, it is difficult to deny the charge completely. The real question is whether the difference makes Messiaen's work inferior, as Boulez clearly believes, suggesting by way of explanation that Messiaen ceased to develop too early – 'Of course, he had an interesting evolution, but his style and way of writing and conceiving music was practically in place when he was twenty-two' – and Boulez makes an immediate comparison with Carter, whose 'gifts were revealed to him through a kind of very methodical approach, and he discovered himself later in life'.[32]

Clearly, there is an implied reproach to Messiaen who, like Carter, felt the postwar winds of musical change in his forties, and also moved into more progressive techniques, but retreated a few years later, as if the loss of

---

[30] Pierre Boulez, 'Proposals', in *Stocktakings from an Apprenticeship*, trans. Stephen Walsh (Oxford: Clarendon Press, 1991), p. 30. See also 'Olivier Messiaen', in Jean-Jacques Nattiez, (ed.) Martin Cooper (trans) *Orientations: Collected Writings by Pierre Boulez* (London: Faber and Faber, 1986), pp. 404–20.

[31] Rocco di Pietro, *Dialogues with Boulez* (Lanham, MD and London: Scarecrow Press, 2001), p. 23.

[32] Di Pietro, *Dialogues*, p. 23.

focus on the consonant triad was an expressive limitation he could not accept. More than that, it seems undeniable that Messiaen's instincts about the primacy of harmony (as described, for example, by George Benjamin) reinforced for him – above all, as a practising organist – the need to retain a distinctive, if ambivalent, role for the bass in non-diatonic contexts. Benjamin seeks 'to get away from the quasi-functionality of the bass line' by 'curtailing the resonance', and using two notes to create 'a sonorous but blurred bass'.[33] For Messiaen (as for Debussy and Stravinsky before him) 'quasi', or ambiguous, functionality, as an allusion to the heritage of tonal scale-degrees, was to be preserved, in keeping with his instinctive sense of the traditional chordal formations behind his harmonies, and in keeping too with the expressive importance he attached to bringing those traditional formations to the surface of the music from time to time.

Resonance and influence

The exploration of resonance, giving primacy to harmony, is characteristic of spectralism, which emerged in France during the 1970s in the music of Gérard Grisey and Tristan Murail, both pupils of Messiaen who went on to enter the brave new world of electro-acoustic experimentation.[34] George Benjamin is an admirer of this music, while remaining sceptical about the ambition, in Murail's case at least, to regard melody as 'a sort of secondary effect of harmonic processes'.[35] But, as Goehr has suggested, such an emphasis is a product of Messiaen's teaching principles, if not of his compositional practice, where he confronts the tensions between linear and vertical, rooted and free-floating. Spectralism also parted company with Messiaen's practice – at least to begin with – in the way it worked with 'the acoustic continuity' that links the constituent sound spectra, 'their relative consonance and dissonance'. Julian Anderson has described an 'obsession with organic continuity' which placed Murail, in particular, 'well outside the 20th-century French tradition of discontinuously juxtaposing *objets sonores*, a characteristic of both Boulez and Murail's teacher Messiaen'. During the 1980s, something of a convergence with 'French tradition' seems to have set in,

---

[33] Risto Nieminen and Renaud Machart, *George Benjamin* (London: Faber and Faber, 1997), pp. 16 and 18.

[34] For further discussion of spectralism, apart from sources cited in other references below, see Julian Anderson, 'Spectral Music', in Sadie and Tyrrell (eds), *The New Grove*, vol. XXIV, pp. 166–7; François Rose, 'Introduction to the

Pitch Organization of French Spectral Music', *Perspectives of New Music*, Vol. 34, no. 2 (1996), 6–39; Julian Johnson, 'An Interview with Jonathan Harvey', in Peter O'Hagan (ed.), *Aspects of British Music of the 1990s*, (Aldershot: Ashgate, 2003), pp. 119–29.

[35] Nieminen and Machart, *George Benjamin*, p. 12.

however, since Murail's *Désintégrations* (1982–83), consisting of eleven highly contrasted sections, and in *Time and Again* (1985) 'the temporal structure is constantly broken up and enriched by echoes and distorted memories of earlier sections or premonitions of future ones'.[36]

The evolution of Murail's music suggests that the core of modernist values which links Messiaen's very personal idiom to musical modernism in general has continued to make aspirations to organic connectedness problematic. It takes the determination of a Boulez to conceive a truly modern (atonal) classicism in which tendencies to 'juxtapose' are made to function as contrasts within an evolving synthesis rather than as fundamental disruptions to continuity. *Sur Incises* (1996–98) might even be seen as the conclusive stage in Boulez's movement away from Messiaen's principles in the way it uses its basic syntactical concept of parenthesis – interruption – as the generator for a sequence of interactive dialogues which are supremely dynamic and fluid in character.[37]

Boulez – even in this non-electronic work – also uses the rich resonance of pianos, metal percussion and harps, in ways which are quite different from Messiaen's more rooted, bass-orientated sonorities. But other composers emerging from a French tradition which now extends to IRCAM have shown a willingness to be associated with the kind of bass orientation of harmony that suggests a degree of affinity with Messiaen. Jonathan Harvey (b. 1939) has not only acknowledged Messiaen as a 'protospectralist', but has described his own commitment to spectralism in terms which makes its interactions with traditional, intervallic harmonic thinking crystal clear. Spectralism can be said to work with 'fundamentals', as well as to allow for rootedness and elements of hierarchisation, and Harvey has declared that 'I found myself thinking again in terms of tonic (no addition to the partials), dominant (the case where 3/2 of the fundamental is added to each partial), subdominant (the 4:3 case), and mediant (5:4). A twist of the spiral indeed ... The mathematically related interval system that has dominated world music from at least Pythagoras on has been reborn in completely new terms. Any child can hear it.'[38] Harvey also shows how tempo as well as pitch can be be related to fundamentals. Yet the most Messiaen-like of his observations comes when the meaning of such technical developments is explained. 'Spectral music is symbiotically allied to electronic music; together they have achieved a rebirth of perception. Yet while electronic music is a well-documented technological breakthrough, spectralism in its simplest form, as color-thinking, is a spiritual breakthrough.'[39]

[36] Julian Anderson, 'In Harmony: The Music of Tristan Murail', *Musical Times*, Vol. 134 (1993), 321 and 323.

[37] See Whittall, *Exploring Twentieth-Century Music*, pp. 191–7.
[38] Harvey, *In Quest of Spirit*, pp. 44–5.
[39] Harvey, *In Quest of Spirit*, p. 39.

Composers who do not share the views of Messiaen, or Harvey, about spiritual values in music display a different level of affinity when they talk of harmony in terms of basses and fundamentals. One of the best, Magnus Lindberg (b. 1958), says of his *Cantigas* (1998–99) for oboe and orchestra that 'the five cycles of the piece ... are based on fifths. ... it's the classical thing of making harmonies of major and minor thirds, fourths, seconds, fifths ... And then there are the fundamentals: the bass line is such that each material has a certain tonal anchorage. So even if the music is by no means tonal, there is that fundamental, open function of the bass.'[40] Such concerns suggest an affinity which may be quite profound at the technical level. Yet the distinctive features of Messiaen's spirituality, and of what Goehr has termed his 'realism',[41] make the prospect of close connections between him and later composers difficult to imagine. Thus, placing Messiaen within the history of twentieth-century sacred music, ranging as this does from functional liturgical pieces to large-scale concert Masses, Passions and Requiems, once more reinforces the different objectives of the 'theological' composer whose organ-loft manner (exuberant toccatas or rapt meditations) can easily be imitated, as it is in the music of his successor at La Trinité, Naji Hakim (b. 1955), but whose contributions to concert music are unique.

Just occasionally, a specific technical and generic feature like the ambivalently functional chorale can suggest style-bridging affinities, and here 'holy minimalism' enters the frame. Something of a Messiaen-like sensitivity to harmonic resonance (including the use of higher consonance) is present in the austere but intense 'tintinnabular' style of Arvo Pärt. For Steve Reich – admittedly not a detached observer – it is the idiom of composers like Pärt, Adams and Andriessen that 'has really become the dominant style today' (1998–99), and he deems Pärt 'the most important living European composer ... He's writing church music ... and he's become enormously popular. What does this say? Obviously that he himself is a religious man who, because of his very compelling, very simple, and also very systematic musical style is able to reach people who seem to be thirsting for the very things his music gives them. And – because he sets religious texts – I think it is extremely positive and much needed in this ultra-secular, radically materialistic world we Westerners now inhabit.'[42] Reich offers no comparisons with Messiaen, and nor does he mention John Tavener, who, in the grandiose climaxes of his large-scale sacred works, might be said to attempt a comparable aesthetic effect to Messiaen – though usually on the basis of rather narrower harmonic and textural perspectives, in keeping with his reservations about the world of concert music.

[40] Magnus Lindberg's notes with Sony Classical CD recording SK89810 (2992).

[41] Goehr, *Finding the Key*, p. 49.

[42] Steve Reich, *Writings on Music 1965–2000*, ed. Paul Hillier (New York: Oxford University Press, 2002), p. 235.

Following up the point that 'Messiaen and Boulez, like Stravinsky and Debussy before them' (and Cage and Xenakis alongside them) 'have drawn on Asian culture, from which aspects of their rituals are derived', Jonathan Cross refers in passing to the music of Toru Takemitsu (1930–96), citing Paul Griffiths' judgement that 'much of Takemitsu's later music "is close to Messiaen, though with a gentler, more yielding character"'.[43] Takemitsu's affinity with French music in general and Messiaen in particular is a central theme of Peter Burt's monograph on the Japanese composer,[44] and a consideration of how this theme is handled is instructive for the ways in which it underlines the challenges and rewards for critical discourse of aligning pairs of composers and assessing their separate developments in terms of types of dialogue between them.

Takemitsu was not a pupil of Messiaen's and their first 'contact' was by way of scores brought back to Tokyo by Japanese composers who had studied in Paris; hence Yoko Narazaki can claim that 'Messiaen's influence is already apparent in Takemitsu's first performed work, *Lento in due movimenti* (1950) for piano',[45] written well before Takemitsu actually visited the West. In his more nuanced analysis, Peter Burt takes great pains to try to separate the general from the particular in relation to Takemitsu's evolving style. Considering *Lento/Litany*, the 1989 recomposition of the 1950 piano work, Burt concludes that it is Takemitsu's extensive use of the octatonic scale (Messiaen's Mode II) 'which is probably most responsible for the "Messiaenic" flavour exuded by so much of his music', though similarities of 'textural layout' can also be detected (p. 32). Still closer connections to Messiaen emerge in *Quatrain* for violin, cello, clarinet, piano and orchestra (1975): 'The instrumentation of the solo quartet here is of course identical to that of Messiaen's *Quatuor pour la fin du temps*, and Takemitsu explicitly intended this work as an *hommage* to the French master, who had given him a two-hour "lesson" analysing the *Quatuor* during their meeting in New York in 1975' (p. 154). Burt identifies various thematic and textural links between Messiaen's quartet and *Quatrain*, and sees that work as having a transitional status. 'Partly perhaps as a result of Takemitsu's intention to pay homage to Messiaen, much of the instrumental sonority has a rapturous mellifluousness which palpably looks forward to the composer's later orchestral manner' (p. 158).

In his conclusion, however, Burt is primarily concerned to defend Takemitsu against charges of random derivativeness. While not denying

---

[43] Cross, *The Stravinsky Legacy*, pp. 151–2, citing Paul Griffiths, *Modern Music and After: Directions since 1945* (Oxford: Oxford University Press, 1995), p. 157.

[44] Peter Burt, *The Music of Toru Takemitsu* (Cambridge University Press, 2001). All page references are given in the text.

[45] Yoko Narazaki, 'Toru Takemitsu', in Sadie and Tyrrell (eds), *The New Grove*, vol. XXV, p. 22.

the similarities, not just of modality, which Takemitsu uses more freely than Messiaen, Burt seeks to establish fundamental differences: he suggests that Messiaen,

> despite his obvious spirituality, interest in Oriental musics, reverence for nature and outstanding sensitivity to harmonic and instrumental colour, was at the same time essentially a 'constructivist', whose music involves the rigorous application of melodic, rhythmic and harmonic schemata to generate materials . . . Takemitsu, by contrast, although sharing certain aspects of Messiaen's spiritual vision, could not by any stretch of the imagination be described as a 'constructivist'. The manner in which he treats the most obvious of his borrowings from Messiaen's 'technique musicale' bears witness to this: the modes are used for the most part simply as a resource from which to draw richly aromatic harmonic progressions, without any consistent underlying rationale . . . Furthermore, Messiaen's rhythmic system based on multiplications of a constant unit-pulse is mostly in complete contrast to Takemitsu's fluidity of tactus.

Ultimately, then, 'if Messiaen is the "theologian", offering a commentary on his spiritual beliefs in terms of rigidly pursued and often descriptive "arguments" of an architectural solidity, Takemitsu is simply giving meaning to the "stream of sound" around him, and in consequence reflecting something of the chaotic and ineluctable fluidity of that medium' (pp. 247–8).

Taken in isolation, this argument risks exaggerating Messiaen's strictness and solidity as against Takemitsu's 'fluidity'. But it shows the matters which can arise in what is likely to prove a relatively rare case of a composer whose resemblances to Messiaen extended from structure into style, from texture into actual sound. Takemitsu was not just one of the myriad of later twentieth-century composers to use the octatonic scale, but did so in ways which call Messiaen (or else a special blend of Debussy and Messiaen) to mind. In the end, what helps to make Takemitsu's own music most distinctive is his profoundly un-Messiaen-like conviction that 'the joy of music, ultimately, seems connected with sadness' (p. 29). The point is not that Messiaen never touches on human grief and pain – the music for the Leper in *Saint François d'Assise* is a powerful example – but that these qualities tend to be resolved out into Christian spiritual fulfilment.

The personal in perspective

Paul Griffiths has offered a basic technical explanation for Messiaen's 'aloneness' during the later twentieth century. 'The segmented and eternal rhythms of Messiaen's music had perhaps been at the root of his closeness to the avant-garde during the 1950s. When younger composers began to concern themselves again more with continuity – both with continuity of process within pieces, and with continuity through musical history – they inevitably peeled away from Messiaen's path, and left him to follow it more or less alone'.[46] As argued in this chapter, the remarkable heterogeneity of later twentieth-century developments indicate that avant-garde convictions evolved and persisted even as more 'classical' concerns with continuity re-emerged alongside them. Messiaen was 'more or less alone' in style rather than structure, and this means that, with splendid and decisive ambivalence, he stood apart at the same time as he stood at the centre, a figure of great importance for twentieth-century music as a whole who remained one of its most individual exponents.

Perhaps what separates Messiaen most starkly from all other twentieth-century composers is the kind of 'realism', which, as Goehr describes it, means that 'a waterfall or a bird was, as far as Messiaen was able to realise it, a real waterfall or a real bird'.[47] Such naivety borders on the sublime; and yet Messiaen's naturalism may have been no more intense than that of Webern, the consistent extra-musical associations and spiritual obsessions of whose apparently abstract instrumental works are revealed in his sketches and confirmed by the kind of audible correspondences discussed by Julian Johnson.[48] To build a bridge between Webern and Messiaen in this way is not to deny Messiaen's lack of sympathy with the aims of the early twelve-tone composers (in other than the rhythmic sphere), or to minimise the importance, for Boulez in particular, of regarding Webern as the kind of source for post-1945 radicalism that Messiaen himself failed to be. In his penetrating account of Boulez's early years, Gerald Bennett quotes a very Messiaen-like 'Theme' for piano (left hand) by the 20-year-old pupil, and he also argues that, whereas with Messiaen, even in 'complex and differentiated rhythmic structures, the effect remains altogether decorative. The interest, excitement, fascination, and the development of the music do not arise from structural relationships', in Webern, 'particularly in the works after Op. 21, the structures become the music'. Yet Bennett accepts that 'Messiaen and Webern share a common wellspring for their music: both write out of a deeply emotional urge, which seeks musical expression', and 'both employ structural devices of varying complexity'.[49] Such comments, simple in themselves, indicate the extent to which, within the supremely differentiated world of twentieth-century music, composers with radically different styles can be aligned, and the ways in which they explored the consequences of living in the modernist epoch compared. In Messiaen's case, such comparisons – with Debussy, Varèse, Stravinsky, Boulez and even Webern – have

[46] Griffiths, *Modern Music and After*, p. 229.
[47] Goehr, *Finding the Key*, p. 49.
[48] See Julian Johnson, *Webern and the Transformation of Nature* (Cambridge University Press, 1999).

[49] Bennett, 'The Early Works', in Glock (ed.), *Pierre Boulez*, p. 82.

all been touched on in this chapter, as ways of helping to define his position in his own time. Finally, I will revert to the comparison with his closest contemporary and most profound complement, Elliott Carter.

In his subtle and impassioned defence of classical music in the modern world, Julian Johnson writes that 'art claims to fulfill what religious icons and the doctrine of transubstantiation once claimed: that a material object becomes more than the sum of its material parts, that it projects a spiritual energy. In this way, high art realizes, in secular form, what was once the domain of religion ... [Art] does not necessarily deliver an experience most people would call religious, but art, even when it is most obviously concerned with the secular, implies something beyond itself, and in this sense it is metaphysical'.[50]

It is important to Johnson's argument that this metaphysical dimension is not seen as somehow dehumanising, a prelude to abstraction. Nor is commitment to religion a necessary condition for apprehending a metaphysical element – 'whether religious or not, we oscillate between the particularity of our lives and a larger, more universal whole ... The capacity to exceed our limits is a basic condition of both art and humanity. It is for this reason that art is profoundly humane' (p. 116) – and Johnson's preferred context for the nature of art seems to turn from the metaphysical to the ethical and the utopian. Near the end of his book he writes that art is utopian in the sense 'that it leaves us altered, tinged with a memory that things might be different or that things once were different. Classical music rarely offers a literal representation of a utopian, harmonious, and reconciled society', but it 'often presents a metaphor of reconciliation, one that expresses the complex competing voices of the self and society' (p. 127). And one of Johnson's boldest declarations is that 'art music of the last two centuries takes on the dissonance of the real world and transforms it. In that way it has a redemptive function' (p. 107).

What might Messiaen's response have been to such arguments? The implication that religion as such might be set aside would obviously be anathema, and, although it will hardly do to describe the character of Messiaen's music as inhumane, his primary intent is to represent those 'illuminations of the beyond' that lead to the vision of 'Christ, light of paradise'. As the Messiaen-Loriod notes for the last movement of *Eclairs sur l'au-delà* ... put it, 'the earth is far away, time has come to an end, and the undying love of Christ lives on in the soul that beholds Him'. The music expresses a sublime sense of repose, inspiring a supremely contemplative frame of mind in the listener, and bringing to mind Johnson's point that 'to function as art, classical music requires a contemplative attitude that the distraction culture explicitly

[50] Julian Johnson, *Who Needs Classical Music?* *Cultural Choice and Musical Value* (New York: Oxford University Press, 2002), p. 87. Further references are given in the text.

forbids' (p. 122). Classical music does not require that contemplation should take place in the context of Christian beliefs. Yet Messiaen, in his characteristically stratified handling of rhythm, harmony, texture and form, still manages to suggest those tensions which, in Johnson's diagnosis, set classical music apart from contemporary culture, insisting as it does 'on the tension between the bodily and the intellectual, the material and the spiritual, the thinglike and its transcendence in thought' (p. 56). In addition, there is a strong contrast between the vision of paradise in Messiaen's finale and the much less stable, more turbulent character of the penultimate movement, which depicts the difficult, often painful ascent of man through death to redemption.

Between 1993 and 1997, Carter composed the three orchestral pieces that comprise his *Symphonia: sum fluxae pretiam spei*. The Latin subtitle comes from the seventeenth-century English poet Richard Crashaw, whose conversion to Catholicism led to escape from England and residence in France and Italy. Carter is not interested in Crashaw's religion, however, choosing a poem called 'Bulla' ('Bubble') which focuses on human ephemerality rather than on the joys of eternal life. The poem seems to depend on parallels between the nature of life and the character of art; also, as David Schiff points out,[51] suggesting associations with images in Italo Calvino and Wallace Stevens, writers Carter has long valued. The Crashaw line which serves as epigraph to the whole work – 'I am the prize of flowing hope' – seems essentially upbeat, affirmative, and, although the central movement, 'Adagio tenebroso', is nothing if not dark, the framing fast movements paint an affirmative portrait of humanity, the end of the final 'Allegro scorrevole' ascending to dissolve blithely into nothingness as the perfect embodiment of Carter's stoic humanism.

Neither *Eclairs sur l'au-delà* . . . nor *Symphonia* pursue programmatic narratives, yet both are richly allusive in radically different ways. Messiaen's vision of heaven is a neat complement to Carter's bubble-spirit floating in space, and in both the purely human is put into proper perspective, as Julian Johnson's criteria for classical music require. Messiaen's particular, personal triumph was to find ways of using his religious beliefs and musical instincts which engaged with modernism, despite his lack of affinity with so much that is fundamental to twentieth-century culture.[52] Yet, whether Messiaen is regarded primarily as a modernist or as something else becomes irrelevant in face of the fact that a history of twentieth-century music without his name and work prominently placed is, quite simply, inconceivable.

---

[51] Schiff, *The Music of Elliott Carter*, p. 317.

[52] For an attempt to contextualise Messiaen's work more broadly in relation to other twentieth-century tendencies than has generally been attempted, see Sandra Corse, *Operatic Subjects: The Evolution of Self in Modern Opera* (London: Associated University Presses, 2000), pp. 192–206.

Index